TERROR TALES OF
THE HOME COUNTIES

TERROR TALES OF THE HOME COUNTIES

Edited by

PAUL FINCH

First published in 2020 by Telos Publishing,
139 Whitstable Road, Canterbury, Kent CT2 8EQ,
United Kingdom.

www.telos.co.uk

ISBN: 978-1-84583-159-2

Telos Publishing Ltd values feedback. Please e-mail any
comments you might have about this book to:
feedback@telos.co.uk

Terror Tales of the Home Counties © Paul Finch, 2020

Cover: Neil Williams

TABLE OF CONTENTS

COPYRIGHT INFORMATION

IN THE ENGLISH RAIN
Steve Duffy

'So what's it like living next door to a Beatle?'

Sally Holden asked me the question, with her usual mixture of mischief and amusement. Sally had come to our school at the start of the lower sixth, after her mother got divorced and left her town house in Highgate for a Surrey maisonette. My dad and I had made a similar journey three years earlier, except in our case it was from Hampstead to a big four-bedroomed house at the end of an affluent cul-de-sac. I'd yet to make any friends either in or out of school.

It would never have occurred to me to seek out Sally's friendship. She was startlingly beautiful – or so I thought, anyway – and I was far too shy to approach her. It was only thanks to Miss Aston's seating plan in English that we were thrown together, and only then because she made us read the parts of Antony and Cleopatra in lessons that we actually exchanged words, even if they were all Shakespeare's at first. I was taken aback at how much of herself she seemed to put into the reading. Everyone else in the class was grunting their way through Charmian and Enobarbus and the rest as if they were reading a bus timetable, but Sally was actually emoting: she was giving it her throaty, husky all, and giving it in my direction, which I found both disconcerting and amazing.

Walking home from school one autumn afternoon, after I had done my hoarse and red-faced best to respond in kind to the serpent of old Nile, Sally had fallen in step with me on the tree-lined pavement. Despite having vowed not half an hour earlier to be treble-sinew'd, hearted, breathed, and fight maliciously, it was all I could do to look up from the toes of my shoes as she buttonholed me. 'Which is the best record shop in town?' she asked me. 'I want to buy the new Blondie album with my birthday tokens.' The album in question being *Eat To The Beat*, which pins the encounter nicely to October 1979, not that I was ever likely to forget the occasion.

'I like SpinDisc,' I said to the drifts of dead leaves through which I was kicking.

'Ooh, I don't know that one,' Sally said. 'Where is it?'

'I'll show you,' I said, not quite believing the turn of events.

'All right,' she said simply, as if we did this sort of thing every day. And to SpinDisc we went; and to the Lite-a-Bite for coffee afterwards. It turned out we both liked cappuccino: what were the odds? Over the next half-an-hour or so we worked out that we both liked Blondie, we both liked Kate Bush (even though nobody else in the school did), and we both identified as New Wave, but were still secret fans of the Beatles. This was the point at which Sally brought up the matter of my legendary neighbour.

'I mean, somebody told me you were supposed to live next door to a house that belonged to one of the Beatles? Something like that?'

I sighed, and inwardly wished for the cracked leather Chesterfield to swallow me. I'd originally shared this titbit in one of my ham-fisted attempts to acquire friends when I first came to the school. It had been met with a mixture of indifference and ridicule, and seemed to have impressed nobody. 'Yeah, it's not ... I mean, apparently, it's only half true. One of them's supposed to have bought the house in the Sixties, but I don't think anybody ever moved in there. Nobody lives there now.'

'It's still pretty good, though,' Sally said. 'We've got a taxi driver in the flat next door to ours, and he tries to look down my top when he talks to me. I think you win.'

It was just as well I didn't have a mouthful of cappuccino.

After that, it was all surprisingly easy. We found ourselves in an easy routine of walking into town after school, meeting up on Saturday mornings. It fell short of actual boy-girl going-out stuff, but for me at least there was a sort of intimacy in it, as unfamiliar to me as it was intoxicating. Our friendship remained steady all through the school year, never more than the best of friends, never any less. When Sally's mother took her to visit relatives over the summer, my holidays lost all their sense of potential, became nothing but a less humiliating version of what school had been like before Sally. For the first time ever, I was anxious for the new term. And on that first day back in September, there she was, with a tan and a new haircut, swinging from the school gate. In Miss Ashton's English class, we moved on from *Antony & Cleopatra* to *The Tempest*, a text with less erotic charge but with a weirdness we both found appealing.

Come the October half-term, I had the house to myself. My father, a widower with an unfussy attitude towards child care and a busy professional schedule, was away on a business trip to Leeds, and would not be back till late on Friday night. So it happened that I was ambling downstairs unusually late on the Tuesday morning when the front door bell rang. The cleaning woman, I remembered, wasn't due until Thursday. I quickly pulled my sweater on, and craned over the banisters to look who was there. Through the rippled glass I saw Sally's silhouette.

For a second I just didn't know what to do, not in the least. For a year we'd been in each other's company almost every day, but on neutral ground: the school, the cafe, the streets of town and the grassy spaces of the park. The thought of Sally actually here, in my home, was at the same time exhilarating and a little bit scary. It would, I thought, be the same as having a proper girlfriend, or at least what I assumed having a proper girlfriend might be like. This thought was almost too much for me to cope with, and only when the bell rang again did I snap out of it and hurry down to the door.

'You *are* in!' she said, and I blushed. 'I thought you were still in kip, you lazy pig. Am I coming in, then?' Apparently she was.

STEVE DUFFY

In the kitchen I made us coffee, surreptitiously checking my eyes for gunk and my hair for flattening from the pillow. She perched on her stool at the breakfast bar, keeping up a stream of chat while inside me my heart bounced around like bingo balls in the blower. My dad was away, remember: we had the place to ourselves till Thursday, at least Thursday.

We took our drinks through to the back room, where I put the latest Kate Bush album – *Never For Ever*, which I knew Sally loved – on the stereo. She sat crosslegged on the sofa singing along, and squinted through the French windows at the garden. All morning it had been drizzling on and off, and the trickle of rain on the windowpanes blurred the leaf-strewn lawn.

'Is that it, then?' she asked, pointing to the high chimneys just visible behind the stone wall at the end of our property. 'Is that the Beatles house?'

'That's it.' In truth, I hardly ever noticed it, unless prompted. It was just a feature in the middle distance, like trees or hills.

'Bloody hell! Brilliant! Which Beatle is it, do we know?'

I'd asked my dad about it, on the off chance it came up again. 'Lennon, apparently. He was looking for a new place in 1968, about the time he was moving out of Kenwood, his house in Weybridge. He sent one of the Beatles roadies round viewing properties – Mal Evans, I think it was. He saw this place, thought John might like it, and the word is that Apple Corps bought it, sight unseen.'

'No!' Sally was entranced. 'So did he move in?'

'Well, no,' I admitted. 'I mean, he still owns it, or Apple do, whoever, but the story goes that he only ever spent a long weekend here, and either he didn't like it or Yoko didn't, or they both didn't, and he ended up buying Tittenhurst Park the year after. And that was it; nobody ever moved in, and it's been empty ever since.'

'Wow!' Sally got up, crossed to the window, and peeked through the net curtains. The sun was coming back out after the rain, and now whenever the weather turns that way I often remember her standing there silhouetted against the nets, her figure edged with golden light. 'I asked my mum about it, you know. She said she thought there'd been a big scandal about it at the time. Apparently there was a rhyme that the kids used to sing, to the tune of *Yellow Submarine*: "We all live in a Quentin Bascombe dream." No idea who Quentin Bascombe was, but she said it had something to do with that house. Have you ever been over there?'

'No,' I admitted. 'Our place and the place next door are the only two houses that actually back on to Shelgrave – that's the name of it. This end of the cul-de-sac is Shelgrave's western edge, there's woodland to the south and the east, and the golf course to the north, with a stream that marks the boundary. We're the only neighbours.'

Sally was still peering through the windowglass. 'I'd have been over that wall so fast,' she said. She looked round at me, and her eyes were bright with monkey business. 'Come on,' she said, and unlatched the French windows. Before I knew it, we were out on the patio.

The raindrops made tiny prisms on the lawn as we ran across the soaked garden, breaking up the soft October sunlight into its constituent colours. There was a wooden compost bin against the biscuit brick wall, and Sally swarmed up it easily. 'Get that,' she directed me, gesturing at the tall ladder we kept around the side of the house. 'We'll need it to get down the other side.' I manhandled it to where she sat waiting, and together we hoisted it up and over, letting it rest on the other side. Joining her on the wall, I looked where she was pointing; across the mossy red ridge tiles on top of the wall into the long-abandoned grounds of Shelgrave.

There were lawns, as shaggy as country meadows, descending from the wall to a reed-filled duck pond. The pond lay at the bottom of a natural bowl, and the ground rose on the far side in a series of overgrown formal terraces to the house. Oh, the house. It took our breath away. A large half-timbered villa in the stockbroker Tudor style, it was all gables and turrets and odd angles. There was no way of guessing how many rooms it might contain, or what you might find inside them. Pine trees clustered up close behind it, hiding any view of what might lie beyond. It looked like a solitary homestead in some magical wilderness land like Narnia, instead of a des res surrounded on all sides by the decorous Surrey suburbia.

'Oh, wow,' breathed Sally. 'It's ... it's unbelievable.' And looking at it, slightly dizzy from the suddenness of it all, I thought, *yes, yes you're right, I don't believe it.* Sitting in the shadows of the tall trees, dense leaden rainclouds above that turning the sky into a baleful backdrop, wasn't there something weirdly stagey about it all?

The thought struck me that it looked more like some insanely detailed diorama than an actual view; the inside of somebody's head, reconstructed in scale model form. However, I had no time to get to the bottom of this curious feeling.

'Sally, hang on –!' But she'd already scrambled down the ladder and had both arms raised, beckoning me to follow. What choice did I have?

She took my hand and led me down through the overgrown meadow towards the pond. The grass came up over our knees in places, wet and slippery, and the bottoms of our jeans were soon soaking. Sally leaned close to me and whispered, 'This is a real adventure.' I don't know why she whispered: our cul-de-sac was never noisy at the best of times, but here beyond the wall we might have been in the middle of the countryside, it was so quiet. No jets overhead, no sound of distant traffic. No birds, even.

The house was confusing; you might almost say devious. It looked different from every aspect, a function, I supposed, of its mismatched angles, those multiple gables and randomly pitched roofs. To this day I doubt if I could draw you a floor-plan of Shelgrave, but I only need to close my eyes to summon up an image of it that's as vivid and improbable as the view through a camera obscura. Its blind windows caught the sunshine, one after the other, the nearer we got to the house, then as we climbed from terrace to terrace they surrendered it, and showed nothing but streaky grime.

The terraces were wildly overgrown, and in some places the brick retaining walls had given way, spilling soil and rubble that had grown thick with weeds. Still holding hands, we picked our way up the levels, till we came out on a broad patio area with monkey-puzzle trees to right and left. The builders had banked the structure half into, half projecting from the slope. If we'd looked back we'd have seen the whole of the landscaped vista across the pond and the lawns, the redbrick wall beyond with the tops of the houses peeking over it. Our world, the world where we belonged; not this place, where we didn't know the rules, or even if there were any. Away off in the distance, thunder rumbled.

Sally had let go of my hand, and was peering through the windows on the ground floor. Some were curtained, thick dusty drapes hanging heavy from runners that were giving way under their own weight, while others were bare and let on to bare interiors.

All of a sudden she started back with a gasp, and I almost fell over the low patio wall in fright. '*What*?'

'Look! In there!' she breathed, and then, as I raced to her side, 'Got you.' Just an empty room. She snorted with laughter, and it is a measure of my devotion that I couldn't even manage to be annoyed with her for tricking me.

There was a large front door with a stained glass fanlight above. Sally tried the handle, and of course it was locked. I was all for leaving it there, to be honest, but not her.

Around the corner of the building stone steps led up to a conservatory on the side elevation. Sally ran up them in a shot, and put her weight to the sliding glass door. It came open, screeching on rusted metal runners. 'Ta-daaa,' she announced in triumph, beckoning me to hurry up and join her.

Inside the conservatory it was airless, muggy. There were wooden trays of potted plants, or the withered brown remains of plants. The greenhouse glass had gone unwashed for years, and a few of the panes were cracked or shattered. Sally poked at one of the trays, and a brood of fat little short-legged spiders scuttled out and ran up the filthy glass. She exclaimed in disgust, and started back so that she bumped into me. I patted her on the shoulders, for all the world as if I was in a position to hand out reassurance.

There was a door giving entrance to the house, with three long panels of frosted glass. Somehow, I knew it wouldn't be locked, which in fact it wasn't; Sally opened it. We stood there and looked at each other for a second, and then she grasped my hand once more and led me inside.

The room was a kitchen, bare and grimy, stripped of all but the basic things: a Belfast sink, an old gas stove, a sturdy little table with wooden drawers, and sea-green cupboards of porcelain steel with their doors ajar, nothing inside except cobwebs. There was a smell in the house that was familiar from the conservatory: the smell of things long dead and thoroughly desiccated, not even the taint of decay lingering about them. 'Ugh,' breathed Sally. There was really not a lot else to be said. She pulled me after her, and we tiptoed through to the inner part of the house.

There was a corridor tiled like a chessboard in black and white diagonals. The walls were panelled in dark stained wood, with empty hooks where pictures had once hung. One painting alone remained: a portrait of a fat, jowly man dressed in a pinstripe suit, perched on an armchair like Humpty Dumpty on his wall. On his face was a smile that was presumably meant to look benevolent, but succeeded only in looking irretrievably sinister, or so I thought. Sally and I exchanged a glance, and I saw in her face that she'd come to the same conclusion. She wrinkled her nose in revulsion, and we pushed on towards the end of the corridor.

Here the way widened into a large vestibule. There was the locked front door, the actual sun picking out the stained glass rays of the fanlight, and there on the far side was the main staircase, winding around the walls to the first floor. Again, what fixtures there had been were all gone now; here and there, the ghosts of the old furniture could still be seen, lighter silhouettes against the discoloured plaster. Above our heads was a Tiffany stained-glass skylight dome, littered with the needles of pine trees that had built up in drifts over many years. There were birds' nests, and in one place a cracked pane that had let in the weather: a little bed of lichen had formed on the tiled floor below.

'This is wrong,' I whispered to Sally – we were both still whispering, for some reason. 'There shouldn't be a skylight there, it was all gable end from outside …'

'I know,' she said, looking up at it with something like wonder. 'This place is *amazing*. Which way should we go?'

'You choose,' I said, hoping that she'd opt for the door that led outside, where the thunder seemed to be getting nearer. I wouldn't have minded the oncoming storm. Instead, she made a pantomime of eeny-meeny-miney-mo, alighting on the door to the side of the entrance vestibule.

The room was empty, dilapidated. Bare floorboards littered with scraps of old newspaper, cobwebs thick in the corners. The only feature of interest, if you could call it that, was a set of step-ladders standing in the exact centre of the room, below a ragged hole in the plaster ceiling where once, I assumed, there had been the rose of a light fixture.

'Look,' said Sally, pointing, but I was already looking. Around the hole, in brightly coloured poster-paint letters, ran the exhortation:

CLIMB THE STEPS – TAKE A TRIP

Of course I knew what Sally would do. Up she went, till she was balancing on the top step, invisible from the waist up. 'Oh my God …' She was whispering still. 'Come here, you've got to see this.'

I clambered awkwardly up the back of the ladder, balancing on slanted props instead of steps, until I had to squeeze my head and shoulders through the hole. There was barely enough space for the two of us to fit, and we were pressed closer together than ever before.

'*Look*,' said Sally, but I didn't need telling.

It was as if the rest of our adventure had been in black-and-white, and the set had suddenly been switched over to colour transmissions. Across every bit of wall-space in that bare upstairs room snaked a maze of illustrations in the childlike Sixties psychedelic style; flowers and rainbows and dancing Paisley people. There were blues and reds and yellows and purples and greens, all as vibrant as the day they were first mixed, or so it seemed.

We might have been on a trip in a time machine, only somehow it seemed we were going back further than the decade or so since that paint had still been fresh. In these surroundings, the decoration was more than just incongruous. It felt – this is the best way I can describe it – it felt like an image of a time when everything had been young, apart from a few very old things that had always been there, and always been old, a time when the distinction between the two had never been plainer or more jarring than it now appeared.

'Is this our man at last, do you think?' I asked Sally.

'Oh yes,' she said, her voice filled with wonder. 'This is him.'

'Look,' I said, as the realisation struck me, 'there aren't any doors or windows, only skylights. How did anybody get in there?' I looked again, to make sure I hadn't missed anything. No doors; not even a crack in the painted images. Sally shook her head, as if the magic of it all outweighed the practicality.

In places the illustrations swirled down to cover the bare floorboards, and in others they spilled across the ceiling. I turned from side to side as best I could, pressed tight up against Sally, and tried to make some sense of them. I soon decided that this was not a place that would ever make sense. In the flow of motifs, I saw bicycles and caterpillars, peace signs and guitars, flowers and long-haired maidens, melting letters that spelled out E-G-O and L-U-V, all the kitschy trappings of high psychedelia. In amongst them were some characters I recognised from Lewis Carroll: Alice, the mad hatter, the walrus and the carpenter.

'Look over there,' I said. 'Lennon wrote "I Am The

Walrus", you know? They say he only knew the names; he didn't realise that the walrus was a baddie …'

'Well,' Sally said, so close to me that I could feel her breathing, 'they were both very unpleasant characters.' Which sounded for all the world like a thing I'd heard her say before, in some other room, or maybe it was somebody just like her. She stopped peering around for a moment, and held her forehead against mine. In her eyes I saw wonderment, and maybe something else. 'This is amazing,' she said, 'this is magic.'

She slipped her arms around me. Hesitantly at first, I followed suit, and we teetered on the top of the ladder, balancing against each other, keeping each other from tumbling down through the hole. It felt like the most natural thing in the world, suddenly not playing a game, or maybe a special game for grown-ups. And yes, we kissed; for the very first time, and as it turned out also for the last. Timidly at first, hesitantly on my part, then slower, longer, deeper. L-U-V.

Was it L-U-V for Sally too? I can't say. Part of me wonders if the whole thing might not have been purely situational, so to speak: what a girl like her might have felt obliged to do in circumstances such as this. Was it her first time? Probably back in Highgate she'd kissed lots of boys; how could she not have? Maybe it was no big thing. But equally, ever since I'd known her, there had only been me. She liked me, I know; did she know how I felt about her? Could she have known? I didn't tell her my side of it, and so she never had a chance to say, or to reciprocate, or perhaps even to make up her mind. Perhaps it was just a kiss in the dream house.

When we broke, I was still breathless. 'You took your time,' Sally said, and kissed me again, first on my lips, then in the hollow of my neck. Abruptly she stiffened, and broke away, looking over my shoulder and behind me. 'Oh my God –' Terror in her voice. I gasped in fright, and twisted to see what she'd seen; the step-ladder rocked and almost fell from under us.

There was, of course, nothing there.

'You are *so easy*,' she said, and burst into a fit of the giggles. 'Every time. Come on,' and she boosted herself up into the room. The stepladder lurched again and this time it actually went over; I was just able to brace myself on the edge of the hole as it clattered to the floor below.

'Oh my God, are you OK? Hang on –' Sally went to grab me, but I could feel myself slipping.

'Let me go, it's OK –' A portion of the lath and plaster gave way, and I fell ignominiously to the bare floorboards.

'Oh no! Are you all right?' Sally was looking down anxiously.

'I'm fine,' I said, brushing the debris off myself. 'Just let me get my breath.'

'I'm such an idiot,' she said contritely.

'No, I'm fine,' I said. 'Give me a minute.' I struggled to a sitting position, and Sally's head vanished from the hole. I sat there for a while, trying to gauge if I'd actually done myself any harm, and I happened to glance at the crumpled newspaper that had been no help whatsoever in breaking my fall.

'BEATLE JOHN BUYS HOUSE OF HORROR,' ran a headline in thick tabloid caps, and beneath it was a photograph of a large house in its own grounds, a scene I recognised instantly. This house; the house we'd broken into.

I've looked up the article since then: it was from the *News of the World* on the 25th August, 1968, and the lede ran thus:

BEATLE JOHN LENNON has shocked local homeowners in Surrey with his plans to buy the house at the centre of a notorious 1963 sex scandal. This reporter has gained exclusive confirmation from sources close to the troubled Beatle that Shelgrave, the luxury home in …

Here the page was partly torn away. I picked it up again where the body text read:

Lennon, currently said to be undergoing marital problems, said:

'You people will write what you always write, and I can't do anything about that. I haven't even seen the house, and I probably won't be moving in to it, so all those stockbrokers can stop worrying, you know? It's entirely a business deal, done through our business arm which as you know is Apple Corps, our new thing, and I don't know what'll happen there just yet. It won't be like anything that might have happened there before, I'll tell you that.' When asked about the house's former owner, Lennon said: *'Look, this guy did what he did, and that's his bag, alright. I'm not going to carry that – I've got my own bag, that's all the luggage I can carry, you know? You can look backwards, or you can look forwards, that's what I'm saying –'*

Sally's voice came from above: 'What are you doing? Are you OK?'

'Yeah, I'm just – there's a bit of paper here, hang on,' I called back. A sidebar caught my eye:

PERVERT WHO PREYED ON CHILDREN

It is ten years since the News of the World *first broke the story of Quentin Bascombe, the sex monster of suburbia. Since then he has been convicted of his crimes, sentenced to indefinite detainment in a mental institution, and scandalously released, despite our campaign to make sure he remained locked away for life. His current whereabouts are unknown, and it is our understanding that his estate has been transferred into the hands of relatives, who refused to comment on the purchase of Shelgrave by Beatle John Lennon. The disappearance of several children in the Surrey stockbroker belt has often been linked to Bascombe, but no evidence was brought at his trial …*

And there the text was torn away again. I've read the whole of it since, and done my own research, and learned about – learned too much about – what Quentin Bascombe got up to in his house of horrors. It was a notorious case of the day back in 1963. Bascombe, independently wealthy since the death of his parents, would drive his Rolls-Royce around the streets of suburban Surrey, parking outside playgrounds with the window rolled down. He'd invite children to come for a ride, tell them there was a tea-party in the grounds of his big house, then lead them inside on the pretext of a game of hide-and-seek. What happened to them in there was not the sort of thing a family newspaper could print, not in 1968, maybe not even today. But even if I'd known all the facts back then in 1980, it would already have been too late.

I called up through the hole in the ceiling, 'Sally?'

An upside-down head lowered itself. 'What?'

'You remember that song you were singing before? The one your mum told you about?'

'What, back in your house?' She sang it again. 'We all live in a Quentin Bascombe dream, a Quentin Bascombe dream, a Quentin Bascombe dream …'

'I've found out who Quentin Bascombe was.'

The upside-down head registered surprise. 'No way! Was there really a Quentin Bascombe?'

I held up the newspaper. 'This is his house. Lennon only bought it afterwards.' I read her the gist of the story. For a while after she didn't say anything. 'They say he was still on the loose,' I said – I don't really know why. Perhaps it was just for the sake of saying something; to break the silence, which was becoming oppressive.

'Then if that's true …' She paused, as if unwilling to make the connection. 'If that's true, then this is really Quentin Bascombe's dream, and we're in it.'

I was trying to frame an answer when Sally gave a little gasp. Her head jerked up and out of sight, as if someone had tapped her on the shoulder.

'Oh give it a rest, Sally,' I said. 'You must think I was born yesterday. You're not getting me again with that routine.'

No answer from above. No sign of Sally.

'Ha-ha, very funny,' I said, loud enough for her to hear. Still no answer.

And then there came a scream, so different to the breathless playacting that had gone before that I had no doubt it was real. I knew that this wasn't Sally fooling me for a third time. All the apprehension I'd felt but could not articulate since we'd climbed over the garden wall and entered Shelgrave found a voice in that scream. It pushed me into full-on panic.

'Sally!' I scrambled to my feet, tried to see into the room above. All I could see was movement; I couldn't even tell of what. A thumping on the floor above dislodged more fragments of plaster from the hole in the ceiling. A stifled noise that I thought might have been Sally.

I grabbed the step-ladder and tried to set it up below the hole again. One of the hinges was broken and I couldn't get it to stand straight; when I put my weight on the first step the whole thing gave way again. The thumps and muffled cries from above continued. Desperately, I jumped for the gap, pulled away another lump of plaster, fell to the floor again. The next time, I managed to hang on to one of the beams in the ceiling that bore my weight, and I pulled myself up on it.

The room was absolutely empty. I looked this way and that, but there was nothing. No sign of Sally; no sign of any other living thing; no sign of a door to open or to close. Only those insane paintings on the wall, and the sound of my own ragged breathing.

I tried to pull myself up all the way, but there was something about that impossible chamber that repelled me. I wonder now what would have happened if I had entered it, whether whatever happened to Sally might have happened to me too. Instead I dropped to the floor again, and tried to overcome for a moment the bursting, toppling terror I felt. I knew I had to do something. But what?

I ran out of the ground floor room back into the vestibule, heading for the staircase. My thought was that there *must* be a door to the room – perhaps it was obscured by the painting or whatever, but there had to be a door. I turned right at the head of the stairs, tried all the rooms on that side of the landing. Nothing. Only empty spaces filled with dust and decay and the shadows of where things once had been. Rooms that existed in the real world, rooms with windows and doors. No paintings on the wall; no sign of Sally.

I went from room to room, kicking open the doors so that they raised little puffs of dust before rebounding against the jamb and slamming back in my face. I shouted her name, and no answer came to me. Once I thought I heard movement, away off in the depths of the house, somewhere I couldn't see and perhaps was never meant to. 'Sally!' I screamed, one last time, and as if to mock me the lightning came, and the thunder right on top of it, and the storm broke.

I looked out of the nearest window. In retrospect what I saw made no sense, because when I try to recreate it now the view was the view I ought to have seen if I'd been looking out from that room with the hole in the floor. The view I should have seen, had there only been a window. There were the terraces, and the grounds spread out beyond, barely visible through the rain. But none of that incongruity registered with me, because I had eyes for one thing only: Sally.

She was lying face down on the patio as if she'd fallen out of the front door, or perhaps been pushed. I shouted her name again, and hammered on the windowpane so hard that the glass splintered. She didn't respond.

I half scrambled, half fell down the stairs, threw myself at the front door, which now seemed to be unlocked, on the inside at least. Out on the patio, I knelt in the rain at Sally's side and turned her face up, saying her name over and over again.

She was breathing; she was conscious, or at least her eyes were open. She tried to say something, but it was aimed at the space beyond me, and she couldn't get it out in any case.

'Can you get up?' She didn't answer, but she did her best when I tried to lift her to her feet. 'Come on, we've got to get away.' She managed a step before swaying and almost falling over. I wrapped an arm around her, and placed her arm around my own shoulders. 'Try now,' I urged her, and she broke into a sort of lurching gait. Like contestants in some dreadful parody of a three-legged race, we crossed the patio and began to negotiate the steps down to the pond. I threw a look over my shoulder.

What I saw has stayed with me since that day, and I'm a middle-aged man now, all too willing to brush away the irreconcilable in any experience. It was what it was, the thing I saw when I glanced back over my shoulder. I only looked for a second, and the rain was in my eyes, and I was filled with a dread that simultaneously made it impossible to move a muscle, and impossible not to run, but I saw it, and I can't rationalise it away, no matter how much I'd like to, no matter how hard I've tried.

There in the open doorway was a figure, half obscured by the dark inside the house, a darkness that was absolute, without any dimensions, just a total absence of light. As I watched, the figure grasped the door with one hand – with one paw, I ought to say – and began to close it. It paused for a moment, no more: just long enough to lean through the aperture, to raise its other paw and wave at us, almost mockingly: *bye-bye*. Then the door slammed shut, and I no longer had to believe the evidence of my eyes, or to cope with the notion that a figure in an animal suit, the costume of the Walrus from the old Beatles' *Magical Mystery Tour*, had manifested in the doorway of Shelgrave for a second, just to wave goodbye.

I managed to get Sally down the terraces and around the water feature. All the while, the storm threw its worst at us, soaking us to the skin while it whipped the surface of the pond into a boil. It was more a case of me carrying her as we struggled across the field, and I practically had to push her up the ladder back into the garden of my house. For a second I was afraid she'd fall over the other side and do herself more damage, but she seemed to realise the danger and clutched at the stonework as I clambered up after her. I tried to take as much of her weight as I could in letting her down the other side, but our hands were slippery in the rain and she dropped heavily – to the grass, thank God. In all this flight I hadn't looked back, not once, after that glance over my shoulder on the terrace. Now I bundled her inside through the French windows, still open from our impulsive exit, and deposited her on the sofa while I tried to work out what to do next. I was in the kitchen, with the stupidly conventional thought of making her a cup of tea, when I heard a muffled crash from next door. I ran back in to find her fallen on the rug. As I looked, I could see a spreading patch of deep red soaking through the sopping material of her jeans.

After the ambulance came and I accompanied her to the hospital, there was a spell in which I sat in the corridor, conscious only of the rainwater dripping from my clothes in three separate puddles on to the linoleum floor. A doctor came to speak to me, asked me what had happened. I told him that Sally had fallen from the top of a ladder. He looked at me, at first impatiently, then with greater attention. He bent to stare into my eyes, pulled out a flashlight and shone it, and when the policeman arrived I was in a hospital bed of my own.

Late that evening, though the passage of time was by this point lost on me, my father came on to the ward. He had a long conversation with both the doctor and the policeman, who I remembered had been asking me questions, though I don't know what they were, and I don't know what I told him. Nor do I know what was said that evening, in the light of the nurses' station, between my father and the police. Eventually, Dad came to the side of my bed and asked me whether I thought I could get up and come home with him. I considered this proposition for a while. Apparently, I could not.

I was released from the psychiatric ward around the beginning of November. My father hired a nurse, who stayed with me the first week back home, and then it was just me and him, alone in the house, me not talking, him not asking. In all this, Sally's name was never mentioned. I remember when I started to come off the medication my nights were bad, and it was after one particularly bad episode that my father came and sat on the bed, and I finally told him what had happened in Shelgrave that October afternoon.

He listened, with a grave attention that I couldn't have expected. He asked a few questions, and received my answers in silence. The matter of the figure in the doorway seemed to startle him, but again he said nothing. He stayed with me until the pills he gave me took effect, and what he did then I can only recreate in my head, for he never told me about it. As long as he lived he kept his secret, but it seems clear to me what happened.

In our garden shed was a two-gallon jerrycan of petrol for the lawn-mower. I believe Dad must have lugged this over the wall and down the ladder into the Shelgrave estate that night, all the way up to the big house. Did he have a torch, I wonder? The moon was the frailest crescent that night, what little of it showed through the wind-driven clouds, so I think he must have lighted his way somehow. I hope so, at any rate. The thought of him in the total darkness I'd glimpsed through the closing front door fills me with disquiet. He had at least a lighter with him, anyway, or matches, because when I woke it was to the sound of fire engines, the rise and fall of their sirens. They were coming from across the garden wall, where the firemen were trying in vain to put out the last of the flames in the wreckage of Shelgrave, now just a charred and broken ruin.

The police came to the house, but my father refused to let them speak with me. I could hear little snatches of the conversation from downstairs; the policemen asking polite if loaded questions, my father poking away every delicately framed suggestion with the straightest of bats. Later I remembered that my father played golf with the Chief Constable, which may have had a bearing on many things. We'd gone to bed early, he told them; neither of us had heard a thing, we'd both taken sleeping tablets. After a while the police went away, and my father came upstairs. 'Do you want a cup of tea?' he asked, and I said I'd come down for it. We exchanged a smile, tentative on my part, all but imperceptible on his.

In the kitchen, waiting for the kettle to boil, my father

switched on the radio. The disk jockey was in the middle of telling his listeners the news; that last night in New York City, December 8th, 1980, Beatle John Lennon had been shot.

I did not go back to school: it was arranged that I should take my A-levels come the summer, that was all. As I left the exam hall after the last of these (English Lit, discuss the dramatic function the storm in *The Tempest* by William Shakespeare), one of my former classmates came up to me. 'Where the hell have you been? Is it right that you got Sally Holden up the stick?'

I shook my head; as usual, the merest mention of Sally's name shut me up like a clenched fist. 'That's what everybody's saying,' he said, scornfully. 'She left school when you did, and Fishy says he saw her about six months gone coming out of the doctor's surgery. None of us thought it could have been you, you're such a virgin.'

I don't remember what I said to him, if anything. I don't remember the bus journey I must have taken to the top of Sally's street – I had a ticket in my hand afterwards, but all the ink had rubbed off it with the sweat of my palm. I suppose I rang the bell, which I suppose went unanswered. I only remember standing on the grass slope outside the block of maisonettes, looking up to the second floor picture window that I knew was Sally's. Behind the blank opacity of the net curtains, ceiling to floor, there was a figure that might have been her, or perhaps I only wanted it to be her. I stared up for a long minute, and then it turned away and there was nothing.

DEVILS IN THE COUNTRYSIDE

Though more famous these days as the affluent 'dormer' district encircling London, the Home Counties were once England's arable heartland, enjoying one of the warmest, driest climates in the whole of the British Isles and yet at the same time comprising rivers, streams and gentle, easily manageable landscapes. A desirable place to live in the 21st century because they share in the capital's regional economy and are largely suburban in nature, in older times the Home Counties were sought out because the farming was good, the villages pleasant and the fairs and markets among the most prosperous in the country. And yet, as so often in agricultural communities in times past, life was precarious, and the response to this could be worryingly irrational.

Even in the Home Counties, it seems that an undercurrent of age-old superstition lingered into the Early Modern Age. Relics of ancient religions remained hidden in folklore and village custom. There was a prevailing belief in and an active fear of spirits, faeries and other supernatural beings, at whose whim crops could fail, animals sicken and wells run dry. In due course, mainly in the wake of the Protestant Reformation, when the ornate, near-magical ceremonies of the Catholic Church were withdrawn and the peasantry left to fend against evil for themselves, a conviction grew – probably out of a desperate need to quantify the problems rural society faced – that these malign forces were all the work of one identifiable enemy: the Devil.

The response, though not as widespread as in other, more desolate parts of Britain, was predictably brutal.

For example, in 1612, at Milton Ernest in Bedfordshire, a certain Mother Sutton and her wanton daughter, Mary, were found guilty of a laundry list of charges, which included using witchcraft to paralyse a quarrelsome neighbour, destroying another neighbour's livestock by driving his animals so mad that they literally cannibalised each other, sending a pair of imps named Dick and Jude to torment an impudent child to the point where he died, afflicting a posse of men who threatened them with a mysterious crippling disease, and most astonishing of all, turning the village pond into a whirlpool before they could be 'swum' in it. How such claims were tested by the court, or even if they were tested at all, went unrecorded, but it's probably no surprise, given the mood of the time, that both women were hanged.

An even more arbitrary display of 'justice' occurred at Newbury in Berkshire in 1643, when a troop of Roundhead soldiers seized an old woman they had seen navigating the River Kennet on a plank, and after deciding that this was against the natural laws, killed her by discharging a pistol into her ear. Enquiring whether or not she was an accomplished boatwoman never seemed to enter their heads.

However, when in the more enlightened 18th century, in 1712 to be precise, the last witch trial in England saw Jane Wenham of Walkern in Hertfordshire accused by a local farmer of bewitching his animals and servants and thus brought before the flamboyant Judge John Powell, there was a different outcome. When the prosecution alleged that Wenham had been seen flying, Powell commented that there was no law forbidding her to do so, which caused much laughter in the court. The case was widely followed by the London pamphlets, most of whom supported the accused, and when Wenham was convicted, Powell refused to condemn her and petitioned Queen Anne for a pardon, which was duly received.

And yet, despite this timely arrival of common sense, tales of sorcery remained strong in the Home Counties until well after 1735, the year when witchcraft in England was finally decriminalised.

The so-called Hellfire Clubs first began appearing in Britain and Ireland in 1718, and were mainly composed of high society rakes, who would use them to indulge in wild parties, ravish local prostitutes and blaspheme as freely and extravagantly as they liked. But the most notorious was the club founded by the famous decadent, Sir Francis Dashwood, in 1755. The so-called Knights of St Francis were a riotous order of drunken, lustful hooligans, whose activities far exceeded the debauches held by their rivals in that, as well as the usual drinking and whoring, they involved women dressed as nuns, mock religious ceremonies and ghoulish Satanic rites.

These sacrileges first occurred at Medmenham Abbey in Buckinghamshire, and later in a network of manmade caves excavated in a rural hillside at nearby West Wycombe by Dashwood himself and christened the 'Hellfire Caves'. Though stories abounded that actual human sacrifices were held there, and that a demonic presence was once summoned, the evidence for such outrages is thin. In fact, one story known to be true concerns a baboon that Dashwood dyed red and produced in the midst of an orgy in the Caves, proclaiming it to be Satan himself. Most of the club members fled in terror, which suggests they weren't entirely committed to the worship of evil.

If nothing else, the main reason for the existence of the Wycombe Hellfire Club, and for Dashwood's activities in general, seems to have been to offend as much as possible against the conservative religious views held by the majority of his fellow countrymen, and to have a thoroughly good time in the process. But the Club certainly left an aura behind it. The Hellfire Caves, which are still open to the public today, possess an eerie atmosphere, while the Club's motto, 'Fais ce que tu voudras', or 'Do as thou wilt', was later adopted by none other than Aleister Crowley.

If the existence of Hellfire Clubs in the Buckinghamshire countryside of the 18th century indicates a playful attitude to wickedness, there were other incidents later on, which imply that some Home Counties folk took a more serious approach. As recently as 1963 and 1969, in the latter case on Midsummer's Eve, apparent attempts were made to perform black magic ceremonies inside the scenic ruins of St Mary's Church on Deadman's Hill, Clophill, in Bedfordshire.

In 1963, a sarcophagus belonging to the wife of an 18th century apothecary was opened, her bones taken out and strewn ritualistically around the interior of the church. In 1969, other ancient tombs were broken open and more bones taken out. The culprits were never found, and Deadman's Hill was shunned afterwards as a place of devil-worship, a reputation that persists even today. Of course, these events took place in the 1960s, an era when interest in the dark arts was rekindled by the arrival of trendy new philosophies, not to mention a glut of horror movies filled with new-

fangled sex and gore. It's possible that the Satanic desecrations at Deadman's Hill were the work of amateurs playing at being bad boys, though scholars were less convinced, thinking that what they saw at the scene were the genuine leftovers of a fully-fledged Black Mass.

MONKEY'S
Reggie Oliver

'The trouble with Soviet Russia,' said Straker, 'is too many chiefs and not enough Indians. That's what's wrong with Socialism in general: all very well in theory, but too many chiefs and not enough Indians. What you want is a small, well-educated, and of course benevolent, elite to run your country.'

Cavendish winked at me and said: 'You mean a Conservative government ruled by a cabinet of Old Etonians?'

'Well, yes.'

'Very sound idea, Straker. We must give it a go.' Cavendish was always amused by Straker's dogmatic pronouncements, and I had learned to be amused too because of my admiration for Cavendish. Very few people are good at finding themselves funny and Straker was not one of them, but he took Cavendish's teasing suavely, by pretending to be unaware that he was being laughed at. Cavendish had once said to me: 'Straker is destined to become one of those Tory Grandees you hear so much about: those secret, hard-faced men who rule the country from smoke-filled rooms behind closed doors. Mark my words.'

I believed him, because Straker was well-connected, ambitious and, in spite of his opinions, far from being a fool. The fact that Straker did not, after all, trouble the history books may have had something to do with what happened on the day the above conversation took place. It is a possible explanation, I suppose.

On a perfect summer's morning in late June 1970 Straker, Cavendish and I were standing on 'Rafts', the name given to a complex of wooden boathouses and landing stages owned by Eton College. Across the river from us towered the stately grey form of Windsor Castle, crowning a steep rise overlooking the Thames. On that bright day it brought to my mind the 'many towered Camelot' of Tennyson's poem. If I remember rightly, the effect was enhanced by the fact that the royal standard fluttered from a mast high above us on the Round Tower, indicating that the Queen was in residence. Between us and the town and the castle of Windsor the river glittered in the sunlight, caressed by a slight breeze.

As I say, that is how I remember it. It is all very vivid to me, but that is no guarantee of accuracy. I have learned over the years to distrust memory, a necessary distrust. All the same, in the light of what has happened, I feel bound to record what I think I remember. I have marked the envelope in which you find this 'To be opened after my death', and it is up to you to do what you like with it. Burn it is my advice; burn it even before you read what follows.

That felt very odd: writing to an unknown someone from beyond a grave that has not yet, at the time of writing, been dug. So, enough of this! Let me just set down what I think I remember, but please bear in mind: it may have been a delusion, or some sort of bad dream.

Straker, Cavendish and I were in our last half – term to the rest of you – at Eton. We had done our 'A' Levels, and our destinies at University or elsewhere were almost sealed. So, while the rest of the school did their end of half exams, or 'trials' as they were appropriately called, we could take our leisure.

That day we had decided to go down to Rafts and take a boat out on the Thames and row upstream to Monkey's, a little island in the river just below Bray. It was known by all of us as Monkey's, but its official name was Monk's Eyot. The story went that there had been a monastery on the site, but at the dissolution it had been donated to Eton College by Henry VIII in 'exchange' for some more valuable land nearer London. The site remained untouched until the nineteenth century when it began to be used by the school's rowers as a place where they could rest and refresh themselves before rowing back downstream to Rafts. A wooden clubhouse and a proper landing stage were built there in the 1920s. In the year 1970, the time I am talking about, there was a man employed to live on the island in the summer months and dispense refreshment to tired rowers. His name was Billy. It was a pleasant place, fringed with trees through which a path from the landing stage led to an oval lawn with the clubhouse, looking like an old-fashioned cricket pavilion, at one apex.

We expected nobody else to be on the island except Billy. In the afternoons on half holidays, the place would be teeming with boys and boats, but we were setting out in the morning, having obtained permission to be absent from 'boy's dinner' as lunch was called. We saw it as an adventure. The expedition had been suggested by Cavendish, not because he was a keen oarsman, unlike Straker who rowed bow in the school eight, but because he had a questing nature and an interest in unusual environments. A private island in the Thames was one such, I suppose.

We hired a 'gig', a leisurely, spacious kind of boat for two rowers sitting side by side and a cox in the stern. Straker insisted on steering. He pointed out that, being by far the superior oarsman, he would unbalance the rowing team and the boat would go round in circles, while as cox he could give us expert tuition in the art of oarsmanship. Cavendish and I accepted with a smile and without protest, but our first attempts at rowing after we had launched the gig away from Rafts were clumsy, and Straker got splashed several times.

'Feather! Christ! Don't you bastards even know how to feather?' He instructed us on how to slide the oar parallel to the surface of the water before dipping it in for the next stroke. After a while Cavendish and I began to be rather pleased with our efforts, though Straker remained critical. As we were passing Windsor Racecourse on our left, we began to tire of Straker's dictatorial manner. We wanted to enjoy ourselves, so Cavendish decided to change the subject.

'So, here we are! *Three Men in a Boat*,' he said.

'I tried to read that book once,' said Straker. 'It turns out the three of them are all lower middle class. And that bit about the dead prostitute is just ridiculous.'

'Remind us about the dead prostitute. I'd forgotten her,' said Cavendish. But Straker would not; instead he continued to give us detailed instructions on how to improve our rowing.

A river cruiser full of trippers passed by, going downstream in the opposite direction. They waved at us. I waved back but Cavendish and Straker did not, so I stopped waving as soon as I became aware of their reticence.

'What ghastly people!' said Straker.

Cavendish said: 'How do you know they're ghastly people?'

There was a pause while Straker considered a reply as we ploughed on, to the creak of the rowlocks and the splash of oars. Eventually he came up with: 'A lot of time is wasted in life by not making snap judgements.'

Cavendish laughed. 'A typical Straker remark! I shall treasure it.'

After we had negotiated 'Locks' which was what we called Boveney Lock, the countryside on either bank of the river became more rural. I began to feel that kind of perfect exhilaration that comes to us rarely, but most often to the young and (comparatively) innocent. It was as if the glitter of the water and the insolently vibrant green of the trees that bordered the river had been made for my delight. I felt, I suppose, that sense of 'entitlement' which is so virulently condemned nowadays, but if it was so, it was of a fairly harmless kind. I began to hum the *Eton Boating Song* until Cavendish and Straker silenced me because it was 'not cool', which perhaps it wasn't.

It took longer than I expected to row from Locks to Monkey's but finally the little wooded island appeared in the stream. We moored our gig at the landing stage and stepped onto the eyot. It was approaching lunchtime and we were badly in need of refreshment.

Once we were off the landing stage we were protected

from any prying eyes on the banks by a dense fringe of trees. On that bright summer day, the woodland felt as humid and intense as a jungle. No birds sang and Monkey's seemed deserted. Such was our carelessness that we had simply assumed that Billy would be on the island, but why *should* he be there?

We came through the wooded area onto the lawn that stood in front of the clubhouse. It was a long low building clad in creosoted weather boarding with a veranda along the front. A clock over the central front entrance proclaimed it to be ten to one. Straker shouted for Billy, but no-one came. I suggested we should row a little further upstream to a riverside pub in Bray and get something to eat and drink there, but Straker was impatient. He seemed to believe that Billy had no right to be absent from Monkey's, the school island. He walked over to the clubhouse, Cavendish and I following. He tried the door and found it open.

'Billy must be here. It's unlocked,' said Straker. 'Billy!'

The whole place smelt of creosoted wood in the heat. It was a smallish, dingy area with a few tables and chairs, and a bar behind which an enticing array of bottled beers and soft drinks was displayed on shelves. Suddenly the place darkened even further. We turned and saw a huge figure framed in the open doorway.

'Hello! What are you lads doing, then?'

Billy was shirtless and dressed in nothing but a pair of baggy khaki shorts and plimsols. He was of middle height but broad-chested and carrying a fair amount of weight some of which hung pendulously over the leather belt that fastened his shorts. His face was bronzed and red from the sun, a great slab of a head in the middle of which his rather small features were gathered close together. Reddish curls clustered on the top of his head and glinted in the sunlight. I suppose he must have been in his late forties, almost the prime of life, but he looked like a monstrous baby. Even today, stripped of the snobbery of youth which looks on anything over thirty as physically unacceptable, I would be repulsed by his appearance.

'Hello, Billy,' said Straker.

'Oh, it's you, Mr Straker, sir,' said Billy who had recognised him as a member of the 'eight', and was accordingly deferential. 'What are you and your lads doing here? I wasn't expecting visitors.'

Straker explained laboriously, and Billy merely nodded, uninterested. The only other time I had been on Monkey's in the presence of many other boys on the usual half-holiday, he had exuded a kind of rough bonhomie and self-confidence, but on this occasion I detected a certain unease in his manner. In spite of this he was very accommodating. He set out a table and chairs on the lawn in front of the clubhouse and found some day-old sandwiches in his fridge for us to eat. We bought several bottles of beer off Billy whom we treated liberally with the same. He sat with us and talked, quaffing his lager straight from the bottle while we decorously poured ours into paper cups.

The slight furtiveness of his initial manner began to dissipate with the sun and the beer. He became expansive and talked reminiscently of his time in the army during the war. 'Those Jerrys, they were real bastards,' he kept saying. He claimed to have been present at the liberation of Belsen. In those days I was very credulous, but there was something formulaic about his description of the event that even made me sceptical that he had actually been there.

'Them Jerry guards. Them bastards. I just wanted to put them up against a wall and shoot the buggers. I would have done too if my sarge hadn't stopped me.'

At that moment we heard a faint banging and shouting coming from behind the clubhouse.

'What's that?' asked Straker.

'Don't you worry about it, Mr Straker,' said Billy. 'Just something I'm sorting out.' Billy's unease had returned, but he continued to talk volubly. He began to expatiate on 'what those bastard Jerrys did.' He went into detail; and now it was our turn to feel unsettled.

From the 'Jerrys' Billy's talk turned somehow to 'women'

whose customs and characteristics, apparently, could be defined with equal ease. It was a hot day and I was not used to so much beer so I cannot say exactly how the transition occurred. He said many things which surprised us but which we, in awe of his experience, did not feel qualified to question. I glanced at my companions. Cavendish had a quizzical expression; Straker appeared actively amused. Billy was apparently very fond of women, but he thought they needed to be kept in order and 'given a good hiding' once in a while. They liked to be treated roughly apparently, and to be given a good 'seeing to' on a regular basis. He then specified various methods by which this 'seeing to' might be applied. At this even Straker began to look doubtful: some of the ways were very strange and unpleasant. We tried not to picture the scenes. Billy said that relations with his wife had taken these forms and that their marriage as a result had been excellent for many years until she left him. He explained that her departure was the result of his having 'gone soft' on her.

In the end, I can only really attribute our lack of protest to the drink and because none of us probably had ever heard an adult talk like this before. During Billy's discussion of women we heard again the faint sounds of banging and protest coming from the direction of the clubhouse. Eventually the noise became so violent and anguished that Billy got up irritably, muttering that he had better 'see to it', and began to walk rapidly towards the clubhouse.

'What the hell is going on?' said Straker. He sounded indignant that the pleasure of that afternoon had been subverted by this strange interruption.

Cavendish, more curious, less set in his ways, said: 'Let's see what all the fuss is about.'

Cavendish and I got up and set off, tracking Billy at a distance; Straker reluctantly followed us after a while. We saw Billy go round the clubhouse behind which among the trees were a number of sheds and outhouses. From the largest of these the noise was coming. Someone was kicking at the door and yelling. The voice sounded young and possibly male, but in my memory it had a quality that was not quite human, like the whine of a machine trying to simulate the human voice. The words spoken sounded English and full of swearing, but, like the language in a dream, were not fully comprehensible.

Unseen by Billy ourselves, we saw him pause before the door of the shed which shuddered from the blows with which it was being assaulted from the inside.

'Hey, you in there!' he said, 'You little scumbucket! You cut that noise or I'll come in and give you the leathering you deserve.'

There was a silence, the shouting and the hammering ceased for about ten seconds, then it began again with renewed vigour. 'Fuck off, you old wanker!' the voice yelled. These were the only words I heard from it that were completely articulate, and even they did not sound altogether real, that is coming from a real live boy. That is how I remember it, because, though my recollections of what happened are disturbingly vivid, there are aspects of them that remain obscure.

Billy's reaction to the creature's insult was unnervingly calm and deliberate. He removed his leather belt slowly from around his waist. Fears that his shorts might ignominiously fall down were allayed by the way the waistband seemed to cut into his barrel of a belly. Billy slid back the bolt on the door of the shed and entered. The belt cracked and cries of pain, unnaturally high-pitched, were heard. I looked at Cavendish and Straker. Their expressions were blank but, like me, they appeared to be held to the spot. I knew that a supreme effort of will would tear me away from the sounds, but Cavendish and Straker did not move, so neither did I. Already we were beginning to feel complicit.

The cracking ceased and the cries had become muffled. Billy came out of the shed, bolting the door behind him. He was putting on his belt and adjusting his khaki shorts to conceal, not very effectively, his arousal, when he saw us. Not put out by our appearance, he said: 'Oh, so you heard?'

We nodded.

'Those little toerags, they swim over here and steal my lager beer. All those little vermin, they come from Monk's Lawn.' We looked blank. 'Over there –' He pointed to the Windsor bank of the river. 'Next to the old Bray Studios where they do them horror films. Monk's Lawn is like a Borstal or approved school, or whatever. The inmates there, they're the real horrors. Little bundles of evil, that's what they are, that's why they're sent there. They swim over here and they make bloody havoc with my island. One of them tried to set fire to the clubhouse. So, when I catch them, I give them a good hiding. That's what they should give them over there at Monk's Lawn, only they don't, the daft soft buggers. My leatherings don't do no good though. They keep coming back. I've caught this little nipper before. He's a right little shitbag.' He paused. 'Tell you what, lads, let's have a little sport, shall we? You young gentlemen wait here, while I get something.'

Billy went into the clubhouse, adjusting the belt around his waist. Straker, Cavendish and I looked at each other. Straker laughed nervously. I suggested we leave; Cavendish smiled.

'Billy is an interesting psychological study,' he said. 'Did you notice the erection? I think we should stay and see what he has for our further entertainment. We might find it instructive.'

That mixture of pomposity and mockery was entirely characteristic of Cavendish. You never knew how serious he was being. His manner was widely admired, but it was also annoying.

'It will afford Straker here, our coming politician, much valuable insight into criminal behaviour among the lower orders,' he added.

'Oh, belt up, Cavendish,' said Straker. For once I agreed with him: this was no time for satire.

Billy emerged from the clubhouse carrying a long coil of rope over one shoulder. He winked at us and put his finger to his lips. We watched as he unbolted the shed. Billy left the door open, but we did not follow him inside. We could hear him talking to what was in the shed and the noises made in reply suggested to us that Billy's prisoner was being gagged. It was some time before Billy came out of the shed with his captive, and I could see why. Its hands had been securely tied behind its back and attached to the long rope, and a rough hood, made, I think, from a large paper bag with holes in it, had been placed on its head.

You will notice that I use the word 'it'. I do this because, however hard I try, I simply cannot remember what the creature looked like. I assumed that it was male and adolescent, but I cannot be sure. I remember that it was smaller than I had expected and that the legs were bare and unpleasantly thin. But was the skin black or white? I cannot even be sure of that: the legs were possibly too caked in grime and mud to tell. I think I saw a little rivulet of blood trickling down the right leg, but I cannot be sure.

'You don't want to see his face,' said Billy, explaining the hood. 'It's like a little rat's face. You don't want to see that.' It was true: we didn't.

The captive began to make plaintive moaning sounds from inside the bag, but Billy jerked the rope sharply, and it nearly fell over.

'Hey! You! Pipe down, or I'll leather you again.'

'Are you going to let him go?' I asked.

'In good time, lad. In good time. But we're going to have a bit of fun first, aren't we, gentlemen? Teach this little article, a lesson, eh? All right, go on, then.'

He pushed the captive ahead of him until we reached the lawn in front of the clubhouse. The sun beat down upon the enclave within the surrounding trees. All sound, except the faint rustle of leaves was excluded. We were cut off from the world on a private island where Billy was king and we were his courtiers. *Le roi s'amuse.*

Billy unwound the long coil of rope and shook it. 'Right you are, little horsey, away you go.' And he lashed the captive's back with the rope's end.

I expect the creature couldn't see very well out of its hood, because it stumbled forward and then fell. Billy jerked the rope.

'Run, you little beggar! Run!' The captive scrambled up and began to run off in the direction of the trees at the far end of the lawn while Billy paid out the rope. Cavendish sat down at the table on the lawn to consider the spectacle and I followed suit. Straker remained standing, enthralled as we were by the strangeness of it all. I felt as if I had entered an alien world where the rules were different. If it was an illusion, it was a curiously satisfying one.

'I can see this becoming a new sport,' said Cavendish. 'What shall we call it, Straker? You are the sportsman among us. You decide.' But Straker pretended not to hear him; he was absorbed by the scene. Billy was urging his victim to run and then jerking him back once he had reached the end of the long rope. Slowly he was driving the captive towards the belt of woodland that fringed the island. Every time he pulled the captive back the creature fell and had to be got onto its feet again with cajolements and threats. There was a kind of savage comedy about it all, like a scene out of Beckett.

'Don't they remind you of Pozzo and Lucky?' said Cavendish, almost speaking my thoughts.

'What the hell are you talking about?' said Straker. He suspected Cavendish of trying to pull rank on him by means of literary references. He may have been right. He strode away from us towards Billy and the rope.

'I think our friend Straker is taking rather an unhealthy interest in the proceedings,' said Cavendish.

I said: 'Aren't we, as well?' and Cavendish fell silent.

Though we could not hear distinctly, it was plain that Straker was asking Billy if he might take over the reins. Billy seemed more than happy to relinquish the rope and watch. Straker took over with enthusiasm, urging the captive to run further into the woods, then jerking him back at the last moment with a shout of triumph.

Cavendish and I had been seated, but both of us rose as one after Straker's second go with the rope and began to walk in his direction. I am not sure whether it was curiosity or the concern that Straker was showing too much enthusiasm in his activities. I believe it was the latter. I hope so. Perhaps it was both. As we approached, we could see the captive in the trees frantically trying to free himself from his bonds while Straker was urging him to run. In his frustration Straker gave a sudden violent tug on the rope. The captive looked as if he was jerked off his feet and was flying through the air for a few seconds until the back of his head collided with a tree and he fell to the ground. Straker pulled on the rope again but could not stir it.

'Get up! Get up, you little shit!' Straker shouted. There was panic in his voice. The captive lay without moving at the foot of the tree. Billy, Cavendish and I ran towards it while Straker remained immobile. Coming nearer we saw blood on the ground about the body; there was blood too on a broken branch protruding from the tree. It would appear that the creature's head had collided with the branch; a deep wound in the back of the neck confirmed it. Billy knelt down to feel the body's pulse. The thing was very still; there appeared to be no breathing.

Billy said: 'Bloody hell, the stupid little fucker's dead!'

By this time Straker had joined us. He said: 'Christ!'

The body was lying face down, the bloodstained bag still partially covering its head. We turned it over and removed the bag, to reveal the face. The shock had been great already but, now, as I remember it, there was a further and even greater shock. The face was not quite human. It was covered in hair, the jaw protruded unnaturally, and the eyes, still open, were black: little round balls of polished jet. The face was like a monkey's; like one but not exactly. The skin, under the reddish-brown hair, was smooth, without the dense network of wrinkles you would see on a simian. The rest of the body, what we could see of it under the dingy shorts and tee shirt, was ambiguous too.

That is what I now remember. I have probed my recollections many times, particularly in these last few weeks and that is still what I see in my mind's eye. In my dreams –

and I have often dreamed a version of what happened – I sometimes see a different face, just the ordinary pale face of a young boy in the throes of a terminal terror. Sometimes in my dreams the boy starts to breathe again, but in my waking memory the body lying there is still, silent, hirsute, and not quite human.

'Christ!' Straker said again.

After a long silence, Billy said: 'Right lads, there's only one thing for it. There's a couple of spades in that there shed. Go and fetch them.'

Cavendish and I raced off to get them. We said nothing: it was something to do. Anything was better than doing nothing. When we returned Billy and Straker had cleared a space a few feet from where the body had fallen under the trees, and we immediately began to dig.

One of us, I forget who, asked why we were burying the body there. Billy laughed and said: 'This is where all the bodies are buried.' Then seeing our stunned faces, he added: 'Only joking, lads, only joking!'

The four of us took it in turns to use the two spades, two of us resting for about ten minutes before taking over from the other two. It was hard work because the soil was crisscrossed with tree roots that we had to cut through, and Billy insisted that we dig a hole at least six feet deep. We did it in a daze of strenuous activity and sheer exhaustion, but it helped to take our minds off what had happened. Billy kept urging us to work harder and dig deeper. He seemed to take pleasure in our hot, sweating, tormented bodies under the tangle of trees.

At last it was done. There was the hole with watery mud seeping in at the bottom. Billy rolled the body with his foot until it tumbled into the grave. Filling in the hole seemed to take no time at all, though we were at great pains in the end to make it look as if the ground had not been disturbed at all. No-one was to know, except us four.

'There we are,' said Billy stamping down a slice of turf onto the grave. 'Rest in peace, you dirty little monkey.' Straker sniggered; Cavendish and I were silent. I think it was only then that the full enormity of what had happened came upon us. We hated what Billy had said, but we hated ourselves hardly any less. At least I did.

Very soon after we were rowing away from Monkey's. Billy did not see us off. When we were several hundred yards downstream of the island, Cavendish said: 'We don't talk about this ever again.' Straker and I nodded and the rest of the row downstream to Rafts took place in silence.

As far as I remember, none of us ever did mention what had happened to each other or to anyone else, so it is strange that my recollection of it – if it is a recollection – is so clear in some respects. I do remember that for a week or so after the incident, I studied the local paper for the announcement of a young boy's disappearance, but there was nothing. That was reassuring in a way. Then came the end of the half, the end of our school life, and the beginning of another.

A few years later I read that the old clubhouse on Monkey's had burned down one summer night, and that Billy had perished with it. In its place now stands a magnificent new building which, in the Etonian vacations, hosts weddings, conferences and 'team building events'. As for me, I took the Civil Service exam from Oxford and went into the Home Office, retiring a couple of years ago with the regulation knighthood and OBE. During my time there I did once look up the file on a Young Offender's Institution called Monk's Lawn near Bray. It had been closed down due to some scandal or other, but the file was so heavily redacted that I got practically no information from it, which was something of a relief; so I left it at that.

Over the years, I came to believe that what I have recorded was an illusion, some sort of dream. Whether my so-called memories are an imaginary torment or a strategy, planned by my subconscious to protect me from a still more horrible reality, I have no idea. Such unanswerable questions should be dismissed from the mind, but they are precisely the ones which never are.

About a month ago Cavendish wrote to me. We had not

been in touch for many years, and I have no idea how he had got hold of my address. It angers me now that he did. The letter told me nothing about himself, but simply informed me that Straker had committed suicide. It was done in a barn on his estate in Norfolk. Cavendish added the unnecessary detail that Straker had hanged himself from one of the beams, at the end of a long rope.

THE OSTRICH INN

Murderous landlords lurking in remote wayside inns is a staple of British folklore. Several counties in England boast such tales, Cornwall, Cumbria and Norfolk to name but three. But it is on the border between Berkshire and Buckinghamshire, in the heart of the genteel Home Counties, where one of the most famous and certainly one of the most ghoulish is to be found.

The Ostrich Inn, which still stands today, was originally erected on the old London to Bath road. It is a familiar fixture in the quaint, semi-rural village of Colnbrook, in what is now Berkshire, where it has stood for more centuries than anyone is actually sure. The present building dates back to around 1500 (when it was still part of Buckinghamshire), but a much older structure had occupied the site previously. This too was an inn, its antecedents traceable at least as far back as 1106, from whence a local charter relates how the Norman baron, Milo Crispin, permitted Abingdon Abbey to provide accommodation in the district for weary travellers. It wasn't called The Ostrich back in those formative days, but The Hospice or, in local parlance, The Osbridge, and it is from this awkward early pronunciation that the modern-day name is believed to have descended. And it's a name that was spoken regularly because by 1600, The Ostrich Inn had gained a notorious reputation. This was thanks mainly to its appearance (under a nom de plume, The Crane), in the novel The Historie of Thomas of Reading *written by Thomas Deloney, a lurid tale in which the author described a series of terrible events said to have occurred shortly after the new building was constructed.*

It seems that in the 16ᵗʰ century, the road from London to Bath was isolated and heavily wooded. It was not the kind of route that wayfarers would happily take in the dark, so The Ostrich Inn, located at the start of it, which offered warm lights and a merry welcome, was always well received. Though not by Thomas Cole, a wealthy merchant from Reading, who one evening happened to be making the journey alone. Having dined well that night thanks to the apparent generosity of the landlord of The Ostrich, a man known simply as Jarman, he was shown up to the inn's prize bedroom, a large comfortable chamber dominated by a four-poster bed.

Later that night, a secret viewing panel slid back in one of the bedroom's walls, and once it was ascertained that the guest was asleep, wooden pegs were removed from beneath the floorboards under the bed, and the bed, which was not a real bed at all, dropped downward at a steep angle, depositing its occupant onto a greased chute, which precipitated him down to a boiling cauldron in the cellar.

Thomas Cole died by being boiled alive in melted tallow.

How long this took is anyone's guess, and it would have been quite a miracle if his screams hadn't been heard elsewhere in the building. Though perhaps it was the case that such assaults on guests would only be launched when there was nobody else on the premises. When Cole was dead, Jarman and his sole accomplice, his wife, disposed of the corpse in the River Coln, and then set about stripping the room of the merchant's valuables. Cole's horse was already in the stables, but apparently it was a skittish beast and when unfamiliar hands were laid on it, it kicked its way free and fled.

The villainous landlord was unconcerned, but that would prove to be a fatal error. The horse did not run far, but entered a field belonging to a local landowner, where it was attracted by the scent of a mare. A few days later, the landowner discovered that he had an extra steed, and a rather fine beast at that. Thinking it might have escaped from the next nearest property, which was The Ostrich, he took it there himself. On the road, he encountered a servant of Thomas Cole, who was searching for his master. The servant immediately recognised the horse. Sensing there was evil work afoot, though still, or so the story goes, not suspecting anyone at The Ostrich, the landowner headed over there with his men to ask some questions. On seeing the armed force approaching, Jarman panicked, leapt onto his own horse and galloped away. The landowner was startled, but suspecting what had happened, he arrested the landlord's wife and demanded an explanation, which immediately was forthcoming.

Jarman himself was captured a few days later while hiding out in

Windsor Forest. Realising the game was up, he too confessed, saying that he had fashioned both the bed and the bedroom deliberately, to make a living from robbing and murdering his guests. Though he kept no records, he claimed to have despatched as many as 60 such unfortunates, maybe more. The story created a sensation even in Tudor England, where bandits and footpads were commonplace, and quite a crowd gathered to watch when Jarman and his wife were hanged.

This account comes to us from Deloney's novel, but the rural population of southern England were in no doubt that these events had really happened. The story circulated widely before the novel was even published. And as late as the start of the 20th century, the elderly landlady of The Ostrich would show guests the bedroom where the terrible deeds were actually done, though by this time the trapdoor had been built over.

THE OLD, COLD CLAY
Gail-Nina Anderson

Another day appeasing the barbarian hordes, thought Viv, as the garden gate closed behind her with a satisfying snick. She started to run through the litany of questions which would definitely *not* make her roll her eyes, lose her temper or descend to sarcasm. Yes, it was indeed a medieval town (and older, much older) but no, there weren't many really old buildings left – you'd have to look underground to find our roots. No, a chapel of ease was not for the comfort of the body but of the soul. Yes, they used to drive cattle and other livestock right into the middle of the town to sell them (and butcher them?, she wondered). It was all finished long before her time, but she could remember her grandmother channelling the memories of a still older generation about dreading the cattle market days, the smell, the sounds, the sense of panic and danger from the disorientated beasts, the blood (had they mentioned blood?).

She certainly wouldn't be repeating that sort of detail to today's coach party of visiting (she paused to check her schedule) American tourists. Why was her mind running along such gloomy lines, when by this afternoon they'd all be back on the bus and she could look forward to a coffee with Susan when she took their tips (Americans expected to tip – a point much in their favour) round to the vicarage to add to the church charity fund?

A couple of familiar figures were deep in conversation further along the street. How good still to have neighbours whose names you knew. Not so chummy as in her parents' day, perhaps, but then not so insular either. One of them looked up, not smiling or waving, and suddenly the memory hit her. Oh lord – last night, of course. An anxiety that had spread from door to door as word went round of a child missing from his home a couple of streets over. Timothy – that was the name. Nice young parents, neat house, quiet neighbourhood. Out to play in the garden, a friend's garden, some other garden and not back by tea time – or bedtime. Or yet, she could tell by the shake of the head one of the neighbours gave her. There had been a search, police cars and torches and later on she had heard a helicopter, and she had pushed it out of her mind by imagining a happy ending, a family re-union of clasped arms and panic displaced by the joy of relief. Or perhaps news of an accident … which might still yield a happy conclusion, plucky lad recovering in hospital. Not a crime, though – not violence, not where everything told you it was safe and you, who had always been here, always felt secure.

Best not to mention it to the tour group; best to put it out of her thoughts. Now, what else were they bound to ask? Oh yes – where exactly was this great Open University? She did have an answer for that one. Right here (pointing to self) – you're looking at it! She knew this didn't compensate for the town's lack of dreaming spires and college greens but she had indeed taken both her degrees with the OU (so much simpler than having to leave home) and for many years had been a tutor for the local branch, grass roots, at the hub of the network.

Duly disembarked from their air-conditioned coach, the Americans were all of a certain age (pretty much her own, Viv mused) and anxious to make it clear that they had read this far in their holiday brochures.

'So we're in Buck-ing-ham-shire,' said one of the women, rolling as many syllables out of the word as was humanly possible. 'Is that named after Buckingham Palace or the other way around?'

'The other way – the Palace was originally a townhouse built for the Duke of Buckingham, who was called John Sheffield.'

Those who had heard of Sheffield laughed dutifully.

'So you go all the way back to the Magnum Charter?' said one of the women brightly, looking around as though she expected to see a certified medieval ice cream stall nearby. Viv didn't bother to correct her.

'Yes, it was signed just a few miles from here, but human settlements in this area can easily be tracked a *lot* further back than that. And we're still making discoveries about our ancestors. A Bronze Age hoard was found not long ago.'

'Is that Celtic? I love Celtic design, don't you? So spiritual!'

'Roman too, I read on the website for this tour. You've got it all kinda piled up through the ages.'

Viv flashed the man what she hoped was a smile of warm, though strictly contained, English approval. 'Exactly. What you can see today is just the surface of century upon century of human activity.'

Which is why you're all looking slightly disappointed, she thought. Lovely spot, lovely location, so it's been used and used and drenched in all the things that people want and need, marinated in sheer unadulterated history but still in use today. And that's why you're looking at the same uninspired urban developments, the same high street chain stores as you'll see everywhere else. You need to look underneath the Victorian re-buildings and the failed Modernist office blocks to see how saturated this area is with ...

She suddenly realised that she'd voiced that last comment out loud. A bad habit; age was clearly creeping up on her, but then any project staffed by volunteer retirees was going to risk the odd senior moment. Viv needn't have worried – the most loquacious of the Americans, having taken in the town centre with a sweeping glance, was anxious to air his own professional thoughts.

'Civic planning, that's what it all comes down to. Get a good spot, decent transport routes and it'll just keep on prospering. You can see it's still a useful place to get to and from. Plenty of cars ...' they were passing by the large central car park that had once been the cattle market. 'Got to have a car, of course – otherwise things do stagnate. And then you're pretty close to London too.'

'By American standards,' Viv added, and raised a laugh. Good – they were back on her side after an initial disappointment that there was no village green complete with maypole, Morris Men and Punch and Judy, all demonstrating the desired level of quaintness somehow lacking from the familiar supermarkets and fast food outlets. 'It's easy to get to London, but round here we don't expect to travel miles and miles across wide open spaces.' She could see some of her audience swelling with pride, thinking big, suddenly homesick for prairies and deserts and mountain ranges and just getting in the car and driving away from things.

'And this is on a very convenient route. One reason the town kept developing is that it was a stopping point for the stagecoaches.'

'When you say stagecoach, do you mean like John Wayne ...?'

Hoping this was a joke, Viv smiled the special smile she reserved for that sort of remark and, so far as it was possible from between gritted teeth, went smoothly on.

'Well your own coach trip isn't so very far from our British tradition of travelling by public conveyances that would pick up or put down at stops along the way, though the terrain around here wasn't so dangerous that we needed outriders armed with rifles.' (Also, she added inside her head, their passengers would actually have been going somewhere, rather than meandering through south England attempting to fit the pieces into some vague and unimaginable picture of ancestral connections and traditional values).

As they were being hustled into the oldest pub in town (allegedly) for lunch, the chatter was interrupted by the clashing sirens of police car and ambulance speeding back in the direction Viv had come from.

'Oh dear – trouble in paradise?'

'Perhaps it's an episode of *Midsomer Murders*!'

That always comes up, Viv thought – but today the joke felt considerably flatter than usual. Lunch took forever – it always did – but the pub was a great success. It was even worth shepherding everyone down the 'no Health and Safety here then' stairs to what Susan had cheerfully dubbed Ye Olde Cellarette, where reproductions of ancient town documents and scenic prints vied with the excellent air-conditioning system and cheerful staff in demonstrating how well the landlord knew his customers. By the end of the meal, though, Viv had caught the buzz passed from phone and mouth among the locals, not yet official but no longer a rumour because someone had taken a call from an eye witness.

'Yes, they've found him. No – definitely dead, dead for hours, carried off in the ambulance. A tree, he'd fallen out of a tree they think, body wedged between trunk and wall. Terrible, terrible accident …'

You just had to avoid dwelling on it, thought Viv. Keep going, get today's job done, see the site of the Eleanor Cross, show them the museum, ending up as ever at the church, which could almost pass for genuine medieval in the dusk with the light behind it.

'Oh this is just lovely – perfect for a wedding photograph! Is it really an ancient Bridal Gate do you think?'

It was certainly the prettiest feature of the place, opening rather disconcertingly from the churchyard to the High Street. A tile-roofed porch set into the wall, extending back far enough to cover a tiny, open-ended room with small stone benches set into the side walls. Today it was decorated with swags of white blossom and ribbons with tiny silver bells that jingled disconcertingly. There had been a wedding earlier in the day, as a scattering of approved bio-degradable confetti attested. Leave it at that, thought Viv: a pretty folly built as a medieval photo-op.

'This ae nighte, this ae nighte,
Every nighte and alle,
Fire and fleet and candle-lighte …'

It was a harmonious young voice but so unexpected that

Viv swung round and almost tripped over the singer. A youngish man, who smiled at her as he passed through the gate with a couple of companions. From the logo on the equipment they carried she could see they belonged to the local radio station (though of course it was mostly online these days.) His face was vaguely familiar, and he clearly recognised her. A professional look of concern replaced the automatic smile.

'Apologies for bustling through but we're *en route* to interview Susan.' (A church connection, then). 'Simply an accident. I realise, but a word from the clergy is always appreciated when it's such sad news. Only five ...' He shook his head as he moved on. 'An appropriate place to pause, I suppose ...'

Their interest piqued, the tourists clearly wanted more than Viv had planned to give them.

'Well it's a traditional feature, though this one was only built in the eighteenth century, at the very start of the Gothic Revival. It's a lychgate, the point where a corpse would be carried onto church ground. It would be laid here while the bearers sat along the sides watching over it, waiting for the burial to be conducted.'

'A wake? I thought they were boozy social affairs – didn't they tell us that when we visited Ireland?'

'Here I think it was the time of transition. Once the corpse is within the territory of the church, the ties are cut with the person who inhabited it. The soul is free, there's just the body to be disposed of.'

She could see the wedding sentiments and trimmings had been much more to their taste. Later on, walking back through the lychgate *en route* to the vicarage, she found herself pausing in the tiny space, suddenly taken up with what it meant. You hoped for the soul but you said goodbye to the body, to the human attachment, to the thing you had known. Far enough back, before this dinky little wishing-well of a gate had been constructed, there must already have been something to fulfill that purpose, a liminal space and not sweet scented with orange blossom. Not even a coffin, just someone you'd held dear translated into a cloth wrapped bundle, earth to earth. And earthy. Maybe stains and seepage from a newly-dead corpse. How could you sit there and consider the change that came to all things, the passage from what was lived to what had to be buried? She shuddered.

Despite the comfort of tea and biscuits, Susan's thoughts seemed locked into the same pattern. Of course – there was the funeral of a child to be arranged.

'There will be an inquest but it should be straightforward. Poor little Timmy – I christened him, you know, only five years ago. And you'll know the parents – not regular attendees but definitely part of the parish. I've spoken to them – still in shock but they'd already begun to anticipate the worst and at least …'

'At least it was simply an accident?'

'Well yes – you have to consider that. No adults involved. They blame themselves, of course. He didn't usually play out unsupervised but there were other children and I suppose he got excited and wandered. It wasn't far. No-one saw him climb the tree. Just toppled out at an unlucky angle. And dead …'

'Dead before he hit the ground?'

'He never did. Body between tree and old wall, broke his neck, stuck there until someone's dog sniffed him out this morning.'

'Don't dwell, don't dwell,' thought Viv trying to clear the image from her mind.

'And who was the bright young thing I spotted heading this way with a microphone in his hand?'

'Surely you remember him, Chris Robson? Wasn't he in your Sunday School class years ago? Elderly parents, used to live in that big house on Stowell Street? He's there alone now, I think. Been back and forward doing the university thing, settled for the moment doing TV and radio. Nice enough but pushy. Wanted details – when was the funeral – burial or cremation – people would want to express grief. Too early for all that.'

'Even if it encourages a few more lapsed parishioners through the gate?'

'Yes, he said that, but I told him to tread very carefully. If it helps the parents that's fine, but everyone takes it differently. And we still have to decide about the Autumn Fayre.'

'It shouldn't have gone ahead, Viv thought.

An annual fundraiser, complete with craft stalls and cream teas, generating that comfortable myth that things had always been thus. Visitors loved it, it fired local memories and of course, it was going to happen regardless. Tim's parents, suddenly more involved with the church since his death, insisted. Once the burial had taken place they thought a sense of continuity mattered more than ever. They were young and proudly brave, thought Viv, with a new baby on the way. Perhaps that helped them to glide over the shadows under their feet. At the funeral, crowded with folk who had never set eyes on their child, their grief had been picture perfect, were such a thing possible. Was there a slight air of … celebrity about them, conferred by their roles in the drama? No, that was unfair – they were clearly distressed, though the swaying form of the bereaved mother, slender yet swelling with an odd self-aware grace, struck a discordant note in the cemetery, with all its associations.

Viv wasn't surprised to see Christopher there too, nodding discreetly at her, their acquaintance now recalled and acknowledged. Gratifying, but it was a relief that he didn't seem to be recording the event. On her way home she was surprised to bump into him again, as she walked past the offending tree, its fate now being debated by residents and council. There seemed to be no diminution of the flowers heaped up around its base, lending it an incongruously festive appearance until you got close enough to smell them beginning to rot in their cellophane wrappings. She had paused more than once to read the sentiments of the neighbours and strangers who'd placed them there, and saw that someone had added a photograph too, perched against the trunk, the image of a smiling child in his red jumper. Christopher seemed to be kneeling in front of the floral offerings. She hesitated before going any closer. Though she knew his name, they still hadn't shared a conversation, and she wondered whether he might be praying. He didn't look the sort – what a prejudiced thought to have! But she couldn't help noticing with fascinated surprise that he reached out and pocketed the photo of the dead child.

By the time he was aware of her he was on his feet smiling and extending a hand, giving no sign of his surreptitious theft. Did journalists just automatically adhere to anything newsworthy?, she wondered.

'Miss Lowell – I thought I recognised you the other day. And Susan supplied the name. It's Christopher. You taught me at Sunday school, remember?'

Viv's memory flickered, but she sometimes wondered if she really recalled anything, or just reacted to prompts and filled in what people expected her to have stored away.

'Christopher Robson?'

'What a memory! You were great friends with Mum and Dad too, but I suspect you heard they moved south a while ago?'

She had, though she doubted whether they had ever been great friends. She had known them, of course, as neighbouring church-goers with a son born late in their marriage. He'd not always been around, she thought – off to university and gap years, she assumed.

'I decided to come back again, permanently this time I hope, and take on the house. I've always really loved it – rooted there. Can't really afford to run it but I'll think of something. Too much of my history in there to give it up. And meanwhile I'm working in local TV and radio.'

'Yes,' she murmured, 'the house must be an anchor.'

It was, she mused, the biggest in the neighbourhood, standing in a vast garden that had become increasingly unkempt. Was it only this year that the Robsons had moved out to somewhere sunnier and more manageable? She couldn't recall seeing them for some time.

'Sad though – very sad that this is pretty much the first thing I get to report on.' He gestured towards the flowers. 'Not much of a tribute to see them rotting away like this, not even in water.'

'And they smell so …' Viv had spoken before she could stop herself but, unoffended, he nodded in amused agreement.

And so something of a link was formed. Or retrieved. The sight of a bright and capable young man lifted everyone's spirits – a fresh focus of attention.

He was going to report on the Fayre, but insisted on helping too. 'Mum would love to think of me doing something like this.' He exhibited no particular piety but the explanation that he wanted to regain some sense of community rang the right note. Susan, remembering his parents and that early attendance at Sunday school, hoped he might become an attendee (she had always hesitated about using the term 'worshipper') but meanwhile his youthful expertise with modern technology was a genuine asset to the preparations. The evening before the event, when there was nothing useful to do except pray for good weather, found him sitting with a small group of the more dedicated helpers around one of the tea tables they had set up in the church hall. Viv and Susan, slightly exhausted from dealing with last minute glitches and fusses, were discussing their efforts over mugs of tea when Christopher, always ahead with anything that might be called local news, brought up the subject of the tree.

'Anyone a member of the Tree Preservation Society – no? There's a right old barney brewing between the Magnificent Mature Growth party and the Hazard to Public Health one. Can't they just put up railings to make it unclimbable? Surely it couldn't happen again?'

'I think it's more than that,' said Susan. 'Whenever anyone passes that spot they're going to think of young Tim. How do you want to remember him, by something that's there or something that's not, a presence or an absence?'

'Do you remember the little girl who accidentally drowned in a pond?' contributed Chris.

'Oh yes – and they filled it in and made a memorial flowerbed. That was quite a few years ago now.'

And, thought Viv, surely it happened while you were away? But reporters of course had access to local files as well as local gossip.

'I gather that Tim's parents were adamant about not cancelling tomorrow?'

'Yes, they even want to be here, if Joanna feels up to it. Sense of continuity, they said.'

'Rising to the occasion,' added Viv, thinking about that slight aura of celebrity their son's death had given them. 'They did handle the funeral very well, though I'm still surprised that they chose burial when cremation is so much more ...' (she hesitated before using the word) '... *popular* these days.'

'Difficult to submit the body of a child to a raging furnace, perhaps?'

'Shadrach, Meschach and Abednigo,' muttered Viv, and was surprised to see Christopher smile at the reference.

'Sunday school did make an impact after all,' he said, picking up on her thoughts. 'But I was surprised too at their choice. I'm not even sure which might be more eco-friendly, the burning fiery furnace or the cold, old clay.'

Viv shuddered involuntarily, but Susan had begun to take a professional interest in the young man's words. 'The churchyard is long since full and the cemetery won't offer space forever. I prefer to leave matters like that to the mourners and the undertaker, but I suppose I might suggest cremation if it came to it – it's certainly what I'd want for myself.'

'It's a matter,' said Christopher, 'of remembrance, of letting the dead take up their due space.'

'We do that in our heads, surely?'

'Of course – but with cremation there's an air of hustling the body out of the way as quickly as possible – and no proper grave. There's nowhere for them to properly occupy.' He paused, clearly gathering his thoughts.

'We had a cat when I was young, very young. A huge grey thing. He was with me all my early life. I don't think there was a time – certainly not a memory – before he was there. Then, in my teens, he had to be put down. He was old and sick and my parents said it was the kindest thing to do. Looking back at it now, I can see they were probably right. I didn't protest – I was numb with grief. But after the vet came in his little white van to take him, to give him the injection, I suddenly realised that I wouldn't have his body. I'd seen pet graves, little wooden crosses, flowers put there for a week or two until the animal was replaced or the family forgot. I supposed I'd planned something similar. But my parents said no – the vet would dispose of him. They said that it would be much more hygienic if he could just be all burned up cleanly and discreetly, sparks and flames, like a firework. In the ground, especially when it was damp, he'd just rot. The earth would be so cold …'

As he stopped speaking, Susan said thoughtfully: 'It's just not a good word, is it? Disposal, disposable … Maybe *kindly* fire and *warm* earth? Maybe joyful aerial dissolution or a peaceful nurturing return? Earth to earth or … bugger, it's raining!'

But the next morning was bright with the kind, fragile warmth of early autumn, so stalls went up and people turned up – and Viv felt it was one of the worst days of her life. She stood behind her craft and needlework stall in heated shame and annoyance. She had never got anything so wrong in her life – how *could* she not have noticed?

She had got there early, helping to set up and decorate the event, and the stall had been quickly filled with the donations she had collected: hand-painted objects, knitted and embroidered garments, the fruits of the local pottery class and anything else that consumed time and added to the clutter.

For her own contribution she had concentrated on making traditional ragdolls, but with a modern style of clothes. Children might no doubt regard them as unappealingly antique but Viv knew the taste of fond grandparents who saw Christmas approaching, and anticipated good sales.

No-one had noticed at first – indeed, the response had been decidedly favourable, with much comment on the lovely hand-made things. Chris was there but, she noted with slight disappointment, clearly in his professional capacity, this time with a camera crew in tow. She hoped this was more for the (admittedly minor) event of the fête itself rather than feeding morbid curiosity by milking one small accidental tragedy.

And yes, Joanna and Luke, Tim's parents, had indeed turned up, quietly dressed and exuding a subdued sense of *noblesse oblige*, as though they were minor royals gracing the efforts of the peasantry. Grief seemed to have conferred on them a certain glamour. Viv noticed that Christopher and his crew never strayed too far from them – she could feel the words 'brave parents' forming in the air – but she returned his smile when the young couple approached her own stall. Obviously ready to be pleased, they were stroking and admiring the items, picking up and exclaiming over each of her ragdolls in turn. It would have been tactless to say 'one for the new baby?' and anyway, she wasn't sure they complied with all the regulations governing toys for new-borns.

Then there was a gasp, and Joanna burst into tears. For a moment the tableau froze, then everyone regrouped round the weeping woman and Viv realised with horror what had caused her distress. How could she – *however* could she not have realised, have been so stupid? The largest of her soft toys, propped at the back of the display, smiling its carefully sewn-on smile, was a boy doll in jeans and a red top. A fringe of dark hair, wide brown eyes and a little snub of a nose. It didn't really look like anyone, just like a stylised doll. But if she had gone out of her way to represent the dead child, the result would have been just this. She saw with relief that the grieving couple were swiftly being escorted to seats and tea, while the camera crew surveyed the stall, looking aimlessly for the cause of this breakdown. Then the situation was rescued without effort by Chris, who must have taken it all in instantly. Before Viv realised what was happening he had bought the Tim doll, pressing money into her hand and catching up a plastic bag to whisk it out of sight.

'Just what I wanted,' he said, too loudly. 'Niece's birthday coming up soon.'

Leaning across to her, he spoke more quietly. 'Can't take it now, kinda on duty. Can you keep it for me?'

He didn't have to add 'well wrapped up and out of sight'.

'Of course – and thank you.' Manners were already smoothing over the fractured surface of the moment. 'Shall I just bring it round to you this evening? You live so close and I'll probably need a natter.'

But the crew were already moving him on, equilibrium must be retained, tea-cosies must be sold.

Christopher's house could come as no surprise. Viv had been inside a few times, years back when his parents had been more active in the church. What *did* surprise her, though, was the fact that although the evening was well progressed (for she had been duty-bound to stay on until the fayre was finished and everything cleared away) the front door was ajar and there were lights on in the porch and the hall beyond. Was he expecting guests, having a party perhaps? Had he forgotten her offer to come round, perhaps because he didn't really want the Tim doll at all, and had bought it simply out of tact – or embarrassment?

'Hello, Chris – it's just me, Viv. I've brought the doll, but if you're busy ...'

There was no sound of music or conversation. Perhaps he had just slipped into the garden, out of sight round the back of the house? She wouldn't have let herself in, but the open door was a temptation. What if something was wrong?

'Hello, are you there Chris?'

The house looked just as she thought it would. Three generations had occupied it successively, so there was an air of continuity, old furniture with modern additions, family photos, a vintage sofa but modern appliances. But no sign of Chris. Had she really just let herself walk right through to the kitchen? She would go straight back, leave the doll in the hallway – but the lights were on and the house didn't feel deserted.

As though she had spoken this thought out loud, a response suddenly came, apparently from below her feet.

'Don't worry Viv – we're not being burgled and the place isn't deserted. I wasn't sure whether you would come but I'm so glad you have. I knew from the start … do you need help with the stairs?'

In what she would have called the utility room, Viv saw that a trap-door had been opened, letting onto a flight of stairs down to the cellars. The older, larger houses did have cellar space, she remembered, remnants of Victorian domestic economy now usually boarded over rather than used.

'It's well-lit and I put in a hand-rail.'

She stepped cautiously down just as he stepped up to meet her, hand outstretched. The cellar was a blaze of light, so that for a moment, carefully watching her step, she couldn't take it in. There was a smell of incense, but a second breath reminded her of the church crypt, damp and more than just earthy.

'The doll is quite lovely – really it was *such* a good thought.' Christopher took the bag containing the soft fabric toy from her hand and guided her last steps onto the floor.

The first thing she focussed on looked like an old-fashioned fairground sideshow, a framework of wooden pillars and curlicues brightly painted, with details picked out in gold. She realised, though, that it was functioning as an altar, with shelves and niches surrounding a carpet-covered tabletop. There were artificial flowers twined with tinsel and assorted ornaments piled and draped, but alone in the very centre stood an elaborate gilded frame. She had to peer closely to make out the tiny image, dwarfed by the overlaid borders and carved edges, which was the mid-point of this gaudy, celebratory fanfare. It was a photograph, faded but still visible, showing a large grey cat.

She knew she would soon have to turn around, for Christopher was smiling at her side, expecting and encouraging her approval. This low room must stretch beneath the whole house. It was set out like a parody of a church service, wooden seats ranged so that a congregation could gaze at the altar. Viv tried to look without registering what she saw. The chairs were not all occupied, and some of them just contained shapeless bundles, damp-stained linen swaddled round an invisible core. Some she thought were animals, inexpertly stuffed dogs and cats or just bones wrapped about with tattered ribbons of cloth to hold them together, with sometimes a desiccated muzzle poking through. But wherever there were clothes, however decayed, she couldn't doubt her worst fears. Slumped like broken dolls were the figures, not just skeletons, which she might have found easier to bear, but remnants of what had once been supple living flesh, some dried almost to nothing, some perhaps embalmed. Rictus grins and strings of hair and features that, where she could bear to look, seemed to have been touched up with cosmetics. She thought that the bloodless, lard-pale white bundle in the corner, a mass of soiled frills and fronded hair, might just be the girl who had drowned in the pond.

Christopher, clearly ablaze with pleasure at her awestruck response, carefully took the ragdoll Tim out of its wrappings. 'That was so thoughtful of you. I knew you had understood.' He placed the limp toy in the nearest chair. 'He'll do really splendidly – for now.'

THE BUCKLAND SHAG

Though it has crude connotations today, the word 'shag' was rarely snickered at in times past. A derivation from the word 'hag', it invariably meant something monstrous and malign. The story of the Buckland Shag, which comes to us from deepest Surrey, is a well-known tale in the region, but quite a complex one as purely in chronological terms it has three distinct stages of development.

The story commenced in the early 1820s with the deaths of two lovers on the bank of a woodland brook running between Dorking and Reigate. This at least is a familiar tale. The boy was son to the lord of Buckland Manor, and in due course would be expected to find a wife of his own social status, while the girl, his village sweetheart, was of peasant stock. He broke the news to her that they must separate one summer evening when they were walking by the stream's edge. The story goes that the girl promptly collapsed and died from a broken heart, which apparently is a medical possibility but only if there is a physical defect in the first place. Equally grief-stricken, and horrified that he had caused his lover's death, the young man drew a blade and stabbed himself in the heart. The bodies were found lying alongside each other, the boy draped over a black rock on the edge of the stream, his blood trickling down it and flowing away in the current.

For a long time afterwards the tragic spot had an eerie aura. People would avoid going there after dark. Those who did would hurry back home again, swearing that they'd seen the black rock bleeding of its own volition, turning the Buckland Brook a vivid red. This legend persisted for quite some time, until it took a turn for the even more sinister.

Often in old country tales, when grave injustices lingered and Man could not fix them, other powers might step into the breach.

It was now the middle of the 19th century, and a different family occupied the manor house. A poacher was taking a short cut along Buckland Brook. It was around midnight when he came to the

Bleeding Stone, as it had become known – and saw something sitting on it. He described it as tusked, humped and shaggy with grey hair. When it turned a brutish, apelike face upon him and transfixed him with a pair of crimson eyes, he shrieked and fled. The horror gave chase, silently but with a hunched, shambling gait. The poacher survived but swore that he was telling the truth. The beast, or 'shag' as it was soon called, was reported several times afterwards. It never harmed anyone, but only because they always fled for their lives. On one occasion it was said to have leapt onto the back of a soldier's horse and clutched him around the waist as he galloped away. In time, the tale became so famous that Lord Buckland could find no-one to work his land in that vicinity. Frustrated, he sent a team of men to dig up the Bleeding Stone, bring it to the manor garden and embed it in an ordinary rockery.

After this, there were no further reports of the beast lurking on the shore of what was now being called the Shagbrook, waiting to attack night-time wanderers. But this wasn't the end of the matter, because yet again the haunting seemed to change form. Lord Buckland himself and several members of his family would report in years afterwards that they had seen a ghostlike figure wandering the banks of the brook late at night, and sometimes standing in their garden alongside the rockery. This was no humped monstrosity, however, but the ethereal, wisplike form of a sad and lonely girl.

BETWEEN
Sam Dawson

The smell of fresh cut grass. The sound of birdsong and the whirr and clack of lawnmowers. Up on the treed embankment a train puffs its way towards Surbiton then fast to Waterloo, but the men cutting the lawns are free of its call today. It's the weekend. In ovens roasts are basting, in garden and road children are roaming freely, their play only to be broken by the summons to eat. Their mothers rest ahead of lunch. Their fathers, dressed in vaguely disreputable old clothes, push mowers, light bonfires or repair tricycles and go-karts, handlessly smoking a Player's as they do, one eye closed, the way they learned in the war. An afternoon of deserved rest – a nap, a drive, a game of golf, a visit to neighbours, a walk to the pub – awaits.

This is the suburbs. This is the Sixties. These are the good times.

The Smiths are strolling back from a coffee morning. David is ramrod straight, but his limp is still noticeable. In deference to the weekend his regimental tie is absent, replaced with a cravat, his weekday suit with slacks and blazer. Shelley, younger than him, is as well-groomed and presentable as ever. She leans slightly into him as they walk, whether through girlish affection or because it eases his injured leg is not clear. Probably a combination of both.

His eyes track the passing London-bound train. She notices.

'Thinking that that should be you?'

He's slightly abashed. 'Not really – more the opposite if anything.'

'Is it something to do with the party? It wasn't Arnold

Janes talking about that new aeroplane they're working on at Hawker Siddeley at Kingston was it? He did rather go on.'

'No, not really. Or maybe it was. I looked around at the other chaps at the party and thought we're all something. Draughtsmen, engineers, managers, public relations officers. All pretty damn hard-working and all part of this brave new country we're building I suppose. And I wondered if it's time we took a break. Took some time for ourselves. Slipped away from the rat race a bit. Narrowed one horizon so we can broaden others. That kind of thing.'

'Running away? That doesn't sound like you.'

'No, changing gear a bit. And not going far. We moved here to New Ditton Close to be nearer our office in Thames Ditton, remember? And it's been a fine place to live. But the truth is, Bob's always been better at the client liaison side than I have, and I've always been better at the copywriting. If we were to juggle the partnership a little, maybe bring in an assistant, I wouldn't need to be there all the time. I could visit just once or twice a week and do the writing at home. It'd mean a smaller cut of the profits, of course, that's only fair.'

'But we've got so many friends here …'

'And we can keep them.' He made two dots in the air. 'Here's the office, here's your parents in Sussex. That leaves all this area in between. All that bit further from London, all that bit cheaper. It'd mean us tightening our belts a bit, but wouldn't it be worth it? I could research that history the regiment's been badgering me about, you could keep up your charity work, not to mention those local history pamphlets you wanted to write. Do some walking, get a dog, learn to paint. I know you're a Surrey girl, that's the point. I'd be relying on your knowledge to suggest a good place.'

'All right, I'll think about it. I will. But you promise that we'd keep our friends …'

Far away in the trees the *tock tock* of a woodpecker. Otherwise silence, save the faint ticking of their car's engine, as it cools from the effort of negotiating the track to the cottage deep in the woods. The smell of damp moss and leaves, with faint overtones of mildew, the inevitable accompaniment to such heavy tree cover. Little light is able to filter through the untrimmed foliage, which divides it into pleasingly geometric broad blades of illumination. Inside them midges dance, scenting sweat.

The single storey house is decayed, its windows blinded with dust, its roof tiles gone and replaced with rusting sheets of corrugated iron creaking under a covering of ivy. The door of the outside privy hangs loosely open, the grass in the garden is waist high and rank with bramble. High banks rise above it, laced with the roots of ancient, light-swallowing yews.

David strides stiffly to the front door, inserts the key with the attached cardboard tag that the estate agent had posted to them, then forces the door open against the pile of leaves blocking it from inside. The tiny hall is carpeted with them, all blown in through broken French windows at the house's rear. There is little inside. Empty tins, a china cup, jars, milk bottles, a few sticks of furniture, a pair of dull monochrome Victorian religious prints escaping from warped and cracked frames to a world of mildew. Long trails of ivy have punctured rusty holes in the roof and hang like vines, then snake across the collapsing wooden floorboards of the living room. Only the stone-flagged kitchen scullery is untouched by the heaving curls of fungi and dry rot that years of incoming rain have fed.

Shelley enters, to report that she has found the well in the almost impassably overgrown garden. 'It seems to be still structurally sound, it's lined with blocks of stone, though there's quite a few of them missing. Fallen in I suppose. Not sure if the gaps behind them are burrows. Hope not. But you can just see water at the bottom. I suppose it'll need to be tested but apparently the last tenant lived till his seventies, so it can't be too bad.'

Gingerly stepping from intact joist to intact joist, David investigates the other rooms, then sums up disparagingly: 'No piped water. But we *could* run a pump from the well. No phone. But that's easy to fix. No electricity. That isn't. It'd cost a fortune to have it extended out to here. No indoor bathroom, only one bedroom, we'd need to build those on the side. No sewerage. That'd mean putting in a septic tank or the authorities would ban occupation.'

There's a slight skip in Shelley's step as she explores. 'It's not wholly without charm, though. The woods are rather wonderful, it's quiet, you could really get some work done here without any distractions ...'

For his own reasons David is not seduced by dense foliage the way that Shelley is. 'The lack of distractions includes the fact that it's four miles from the nearest village, and at least two from the closest farm. Completely isolated. Every winter the hamlets in these hills get snowed in for weeks at a time. This isn't the suburbs anymore, conveniently located between town and country. This place is small. It's up a mud track and it's pretty near falling down. There's a reason why they're asking next to nothing for it.'

That fact hasn't escaped Shelley. Empty for years, the cottage had for centuries been the home of generations of lone foresters tasked with managing the hundreds of acres of forest owned by a local grand house. It is of little use now to its new owners, the Forestry Commission, who have been handed the entire estate in lieu of death duties.

'I'd rather thought that the price might mean we could take out a loan to cover the purchase price and stay on at the Close till the work's done. I must admit I've become rather fond of an indoor bathroom and hot and cold running water.'

David picks at the wood of a window frame and is rewarded by a great strip of it peeling damply away in his hands. He looks at Shelley and raises an eyebrow.

Unabashed, she continues: 'Oh, and you didn't see, under all that undergrowth there's a big brick outhouse for sawing wood and storing tools. It could be made into two rooms. With skylights. One for you to write in and the other ... well, do you know I don't think I'd realised till now how much I'd love a studio?'

This is the countryside. This is the Sixties. With some work, with patience and farsightedness, these too could be the good times.

He's up to his waist in the hole he's dug when their Hillman Minx once again grinds its way up the rutted track and parks in the near permanent shadow of the trees that overgrow the house and garden. His back is stiff and painful as he puts aside the shovel, but that doesn't disguise the fact that a certain athleticism has returned to him during these last months of restoring the building every weekend.

Shelley is carrying two paper bags of groceries. She uses her bottom to shut the car door, steps over and peers into the hole.

'I say, you've gone deep. Surely the foundations don't have to be that far down, do they?'

He climbs out, sweating slightly, and puts on his cardigan. 'No, they don't, but it was so easy to dig that I thought I might make myself a little wine cellar while I was at it. But I'm thinking of giving it up. Look, once you get below about two feet you start finding these damn little tunnels everywhere. Badgers I suppose, though they must be pretty ancient. No spoor. No fur. Like those ones.' He points at the cavities that pockmark the yew-heavy bank that towers over the bungalow – where he never feels quite comfortable – and puncture the earth between the endlessly overlapping serpentine coils of millennia-old roots.

'Oh, that's typical,' she informs him. 'Didn't you know? Lots of Surrey is chalk or sandstone. Easy to excavate. Nature's answer to the fact that refrigerators hadn't been invented. Anyone who wanted to store food or needed refuge from war and riot and religious persecution could dig a space out. Towns like Reigate and Godstone and Dorking are famous for it. Beneath the cobbled streets they're absolute warrens of tunnels. It'll be the same here.'

He can see that she has more to impart than just that. He helps her in with the groceries, puts a match to the spirit stove and draws water for the kettle, then tells her: 'All right. Give. What have you discovered this time?'

She narrows her eyes at him and begins to talk.

'Well, I've been to both Felday and Hawkesview – slightly funny place, that, though I can't quite put my finger on why. There's something missing though, but I'm not sure what. Anyway, so far as both are concerned, we're nothing to do with either of them. We just happen to be placed in the middle between them. It's not that Felday thinks we belong to Hawkesview and vice versa. They both know about this place. And us. In the post office they called us the new tenants. Not owners, note. I get the strong impression that we're on test as it were. They're waiting to see if we can make it. On our own, that is. They're not going to get involved one way or another.'

'Well that's good of them. Don't like outsiders I imagine, or anyone who hasn't spent their working life watching a plough horse's rump.' (In deference to her gender he holds back from saying 'arse'.)

'Oh I don't think it's that, as such. They're certainly happy enough to serve us in the teashop at Felday or the grocers at Hawkesview, I think. But there's something about *here* to them.'

'Mysteries upon mysteries. You're not put off?'

'Me? No, you know I love that kind of thing. Do you know, one day I think I'd like to write a book on this county and its folklore. You practically can't find a town or village without something a little eerie sheltering just behind it. Look at beautiful Shere and its church, where an anchoress had herself walled in. And what about the Silent Pool, where they thought Agatha Christie had drowned herself, and the Devil's Punchbowl, and Mother Ludlam's cauldron at Frensham? Practically every old church has a squint so the poor dying lepers standing outside could watch the priest genuflecting to the God who had abandoned them. Then there's Sir Walter Raleigh's mummified head at West Horsley and the ghosts of crashed coaches rising up out of ponds. And Druid's Grove – have you heard the rumour that they hold Black Masses there? Historically this was a county of hill-mounted gibbets creaking with the corpses of flogged, hanged and tarred highwaymen. It's lightly hidden, it's partly forgotten, but it's still there in stone and wood – maybe even in grave and grove.'

He hands her a mug of tea, and between sips, she continues.

'Speaking of which, since it's going to be our nearest market town, just look at the history of Dorking. Millennial cults, riots, bloodletting, religious persecution, priests' holes. They've got a funny stone there. Glauconite, or something, but they call it 'carstone'. It rusts. I mean it really rusts. Looks like dried blood. It's full of iron. They cube it and mount it in buildings as decoration. Witches can't pass iron, so you see it there in old houses, in the walls and surrounding the doors and windows so they can't get in. Imagine!'

David has already finished his tea. His cooling muscles are knotting slightly. He wants to resume digging before they do. She senses his impatience but can't resist telling him more.

'Don't you want to know the best thing? I saved it till last. I got it from the vicar at Felday. He was a bit embarrassed about it. Up to a couple of hundred years ago they used to release a lamb into that field down by the crossroads just five-hundred yards from here. A nice juicy, expensive lamb. Then they'd leave. Go back to their homes. Leave it to its fate. The vicar didn't know what that might be. But personally I don't see any fields full of sheep round here.'

Sometimes David and Shelley disagree on what constitutes 'the best thing'.

'Well, that's all firmly in the past,' he tells her, with finality. 'Did you follow up that card about the litter for sale?'

'Yes, but you won't like it. Everything seemed to be going well until I said that we were based here. The owner backed out, gave some excuse that the pups were village dogs, they wouldn't take to the dark woods. Well, I said it would spend half the week in suburban comfort and the rest being taken for

SAM DAWSON

lovely long walks, and that the advertisement said the pups would make good ratters, but she wouldn't have it. Even said we'd have no trouble with rats here.'

She takes out her packet of Peter Stuyvesant, then notices that there is only one left. Wordlessly David gives her one of his Senior Services.

'She's right though, there aren't any rats. Though something's been going through the compost I've been putting out. Fox, I suppose.'

'I thought there are always rats.'

He knows the answer already. It's wrapped up in his memories of the jungle war. 'The foliage is too dense. It prevents growth below. What is there to eat? Some nuts, I suppose. Fungi. Very few berries; non-poisonous ones, that is. Saplings for the deer, though come to think of it, I've not seen one yet. Funny that. And it'll get worse when the Forestry Commission flattens it all and puts in miles and miles of ranked pines. Though it's so dark and crowded now round the house that I wouldn't mind having a few ...' He looks momentarily for the right word then settles on '... sightlines'. But he's not being entirely honest, the first phrase that came to his mind was 'lines of fire'.

He continues his explanation. 'This is what we used to call a "food-poor environment",' then shivers. He is unsure whether it is the long icy fingers of the malaria he picked up back then making one of its periodic returns or just the fact that the nights are beginning to draw in, the work is mounting up on the cottage, and so is the interest on the loan that paid for it. He makes what for him is an unusual decision.

'Tell you what. Why don't we just chuck it in for one day? Let's go to the pub. On foot, I'm getting a bit worried about the car's springs. You can tell me more about your research. They take guests there so there must be a kitchen. Let's make them rustle us up something for our dinner.'

Her face lights up. 'Oh yes, what a good idea! But let's go to The Falconers, even if it's farther. Not The Woodsmen, please. Not if we've got to walk home in the dark afterwards.

74

That old inn sign positively gives me the heebie-jeebies. All those awful dark painted little faces covered in hair and hiding among branches. But I can just about bear that. What I can't bear is going inside and finding their real life cousins muttering and playing shove ha'penny and skittles.'

The following morning David rises early to pack the car for their return to work and the Close. With a quick look back to see that Shelley isn't at the window, he strides as quickly as his leg will allow into the woods. There was something he saw on their walk back last night, nuggets of sickly white barely visible in the buttery light of their torch. Something Shelley hadn't spotted, and which he wants to check.

A natural depression among the trees. Fifty yards from the house. Shallow and wide. Full of fallen and rotting timber and the spongy mass of centuries of autumn leaves. And atop or half buried among them what he thought he'd seen the night before. A charnel house of bones.

He is no veterinary surgeon, but after what Shelley told him he can guess they're the skeletons of lambs. Scores of them. One a year, she said, and he can believe it. Right up to two-hundred years ago.

Thing is, he's seen death and what time does to those it falls upon when their bodies are left in the open. And he knows that these remains are much, much newer than that.

Light morning mist. Condensation coats the inside of the windows. Indoors, the smell of the paraffin heater and the breakfast cooking on it. Outdoors, of rain, fresh fallen onto already sodden leaves. Autumn is here. A cold and wet one.

The cottage is nearer to completion. Once again it is time for the Smiths to return to their other life. Except that this Monday there is a problem.

'I feel so guilty. He'll be lost and alone out there. He's only a puppy.' Once again she stands in the doorway in her robe and fruitlessly calls: 'Boyce! Here boy! Here Boyce!'

'Better come in now, we're on a schedule, remember?

Home first, then the station.'

'Oh, David, he'll be all right won't he? Could a fox have killed him? And how did he get out, anyway?'

'In a house this age and with work going on in it there are any number of possible small entrances and exits. Especially with half the floorboards up. And remember what the sweep told us when he forbade us to use the kitchen range and chimney: what should be open is blocked up and what should be blocked up is riddled with openings.' Then, with a look at his watch and a sudden decision: 'Look, when we get home I'll telephone Bob. Tell him I won't be in today. Then we pick up your bag and get you to the station and afterwards I'll come directly back here and mount a proper search for our little canine Harry Houdini.'

'Oh would you?' Shelley clings to his arm and looks up into his face with relief. 'That would be wonderful. What a time for Mother to have that operation on her bunions. She won't be able to walk at first and you know Father, he's incapable of looking after her and managing the house as well. All right, give me half an hour to get washed and dressed then we'll be off. And thank you, darling, you are good.'

Still in his pyjamas and dressing gown, David again scans the undergrowth for their errant puppy. He stops suddenly, noticing freshly dug earth around one of the badger holes in the bank. Probably looking for rabbits, he thinks. Exactly the kind of thing a young dog would do after giving its owners the slip during the night.

Holding on to the roots David labours his way up the steep and slippery slope and, stooping below the overhanging branches, explores the gloom of the yew grove. On the other side of it is the depression where he has, unbeknown to Shelley, concealed the mass of scattered lambs' bones he found there beneath a covering of leaves and branches.

Which makes it easy to spot the fresh corpse.

It's impossible to say what has eaten it, leaving just the skeleton and some of the pelt and head complete. Or mostly complete. As with any animal left for dead, the eyes have gone first, but the muzzle more or less remains. On it is caked earth from where it had dug into the burrow on the bank.

David does not share the discovery with his wife. There are things he has to do first.

He is unusually quiet on the drive back to the Dittons. Shelley doesn't notice, too busy fretting over the fate of Boyce and her need to abandon the search for him in order to tend her mother and save her father from burning their kitchen down. When they arrive she hurries in, changes into her smarter, non-weekend travelling clothes and picks up her bags. In the rush to be ready for the train she pays no attention to what David may be doing. As they set off for the station she does not register that he is taking his briefcase with him, does not notice that though washed he has used no soap, though shaved no foam. Nor does she detect a new scent in the living room. Not furniture polish, or pot pourri, or her Yardley's English Lavender perfume, but the whiff of gun oil, freshly applied.

He promised that he would go straight to the cottage after seeing her off and he does. But not quite by the usual route. Instead he parks in a quiet lane well outside Felday, still wearing his old brown weekend corduroy trousers and frayed tweed jacket. They smell faintly of the cottage and bonfires and earth. The colours blend well with the forest floor. Before he locks the car and sets off on foot he puts on a similarly battered and camouflaging tweed hat, and distributes about his person a number of items taken from the briefcase: a hipflask; a cheese sandwich; a cork, burnt at one end, which he will use later to blacken his face, neck and the backs of his hands. The kukri dagger he pushes into the back waistband of his trousers where it is concealed but easily reached. The revolver he puts in his right jacket pocket; the box of spare .38 rounds for it goes in his left. They balance nicely that way.

It is heavy going through the dense woods, especially as he may use no path and must move quietly at all times. But he has all day. What he expects to meet he expects to meet by night.

Half a mile from the cottage he drops to the ground and begins to crawl.

There was a turning point in the war against the Japanese when the British began to learn from and improve on their enemy's tactics. Always use the least expected route. Eschew toiletries whose smell might give you away. Make ambush king, but to strict rules: find a route the enemy needs to use, get to it early, quietly and untraceably. Take up position, sight your weapon and move for nothing for days. Not to urinate, not because animals or insects are crawling over you, biting you or nesting in your gear. Not because your skin is growing mould or your clothes rotting on you.

David has not forgotten those lessons. His agonisingly slow and undetectable progress continues. Periodically he stops, waits, listens and watches. Then resumes his journey, crawling all the way.

In this way hours pass before he reaches his objective, a fallen tree within sight of the cottage, the bank and the garden. He flattens himself in the slim space between its decaying trunk and the ground, and worms himself into the damp leaves until he is completely concealed. With a piece of chalk he has picked up along the way he whitens the foresight of his Enfield service pistol, the better to sight along in the darkness, adopts the prone shooting position. And waits.

Twilight. A pattering. No more than that. Just a sound like a few tiny pebbles dropped down a long stony slope. Coming from the well. Resolving itself into the scratching of claws (or nails) on stone as it nears the surface.

Something (or someone) stops just below the brim of the well. Listening. Sniffing. Then raises itself onto the parapet. Hops down to the ground. Bent over, hairy backed, on all fours. Then raises itself onto two legs, and David almost shoots it just for that, for its repulsive transgression of the species barrier.

So that is how alone and shameless some past foresters had been, then.

That they had actually sought sexual solace with the

woods' shunned and propitiated animal inhabitants, giving birth to a breed of creatures like the one he saw before him.

In the dwindling light it is difficult to make out its exact form and features. But he can see that it has a vestigial tail. And that it wears scraps of decayed clothes. Then it turns its head and he is shocked to realise that its face has skin rather than fur, and that it possesses something between a nose and a snout. Its deeply sunken eyes shine red and dangerous in the dying light.

It moves towards the bank, taking one step with its legs then the next with its long arms, the way he remembers legless amputees doing in India. He only has to move the barrel of the pistol a fraction of an inch to keep it in shot.

At the foot of the slope it begins to sound, a horrid, wet mewling noise, like a toothless mute lecher asking to suckle. From within the burrow that Boyce had disturbed comes a low angry chittering, then another of the beasts, this one wholly unclothed, emerges and scrambles down, using its talons for purchase.

David could get both of them with the same bullet.

He has no fear. He can drop both and if more appear – and there surely are more – pick them off before they can even identify where he is firing from. And then …

And then?

He hasn't planned that far ahead, he realises. Kill these two and he will have to kill more. It won't be difficult. They'll go to earth, no doubt. Use their tunnels to try and flank him. He's sure there is at least one that emerges somewhere in the cottage. Which is why he is where he is. Where he can cover all the exits. Which he can, of course, block. Then in the morning go to a farmers' store and buy what they use for gassing badgers.

So it's kill one, kill them all. But why? For being repulsive? For murdering a dog? Because he can't sell the cottage knowing that he would be endangering any buyer? It seems that there are only two choices: tolerance or genocide. And hadn't that spot of unpleasantness he'd been in that ended in

1945 been about standing up to those who embraced the latter?

He has to make a decision.

He edges out from cover and stands, keeping the gun aimed. The creature by the well sees him, starts, then drops to all fours and hisses menacingly at him, like a cornered cat, revealing vile rows of yellowed, rat-like teeth. The other one leaps in shock and edges backwards towards the burrow, it too baring its filth-encrusted fangs and making darting glances at its companion. It is ready to attack left if the other attacks right.

Watching them both, unflinching, David lowers the gun to his side. For a whole minute he holds their gaze, keeping the weapon ready for use if needed. Then turns his back on them and walks to the cottage.

He pulls the curtains and treats himself to a cigarette. He knows the house is not inviolable. When he sits he keeps the revolver, cocked, in his hand. If he stands up for something he takes it with him. He does not sleep. He listens for the slightest movement: for the rustle of leaves outside, for the fall of soot in the chimney, for the merest creak of a floorboard. There are a couple of quart bottles of pale ale in the kitchen. Sitting with a travelling rug around his shoulders he drinks one, pondering. Sometime before dawn, still holding the pistol, he goes to the front door. Opens it. Steps out into the garden. Then lobs the second bottle of beer over towards the burrows and goes indoors again.

At daybreak he leaves and walks to the car. The bottle has gone. David has made his decision. Now it's Shelley's turn.

The following spring they sold their house in the cul-de-sac and moved into the cottage. They quickly became a familiar sight in the area: David on the long daily walks that he came to love and which helped relieve the pain of his wounded leg; Shelley driving the Land Rover that became their regular transport, and under whose bonnet David willingly spent many weekend hours tinkering. They quickly developed a number of favoured destinations, reached down those Middle Earthian lanes, the old, high banked, tree-rooted medieval holloways that still weave through that part of Surrey southwest of Dorking, steering narrowly between hill clinging villages. One weekend enjoying a drink in the garden of the King William IV at Mickleham or lunch at The Volunteer in Sutton Abinger, the next walking to Leith Hill or taking tea in Abinger Hammer. In the coming decades Shelley did indeed write widely on local history, including on Surrey folklore and customs. Thanks to evening classes, she became a competent watercolourist and had some modest success with a small exhibition at the Thorndike Theatre in Leatherhead. Her painting of the view from Prospect Hill was much admired, but it was her tree pictures that sold best.

As David had promised, they did keep their friends from the Close, still busy building that 1960s Britain whose confidence was so great that they only needed initials to label its triumphs: VC10, DB5, EMI, GEC, BAC-111, ICI, Hawker P1127, E-Type. They often came to visit, to stay for lunch and then a long walk through the fields and woods to some local pub. If they had a dog David would always ask them to keep it on the lead, 'For the cattle, you know,' and if anyone ever noticed that there were none, they never thought to mention it.

Theirs was a good and a long life together, and if their friends ever jokingly asked them what the secret of it was they would modestly disparage the idea and reverse the compliment. But even as they did so they might give the merest of conspiratorial glances at each other and maybe at the old painted sign they had found in a Guildford antique shop and mounted above the fireplace. It was from some old and forgotten pub, The Live and Let Live.

The smell of fine perfume and expensive moisturiser. The sounds of a neighbour's cellar being excavated for a spa and underground garage, and of Nigel slamming the front door.

He's in one of his aggressive moods, Esme realises. It means he wants an argument, sex, or to boast.

'How was the cycle race?' she asks.

'Pretty bloody good, actually,' he says (so it's the third option), and gives her a token peck on her proffered and newly facialled cheek. 'Tore a strip off some yokels on Box Hill. Thought we'd got them trained up by now, the old farts who live there. Thought they'd learned to stay at home on the weekends when we want the roads.'

He begins to strip off his red and black lycra cycling club gear and drop it on the floor. She wishes he wouldn't do it in the living room, not when the children are still up and the nanny could walk in. He stops to admire his muscled torso in one of the many antique mirrors. Absentmindedly passes a loving hand across his waxed chest and stomach. Finally tears his eyes away from himself and resumes. 'So there we were, going up the Zig Zag *en masse* and some plebs in a shitty little Corsa actually beeped us. Wanted to pass. One of those idiots who actually think we're not allowed to ride as many abreast as we want. His car would be worth less than one of the wheels on my bike. Do you know some of those pensioners actually live in *caravans* up there? Incredible.'

'So what did you do?'

He smiles knowingly. 'One OAP couple in a car? And a cycle club of twenty superbly fit men – currency traders, new media entrepreneurs, city lawyers, brokers, finance wizards – with an average age of thirty? We're the people who're making something out of this country,' he smirks, 'in every sense. What do you think we did? We *remonstrated* with them.' He gives a thinly cruel smile. 'They'll be cleaning the spit off their car for a week.'

The memory has excited him. He looks at his reflection again, unconsciously tensing his muscles, then at her. So it's to be option two after all.

Afterwards he remembers to ask her how her day has gone. He quickly switches off as soon as she complains about the work next door and why aren't they planning a similar subterranean extension to their house? Luckily the nanny interrupts her by making noise in the hall outside to discreetly signal that she is putting the twins to bed.

After they have kissed Crete and Toby and left her to it, he remembers another incident.

'Had an excellent row with some old biddy in Westcott as well. We'd all parked up in this little car park at the church there and were getting our bikes off the cars when this old dear pulls up and says she needs to stop there. Sunday service or something. Claims she can't walk and that's what the church car park's for. Silly bitch. These people just don't get what we're doing for the environment. And the local economy. Twenty of us drive down from town every weekend and we always eat in some pub or café. Not to mention the charity rides. What in God's name are they complaining about? Still, it got me thinking, wouldn't it be good to have, like, some kind of place of our own down there?'

Esme likes where this is going. She immediately thinks of the footballers and their wives who live in Oxshott. And Sir Michael Caine at Leatherhead. Not to mention Antonio Banderas in Cobham. A second home in Surrey could have real cachet.

'And lo and behold. What should we pass an hour later when we were on our ride, but some half hidden old house with parking, substantial room for expansion and an auction sign outside it?'

The next day they drive down to see it.

'Apparently it belongs to some old woman. Local author or painter or something. Popular. Lots of charity work. Husband died ten years back and she's had to go into a nursing home: too old now to live alone bang in the middle of the country. Dead set against selling. Really dead set, but it's out of her hands now she's being forced to pay for the home fees.'

Esme is all questions. A strong picture of what this house is going to be like and what it's going to mean for them is crystallising in her mind, and it needs to be fed with details. 'How big is this place? How many rooms? And where's the money for it coming from?'

He's driving one handed. He waves the other one airily. 'Minor details. It's being auctioned by some little local firm. No real publicity. So it'll be cheap. Probably less than a garage in our road. We can remortgage one of the buy-to-lets. Agency the new place when we're not using it. Maybe put a few clients up in it from time to time, set it against tax. We'll let Max loose on it. I told him about it and he's like "Before you know it I'll have HMRC paying *you* tax on it."'

'Max?'

'From the cycling club. Oh, you know. They went on holiday to Treetops. Wife ran off with a Kenyan beachboy. A week later he ran off with her salsa instructor.'

'Yes, I remember him now. So how many bedrooms?'

'Two, I guess. Living room, dining room, bathroom, toilet. Kitchen, utility room, conservatory. That's about it. It's a bungalow. Oh, there's a sort of, like, studio block. We'll rip that out and make it a garage.'

'Two bedrooms. Jesus! Are you joking?' Her dream of a Virginia Water style Surrey mansion is quickly disappearing. 'I bet they're not even *en suite*. Where are we meant to put us and the children and the nanny and any guests?'

His patience is wearing thin. He can't see why she can't understand what seems so simple to him.

'Look, right? Whatever else you might say about the last two governments, they both freed up planning permission nicely. It doesn't matter anymore if the locals or the council try to block you. You spend a bit of money, take it to court and next thing, the steamrollers are moving in. I'll go to Sunil. From the club. It's what he does for a living. Job over.'

Now she sees it. Maybe not a mansion, but keep the outer shell, rip out all the interior walls, build a huge glass kitchen and living area on the back. She's seen it every week on *Grand Designs*. In fact, maybe *they* could be on *Grand Designs*. That'd be one in the eye for her girlfriends.

They arrive. Beneath an honour guard of overarching branches the car lurches up the long, sunken lane to the cottage. Esme does not hide her disappointment. 'Is this it? All of it I mean? I thought it would have a bigger garden.' Her dream of playing tennis with Antonio Banderas on a classically proportioned lawn dies a sudden death.

'Can you see me pushing a lawnmower? Forget the garden. We'll be paving it over for parking.'

She still hasn't grasped his vision. His cycle club is maybe thirty or forty strong. Despite appearances, it isn't all just rich white men in matching lycra. As you'd expect from a London-based club there is some diversity. It's multiracial (just). There are some women members and two identical and very rich hipsters, who are completely unrelated, but whom everyone assumes must be twins. The one thing that unites every member, apart from possessing eye-wateringly expensive bicycles, is that they all have very, very large cars, made larger still by the addition of bike racks. Almost every week this expeditionary force of estates and four wheel drives – CX-90s, Q7s, Cayennes, RX450s, X5s – sets out from London to the Surrey Hills and parking spaces in which they cannot fit, down lanes built for carts and gentlemanly motoring, not for vehicles that are actually now larger than the tanks that manoeuvred with such difficulty to defend them in 1939. To Nigel it's so simple. Therein the problem. Herein the solution.

He decides to explain it, quite slowly, to Esme. 'You see that lane we came up? It will be ours. You could get ten cars on it, at least, plus four more on the garden. Prudential Ride London is next summer. Shutdown. We take over Surrey. Bikes only. Everyone in the club will be riding it. Now imagine. We'll be right here, in demand, in the middle of it. A daylong party. A giant screen on the patio for the wives and partners to watch us taking part in it live. Then all the men back here after the ride for the second half of the party. We'll get it catered, of course. It'll be perfect. And the most fantastic networking opportunity you can imagine.'

The traffic down from London had been better than expected and they've arrived early, ahead of the estate agent who is to show them the cottage. Esme crosses the garden to the well and peers down it, sniffily. 'I'm not having the children falling down this. The first thing we do is concrete it over, do you hear?'

He hasn't. He has climbed the high bank and is standing, hands on hips, surveying the forest that surrounds the cottage. He's trying to remember when he and his friends last did any mountain biking. Years, probably. They pretty well gave it up after seeing the road racing in the 2012 Olympics.

'Hey Esme,' he calls down to her, 'Look at this. It's mountain bike heaven. Me and the boys are going to tear the *arsehole* out of these woods.'

Nigel had been right. The cottage had been cheap. The rebuilding she envisages won't be, though, Esme will make sure of that. Last night hadn't been too bad, actually, she has to admit it. She and Nigel in one bedroom, the children in the other. Ania, their Polish nanny, on a camp bed in the dining room. All the plants chucked out of the conservatory so Crete and Toby can use it as a playroom.

This is their first weekend in the soon to be transformed property. For now the only changes have been the filling in of the well, the dumping of a vanload of gravel over the garden to make more parking space, and the addition of a catflap for her two Siameses, Vivienne and Westwood, and her Sphynx, Barcelona. Not that they need have bothered, it seems. All three refuse to go out unless she's with them, and even when they do they have a quick crap and then bolt back indoors to find some shelves to hide on. They don't even seem to want to enter the kitchen to eat their food.

She wanders out onto the patio. The two hipsters had monopolised it all morning for their vaping, but thankfully they and the others are out now riding a road race. She knows the timetable. They'll all go to a pub afterwards for dinner, as agreed with Nigel – they simply don't have the room to entertain yet – then be back at nightfall to pick up their cars.

Darkness comes early to the cottage, particularly now in

early winter, the trees and the shadowing banks ensure it. She sees the lights come on in the conservatory where Ania is entertaining the children. There's a chill in the air. She goes in. As she passes through the kitchen she notes approvingly that the cats have, after all, consumed all the food she had laid out for them.

She puts some more in the bowls, just in case.

The smell of Highgrove scented candles. The sound of a muffled bang. It is unfamiliar, as sounds usually are in a new house. In the living room, Esme half-heartedly pecks at a copy of *Country Life*, which she feels is more appropriate to this new environment than her usual *Vogue*. She has kissed the children goodnight and left it to Ania to put them to bed and read them a story.

The noise can't be the men back, she decides. Too early. And the cats are all in the room with her. *That's* what it was, she realises: the catflap closing.

So that's why her darlings are so scared. There's another cat here. Probably bigger and wilder. And it's been coming in and eating their food. The poor things! Well, she's going to teach it a lesson.

As she gets up it occurs to her that there may be things bigger than felines that can still pass through a catflap. On stockinged feet she heads very quietly to the bedroom. Nigel hasn't lost his London habits. Beneath their bed he keeps an aluminium baseball bat. She arms herself with it and creeps to the kitchen door.

She flings it open. The counter obscures the view of what's hunched over the catbowls. But she can see an arched back. Heavily furred, much bigger than one of her cats'. An almost primeval 'Get OUT!' erupts from her and without even thinking about it she stabs the end of the bat into its matted flanks.

What turns angrily to face her is beyond all her experience.

It is crouched, filthy, dirt and grease-stained. The head is child sized. Its eyes flame at her. Impossibly thin lips draw back over inches of livid and spittle-flecked gums, revealing row upon row of rodent-like teeth, yellowed like old ivory and sharpened by years of digging and snapping bone to reach the marrow within. The horrid stump of a tail beats the floor in anger or warning. But what pushes Esme over the edge isn't that, not even the fact that it is wearing the tatters of a discarded tweed jacket. What moves her to total, unplanned violence is the sight of the ranks of swollen teats on the thing's chest and the realisation that, like her, it is a mother.

The bat is a superb weapon. She swings it. Brings it down, axe-like, with all the force she can manage.

Esme has never had to lay a rat trap. She has been spared the noise when one triggers. The frantic scrabbling that follows the *snap*, as the animal's back legs reflexively pump at high speed, as though trying to dig its way out of death.

Its back broken, that is what this animal does. And all the while its head is turned to face her with pure hatred. It screeches. Long and high and loud. The sound of pain and anger. Warning and summoning.

Something pushes at the catflap, blocked by the crippled creature.

There's the sound of something jumping from the bank onto the bungalow's roof, then of claws traversing the tiles.

In the scullery the grille covering the drain grates, rotates, then begins to lift.

The chimney flue to the antique and now never used kitchen range clanks, bends, shakes. Soot falls from newly opened joints. Then the oven doors begin to move. Opened from the inside.

Esme turns, round and round, waving the bat at the growing shadows that surround her. She hears Ania, panicked, calling to her in Polish, the childrens' querulous voices asking *her*, not their mother, what is happening, the yowling of the terrified cats.

The smells of flesh and fear. The sounds of a food-rich environment.

THREE MORE FOR THE HANGMAN

The Home Counties of England have long enjoyed a reputation for being affluent. Even in the days before they served as London's stockbroker belt, they were known for the richness of their harvests, the quality of their produce and the prosperity of their farmers. But though there's a general rule that where there is good living there is relatively little crime, the Home Counties, like so many other districts in the British Isles, have seen more than their fair share of grisly felonies.

Horrible acts of criminality are not restricted to inner cities. Three particularly terrible Home Counties murder cases amply illustrate this.

In 1751 in the scenic village of Gubblecote, Hertfordshire, a certain John Butterfield, who was landlord of the Black Horse Inn, began to stir up his neighbours against an elderly couple, the Osbornes, who lived in nearby Long Marston. Butterfield claimed that Ruth Osborne was a practising witch who many years earlier had hexed his cattle. Whether Butterfield actually believed this or simply had some other grievance is unknown, but this was 17 years after the abolition of the death penalty for witchcraft, for which reason it is surprising that so many were easily swayed by him.

The rumour spread fast, and a short time after the town-criers of Winslow, Hemel Hempstead and Leighton Buzzard announced that the Osbornes were to be 'swum' in order to test their guilt or innocence, the elderly couple fled first to the Tring workhouse and then to a local church. Neither provided the sanctuary they sought. A day later, a posse seized them, stripped them naked and dragged them for two miles amid jeering crowds to a deep stream called Wilsone Wear. Both man and wife were bound in the traditional fashion, thumbs to toes, and thrown into the water repeatedly. When they failed to sink, a chimney sweep called Thomas Colley grabbed a wooden pole and continually pushed Ruth Osborne, who was over 70 years old, beneath the surface. A wiry countrywoman, she survived even this ill-treatment, but was in a very poor state by the time she and her husband were finally hauled out, having inhaled much mud and water. The enraged crowd weren't pleased, and proceeded to beat her with clubs, under which savagery she eventually expired, much to the satisfaction of Colley, who then made circles of the onlookers, collecting money for what he considered his own exceptional efforts in bringing a witch to justice.

What lay at the root of this barbarous attack is unknown now and was unknown back in 1751. At least that was the conclusion of the Coroner, who expressed bewilderment and disgust at the lingering beliefs in the power of witches. But it must still have come as quite a surprise to the local community when some 30 of them were arrested and charged with Ruth Osborne's murder. In the event, finding reliable testimonies was difficult – unsurprising when so many bystanders could themselves have been charged with aiding and abetting simply by their inaction – and only Thomas Colley was convicted.

Though a clear scapegoat, he was undoubtedly guilty and was hanged at Hertford, his body later gibbeted at the spot where the crime had occurred.

Just over a century later, in 1870, an even more vicious crime was perpetrated in the Home Counties, this time in Denham, Buckinghamshire, when a brutish travelling man called John Jones, aka John Owen, a former blacksmith from the Midlands, decided that violent crime was more profitable than working for a living. He was already known to the authorities, having served various prison sentences for theft and assault, but he either hadn't learned from these experiences or had simply reached a point where he no longer cared.

It was another blacksmith, Emmanuel Marshall of Denham, whose family were unfortunate enough to encounter Jones while he was in this deranged state. The criminal attacked Marshall first, having approached his forge on the edge of the village late one April evening, entered uninvited and demanded money. When he was refused, he slaughtered Marshall with his own hatchet. Now armed with tools, Jones then forced open the blacksmith's undefended house, where the rest of the family were stirring from bed, having been woken by the shrieks outside. First, in the front parlour, he killed Charlotte Marshall, Emmanuel's wife, and his sister-in-law, Mary-Ann, battering their heads to pulp with an iron bar. The elderly Mary Marshall, Emmanuel's mother, was assaulted in the back parlour, her skull also crushed by repeated blows, this time from a sledge-hammer. At the time, she had been attempting to protect Gertrude, the family's four-year-old daughter, but Gertrude went the same gruesome way as her grandmother. This left only Mary and Thirza, eight and six respectively, whom Jones found hiding in a closet, and also hammered to death.

The miscreant then looted the house, and as he was saturated in blood and brains, found himself a new suit of clothes, which he wore for the remainder of that weekend in nearby Uxbridge, where he cheerfully spent his ill-gotten wealth. Such profligacy from a man who until recently had been known as a vagrant aroused no end of suspicion, but it was several days after the murders were detected when Jones was finally traced to Reading in Berkshire, at which point he resisted arrest with extreme violence. Even after conviction, Jones showed more of the same spirit, begging the officers charged with transporting him to Aylesbury Gaol to give him just five minutes with a sledge-hammer in the midst of the unruly crowd awaiting him there.

His wish was not granted. Nor was his angry demand that hangman William Calcraft run ahead of schedule and make swift his execution. Calcraft despatched Jones to eternity in his own good time (which apparently was excessive).

But there are some crimes in comparison to which even the mob-lynching of a terrified old woman and the unprovoked massacre of an entire family pale to near-insignificance. And yet the perpetrator of one such was the least likely mass slayer anyone could imagine: a pleasant faced nurse and child-minder, who hailed from a good family and a respectable middle-class background.

In 1895, Bristol native and child-care professional, Amelia Dyer, began advertising her services from her new home in Reading, expressing a particular desire to adopt and foster illegitimate infants. It seemed a benevolent attitude, but what no-one knew at the time was that Dyer, despite her civilised upbringing in the cosy village of

Pyle Marsh, had a long criminal record, having been sentenced to hard labour at least once and even spending time in lunatic asylums because children she had looked after in other towns had always suffered at her hands.

Even in that era before the Social Services were formed, it was understood that particularly callous foster-parents, while benefitting from the money provided for their charges – especially illegitimates, as embarrassed families tended to pay more to guarantee secrecy – would withhold food and medicine from them and maybe even try to bring about their 'natural deaths' by plying them with opiates and alcohol, but this was always difficult to prove. Dyer had undoubtedly employed these methods in previous towns, but once settled in Reading, she let greed completely overcome her common sense.

Within a year of her arrival, the bodies of seven babies had been fished from the River Thames, all strangled with tape and wrapped in brown paper. Even so, suspicion only fell on Dyer because her home address was still recognisable on the last of the sodden parcels.

With several corpses identified and matched to those children trusted to Dyer's care, there was little possibility she could save herself. Though her solicitor attempted to lodge an insanity plea, the hostility the case aroused was overwhelming. It took the jury only five minutes to convict her as the 'Reading Baby Farmer'. Even as Amelia Dyer climbed the scaffold at Newgate Prison, with the hatred of a nation ringing in her ears, the investigating police team were revising their estimate that she was responsible for the deaths of seven children. Their new figure was closer to 20. But modern investigators suspect that Dyer actually murdered about 400, which would make her by far the most prolific serial killer in British history.

MY SOMNAMBULANT HEART
Andrew Hook

That was it. John Harris. Such a name could only be forgettable.

My approach to Surrey was blocked by the removal lorry. A large yellow rectangle: a post-it-note stuck to the horizon. Either side, considerable tracts of London clay were covered by the heath-bearing Lower Bagshot Beds and these eventually gave way to mature woodland as they pushed further into the green belt.

I kept a steady fifty behind the lorry. It contained my life.

Local radio kicked in and that was when I heard the voice.

John Harris. A salute of blond hair, a twisted leg, angled body, worried face. Some children are bred to be bullied and if it wasn't him it would have been someone else. That it was *him* was a relief to many other boys at school. It was only afterwards, with precious hindsight, that I'd begun to realise just exactly what we might have done to him.

None of this was evident from the radio.

'That was Anita Ward with "Ring My Bell", classic disco. And we continue the theme with "Lost In Music" from Sister Sledge, a hit in the same year: 1979.'

1979.

I had imagined that was a year Harris would have been keen to forget.

The day was gusty bright. Occasionally the lorry rocked sideways. I imagined my belongings – furniture tied to the interior with thick rope and stacks of boxes containing books and brittle things – shifting almost imperceptibly inside. For a moment I became one of them: a confused copy of DH Lawrence's *Selected Short Stories* wondering with its paper brain if it were taking a sea voyage. My records were contained within plastic black cases. I had considered dumping them, given the impetus of the move and the absence of a record player. But some memories are meant to last in physical form. I wondered if they had any value.

A kestrel hovered to my left. Something was in the grass. I remembered our tutor, August May, addressing the form with good intentions – *It seems someone thinks you're very happy, John* – before gesturing towards the graffiti proclaiming *Harris is gay*. Even then, I knew the situation to be toe-curlingly misappropriated. Perhaps that was May's aim: to offset us. But my discomfort arose from the knowledge that those who hadn't even seen the graffiti were now aware of it. Baiting Harris became public.

He returned to the radio. It wasn't so much that his voice was distinctive, simply that it touched a memory as succinctly as an epidural grazing the spine.

Any doubts flew as he concluded, 'You've been listening to John Harris on County Radio. 104.9 FM. We switch over to the news with Anna Letham. Be seeing you.'

Fucking idiot. I couldn't help the words that forced their way from my mouth. It seemed ironic that Harris had a face for radio.

I once told a girlfriend that I never cried at documentaries. The subject matter was irrelevant. But put it in a movie – *fictionalise* it – and I was there. She gave me a hard look. The credits were rolling on a yawnfest about terminally ill children. You know the kind of thing. The sofa was littered with tissues I had other uses for. Mascara ran down her face as though she were auditioning for *Stars In Their Eyes* as Alice Cooper.

'If you think it, don't say it,' she said.

I shrugged. 'I'm only being honest.'

'Sometimes honesty *isn't* the best policy.'

It was one of those evenings where creating space would have been useful, but our shared London flat was so small that one of us could only star-jump when the other wasn't around.

I dug in. 'I think it's because real life is meaningless. We meander from one situation to another. There's no context. But when you put it in a movie then you have a beginning, middle and end. Even something open-ended, deliberately obfuscated or unutterably arthouse concludes one way or another. That's why a movie touches me and real life doesn't.'

'Kids in movies are fictional,' she said.

I sighed. 'And your point is?'

'A documentary is also art.'

'It also isn't,' I said.

The conversation had the potential to spiral, but she stood and said: 'I'm going to bed.'

I remember holding back on, 'Me too.'

Now my bedroom is larger than the London sitting room and kitchen knocked together. If she hadn't have left, allowing me to buy out her share of the flat at a fraction of its market value due to the speed of our animosity, then twenty-four years later I wouldn't be standing in my new Surrey home. I trusted it would be something to thank her for.

Space. My final frontier.

I moved in gradually, reassembling my belongings until the house seemed less spartan. Sometimes I stood at the window and looked out at the gardens – front and back – which had been meticulously maintained by the previous owner and wondered how long it would take for me to fall into disrepute. I had read a book once, Laurence Urdang's *Names & Nicknames of Places and Things*, which had described Surrey as being *inhabited on the whole by 'nice', comfortable, and conformist middle-class people* living in *a plasticized commuterland with respectable villas and neatly mown lawns interspersed with patches of mild scenery*. Remembering that description I found myself re-evaluating my decision to move. What had happened to me over the years?

The mirror suggested I had aged.

On sunny days I ventured out to Box Hill. Avoiding the visitors who tended to flock around the Salomons Memorial I usually headed to the highest point at Betchwood Clumps where I would wrestle with *Pret a Manger* sandwiches whilst looked down on by occasional residents who ate their lunch unwrapped from greaseproof paper.

There was no doubt the scenery anchored me. London had its history but it was almost entirely manmade, whereas Surrey was the most wooded county in England. Box Hill itself had the oldest untouched area of natural woodland in the UK. Where mankind had encroached it was quirky: the Bronze Age barrows, the grave of the eccentric Labilliere who in accordance with his wishes was buried head downwards on the western side above The Whites. Then there were the Wicca and Pagan witches whose covens claimed the local Box Trees improved interaction with the spirits required for their spells and enchantments. It would be gauche to suggest I had found my spiritual home, but in some ways I knew I wouldn't leave.

Curiously my neighbours to the left seemed disdainful of my London career. Whilst nothing was *actually said* I gained the impression they believed I had bought my way into Suburbia with dirty money. On the right, my neighbours were almost too effusive: Margo and Jerry Leadbetters for the modern age. Roger (Jerry) was cultivating a red nose whilst his wife, Samantha (Margo), did her best to flirt with me in such a way that advertised her monogamy. One summer morning Roger encouraged me to take Samantha to Box Hill and she looked aghast as I disparaged the nine members of the RAF Aerobatic Team as they roared in formation overhead in some spurious flypast.

'Always the bloody Red Arrows.'

'That isn't very patriotic.'

'It has nothing to do with patriotism. I just can't stand ceremony. It's too wrapped up in tradition.'

'Traditions built this country.'

'Maybe it's time for it to be unbuilt.'

Her brow furrowed. 'Whatever do you mean? You're not a communist are you?'

'Oh Samantha. There haven't been any communists since the 1980s.'

Her hair fairly fizzed in the sun, her blonde locks curling like metal shavings. I thought of gripping the back of her neck and pulling her forwards in a kiss. It would clinch our relationship. She would push me off, huff, and perhaps a year later, one afternoon when Roger was playing golf, she would let me have her over her dining room table whilst leaves of edelweiss fluttered in a cut-glass vase.

It was at one of Roger and Samantha's parties that I became reacquainted with John Harris.

The evening was September dark. Samantha had knocked on my door, all over-dressed elegant, and insisted I pop over for at least a drink considering I had tactfully managed to avoid her previous invitations. Her fingers that gripped the tips of mine were warmer than I had imagined. I made the usual excuses of not being dressed for the occasion, but found myself hustled from my house into hers with insufficient ceremony for someone who approved of tradition.

Harris stood with his back to me, in front of the canapés. I later found to Samantha's embarrassment that some of them hadn't defrosted. *It* was *a Delia recipe.* I recognised him instantly. A barely perceptible hunch spoiled the cut of his jacket, as though he wore a tortoise as a back pack. He affected a casual stance, a conscious attempt to negate his gammy leg. I wondered for a moment what disability he actually had. Perhaps it was no more than appearance. It crossed my mind for the first time that he had never attended what were known as Special Schools. Yet even from the rear I knew he had regained some poise. If that hadn't been evident enough from the radio it was clear in the flesh. He was flanked either side by two beautiful women, both of whom I would have had in an instant.

I was sleepwalked across to the table, Samantha's fingers digging into the cotton of my right forearm through my shirtsleeves. I realised Harris was the star turn: her main guest. As though underwater I heard her say, 'John, this is Ian Baxter. He lives next door.'

Harris turned in slow motion. I wished I were a woman with the luxury of a married name. Even so, recognition was instant. Harris stuck out a hand; each finger seemed independently alive.

'Why Ian,' he said, 'I do believe we've met.'

In 1979 any thoughts of touching Harris would have been abhorrent. He was a leper bar the disease. The only exceptions would have been to furiously flick his ears until they were so red they could be seen from space, or the time we gave him the bumps on his birthday within a patch of stinging nettles.

I glanced at his hand in the way a vegetarian might regard raw meat.

I remembered an instance in PE where the teacher made Harris repeat the triple jump over and over again because he couldn't hop, step or jump in the right order. The sequence was lost on him, and with each mistake our laughter rose.

I realised I associated disability with Harris. *Unclean.* I then realised that unlike Harris I hadn't grown up. I found myself extending my own hand, until it touched his in a firm shake just like every other. There was no malice, no aversion. It just was.

'I hadn't realised you two knew each other.'

Samantha was disappointed. She had hoped to impress me with the local radio star.

'It was a long time ago,' I heard Harris say. 'We were at school together. I was the cripple and he was one of the bullies.'

I glanced at Samantha but her face revealed nothing. I then realised Harris hadn't said anything at all.

'It was a long time ago,' I said. 'We were at school together. I'm surprised he remembers me.'

My attempt to play down my role was clumsy, but heartfelt. I certainly hadn't been the main protagonist. Just another boy who jeered and never reported it. Just someone who knew they had to blend in or find *themselves* a target.

'It's been some time,' Harris said. He smiled and there was something behind it. I glanced at the clock. Then Roger thumped my back rather harder than intended and said in an overly loud voice, 'I see you've met our local celebrity.'

The usual pleasantries were exchanged and I slipped into a corner of the room where I was set upon by one of Samantha's predatory friends. In her black suit and red sash she resembled a toreador and in the next twenty minutes I was gored to death.

Harris caught up with me at the end of the evening. 'I see you fell out of London too.'

'They say if you get tired of London you get tired of life.'

I had no idea what I meant by the statement.

'It's easier to fit in here,' Harris said. 'There's eight million people in London but it's easy to be alone. These people are charming even if they don't know they exist.'

Now I was puzzled by his dialogue.

'You remember *The Stepford Wives*?' he asked, suddenly conspiratorial, bending close enough that the acrid smell of brandy carried with his breath.

'Of course.'

'It's no different here.' He gesticulated to the room, one arm swinging out to encompass them all, a smile on his face indicating acceptance even if at heart it were disingenuous. 'None of them really *feel* anything. Do you remember what it's like to feel anything?'

I scratched my head. Since moving to Surrey I hadn't gone to the movies, and had barely kept up with films on television.

'You'll become one of them,' he said, venomously. 'You're no *different*.'

I thought over the emphasis as he gathered up the two beautiful women and air-kissed Samantha a good foot away from both cheeks.

Roger sidled up to me. 'I always think you have to be a bit of an arsehole to be a celebrity.'

The Old Fort on Box Hill cannot be entered by visitors. It is inhabited by bats. A protected species throughout the UK.

It was too cold to be comfortable. I kicked fallen leaves under my feet and considered the façade. On the journey from my home to the National Trust car park Harris had regaled me with more music from 1979. Tubeway Army's 'Are "Friends" Electric?', Lena Martell's 'One Day at a Time', The Bee Gee's 'Tragedy' and Gloria Gaynor's 'I Will Survive'. I hung out for Blondie's 'Heart of Glass', but if he played it then it was after I switched off the ignition.

On the side of the Old Fort some vegetation made a face. It struck me that pareidolia wasn't restricted to finding order where there was none, but it also collated a series of random events into something that might be perceived as significant. Hindsight made it easy to fictionalise reality, to find signs and connections which don't actually exist. Yet underlying my dissatisfaction was the knowledge that Harris had somehow managed to step outside of the persona we had granted him. However it had happened, Harris was somehow more successful at being a person than I was.

At school we had despised Harris for being different, but of course, he was correct, being different was a strength. Suddenly I was reminded of a paragraph in a MJ Harrison story, *Gifco*: *Suppose there was something so deep inside you that you never heard from it, something so intricately woven into your personality that it was hidden, something which had nothing but contempt for you. Suppose one day it spoke quite clearly to you, with perhaps a shade of an echo, as if it came from a well, and told you in a clever voice that the things you did were shit. Would you want to hear it speak again?*

I drove back to the house. Harris span 'I Don't Like Mondays', 'We Don't Talk Anymore' and 'Another Brick in the Wall'. All those number one singles indicated that 1979 was much darker than I had believed it to be.

Harris was leaning against my front door as I pulled into the drive. I had the weird sensation of seeing him in one place and hearing him in another. *Be seeing you.*

He must have caught the end of the show as I opened the car door.

'It isn't live, you know. I record the whole lot on Tuesdays. The rest of the week is free time.'

'Did you want something?'

If he caught me being abrupt he didn't say so.

'Just a word.'

I looked about. 'I suppose you better come in.'

I had to get close to him to unlock the door.

'Drink?'

'Tea.'

My palms were wet.

As the kettle boiled I watched him examine my property. He flipped open the black record cases and exhibited genuine interest in the collection, then became amused as he realised I couldn't play them.

If that was staggering then it was nothing to my realisation that he walked without a gait.

He took the cup and saucer from me.

'You noticed.'

'I ...'

'I affected it,' he said. 'I was already the target for bullies in primary school, and when my parents moved to a different part of London and I transferred to secondary school I knew what to expect. There was a good reason for me to walk to one side. I had a hammer sewn into the lining of my jacket.'

He raised the cup to his lip. Sipped. 'Still hot.'

'A hammer?'

I considered the possibilities.

'Yes. A hammer.' He sat, rested the saucer on my glass coffee table. 'Not that I ever used it. And after a week I removed it. It became superfluous.'

'I don't know what to say.'

'You never did.' His voice trailed away. 'Have you never thought you might live your life differently? There's a lot of magic in these hills.'

My fingers gripped the edge of the draining board. 'I don't understand.'

'Weekends my parents would come here. We had relatives in the area. Summer holidays, Easter, those one-week half-terms. All spent here. No wonder I came back, really. What drew you here?'

I couldn't answer. And then I did: 'To find myself.'

He laughed. 'You might do that. You might just do that here.'

'Look,' I began. But there was nothing to say.

'A few years ago,' Harris said, 'the website *Friends Reunited* was popular. I know you visited it. Did you ever wonder what became of the other bullies?'

I admitted to myself a cursory interest. None of them had amounted to much. One of them had died.

'There's not much to you, is there Ian Baxter?'

'There never has been,' I mumbled.

'What was that?'

I faced him. 'There never has been.'

He drained his tea. Stood. 'You might like to think that it's guilt, Ian, but you don't even have that emotion.' He reached into a pocket. 'I told you, there's a lot of magic in these hills.'

I watched as he pulled out a small carved box. From a distance I couldn't see my name etched into the side, but I knew it was there.

'I'll leave this with you,' Harris said. 'Time the past was buried, wouldn't you say?'

He closed the door behind him. It took me a while to realise his car had never been in my drive. In their back garden Roger and Samantha were hosting a barbecue. I watched Harris sink his teeth into a burger which oozed hot chilli sauce around the sides.

I considered my appreciation for the Surrey countryside. For the ancient wood.

I knew what was inside the box.

THE HORNED HUNTSMAN

One of the most recognisable and iconic spirits in the annals of British folklore is Herne the Hunter, the antlered half-man/half-stag of ancient English myth, who rides a furious steed through the night-time forests at the head of a baying pack, with demonic owls and ravens soaring overhead. According to Tudor-era fable, this ferocious entity, constantly on the prowl for the unwary and unworthy, whose souls he will steal, withers trees wherever he rides, infects cattle with illness and poisons and bloodies milk. His terrifying appearance is also said to presage national disasters or the demise of monarchs; he was allegedly sighted in the days leading up to the deaths of Elizabeth I (1603) and George III (1820).

In recent times, neo-pagans have made attempts to link him with the legendary Wild Hunt, a phantom horde of huntsmen who ranged across stormy winter skies at the heels of a formidable leader, whose main quest was to conquer and destroy and who in earlier ages was held to be a non-Christian deity, Woden of the Norse or Cernunnos of the Celts.

In reality, though the Wild Hunt was a feature of medieval mythology allegedly witnessed by real people all across Northern Europe, the actual story of Herne the Hunter is much more localised, the spectral horseman said to ride primarily in Windsor Great Park, in Berkshire, usually emerging at night from amid the twisted, fungus-riddled roots of the great oak tree on which he died. And it wasn't just in olden days when this story appeared. As recently as 1962, a gang of youths supposedly enraged him by blowing on a hunting horn they'd found in the park and subsequently were chased back to civilisation by the horn-headed horseman, who loosed arrows at them, which whispered away into evil black smoke as they struck branches and tree-trunks.

A fantastical sounding story for sure, and in fact there have been melodramatic elements attached to the story of Herne since its very beginning. The earliest written references we have come from

104

Shakespeare, whose 1597 play, The Merry Wives of Windsor, *contains the following passage:*

> *Sometime a keeper here in Windsor Forest,*
> *Doth all the winter-time, at still midnight,*
> *Walk round about an oak, with great ragg'd horns;*
> *And there he blasts the tree, and takes the cattle,*
> *And makes milch-kine yield blood, and shakes a chain*
> *In a most hideous and dreadful manner.*
> *You have heard of such a spirit, and well you know*
> *The superstitious idle-headed eld*
> *Receiv'd, and did deliver to our age,*
> *This tale of Herne the Hunter for a truth.*

Shakespeare was referencing a tradition that his audience were already very familiar with, even down to the tree, which they clearly also recognised. (In fact, the oak tree in question – a huge shambling monstrosity known locally as Falstaff's Oak – was so well known, certainly in the Home Counties, that its final death and felling was noted in 1796, some 200 years after the play was first staged, while a younger but similar tree, which inherited the title, collapsed in a gale in 1863.)

According to the myth Shakespeare drew upon, Herne was a trusted gamekeeper and huntsman during the reign of either Henry IV (1399-1413) or Henry V (1413-1422). Given Windsor Great Park's proximity to Windsor Castle, which has been an official residence of the monarch since about 1076, we must assume he was a royal gamekeeper, but one day he forgot himself and committed some unspecified crime for which he expected to lose his position. In one version of the story, his grief was so intense that he used a chain to hang himself from the greatest oak in the forest. In another, he attempted to flee but was captured and hanged from the same tree with the same chain as a form of impromptu execution.

Why his ferocious revenant, which was being reported in the Park long before Shakespeare institutionalised it, was deemed to be so evil, and how it came to possess the antlers and other features of a wild forest stag are unknown. It is even possible that Shakespeare was making a joke of the demon, The Merry Wives of Windsor *being a raucous comedy and horns on the Elizabethan stage often used as a symbol for cuckoldry. However, the local peasantry of the day were wary of entering Windsor Great Park; it was no laughing matter to them. So, it seems more likely that those propagating the myth (possibly the authorities, who didn't want trespassers on the royal hunting estate), were happy to merge the features of a man with those of various fearsome animals, stags, hounds, ravens and so forth, to create a monster in the traditional hybrid style of the Middle Ages.*

This is still the figure we are familiar with today, though the conflation of this character with the legend of the Wild Hunt has now rendered him a godlike being, a pillar of wisdom and woodland worship wreathed in mist and mystery, even if this more dignified status is strongly at variance with the origins of the story, in which he is an executed criminal or suicidal sinner.

THE GRAVEDIGGER OF WITCHFIELD
Steven J Dines

'You're white as a sheet, Ben. Where have you been?'

I am standing in front of my father in the graveyard of the Holy Trinity church in Witchfield, Buckinghamshire. It's mid April, eighteen degrees out, and almost everyone is in lockdown due to the coronavirus. My father works for the church in a janitorial capacity, tending the grounds, fixing this and that. The coolest part of his job, he once told me, is the digging of the graves. There will always be a need for holes, he said, and there is never a shortage of folk needing to be thrown into one. I never quite understood what he meant by that but then there was a lot about him that could be read two – or more – ways.

'Still waiting for your answer, son.'

He is. Leaning on the spade handle, muddied black jeans and a green plaid shirt, completely bald but with that showpiece of his – the thick moustache he calls his Magnum PI and which mum said made him look more like the Butcher from *Gangs of New York*.

And I know he is waiting, because I *know* I am stalling. Weighing up my options: truth in one hand, lie in the other – neither of which has a hopeful outcome. It's like choosing between staying indoors and going mad or venturing outdoors to risk catching this thing. Me, I'll take my chances with the virus. Why? Because people indoors are losing their fucking minds. I've seen it with my own eyes. Should I tell him what happened?

'I went for a walk,' I say, wringing my hands. I feel like I need to give him more to justify my hour-long disappearance. I always do with my father. He asks a lot of questions, and even when he doesn't, you know they're gathering in his mind, readying to ambush you later. 'I just needed to clear my head. That's all.'

'That's all, hm? How's school?'

I almost laugh at that. Firstly, because parents *always* start there, with the human petri dish that is the education system. Secondly, because the government closed all of the schools in March and my father doesn't seem to know it.

'Dad, schools are shut till September. Besides, school is fine.'

It isn't. These extended holidays are merely a stay of execution for me. I'm fucked. Well and truly. I won't be going back. Ever.

'You must be, what, in Year 10 by now?'

'No, Dad. Year 11. I'm sixteen.'

He stops digging to massage the knuckles of his right hand into the base of his spine. The slight but noticeable kyphosis adds at least a decade to his fifty years.

'So how did your mock exams go?'

They went, hence the stay of execution, but it would seem my father doesn't know that either. Rumour has it that in lieu of the proper exams this year our grades will be based on teacher assessment and past performance. My whole plan, such as it was, had been to catch up by cramming. Now there is nothing to cram *for*. Will it be death by hanging or will I swallow a handful of mum's old antidepressants?

'I'm not going to lie, Dad.' Which is a lie. 'They were a bastard.'

Dad is looking at me. I blush and look away. Behind him, the parish church looms in silent judgement, its spire intensifying my shame.

'Well, at least the colour's come back to your cheeks,' he says. 'How about I take a break from this so we can have ourselves a little chat? What do you think?'

'Sounds good,' I say, and it is perhaps the first truth I have spoken since I returned, running and out of breath, from the house behind the trees.

'I'd offer you a cuppa but I seem to have lost the old thermos.'

'Oh, I brought one,' I say, pointing at a stainless steel flask I left sitting on top of one of the granite headstones earlier.

'That's not mine, is it?' he asks.

'No.'

'Sure? I have one just like it.'

'Positive. I knew you wouldn't have yours so I brought my own.'

'What happened to mine, then?'

'You lost it last month.'

'Why didn't I buy a new one?'

'I don't know, Dad,' I say. 'I don't think it was important at the time.'

He gets confused sometimes, like grandpa Keating did right before dementia swallowed him and refused to give him back. It's like walking into a maze after midnight. And after grandpa died a couple of years ago from complications it was like Dad followed him inside, willingly, wanting to get himself lost too. He grew distant, forgetful. Cruel. His gait changed, accentuated by his kyphosis, so that he began to walk like a man who wanted to forget but who still carried the weight of all the memories in the world. A maze of confusion and of Mum and Dad not getting along at every turn, becoming like strangers in fact, as though he not only began to forget the small day-to-day stuff like shopping lists or paying the electricity and gas but the love he once felt for her, for both of us. You can write some things on a memo board but you cannot write that. You cannot write that.

'I brought your mug too, Dad.' Skirting around the hole in the ground, I pick up the rucksack I brought and left leaning against the headstone I sat the flask on. The mug is plain white with an initial 'R' stencilled on it. 'I'll just use the flask lid,' I say.

'But the mug's all cracked,' he says. 'How'd it get in such a state?'

'You don't remember?'

He threw it at the wall during an argument with Mum. It was around the time she lost a lot of weight. She died three weeks later in the house fire. Smoke inhalation, they said. Choked to death, they said. I don't know if Thames Valley Police believe he started the fire or not, but they had never listened to him through my bedroom wall, never heard him threaten to torch the place every single night he and Mum got into one about money or just the fact she wasn't eating enough.

Dad swats the air dismissively. 'Just throw that thing in the bin when you get home, Ben. I'll buy another.'

'But I fixed it with Super Glue,' I tell him. 'Took me ages. It's good as new now – look. Doesn't leak at all.'

'Why would you do that?'

I'm not sure if my father is impressed or exasperated. 'Because it's your favourite mug,' I say. 'And you can't just replace your favourite things.'

You can only imitate them, I think. Like fathers who invite amnesia into their minds because they want to forget who they are and what they've lost. Munchausen's syndrome for the bereaved was how my counsellor put it. She was full of shit about most things but about that, about my father – she was on the nose.

I pour the tea from the flask. No sugar, no milk. Tea in its purest form. Black.

Dad sits on the edge of the hole, swinging his legs and dislodging clods of earth and the occasional worm from its walls with his thoughtless boot heels. I sit on the grass at the nearest headstone, back to granite back, sipping my tea. Thinking of the opening lines to my favourite novel, *The Hobbit* – of the ends of worms and oozy smells. Smiling as the sun warms my face. Its light comes filtered through the high, thin branches of a singular tree that stands above the graveyard. There is a word for what this moment could have been: *beatific*. It means feeling blissful happiness. This could have been that. *I* could have been that, blissful, happy – if it wasn't for what I've seen. Look a little closer at that word. *Beatific.* It doesn't speak of violence so much as say it under its breath.

'What kind of tree *is* that?' I ask, pointing at its tall, branchless trunk and its sparse crown of branches. 'It's not a pine, is it?'

'Monkey puzzle,' my father says without looking up. 'They used to plant them at the edge of graveyards long ago … The belief was it deprived the devil of having somewhere to hide during funeral services. Meant he couldn't go round stealing the souls of the departed.'

Peering over the rim of my flask lid, I look at the tree again in the light of this new superstition. New to me, that is. Despite the heat of the day, a cold chill traces my spine. I shudder and glance away.

My father looks at me from his graveside perch.

'What?' I ask a little too defensively.

His eyebrows rise, hold for a moment, then fall back to their usual resting place. 'Walk, my arse,' he says in a humourless voice. 'Something happened. You were away for too long and when you came back you looked terrified. You look it now. What is it?'

'Nothing.'

He shakes his head. 'There's no such thing. You went up to that house, didn't you?'

One thing I have never been able to do is lie to my father. To him, lies are the red cape to a bull. He charges them down. Gores anyone who tries to hide behind them.

'Yes,' I say.

'After I told you not to, you still went …'

'Sorry.'

'Why?'

'Why what?'

'Why do you not listen to me? You listened to your mother but never to me. *Why?*'

'You get angry. Like – like you are now.'

'So what? When someone does something wrong it's a natural response, no?'

'Sometimes.'

'Why only "sometimes"?'

'It depends on what they did wrong.'

'Wrong is wrong, Ben. Wrong is wrong.'

I close my eyes and tilt my face up to try and let the sun find me but there's nothing *beatific* about it now: there is only a prickly heat and sweat pooling in my pores; a growing itchiness across my face that simply won't ease on its own or by blinking or pulling faces or …

'What are you doing?'

'It's too hot,' I say.

'No wonder you're hot. You're wearing a wool sweater over a polo shirt on a day like this. Take it off.'

I remove the sweater and lie it flat on the ground beside me. The polo shirt is yellow and badly creased. I never iron what people cannot see and I tend to overdress to cover my arms, which are too long and too thin. It's like having a pair of oars when there's no water around to paddle.

'Feel any better?' he asks.

I look around the graveyard. It's hard to tell that the world is spinning off its axis but there is something seriously out of kilter. I can't see it at first; it's only when I look and *keep* looking that it slowly becomes clear. Clay Lane, visible from where I sit with my back to this headstone, is all but deserted. No people; very few vehicles. A virus that originated over five thousand miles away in Wuhan, China, has sent most of the residents of my little village of Witchfield, Buckinghamshire, scurrying behind their doors. People are dying everywhere, but mainly on the news, not only from COVID-19 but at the hands of their partners, loved ones for whom the lockdown – this new normal that has been thrust upon them – is so much to bear they are finding new and bad things to do with their hands. Like what happened in that house behind the trees. Bad things with hands and more than hands. People losing their shit. This new normal, this *Tiger King* normal, and maybe that is okay, maybe that is fine, but leave me out of it. I want to walk outside and have the streets to myself, besides joggers who veer around me anyway, confirming what I already knew – that I have some kind of deflective superpower. It isn't so bad, really. I can be alone or I can sit here with my father, drink tea with him, talk to him, and listen to birdsong I could never hear until the virus came, because Clay Lane is a main thoroughfare and usually grumbling with traffic. Now, I can hear the firecrests sing and watch them drop from the branches, bold as brass, to choose from the graveyard's insect menu. Now, I can feel connected to the world and to the world beyond this one. I just lean back and touch my head to a headstone of paradisio granite, a granite that originates in India, and we're connected. We're all connected. India. China. The Upside Down. By granite and COVID and Netflix. Invisible connections to faraway people, and the best kind of people, as the world is only just beginning to realise, are the ones who are just that: *far-a-way*.

'I need to tell you something,' I say. 'I'm ready to talk.'

'About the house?'

'Yes. About the house.'

Dad and I have spoken of Burnwood before; on many occasions, in fact. Sometimes, he'd be working in the grounds of Holy Trinity, mowing the grass or removing the dead flowers from the grave vases, and we'd hear music playing from the house. Thumping music, like a heartbeat on ketamine. There were a lot of big houses in Witchfield, but they seldom drew attention to themselves like Burnwood. They sat at the end of long private driveways behind walls or fences and observed a kind of reverent silence. Burnwood had the driveway and an entrance lodge (or guardhouse) but there was nothing reverent or silent about the place. It was owned by a former celebrity DJ who'd enjoyed some fame and notoriety in the early 2000s. He had a string of Top 5 hits, including a trio of number ones in the UK and one in the US.

Most of his fortune, I'd read, was made through lucrative gigs all over the world, including a twelve-month residency in Las Vegas. Now, he was here of all places, playing EDM for his select guests and those unfortunates buried next door in the grounds of Holy Trinity.

On my father's behalf, the Reverend Brian Steele, who lived in the vicarage on the other side of the church, sent some letters of complaint about DJ Kool Ade to both Witchfield Parish Council and Buckinghamshire County Council – to no avail. In fact, a month after the complaint, work began on a new stained glass window for the Holy Trinity and double glazing for the vicarage, thanks to an anonymous donor. My father was livid. The East Window, he said, was where the sun rises. It's supposed to remind us of the Resurrection of Jesus *not* some has-been pop star's feeble comeback to a legitimate complaint. Corruption is everywhere, he said. They *drank* the Kool-Aid on this one. I only had a vague idea what he meant by that. There were rumours too of pay-offs to keep certain stories out of the local newspaper. What stories, what people, I didn't know.

My father had worked for the church for over twenty-four years. He was a proud and principled man; a man not prone to backing down. When he found out that the new window was to be based on a passage from Revelation 19 ('*His eyes were a flame of fire, and on his head were many crowns.*') he felt a message had been sent. A winner announced. That same night, he sent a message of his own when he beat my mother and I both senseless.

I have always wanted to see Burnwood with my own eyes and not just on the Rightmove website. Better still, to sneak into its grounds and see what the bfd was about the place and this Kool Ade fellow – or how those two could turn a once good man against his family. Today was just the day that it happened.

Dad was standing in a deep hole and droning on about the coronavirus, about how it was a punishment sent to us all. A punishment for what, I asked. Sent by whom, the Chinese? He looked up at me like he wanted to beat some sense back into me. 'A punishment for everything. Poor choices. And sent by ourselves because we're too stupid to learn anything without people dying.'

That was enough for me. I grabbed up my bag. 'All this – *this* – about people dying while I'm in a graveyard surrounded by … I came out for some fresh air, Dad, not this. I'm going for a walk. Won't be long.'

I walked across the lawn and through the gate onto Clay Lane. Turned left. Out of sight of the graveyard, I immediately ducked into the yew tree bushes that separated the Holy Trinity's land from the Burnwood estate. I felt like one of the children in the Narnia novels, entering a new world. I wove a path through the tall bushes, careful to remain unseen by my father in the narrow spaces between. I avoided stepping on sticks and twigs on the ground. I wondered if I should have brought a coat. But when I emerged from the bushes on the other side, it wasn't into some snowy otherworld but a perfectly manicured green lawn and, to my slight disappointment, the same old sun and sky overhead.

The garden was huge. My garden at home was too small to throw a tennis ball across and put any real *welly* into it. It had to be underarm throws and you had to hold back, even when you wanted to let fly, otherwise the ball just went over the hedge and onto the road. Here, I could throw a tennis ball and it wouldn't even reach the swimming pool never mind the pool house, never mind the *main* house or the tennis court on the far side. It was a vast open space surrounded by tall trees, their long shadows stretching across the sun-kissed green until even they could reach no farther, leaving a smaller but still generous expanse of garden where the sun could find you whichever direction you turned.

Sixteen acres, according to the internet. An eight bedroom country house, built in 2008, within its own grounds. Mellow red brick. Tile roof. Wonderful views of the countryside. Lutron lighting. And the *pièce de résistance*, what probably sealed the deal for DJ Kool Ade: an integrated music system.

Guide price, a cool six million.

You do not belong here.

This feeling came at me from both inside and out. I felt it in my bones but I also heard it in the heartbeat of the electronic dance music that carried across the pristine lawns and forced itself inside my ears. It was as though Burnwood had a pulse, a life separate and distinct from the rest of this dreary village with its resident solicitors and doctors, its retired this or retired that, its bookshops that sold only expensive first editions, its entitled born into freestanding baths full of family-inherited money. The ground shuddered with it – EDM, *life* – the sound of the outside burrowing deep into the foundations of Witchfield without any of them really knowing it. As I stayed within the shadows of the trees, creeping across the lawn toward the pool house, I felt its pulse enter through my feet, travel up through my body, and settle inside my chest, where my heart raced in an effort to keep up. *You do not belong here.* But I want to. *You do not belong here.* But I want to.

Someone was in the pool.

I stopped moving, stopped breathing, and crouched low to the ground. I felt dangerously exposed despite the cool shadows clinging to my skin. The temperature soared in an instant and the trees seemed to move away like the forest of Ents in *The Lord of the Ring*s. Off to attack Isengard, perhaps, while leaving me here, alone and exposed, staring at the two people in the pool.

They were at the far end. In the deep. The man's back was to me, broad and strong. He was treading the water immediately in front of a tanned woman who wore a black lace mask with a soft explosion of feathers on one side. Something lay poolside at the shallow end. I couldn't make out what it was. The man's hair was dark and wavy. Hers looked like honey in the sunlight. A sense of panic fluttered through me then. I could not breathe but I *needed* to breathe. My body demanded it. I anticipated a gasp, like a swimmer coming up for air, and then the two people in the pool would hear me above the music, above their own private conversation, and they would turn.

Two things happened.

He kissed her on the mouth just as someone, a third person, walked past the glass sliding doors of the pool house. That person was a male, naked as the day (which is a phrase my mother often used to describe how I came into this world, although why it should come back to me at this time I do not know; maybe I am grasping for what is familiar in the strange). He wore a mask that covered the upper half of his face. A red mask of a rough texture with small, curling horns like those of a goat. His body was hairy, certainly hairier than the man's in the pool. His legs, chest, even his shoulders were dark with the stuff. His penis sat in a nest of hair, a flash of pink, like someone stuck at the bottom of a deep hole waving for help. I laughed. A nervous reaction.

He was visible through the glass doors for only a moment, a few steps as he walked by, and then he disappeared into another part of the pool house, carrying an empty champagne flute.

The couple in the pool were kissing vigorously. The woman wrapped her arms around the man's back, caressing the muscles around his flexing shoulder blades. He lifted her by the waist, out of the water, and I glimpsed her small breasts and the white teardrops where a bikini had kept the sun from reaching her. She wrapped her legs around his middle and they swam as one, the man forward, the woman backward, toward the pool wall, kissing as they went. I finally breathed as she started to moan between kisses.

What was happening here?, I thought. Most of the country was locked down and social distancing and these people were flagrantly ignoring the rules. In broad daylight. I had entered another world, alright; maybe not Narnia but definitely somewhere else. I tried to decide what to do next. There seemed to be only two options: retreat back into the trees and return to my father or wait here until I was inevitably caught and – then what? I didn't know.

The man and the woman started having sex in the pool.

117

She extended her arms along the pool's edge and leaned back in the water as he kissed her taut neck and licked those pale teardrops and thrust like a man possessed. His grunts elicited breathy moans from her. Between these, she encouraged, no she *goaded* him to fuck her harder. I blushed. Wavelets slapped against the edge of the pool, spilled onto the concrete surround, and trickled into the grass. I had to do something soon, before the man inside the pool house, the man with the red goat mask, returned and looked outside.

The thing that lay at the poolside …

The man in the pool house had been wearing a mask; the man having sex in the pool had not. His mask lay beside the pool. He must have removed it at some point after getting into the water with the woman.

Instead of retreating to the trees, I crept closer to the pool and the mask. There was no clear thinking involved, no sequence of thought at all other than I needed cover and that meant either run away or find a way in which to hide in plain sight. As I lay my hand on the mask, the man in the water stopped and turned the woman away from him so that she faced the main house. She gripped the edge of the pool as he began fucking her from behind, against the pool wall. The rhythm was different, slower, stronger, determined, like he was trying to reach some elusive thing hidden deep inside the woman's body, driving toward it as she pushed against him, both of them somehow finding pleasure in this mutual aggression. He pulled on her golden hair, drawing her head back so that she looked straight up at the clear sky over Witchfield, and when he joined her in looking skywards it was as if they were both worshipping that empty blue even as they worshipped each empty other. I had watched my fair share of internet porn, but on a phone or laptop screen it seemed less … *threatening*, more removed. In truth, the violence of it felt intimidating.

Ignoring my thoughts, I grabbed the mask and ran for the cover of the nearest trees. A broad yew bush offered me a hiding place where I could catch my breath and inspect my dubious prize. Immediately, I understood why the man in the pool had removed it to focus on the woman. It was a gas mask hood, black leather, circular lenses. Instead of a filter cartridge there was a large black cap that could be removed to allow access to the mouth.

I looked at the thing with wonder and fear. What had I stumbled into?

You do not belong here.

The words never rang so true but at the same time, like an undertow pulling me down and down, I wondered if I would ever belong anywhere. I swam against it. I put on the mask.

It was cumbersome. Hot inside. Tiny vents cut into the leather allowed air to enter and exit the mask but they did not seem to allow quite enough. The air tasted leathery and second-hand. My breathing became heavy. But ... I felt different. Like somebody else.

Within moments, I had stripped out of my clothes and left them in a folded pile behind the yew bush, my trainers sat side-by-side on top. I was hidden from the couple in the pool, the masked man inside the pool house, anyone who happened to peer out through the windows of Burnwood itself, and, of course, I was invisible to my father waiting for me in the graveyard next door. And yet, unseen as I was, I was also something *to* see: a sight to behold. Naked as the day, yes, but for my gas mask hood. I laughed, and even my laughter sounded changed somehow, muted as it was by the warm press of leather.

Strangely, I did not challenge myself. I accepted what I had done so far with relative ease. We can accept anything if it is delivered in stages. A baby starts with a crawl, begins to pull itself up on furniture, graduates to cruising, before it takes its first unassisted steps. A hand lands flat on the face before the next time it curls into a fist to fracture the cheekbone.

Stages.

Master one before moving on to the next.

I stepped out from behind the yew bush, leaving the old Ben behind along with his white trainer socks and his Asdabought jeans, his un-ironed polo shirt and his jumper with more holes in it than a Swiss cheese, all of it unflatteringly crowned by a father's handed-down trainers – and I emerged onto Burnwood's sun-kissed lawn, if not ready then at least opening myself – in stages – to what it had to offer. The air felt different on my skin, like there were no layers of lies between us.

I walked across the lawn, past the pair in the pool, who seemed too lost in their activity to notice me, and approached the sprawling Burnwood. The music grew louder as I drew closer, the driving beat of EDM; the soundtrack to this private event. I began to see other people in the windows overlooking the rear lawn, most of them passing from one room to the next as though taking a tour of the house. They wore masks of all sorts and little else from what I glimpsed. Gravel paths surrounded the property, crossing each other like limbs. A cluster of rattan lawn furniture sat on a patio area, next to a colourful garden of mixed flowers surrounded by box hedging. To sit next to such low hedging would surely give a false perspective, I thought. Make you feel bigger than you are. Perfect for a former celebrity, I concluded.

A woman sat on one of the rattan chairs, naked, legs crossed, smoking a cigarette alone. She wore a black lace mask that resembled a butterfly. There were no eye holes; she looked through the spread wings. Her hair was fiery red, her skin pale and heavily freckled. She had full lips and wore no lipstick, or rather wore none *now*; there were traces of it around her mouth and smeared across her face. In the seconds before she looked up and saw me approach, I thought she looked tired, run-down, like someone stealing a cigarette partway through a difficult shift. Then she saw me and smiled, but the switch from one state to the other, from truth to fiction, was so dramatic that her smile filled me with a momentary sadness. Inappropriately or not, I could not help but think of my mother when she had smiled at me. With her it had got so that when I looked at her I saw a closed door with an open room painted on it. There were times, too many times, when I would drop my school bag on the kitchen floor after school and head to my bedroom to play PlayStation, passing her and seeing only that open room of her face, bright and untouched, not realising that all I was looking at was what was painted on the other side of a closed door. I never tried to open it and get a peek inside because I was too afraid. Afraid of what I might find. Afraid of what I might not.

I nodded my head in greeting at the woman. She continued to smile at me as I passed her and entered Burnwood through a pair of glass doors, after which I imagined that smile, like a dream of something that never existed, was gone in a snap.

I walked into a games room full of people moving to the bubbling synth of Martin Garrix' *Animals*. The room's centrepiece was a pool table and a naked woman posed like a frog upon its blue felt. She wore a Venetian mask of cracked white overlaid with gold lace and a mane of black feathers. Since she was facing me as I entered the room, I could not see what the commotion was behind her. A small group of four or five people, men and women, all naked and wearing masks, stood back there, their attention clearly on her raised backside which she shook in their faces. On either side of the pool table, there was a three-seater sofa with at least three people on each. It was hard to see how many people there were at a glance; they were tangled together like naked wrestlers. As I moved around one side of the pool table, a head appeared on the couch, at my thigh level, sliding out from between the legs of a male who was fucking a woman from behind. This third person lay beneath the other two, his cock throated by the woman as he licked the balls and anus of the man fucking her. I felt a dizzying combination of excitement and revulsion. An urge to look *and* to look away. I decided to keep moving – around the table towards the door, which revealed to me what the crowd of people behind the table were doing. Attached to the end of one the pool cues with duct tape was a very large sex toy; a dildo bayonet. They were taking turns in stimulating the woman, who rolled her hips appreciatively with each stroking motion of the cue. I glanced at the other sofa on the other side of the pool table and two men were having rough sex with a third. I reached the door and looked back in stunned disbelief. Sunlight streamed inside the room. It felt like it had no right to be there. A red brick fireplace and chimney stretched up to a ceiling of exposed oak beams. Suspended from these beams was a long vinyl banner with a stark message: #fuckcorona. And dotted around the room, not quite hidden but inconspicuous, I counted at least four webcams.

On the landing outside, I caught my breath.

Underneath the stairs was a cosy alcove lined with bookshelves. A high back Victorian leather chair. On any other day, a perfect spot in which to sit, think, read. When I sat, the cool leather stuck to my bare skin and the only thought I had was to get up and flee this house before I was caught. Before the man in the pool outside finished having sex and went looking for his mask. My legs were restless, refusing to be still, shaking through the balls of my feet. In the end, I convinced myself that if I kept moving, nothing would happen; I would be like a ghost passing through this place. I stood and continued with my haunting.

Every room was the same.

Sex.

Naked people wearing masks.

Sex.

The only thing that changed from one room to the next were the masks and the positions. Everything was built on a foundation of sex. Sex in all its forms. I became a little intoxicated by what I saw. Maybe it was the second-hand smoke from the weed. Or maybe it was the heat inside the gas mask. I dared not take it off, though.

My vision blurred several times. Whenever I stumbled, someone was always there to catch me; someone naked who wore a mask and spoke with their hands, touching me in a way I found almost as disturbing as the sex being had in every room. The music was too loud for conversation but the guests were somehow able to communicate with each other, to offer and invite, accept and refuse, as though they had developed a shorthand over time, during many gatherings like this one, and it only underlined that I was a stranger here, an intruder; a strange intruder. My own hands seemed useless. Dead weight on the ends of my arms, such that when a woman appeared beside me, wearing a mask of pink lace, and she took my hand and led me toward the stairs to the second floor, I could only obediently follow. All I could look at while we climbed the carpeted stairs was her hand holding mine, like some bony spider wrapped around its prey.

She led me to the only room on the second floor – in the entire house, it seemed – with its door closed. She waited outside and rapped a secret knock. There was no reply but the door was opened a few inches from the other side. She turned to me and gave me a gummy smile. It was only then that I took her in, my brain finally acknowledging her. She was tall but pale and thin as a sickly moon. Not so much flesh and bone but bone and flesh. Her ribs visible underneath her skin, like bodies lined up along the floor of a morgue. Tiny breasts. Jutting hips. Her body spoke of a poorly-hidden eating disorder. More immediately worrying were the finger marks on her neck. Her own, I wondered. Or somebody else's? Before I could begin to ask, she led me inside.

I hesitated as I entered the room. A man lay on a king-sized bed with his hands behind his neck. He wore a full black-devil mask with gold paint around the eyes and running down either side of the face like tears. The horns and lips were painted red. Like everyone else at the party, he was naked except for the mask he wore. His body was muscular and hairy; his penis languished on his thigh like some fat, half-asleep serpent. I held my hands over my privates, consciously shielding them from comparison.

The woman closed the door behind us. The room was a pocket of relative quiet. The dance music playing throughout the house did not reach here but seemed to stop outside the door; I was conscious of it only distantly, as I might be aware of my pulse after an unexpected run. I stood and listened to myself breathe inside the gas mask. The man in the black-devil mask nodded at the emaciated woman. She approached the bed and climbed on – the mattress was several feet off the floor – straddling him at the knee. Then, she bent forward over his groin and worked him with two hands. Her hair fell forward in black ropes, brushing his skin. His hips rose in response, alluding to her face. Her back curved as she leaned further over him. I could count the ridges of her spine. When she ate him, she choked.

I turned to leave. My hand made it as far as the door handle before he spoke in a menacing if partly breathless voice.

'Don't leave, son. I'll get to you next.'

I turned around to face the bed again. He was sitting now, legs spread, the woman lying on her front like some pale extension of him, face pressed into his groin as though he had nothing down there at all. He had both hands gripped to the back of her head, pulling her into him, pulling her into him, holding her in place. His eyes would not leave mine. I tried to move a couple of steps and they followed me like some terrifying portrait.

The woman was struggling to breathe now. At first she tapped his thigh to signal she'd had enough. Then she slapped him repeatedly on the abdomen. When she scratched him and drew blood, I stepped forward to protest, but before I could find the words he grunted and pulled her in with a renewed enthusiasm. Snot bubbled from her nose; I heard it rather than saw it. All I saw were my feet as I thought of my trainers sitting on top of that pile of clothes in the trees. I wanted to be anywhere but where I was and who I was at that moment. A coward trapped in a room with the devil.

I wondered if he would kill her in this place, and if she was to be some sacrificial lamb singled out from the other partygoers. Was he the owner of the house, this DJ Kool Ade? The name sounded too whimsical beside the crime I was witnessing, even knowing a little about its sinister origins.

She began to flail. The woman was choking to death. Her

arms reached for something that did not exist in that room: help. Finding none, she thrashed like someone who saw their final moments looming. In her throes, her hands found his face and gripped his mask with skeletal fingers. He looked away from me momentarily, glancing out of the window at a bright day and green leaves shifting in the breeze. Taking in the view. When he looked back at me, his eyes were black, the pupils engorged as though they wanted to consume all of the light in the room. And somehow they did – as her nails found some purchase on his cheek and raked at the flesh, opening a wound and drawing blood. As he smiled – *leered* – at me and I realised the mask he wore *moved* to form that smile and that it was in fact the actual face of this thing. And as I ran screaming from that room, that house, hearing laughter at my heels, both a man's and a woman's.

There is a moment after I finish telling my father what happened at the house behind the trees when we both just sit there and listen to the firecrests sing; listen to the wind sough between the graves; listen to the devout and comforting silence of the Holy Trinity church. It is a moment in which the tornado of feelings inside me falls apart and I begin to feel like my old self again. Until, that is, from his perch on the edge of the hole, my father says, 'You shouldn't tell lies in a graveyard, Ben. It's not the place.'

'I wasn't *lying*, Dad. That's what I saw. It was real. All of it.'

'You weren't smoking anything, were you? Maybe took one toke too many and fell asleep in the bushes. Dreamt this whole thing up. It's possible, you know.'

'I didn't fall asleep. Besides, I don't smoke that – or anything. She scratched his mask, Dad – and it *bled*. How is that even possible?'

He climbs to his feet. Works the kink out of the small of his back. Gazes at the trees separating the graveyard and the Burnwood property. Then he laughs to himself as he shakes his head. 'Sex parties,' he says. 'Masked orgies … Right here in

Witchfield. These rich types are all the fucking same. The world is burning and they just want to fuck each other and fuck us. Well, burn it all.'

'Dad, did you hear what I said – what I *saw?*'

'I did, son.'

'And?'

He thinks for a moment.

'Sometimes things overlap.'

'What? That's it? That's all you've got to say?'

'No, but you need to be quiet and give me the chance to say it.'

'Okay, go ahead. I'm sorry.'

'Imagine two circles intersecting,' he says. 'They create this … *area* where they overlap, okay? It's like an oval, or something else, but let's stick with oval. They overlap – life and death, rich and poor, your mother and I – and out of that oval comes … well, the likes of what happened to you today, that's what. It's a kind of … *turbulence*. You shouldn't mess with these things, Ben. I warned you. You shouldn't have been in that house.'

I find myself on my feet, hands clasped together, when usually you would kneel to pray. 'So you believe me?'

'I've seen and done too much to doubt anything these days. Look at what's happening with this virus. Talk about an overlap.' He holds his fists up. I imagine a magician presenting a pair of metal rings to his audience. 'This is the old, this is the new.' He moves his fists closer to each other, the invisible rings locking together, unable to separate. 'This is *now*,' he says, looking at me through the narrow gap between his fists. 'Nothing but turbulence.'

He lets his arms fall back to his sides.

'So what do I do now?' I ask.

'Firstly, don't invite yourself to any more parties at that house. You're sixteen years old – you're in a bit of an overlap yourself. Secondly, try to forget what you saw. Bury it, fill in the hole, walk away.'

'I think he was hurting her, Dad. I *know* he was. Why

would she let him hurt her like that? Why didn't she leave him? Divorce him. She had the chance.'

'Bury it, son. Walk away. Why will eat you up in the end.'

'What if he tries to find me?'

My father looks at me and for one startling moment all I can see are that other's black pupils staring back. I look away from him hurriedly.

'He won't *try* to find you. He will. There's no question.'

As I stare at the ground I wait for him to say something else, offer some kind of reassurance, but instead I see him from the corner of my eye, searching for the spade in the grass.

'Is that it?' I ask. 'No advice? No ...'

'He'll find you. Just like he found me.'

He says it while looking for a fucking spade in the grass, like some throwaway line or the thousand times he told me to brush my teeth unless I wanted to lose all of them. Finally, he sees the terrified look on my face. 'The thing is not to worry about it – or him,' he says. 'Things like this, the bad things that happen, the turbulence, they're always around, waiting around every corner, hiding in every crack. This virus. What you saw at the house. The only difference is you got a good look at him first. You could have gone your whole life and not seen him, not known him. But you did, and you do. Damage is done, son. How you let it affect you is entirely down to you. Things happen that you'll never understand. Don't send yourself into one of these' – he points at the hole between us – 'by trying.'

He finds the spade and picks it up. Leans on the handle like a walking stick.

'What will he do?' I ask. 'When he finds me ...'

'Ben ...'

'Dad – what will he do?'

My father sighs; a familiar, forceful exhalation that signposts the path this conversation is about to take. I want to take the question back, I want to leave the mask at the side of the pool and walk away, *run* away, but sometimes it's too late to go back and change what has happened; sometimes, the mask simply refuses to come off.

Tears fill my eyes. 'What will he make me do?'

'Bad things,' he answers. 'Some of it worse than what you saw. That's how he works. In stages.'

'Don't …'

'You'll say that. At first.'

'Stop!'

'And that too.'

'I don't want to hear this.'

'It's already started, Ben.'

'What has?'

'He's already inside you. You just don't realise it yet.'

'I don't understand!'

'You won't. You'll try to figure it out but it will only make things worse, because the harder you try to pull him out of *there*, the deeper he burrows.' He taps the side of his skull and a clump of hair falls onto his shoulder.

'Dad, your …'

'What can you do?' he says, guessing my next question incorrectly.

'No, I –'

'Nothing. There's nothing you *can* do. The world is going to be a lot darker from now on. People will be like strangers to you. Even your loved ones – *especially* your loved ones. You won't get the same pleasure out of anything. You'll look back and long for the old days, and for all the days that came before those. You shouldn't have been in that house, Ben. You shouldn't have seen the things you saw in that house.'

'*What* did I see though, Dad? Was he hurting her? Or was it a joke? Was she in on it? What did I see? Tell me. I want to know what *you* think I saw …'

He shakes his head. 'He's here. It's time for you to leave. Don't be like your old man, son. I was good at only one thing my whole miserable life – putting other people in the ground. Don't be like me and don't you *ever* think of coming back here. Now take the spade. Take it. It's time to put your old man back.'

Part of me knows it from the goose bumps on my arms but they spread like cold fire when he says those words. I turn and look toward the trees and there *he* is, standing in the shadows beneath the monkey puzzle on the edge of the graveyard. Black pupils staring back at me from a face that has burned so long it has carbonised. Blood drying on his cheek from the woman's struggles to free herself. Penis flaccid but stirring into new life at the sight of me, ticking upward in stages. I don't know if it is the broad daylight that prevents him from stepping forward into the graveyard or if there is some truth to the monkey puzzle superstition. I don't know and I don't *want* to know.

'It's time,' my father says again.

It is. And as I use the spade to push the piled earth on top of him, I am conscious of the thing watching me from the shadows of the nearby trees. Of the smoke rising from a house behind him. *He's already inside you*, my father said. *He's already inside you. You just don't realise it yet.*

No, Dad. I think I do.

THE NAPHILL DEATH OMEN

Naphill is a typically bucolic Buckinghamshire settlement, a quaint, rustic village running in linear fashion along the road to High Wycombe in the shadow of the Chiltern Hills. Yet weirdly, for reasons no folklorists can explain, it is, or once was, strongly associated with a bizarre but recurring death omen.

How far back in time this event dates to is unknown, but in 1910 a local woman, known today only as D G A, collated a number of such occurrences that she herself had had personal experience of during the latter half of the 19th century, and compiled them in book form. Four in particular stand out as especially weird, and yet all are verifiable as relating to deaths that are traceable in the historical record.

The first one concerns a farmer's son, who lived outside the village, and sometime in 1885 complained to his family that he'd suffered a particularly vivid nightmare in which he'd turned his own shotgun around, and despite resisting with all his strength, blasted himself in the chest. Dismissing this as nothing but anxiety, his father bade him forget it and be about his work, but before the week was out, disaster had struck: the farmer's son was indeed dead, having accidentally shot himself with his own gun.

It would be possible to write this off as a coincidence, albeit a very rare and unusual one, but the next death omen connected to Naphill is harder to explain.

One evening, a young village girl returned home to her cottage in Naphill in a distressed state. She said that she had been walking down the lane when she'd spied a diminutive figure skipping along the top of the wall parallel to her. Astonished, the girl had taken a closer look, and saw that she hadn't been mistaken. This figure, she said, was a doll, a living doll, dressed in silk and satin, and that it was moving stiffly but jerkily, and of its own volition. She called to it, but its only response was to run as far along the wall as her mother's gate, and then vanish from sight. The girl's mother waved the tale away as stuff and nonsense, but the following day the mother died unexpectedly from natural causes.

The most interesting aspect of these events so far is that there is no comparison between them. They simply don't match. And yet the dissimilarity of these incidents is perhaps their most curious and striking feature. For example, a short time later, the omen took another very different form.

A resident of Naphill known to D G A as 'Uncle Alf', was in his cottage kitchen one night when he heard heavy feet clumping up his garden path to the back door. Surprised by this because it was the normal custom for visitors to approach the front of the house, he stood up. He was even more surprised to see the latch on the door lift as if whoever it was intended to enter unbidden. Annoyed, Alf yanked the door open, but there was nobody outside. The following night, the same thing happened again. Alf was seated in his kitchen when the sound of heavy feet, this time running, came thumping along the path towards the back door – with such speed that he expected an impact. There was no impact, but again the latch lifted. Alf asked who was out there. There was no response except that the latch dropped. Alf opened the door, and, as before, found nobody there. The following night, assuming that some local fools were making a game of him, Alf armed himself with a club and waited. Exactly the same thing happened. Heavy feet came running up to the door, but this time Alf pulled the door open before the latch could lift. Still, there was nobody outside. The following day, Alf's grandfather died – and after that there were no further incidents.

The fourth occasion is perhaps the eeriest of them all. A different Naphill villager was walking home one night to his farm, when he became concerned that he was being watched. In an increasingly agitated state, he quickened his pace. But then was amazed when some other person he hadn't heard on the road behind fell into stride alongside him. He was even more surprised, if not horrified, to see that the stranger was nothing more than a shadow-form, without any distinguishing features. Whatever this creature was, it made no response when the villager addressed it. Terrified, the man ran the rest of the way home, the shadow-figure running alongside him.

When he reached his home, the villager veered away to the outhouse to get a lantern. To his consternation, the shadow form continued to the main house and entered. The villager told a lodger in the outhouse what had happened, and the lodger felt this was some kind of warning. They dashed to the main building together, wherein an old man who lived there was about to commit suicide with a pistol. They talked him around, thus taking heed of the death omen in time to prevent a tragedy.

Folklorists are most interested in the overarching story here because of its apparent lack of pattern. The individual incidents are so anecdotal and even taken together, fail to create a coherent narrative. Certainly, the woman who collated the tales into one made no effort to give it a beginning, middle or end. Nor did she use common rural terminology to try and explain anything. The diminutive figure on the wall, for example, was never named as a faerie, nor the shadowy figure on the lonely road as a fetch.

It remains a bemusing mystery, though in later years comment has been passed on the proximity of Naphill to Grimm's Ditch. This Iron Age earthwork, now little more than a pleasant woodland walk, was in pre-Roman times a dividing line between the domains of the Catuvellauni and the Atrebates tribes. In Celtic Britain, such political boundaries were also held to be spiritual, in other words they created an edge between one belief system and the next. It is certainly the case that in later centuries, during the Dark Ages, when Grimm's Ditch was so-named by Christianised Saxons, 'Grimr' being their own name for the Viking god, Odin, many mysterious things were said to have occurred there.

WHERE ARE THEY NOW?
Tina Rath

Ah. Hallo. Yes. No, not at all, I've only just sat down ... oh, no
problem. Just followed your directions ... Ah, no, if you don't
mind what I'd really like is a tea. I noticed they were doing it
as I came through. Oh, yes, please, ordinary tea, with just a
splash of milk, none of that herbal sludge ... they probably call
it English Breakfast tea although strictly it's Indian and you
can drink it any time ... Ah, thank you. 'The cup that cheers,'
you know. Good old Pope ... Oh. Sorry. Alexander. No,
Alexander Pope, certainly not Pope Alexander. Quite different
sort of cup from *him*. Oh dear, I'm wittering. I'm doing my
'kindly old school master' character. Did it for years. Theatre.
Television. Especially in those costume thingies the BBC used
to do a lot of. Couldn't do it now of course. No. The idea of
playing any kind of teacher makes my blood run cold ... well,
you know he's going to be a wrong 'un, and there will be a
horribly embarrassing scene with a Young Person ... You can
tell I'm nervous, can't you? No, no, I want to do this, I
definitely want to do it. But when I start wittering, or being
school masterly just stop me. OK?

I owe it to Chloe to do it you see. I feel a bit guilty ... mark
you, there's nothing like talking to the police – what do they
call it? 'helping them with their enquiries' – to make a chap
feel guilty ... I mean, I know they're on our side really, and the
last thing they want to do is pick on the wrong man, but I did
get the feeling they would have liked me just to say, 'I did it,
you've got me bang to rights, I'll tell you where the body is,
and we can all go home.'

Well, almost all of us. Not me of course. Oh, no, it wasn't
just me, they talked to all her friends. You see, I don't think

133

they really 'got' Chloe. Didn't understand her. Well, part of the problem was that I know they saw some footage of the kind of stuff she does now. She used to laugh about it – five Alzheimer's patients and counting, she used to say, one being ripped off by her son, one neglected by her carer, one actually knocked about by a nurse, and one being very kindly treated in spite of being a bit difficult ... I forget what the fifth one was. She might have been a vampire. I know vampires came in it somewhere. But, you know, if you see enough of that sort of thing and you start to identify her with the role – if you never met her in the flesh – and you start to think that she *wasn't* quite right in the head. And nothing could be further from the truth. Chloe was bright as a button and sharp as a tack.

But then there was Facebook. Yes, most of us old codgers stick to Facebook, more or less. I never did get the point of putting a photograph of my breakfast on Instagram. Especially as breakfast used to be a cup of instant coffee and a ciggie, until I gave up the gaspers and now it's just coffee. Oh, yes, I've been clean for about five years now – only a couple of lapses, and that's with someone else's cigs, and that doesn't count, as we all know ... to be absolutely honest, it was the expense as much as anything else. I just didn't have money to burn ... yes, a joke. Sort of ... Now, where was I? Smoking – breakfast – breakfast, photographs of on Instagram – ah, yes, Facebook. Well Chloe used to have these little, well, comic mishaps while she was out and about, often on public transport. Just odd things that happened to her and she'd make them into short stories to amuse us – her friends on Facebook that is. Well ... there was the one where she was looking *at* Facebook on her phone on the tube, and she scrolled down and suddenly came to an ad, and the carriage was filled with this gloopy music and the voice of an American woman talking about incontinence pants. Well, everything went quiet as it does at inconvenient moments and she panicked and kept pressing keys to try to turn it off, but it wouldn't go away, and as there was a station coming up, although it wasn't where she actually wanted to get off, she shoved the phone in her handbag and made for the door. And, she said, the train was quite crowded but no one seemed anxious to take the seat she'd vacated. Things like that.

Oh, no. I'm quite sure she didn't make them up. She may have embellished them a little, but she was just the kind of person that stuff *happened* to. I was with her once when it did. We'd both gone to a casting together. It was in Northeast London – a bit out of the way for us. Most castings are more central, of course, and though I'd been to the area before, there's a good little pub theatre there – I hadn't gone quite as far out – or in, I suppose – as we did that day. The actual place turned out to be what they used to call a scout hut. No, I didn't know they still had them either, and it was *underneath* a flyover ... anyway we found it all right – Chloe was very good at finding her way about, that's why I can't understand – well, we got there and did our bit ... it was for an Indie film, I remember and they asked us to do the Hamlet/Ophelia scene – you know the 'Get thee to a nunnery' one, improvising the words, but doing it as if we were rabbits. Yes. Two of the younger people were struck virtually dumb when they heard that. Oh, no, not by the rabbit idea. But they didn't know the scene. I rather got the impression that they'd never heard of *Hamlet*. Good old Chloe whispered the details of the play to them, and gave them a few phrases, and I have to say they made a jolly good fist of it. Under the circumstances. Of course, it was their idea for the girl to take Hamlet's lines and the boy to play Ophelia, and directors do like that kind of thing nowadays ... No, I never found out if either of them got the job. I know *we* didn't, and quite honestly, I wasn't too sorry.

Oh, no, the film was nothing to do with Shakespeare. Or rabbits. Sometimes, I think these casting directors just get bored ... anyway, we did our little best, and off we went to get the bus back to the tube station. Oh dear. I very nearly said back to civilisation. The bus was one of those little one-storey jobs, and quite crowded, so I stood up, while Chloe got the last seat. And we were pootling along quite cheerfully when suddenly the chap sitting just behind Chloe stood up and roared, 'I am Say-tan.'

Yes. Just like that. Now, no one else took much notice. I don't know whether they were used to that sort of thing round there, or they just didn't find his Satan particularly impressive. This seemed to make him really cross because he shouted a few names of Demons of the Pit – or that's what he said they were, and then he began to swear. Quite loudly. I was getting a bit worried, because Chloe as I said, was sitting right in front of him, and – well – these days you do ask yourself 'Has he got a knife?' and even if he hadn't he was quite a burly chap … I doubt if anyone else wanted to tackle him any more than I did. And something else, which you'll think is really ridiculous – I have a bald spot right on the top of my head – like a tonsure – and it was one of those very hot days we had this year, and my scalp burns awfully easily so I was wearing my old linen sun-hat. I have no doubt I looked rather silly, and it's very difficult to make up your mind to be heroic if you're wearing a silly hat … sounds daft I know, but that's the way the human mind works. Or mine does anyway. And then a small woman right in the front of the bus put us all to shame. She stood up and told his Satanic Majesty to stop swearing at once, or get off the bus, and when he carried right on, she ordered the driver to stop the bus and *put* him off.

Well, the driver did as he was told, as far as it went, but he claimed he wasn't allowed to leave the driver's seat … and for a moment I really did intend to do something, but the chap suddenly seemed overcome simply by the woman's hard Paddington stare, and he got off on his own volition, and wandered away muttering. I led a round of applause, the little woman sat down and we were off again.

Chloe got up and came to stand beside me. She knew I felt I'd let myself down by leaving the little woman to deal with Satan, but all she said was, 'I think we could both do with a coffee – look there's a nice place just coming up …' and she rang the bell – it was one of those buses where you can choose

your own stop, and we got off and went to this little café she'd
spotted. I don't suppose it would have looked anything at all
on a rainy day, but it was rather jolly and Parisian in the
sunlight, with tables outside and a candy-striped awning, and
– well it was quite delightful. There was only one thing that
struck me as a bit – well – odd is too strong, but it was just
something I remembered later, when … well … when it
happened. The waitress said there was a garden at the back,
and asked us if we'd like to sit out there. And we said, thanks
very much, but no. Mainly because of a rather childish feeling
on my part that I'd like to stay where we were, and pretend
we were in a street café in Paris but also because I knew Chloe
had an emergency store of ciggies, and I thought she might
break them out, and while you can still smoke in the street, I
thought perhaps we couldn't do it in the garden which was
technically café premises. And I know Chloe had the same
idea, because she brought the cigarettes out as soon as the
coffee came … but I thought the waitress was a bit over
insistent. And she seemed really peeved when she finally took
no for an answer and went off with a bit of a flounce. I was
afraid she'd spit in our coffee, but we didn't see her again. An
older, rather motherly type in an overall brought us a cafetière
of really good coffee – hot and strong, with some delicious
little cakes and it was all fine. Chloe, who'd noticed that the
girl was a bit pushy too, said it was because she was so good
looking, she was used to getting her own way, especially with
men, but I hadn't noticed that. Chloe said she had a mane of
white blonde hair, almost down to her waist, which, come to
that, shouldn't have been worn loose like that in a café and I
said I hoped we wouldn't find any in the cakes, but of course
we didn't, but that set Chloe off giggling and we had a good
giggle about the whole thing, Hamlet, rabbits, Satan and all.

I suppose – in view of what – well what we're talking
about you'd expect me to finish the story by saying that we
went back the next week – had a recall, you know, and we
couldn't find the café. It had either vanished completely or
turned into an ordinary greasy spoon, but we weren't called

back and we never did try to find the place again. Besides I'm quite sure it was real.

Chloe was a wonderful giggler. Rather too wonderful sometimes, because she and I had a terrible tendency to set each other off when we were working together – oh, yes, that's how we met. In pantomime. It was a seaside town, and I don't even remember where it was now. We always called it 'The Last Resort' when we forgot the right name. I was mostly doing scene shifting, but I also played one of the Broker's Men, which involved splashing flour and water all over the stage, and then of course cleaning it up afterwards while the Ugly Sisters sang a duet front of curtain, and then I was part of the Crowd in the Ballroom Scene. I had the unforgettable line, 'Oh, look at her, oh who is she, who can that lovely lady be?' Sadly there are quite a number of ways you can say 'Oooh, look at her' and I'm ashamed to say I exploited them all. In rehearsal anyway. Oh, yes, it was *Cinderella*. No, Chloe was one of the dancers. Not a very good one, as she was always the first to say, but it was a job.

We met, we 'clicked' as they used to say, and we never looked back. Oh, no, nothing like *that*. We were *friends*. I was married for a while – it didn't work. She wanted a mortgage, and children, and I'm afraid I didn't, well, not enough to give up the theatre for them, and of course I would have had to do that. And Chloe had a few affairs. Well, so did I. You know what they say, what happens on tour stays on tour … Or, no perhaps you don't … But we never lost touch. And as we've got older, we've seen more of each other. You could say our careers, such as they were, slid gently downhill together.

Ah, Chloe's stories … Oh yes, there were plenty more. In one she went for a casting in one of the most mundane parts of London, rang the doorbell, and they buzzed her in … and there was a notice written in biro, stuck to the wall with Sellotape, telling people who were coming for that particular casting to walk straight through the house (it had been a house of course before it was turned into offices), through the back door, across a courtyard and through another door … she said she felt like the girl in the fairy tale, who had to take a flask of oil for the creaking gate, a crust of bread for the fierce guard dogs and ribbons to tie up the branches of the birch tree ... but for her the gate had been oiled, the dogs, mercifully, were off duty and there was no birch tree, so she passed all the dangers and got away safely. Although she didn't get the job.

Oh, from a folk tale. It's quite an old theme, you know, a coin for the ferryman, a sop to Cerberus – you have to pay your passage from here to the Otherworld, and they'll let you in, and hopefully, out again. Oh – Cerberus – I'm sure he turns up in *Harry Potter* except that there he's called 'Fluffy.' Greek and Roman mythology. Three-headed dog. Guarded the entrance to the Underworld. The classical story being that when the Sibyl was guiding Aeneas into the Underworld, she threw a drugged cake to Cerberus and he ate it and went to sleep so they could pass him safely. But in the story Chloe was thinking about a girl is sent to visit a witch, or some such supernatural creature and she gives the dogs a bit of her lunch on her way, and does various other acts of kindness, and when she has to run for it no one will help the witch catch her *because* she's been kind. There's a weird bit of a rhyme my mother used to say:

> *Oh, hide me, cherry tree hide me*
> *For fear the old witch should find me*
> *For if she do she'll break my bones*
> *And bury me under they marly stones.*

I used to ask her what it was about, but she'd heard it from *her* mother, and she had no idea it was attached to any story. Or that 'marly stones' must have been 'marble.' Now I come to think of it, I wonder if great gran had heard it from a nurse, or a nanny ... it's not the kind of error she would have made ... oh dear. I'm wittering again, aren't I?

Kind of you to say so. Ah – Chloe collected that sort of thing. She was a *professional* story teller you know and because she was interested, I got interested too. Folklore, of course and

… other things. Yes, she did the stories as a bit of a side-line for some extra cash if the jobs were slowing down. Oh, no, not just for children. Few folktales *are* for children really. I mean – well, there's one called *Jesper that Herded Hares* and there *is* one version intended for the young. It's in one of the coloured *Fairy Books*, I think, the ones by Andrew Lang, but the other versions … well … *Quite* rude … Not that Chloe told any of those. But of course, her *being* a story-teller … as I say, I don't think the police understood that she could always tell the difference between fact and fiction.

Yes, well you want my version of what happened. I think that's partly why I've been wittering. I don't really want to – to put it into words. Silly I know. And that's what I'm here for. So. Here goes.

Chloe had a couple of days film work – yes, she was going to be an Alzheimer's patient again, I'm afraid. And it was in Barnes. Not Barnes Bridge, just Barnes, *tout court*. Now if you'd asked me I'd have said, well, that's in London – it's covered by the Old Crumblies' Free Travel Pass and that's what matters to me. But it's not really London. It's Surrey. I looked it up when Chloe and I were mapping a route for her and Wiki is very positive about that. And – this will mean nothing to you, of course, but it's surprising how far the Old Crumblies' Pass will take you – and how far the tube goes, come to that. There's one underground line that just ends in green fields. Right in the country. No, I'm not saying *Barnes* is in the country but it's not so long ago that it was … and another thing, it's bang next to Mortlake, yes Mortlake used to be part of the Borough of Barnes, in Surrey.

And – well Mortlake …

Well – there's the name for starters. It's supposed to be derived from 'salmon stream' but it *sounds* like 'Dead Lake', or 'Dead Water'. And yet there are no stories to explain it, not even daft ones, like the one about Nunhead which someone told me once, and insisted it was true, whatever I said.

Well, the obvious, of course. He claimed that there was a convent at the place, and during the Dissolution of the

Monasteries the nuns defied Henry VIII and refused to leave, so he had the lot beheaded, and their heads set up on stakes – *pour encourager les autres* no doubt. Another version says the place – and the name wasn't recorded until 1680 – was named after a local pub called The Nun's Head and that referred to just one nun who got herself beheaded. Now I'm not denying that the Old Beast would have beheaded any number of nuns if they caught him on a bad day, but the simple fact is he didn't. He was a bit sentimental about nuns, apparently, like a lot of blood-thirsty tyrants, and he treated them reasonably well, nothing like that horrible business with the Carthusians, or the Abbot of Glastonbury. And certainly not a mass beheading. Not even one small one.

Ah. Yes, well, I read history at Cambridge. No, I didn't go to drama school. Oh, I got quite a good degree, I had my pick of careers – I could have been a spy – they were recruiting for both sides at the time, you were spoiled for choice – Oh, yes, a joke – sort of … or I could have just gone into the FO like my father. Oh. Sorry. Foreign Office. Or taken up teaching. Funny really. I hated the idea of being a teacher, and then spent a good part of my career pretending to be one …

But never mind that. Mortlake. Well, of course, *that* was where Dr Dee lived. Oh, good heavens no, he wasn't that sort of doctor, he didn't murder his patients or his wife – wives actually, he had three of them … He wasn't a medical doctor. I'm afraid I'm going to have to be a bit school masterly, but I promise it's the last time. John Dee was Queen Elizabeth's Court Magician. No, I doubt if that was his official title, but I think it's a pretty fair job description. He was an alchemist and an astrologer, both quite respectable professions at the time. Possibly more to the point he was an authority – probably *the* authority – on navigation. Yes, all those voyages of discovery relied a lot on Dr Dee. He's credited with pretty well inventing the British Empire, even with being the first to use the phrase, British Empire, which is either a bad or a good thing … I'm not sure. Elizabeth was probably more interested in the alchemical side. Well … yes, people did believe in it. I daresay there's all sorts of things that *we* believe in that later generations will laugh at. But she needed money. North America hadn't turned out to be the Tom Tiddler's Ground that they'd hoped for … Oh, the children's game '*Here I am on Tom Tiddler's Ground, picking up gold and silver…*' well, they certainly weren't doing that. But although Dr Dee did his best he couldn't come up with the goods. Well, naturally. And then he came across a man named Kelley who helped him to contact angels …

Yes. By scrying … that is staring into shiny or reflective objects – we'd probably call it crystal gazing, but while Dee seems to have had a ball of rock crystal, he used other things for his 'shew-stones' as well. There's a black mirror, made from obsidian, in the British Museum which is supposed to have belonged to him. It must have been brought from Mexico, and had probably been used by the Aztec priests for much the same purposes as Dee's in their worship of the god Tezcatlipoca – Smoking Mirror.

Yes, I see what you mean – perhaps it *was* all smoke and mirrors. It is possible that Kelley was a con-man, and perhaps he managed to con himself. But Dee believed in him and his angels. They went to Europe together, but parted company. Kelley entered the service of Rudolf II, the Holy Roman Emperor, as an alchemist. But when the gold wasn't forthcoming, he ended up in prison in Hněvín Castle. Literally ended up because he died there, after breaking his leg while trying to escape …

Dee went back to England to find his house vandalised, and a cold welcome from Elizabeth and her successor James. He died in poverty at his Mortlake house … I wonder now, did they contact *something* – something that Kelley claimed was angelic, which Dee really believed was angelic, but which led them to danger, poverty – death?

And what was it?

I don't know. Yes. I think it might be relevant. Perhaps you'll agree.

Well – Chloe had this job, and on her first day, and this is the way she told it on Facebook that evening, she got up rather earlier than she wanted to, and took the underground to Vauxhall and then the train to Barnes Station. She climbed the stairs from the platform, and crossed the bridge, wondering, she said, why you *always* have to climb a flight of stairs and cross a bridge to get into or out of a station – sometimes both when you arrive *and* when you leave, which theoretically shouldn't be possible. Well, fair enough. I've noticed that myself. But then things started to get just a bit – well – weird. A frantic girl ran up to her on the bridge, asking how to get to Platform One. They both leaned over the parapet, and Chloe agreed, you could *see* the platform but there seemed no visible way of getting to it. She was wondering how she could help when the girl darted off. Well, she was obviously desperate to catch her train, and she wouldn't do that on the bridge. Slightly disturbed by this, but still game, Chloe followed the notice on the wall of the bridge, telling her which way to go for the bus she needed. Down the stairs she went, expecting, not unreasonably I thought, to find herself within sight of a bus station, or at least a bus-stop. Or a road. Instead she found she was, quite literally, in a wood. There were a lot of trees and a decrepit wooden sign-post directing her to Mortlake, where she had no wish to go, but nothing else.

At this point, she said, she looked back to make sure the station was still there and she hadn't been transported to the Black Forest, but honestly, this was a joke. I mean, she *was* in a wood, and there was no visible bus, but she didn't really believe she might be anywhere else but Barnes. Nor did she think she was really at risk from wolves, although she says it looked like wolf country, but when two people came jogging out of the wood, she didn't really think they might be running away from a wolf. She stopped them anyway and asked where she should go to find a bus. Now, there were three paths – just tracks, beaten earth, not actual roads – and after a hasty, whispered discussion, the joggers suggested the middle one and she set off.

The trees seemed to get thicker, and it was rather a long

way. She joked about keeping an eye out for grey muzzles appearing out of the bushes, or even a gingerbread cottage, or a little house with an open door and three bowls of porridge on the table turning up at the end of the path, but she finally made it out of the wood to a stretch of pavement, and a road filled with traffic. There was even a notice, announcing that what she'd just walked through was Barnes Common. She found a bus-stop, but it was for the right bus going the wrong way, so she crossed the road to find another one … which she did, the only problem being that it had a notice on it saying that buses wouldn't be stopping there 'because of a fire'. Well, she couldn't see any signs of fire, and she was sure she'd seen a bus stop to let people get off there while she was waiting to cross, so she stayed put, and indeed the right bus duly arrived and she got on.

There were a few residual bits of weirdness on the bus journey. A tempting sign showing the way to the Old Mortlake Burial Ground (I checked on this – apparently Dickens is buried there, but Dr Dee isn't) and, at the bus-stop for the evocatively named Priest's Bridge, a building was protected with a line of rowan trees. Oh, rowan, both wood and berries is supposed to be a good supernatural repellent – there's a little Scottish rhyme, '*Rowan tree and red threid, Gar the witches tyne their speed.*' Well, basically it means it frightens them off. And – other similar creatures I would suppose. So, it really looked as if someone had put up a barrier against – well – weird stuff. But the rest of the day was quite normal … she was rather cross to discover that her phone wasn't working when she got to the location, but it had happened before – and the filming went well … and she got the same bus as she had in the morning going in the opposite direction, but it didn't quite follow the same route … she found it stopped at what the display told her was certainly Barnes Station, but turned out to be a bridge with a lot of trees on either side … and rising above the trees six slender, quite elaborately ornamented Gothic brick built chimneys … well, there was a flight of steps near the bus-stop, going down, and down she

144

went, reasoning that they must lead to the station. The stair rail and bannisters were covered with pink convolvulus, which was quite pretty, but unexpected and at the bottom she found herself in a wild meadow with a stand of trees at the far side. A little trodden path led across it, but she ignored that, and just walked until she came to a kind of tunnel, went through that – and YES, there was the station. And there was the house which was attached to those Gothic chimneys, a miniature Gothic mansion, in red brick, all pointy arched windows … and next to it a kind of hole in the brick wall which led onto Platform One!

So she went home, made a cup of tea and told us all about her adventure on Facebook. She said she'd try to get a photo of the Gothic House, which she thought might be offices now, next day, and said goodnight to all her readers.

And that was the last entry she ever made.

Oh, we know she went back to work next day. The film people said she seemed quite normal … the police had got the idea, you see, that she'd been taking drugs, and hallucinating, but the director insisted that she wasn't. No way. You don't do a day's filming if you're off your head on some mind-altering substance, she said, and quite right too. I've seen people under the influence. You can always tell. Besides Chloe wasn't one of those women who have half a chemist's shop in their handbags. She wouldn't even take anything legal unless she was at death's door. A cup of tea was her drug of choice, coffee for special occasions. So, everything went off as normal. They'd wrapped fairly late in the afternoon, and Chloe said goodbye, thanked everyone, and went off to get the bus.

They – oh, the police – think she might have caught it, because they found a driver who said he remembered her from the day before. Not surprisingly she'd checked with him to make sure she *was* on the right bus, after all the trouble she'd taken to find it, and he said she'd struck him as being a nice lady, which is why he remembered her when he saw her the next day. And Chloe *was* a nice lady … that's why … well you understand. She was a *very* nice lady … I'm so sorry. No,

I've got some tissues. Can you give me a minute? Oh, that would be very kind. Yes, the same again. No, nothing in it, just a splash of milk ... thank you.

Right. Sorry. Won't happen again. Well, I do feel guilty. You see, I'd been ... disturbed by her story. No, I didn't think there was anything wrong with *her*, not at all. I just didn't like ... well, it gave me a funny feeling. You're going to think I'm a silly old fool, but I thought – *danger*. That red-light signal – metaphorically speaking, that you sometimes get. I've had it before and ignored it, and I've been sorry. I should have gone to collect her. And the reason I didn't wasn't that I couldn't be bothered, but because I knew she'd be cross, and call me a silly old fool, and *mean* it. We'd fall out and I'd lose her for a while, and at my age ... you can't afford to lose friends. And of course, I didn't go, and now I've lost her forever.

I don't know!

Sorry. Didn't mean to shout. Forget, sometimes. I started in the theatre, in the days before throat mikes, and I don't realise how loud I can be. Well ... yes, thanks, the tea helped a lot. Well, the police weren't at all sure that the driver really had seen Chloe again, that afternoon. Apparently the public don't usually lie, but they can be too eager to be helpful. When people go missing, they get sightings reported from all over, often long after the ... the missing person ... must have died, too. So they don't think she necessarily got as far as the station. She could have been standing at the bus-stop, they say, and someone – with evil intentions, you know, driving past could have stopped and offered her a lift. You'd think at Chloe's age she'd have been safe from ... from that sort of thing, but there have been cases ... He might just have had robbery in mind. She was always well-turned out, and carrying a nice handbag ... or it could have been something worse, but not necessarily murder. But Chloe would have resisted, and ...

I don't believe that actually, because for one thing she would never have got into a car with a perfect stranger, on a sunny day, when she knew a bus would be along in a few minutes. It's not as if it was pouring with rain ... I mean, she wasn't an idiot. Sharp as a tack ... and they never found *anything.* Not a trace of her or her belongings. Her bank card's never been used, her phone wasn't recycled ... *Nothing.*

Of course there's been a lot of speculation ... some people thought she might have had a stroke, or a fall, and wandered off, but at the time of day there are always people around. Someone would have seen her looking a bit *distrait* and helped her. Probably called an ambulance. And she had her handbag with all sorts of identification in it, including her Equity Card. And her diary, with the name of the person to call in case of emergency, who, incidentally, was me. Well, yes, I suppose she could have dropped the bag, or someone stole it from her while she was helpless, but I *know* she would have had her call-sheet stuffed in her coat pocket, and there were only two actors working that day, Chloe and the young lady playing her carer. And they would have been listed with their respective phone numbers. She would have been identified in five minutes. And naturally the police checked. No hospital reported seeing or treating an unknown woman in a confused state that day or even that week.

Well. Yes. I think she did take that bus to the station and she went down that flowery stairway and ... all right. This is where I make an utter fool of myself, and you decide I'm a complete nutter ...

I think she was *taken.*

Again, I don't know. But ... perhaps there was someone, some *thing,* waiting for her, at the foot of those steps, to lead her down that narrow path across the meadow and into the trees. Or perhaps she got as far as that little Gothic mansion – it's quite real, by the way, I looked it up. It was originally part of the station. There were four Gothic stations on the Richmond branch – one at Mortlake, by the way, all built around 1846 by an architect called – well – called John Thomas Emmett. Yes. He was a Gothic nut, apparently. This is the only one that survived, and it's Grade II listed now. She mentioned on Facebook that she'd try to take a photograph, although she was having trouble with her phone, and perhaps she stopped outside for a moment to see if she could get a picture. And ... the door opened. No. I don't mean any of the people who really were inside invited her in, or that, if she did go through the door that she went into the real place. And perhaps she didn't go in at all. No one remembers her. She could just as easily have walked into the wood ... and crossed a threshold into – well – all right, into another world.

Oh. I thought you'd be discreetly making for the exit. No, that's all right. I can tell you're not humouring me. You don't believe me, but you know I'm not mad, or pretending. I might as well tell you the rest, so here goes. I think ... that there have always been these encounters, between humans and – others. Some of the recent ones have been re-worked into something that fits in with our 21st century ideas. We call them Aliens, or Greys, or whatever. We meet them in lonely places, or at night, half-way between sleeping and waking – often they want to take us somewhere. Oh yes. There was an encounter in America between a sheriff who was riding out with a posse, after some outlaws. It was a filthy night, pouring with rain. What seemed to be some kind of airship (in those days before airships) landed in front of them, and one of the chaps inside offered to take them 'somewhere where it wasn't raining' but according to the sheriff, 'We allowed we'd ruther stay where we wuz.' I think he made a wise choice.

Poor John Dee thought those who appeared to Kelley in that mirror of black volcanic glass, which might have reflected who knows what before it came to England, were angels and he followed their advice ... The people from whom the Reverend Robert Kirk, minister of Aberfoyle, gathered his folklore in seventeenth century Scotland thought they were spirits somewhere *between* human beings and angels. When he wrote about them in his book *The Secret Commonwealth*, he called them 'fauns' and – 'fairies'.

Oh yes. It's a bit of a joke-word now. Or it calls up rather sickly images of rainbows and unicorns covered with glitter and pink sugar sprinkles, and little girls in tutus. But it was different once.

In Scotland especially, they took them very seriously indeed. A woman in Orkney, Elspeth Reoch, met someone she described as 'a Farie man' when she was around twelve years old. He taught her magic, and later, when she was older, he would appear at her bedside at night, and ... well ... they would do what you might not expect if you'd been brought up on Disney. Yes, of course the poor woman was deluded. She was probably being exploited by a perfectly human villain or re-working an actual episode of incestuous assault ... But ... she was charged with witchcraft by Robert Coltart, the then Procurator Fiscal, the authorities maintaining that she had consorted with the devil, under the guise of a fairy, but her own story was oddly different. According to her he certainly wasn't a devil, and not just a fairy either, but a relative of hers, named Johne Stewart, who had been fatally wounded somehow or other, who told her 'he was neither alive nor dead but was forever trapped between Heaven and Earth.' ... What? Oh no – not medieval at all. Poor Elspeth was found guilty, strangled and her body afterwards burned in March 1616. That's well into the seventeenth century. But, yes the idea that the King of the Elfland presided over the Kingdom of the Dead was known in the Middle Ages – there's a description of a fairy castle in a Middle English poem, *Sir Orfeo*, and it's quite horrific. It's full of people who *'were thought dead but were not'* who had been taken into – well, Fairyland, just at that moment when they were between life and death, some headless, some limbless, some drowned – well you get the picture. All trapped. Ah, yes *Orfeo* is a Middle English version of the myth of Orpheus who went into the Underworld to bring his wife back from the dead, and lost her again, because he looked round to see if she was following him, in spite of being warned against it. But in the medieval poem he rescues his Eurydice – or Heuridis as she becomes to the medieval reader, and takes her home.

And that's what I've been thinking about. There are stories of rescue. Two farm labourers, walking home from work one night heard sounds of music and dancing. There was nothing necessarily uncanny about that. Young people being what they are, there were always some of them up for a bit of a dance on a moonlit night, and one of the men, who fancied a dance himself, went to see what was going on. His friend followed him a bit reluctantly and saw him join the dancers, but was disinclined to do the same. Perhaps he was tired – or perhaps *his* red-light went off. Because he went home, leaving the other to it – and next day discovered that the other man hadn't come home. He told his story, but no one knew anything about a dance that night, and he was under some suspicion. And when his friend hadn't turned up after nearly a year there was talk of charging him with murder. In desperation he went back one night to the place where he had left his friend. It was a year to the very day. And there he saw the ring of dancers, and his friend with them … he rushed in and pulled him away, and he had quite a struggle to get him free. And when he did, the man wasn't at all grateful. He'd just been having a bit of a dance, he said, and he wasn't ready to come home yet. It took a long while for his friends and family to persuade him that he'd been away for a year …

It seems time goes differently there. Well, that's the other thing, you know. You must never eat anything in the other world, whether it's Fairyland, or the Land of the Dead. Remember Persephone? Once you've eaten their food you can never come back. But if you can be there for a year, and it seems like a few hours, and apparently be none the worse, then perhaps I could still get Chloe back. She knows the rules as well as I do. She taught them to me after all. She won't eat a bite.

Oh. Yes. That's what I want to do. Or at least try. I went to look at the place, you know, and everything was pretty much as she said. The stairs, the bridge, the tunnel – liminal places you know, places of crossing. And the strange house dropped in amongst the trees. Although I suppose it's just an office. And the three paths leading into the wood like the three paths in that ballad about Thomas the Rhymer … no, I don't know why they took her. They usually want nursing mothers, to feed their own children, or pretty girls, or strong young men ... but one of the stories people told about Robert Kirk when he died very suddenly was that he'd been taken by the fairies because he betrayed their secrets ... perhaps they felt she was a danger to them ... I don't know. And yes, I know I sound like that chap in Ireland who was convinced that his wife had been taken by the fairies and replaced by a look-alike, and killed her when he tried to get her back. I don't know. Perhaps I am.

Yes, I think there are certain places where the barriers between their world and ours have become weakened, somehow. I think Barnes Station and its environs is one of them. Perhaps because of its nearness to Mortlake. Who can tell? And I think, because of her interest in Story, Chloe was particularly vulnerable. I think they tried to trap her several times. One was on that day at the café. The girl who wanted to lead us into that garden ('up the garden path' perhaps) was not a waitress. She was trying to do what they call 'glamour' us, but it didn't work. Perhaps because there were two of us. Then there was that weird passage through the house and across the courtyard to the casting studios, but she escaped again. And the last time, the fatal third, she succumbed.

But I can't live with that picture of Chloe trapped for ever in a castle full of zombies.

So I shall go there on Halloween – it's supposed to be a good time to try this sort of thing. And just between dusk and dark I will go down those stairs – although I expect the flowers will have died off. I'll pass through the tunnel and cross the bridge and take the path she took through the dark wood. And perhaps I will bring her back.

Re:WANT. Interview 9

Look I don't think we can use the attached. I mean, the chap's evidently as mad as a badger. Of course, I don't mean he wasn't very convincing. He was giving me the cold grue towards the end of the interview but that's the problem. We're doing 'Where Are They Now? – True Life Disappearances', not 'Tales from the Twilight Zone'. Still. I agree he was effective. I don't think I want to lose him completely. Old actor laddie, wasn't he? Look, tell you what. We've got time. Get him back in, get him to rein back on the weird detail and cut the bit at the end, he's a professional, he'll understand and we'll see. Next week?

'Hi, Clive. Problem with your old actor?'

'Yes. I … sorry to phone, but email didn't seem …'

'What's wrong? You don't sound too good.'

'I tried to contact him. His agent can't … he said … he hasn't heard from him since the end of October. He's not in his flat … the police are looking into it… Clive, I think he did go into that wood. And God help me, I don't think he will ever come out again.'

LAND OF DARK ARTS

Hertfordshire is probably one of Britain's most inoffensive counties. Only a short drive from London and yet exceedingly rural in character, well over half of it has been classified as 'green belt', while the majority of its conurbation comprises scenic villages, pretty market towns and thriving young cities where innumerable blue-chip companies have set up. The standard of living here is high and crime rates are low. Hertfordshire even boasts its own patron saint, one of the few British counties to do so: St Alban, who was martyred here on the orders of the Roman Emperor, Septimus Severus, in 209 AD. The impressive medieval edifice of St Alban's Cathedral stands on the very spot where his head was severed.

And yet there is one other thing, something much darker, for which Hertfordshire is also well-known, or at least it was in the distant past.

Alchemy.

A form of protoscience practised all over the world in times past, alchemy interwove occultism and philosophy with early forms of chemistry in the pursuit of various fantastical aims, such as the ability to transmute 'base metals', like lead, into 'noble metals', like silver and gold, and the discovery of the Philosopher's Stone, from which it was believed an elixir of immortality could be derived, but also – and here's where it gets respectable – the development of medicines and remedies for common ailments.

Alchemists were rarely persecuted by witch-hunters or inquisitors. This was partly because they were not seen as being widely different to apothecaries, whose origins could be found in the Catholic Church itself, but also because they often had powerful patrons who shared in their ambitions; Dr John Dee, for example, was famously under the protection of Queen Elizabeth I of England. But there is no doubt that many ordinary observers considered it a 'dark art', seeing no difference between alchemy and sorcery. And they may have had a point. A significant number of alchemists were charlatans, who lacked even crypto-scientific knowledge and yet thoroughly enjoyed their reputations for being wise and mysterious men, not least because it enabled them to earn money without actually doing any work.

But there are one or two cases, particularly in Hertfordshire (of all places!), where more sinister circumstances seem to have prevailed.

Aldbury, in the beautiful Bulbourne Valley, is one of the most picturesque corners of the county. An archetypical Home Counties village, it boasts a central duck pond, a Norman church, a couple of medieval ale houses and numerous well-preserved Tudor cottages. It was also once home to the notorious alchemist, Guy de Gravade.

Reputedly the pet magician of Edward III (1312-1377), a warrior king who on the battlefield could not imagine defeat, De Gravade's speciality was supposed to be the overnight creation of dykes, earthworks and other fortifications. You can imagine why this skill would be useful to a potentate much concerned with war, but the fact that De Gravade is also credited with having created the impressive Grim's Dyke, which runs the 20 miles between Bushey and Tring, always casts him in a vaguely menacing light.

As referred to earlier in this book, there are many notable ditches or dykes crisscrossing England and Wales, most of them prehistoric in origin, thrown up originally as tribal borders, but the pagan Saxons, who came later, were always wary of such unnatural land-forms, and their name for them, Grimr, a reference to Woden, the ruler of their Teutonic gods, indicates the awe with which they held them. Later of course, once the Saxons were Christianised, and Woden became Odin, the demonic godhead idolised by the insurgent Vikings, the dykes and ditches were actively shunned. It's not difficult, therefore, to understand why assumptions were made, both during his life and afterwards, that Guy de Gravade, whose abilities far surpassed those of other alchemists, had made a pact with the darkest powers, maybe even had sold his soul to Satan, and his eventual death and the complete destruction of his property were seen as a just dessert.

Apparently, the alchemist's fortified house stood on the site now occupied by Tring Railway Station, but was demolished in a devastating explosion when his apprentice, John Bond, entered the *laboratory while his master slept and sought to enact some spells of his own. As a footnote to this fascinating tale, both men's ghosts are said to appear on the site on the yearly anniversary of their deaths.*

Another Hertfordshire alchemist who was held in similarly fearful regard comes to us from more recent times.

John Kellerman was a 19th century occupant of Lilley in the northwest of the county, and often designated 'the last of the alchemists'. A certified real-life person, and something of a recluse, he was visited and written about by the author Sir Richard Phillips in 1828, who'd heard of no actual evil deeds that he had done, but who was struck by Kellerman's cottage, which externally was encircled by the sort of defences that would be illegal today, mantraps, spring-guns and the like, and internally was given over almost entirely to bizarre experimentation. Phillips described a litter of 'crucibles, alembics, jars, bottles in various shapes, intermingled with old books piled upon each other ... with a sufficient quantity of dust and cobwebs.' In short, all the typical accoutrements of the alchemist's lair.

However, it wasn't this that made the nearby villagers fear Kellerman. Few of them ever got inside his house, anyway. Most wouldn't even have wanted to, though gathering on nearby roads and watching from a safe distance became a night-time sport for them. Apparently, all manner of strange things could be seen: different coloured flames flaring behind the cottage windows, plumes of rainbow-patterned smoke issuing from its chimney; there were thunderous bangs and blinding flashes. But the crowning glory, which actually occurred several times in front of dozens of witnesses, involved an intense cloud of flame bursting upward from the chimney pot, and assuming a colossal human form, before being sucked back down again.

Trickster stuff? The work of a clever conjuror? Or evidence of someone genuinely pursuing arcane powers to improve his lot?

We will never know, but one thing is certain: Kellerman, who lost a fortune during his early years by gambling, never seemed short of money later on. Rumours spread that he had indeed discovered the Philosopher's Stone and even the Universal Solvent, and that this could only have happened had he struck bargains with ancient, eldritch beings.

Despite all, more educated observers remained doubtful. And when Kellerman allegedly approached several different governments offering them the formula for 'making gold' they curtly ordered him away.

He died mid-century in the same manner that he'd spent most of his life: quietly, unobtrusively, and shrouded in mystery.

THE DOOM
Paul Finch

Considering the age of St Bronwyn's priory church, it struck Reverend Bilks as odd that he hadn't previously considered that there might be a treasure hidden inside it.

This was his first thought when he woke that fateful morning. The bedroom was fragrant with the smell of chopped summer grass. Somewhere in the eaves, birds were twittering. But seriously – why, he wondered, hadn't he initially suspected that so old and venerable a church might have something interesting to hide?

Built in the compact Norman style of the early twelfth century, St Bronwyn's still retained much of its evocative medieval character. Various refurbishments had been made over the centuries: the transepts and tower were modern, while it's more exquisite features – the stained glass in the windows, the carved oak with which it's interior was adorned – dated from the sixteenth and eighteenth centuries respectively. But the essential structure, the main body of the church, its aged exterior now weathered and thick with ivy through which the occasional Green Man or Sheela na Gig would mysteriously peep, was original. He should have realised from the outset that a majestic piece of antiquity could be concealed in its fabric.

He rose between nine and half-past, showered and went downstairs to enjoy a leisurely breakfast of eggs, bacon and sausage followed by toast and marmalade. Mrs Coulson, the housekeeper provided by the parish, was an excellent cook, but she'd now finished for the day, and had left the meal for him under a polished metal lid. It was a glorious June morning. Sunlight streamed through the kitchen window, casting myriad reflections of flowers onto the ceiling.

Bilks had certainly landed on his feet here.

As rustic churches went, there were none prettier than St Bronwyn's, and few in more scenic a location. Chiddingworth was vintage Surrey. Surrounded by acres of farmland, it centred on a small green and consisted mainly of period cottages, many thatched, some timbered in the Jacobean style. With its timeless aura and sedate pace of life, little wonder it had won 'Village Of The Year' a record number of times.

Ironically, his initial response to being posted here had been disappointment. For his first parish, he hadn't felt it would challenge him. There'd be few social problems to get his teeth into. The church would always be full on Sunday, as, no doubt, would the vicarage tea-room afterwards. But after several months' incumbency, he'd found that quaintness had its own rewards. It was nice to be able to arrange fêtes where everyone in the community attended, or to host bring-and-buy sales where the contributions were not only plentiful but of high quality. And it was nicer still that these events cost virtually nothing, local people being so generous with their time and talent. More important than any of this was Pamela's attitude. Bilks's sweetheart since college, she'd at times expressed doubts that his vocation was something she'd be able to acclimatise to. But on first sight of the rambling old building that would be his home, a handsome remnant of the original priory, and then the picturesque village in which it was set, she'd instantly agreed to be his wife. Bilks, who for all his early reservations had now acknowledged that he'd never been much of a crusader, had finally had to admit that his lot was a happy one. But the discovery of 'the Doom' was the icing on the cake.

It had happened by accident. A local man was restoring the fading whitewash on the walls of the nave. As he'd stripped the original decayed material away, he'd been startled to find images underneath. Experts were called in, who quickly became excited. St Bronwyn's, like many medieval churches, had once been decorated inside with vivid religious murals. However, on this occasion, the Reformation-era vandals had elected to cover these pictures rather than scour them out of existence. This was unusual, given that the same vandals had extended their energy to dissolving the Augustinian chapter that had once occupied the priory and then to pulling down at least half of the priory building. But it was an oversight that was now to be welcomed. The remainder of the whitewash was removed with extreme diligence, finally revealing what could only be described as an impressive if maleficent piece of baroque artwork, twenty yards across and stretching from the floor almost to the church ceiling.

'A classic,' in the words of Doctor Rupert Black, senior curator at the National Gallery and a renowned expert on so-called Dooms. 'The best and most hellish example of a Judgement Day scenario that I've ever been witness to.'

Even now, two months later, Bilks couldn't get over his good fortune.

He glanced out through the window and saw Pamela, looking unconscionably desirable (for a vicar's wife, that is) in a short-skirted summer dress, high-heeled sandals and a broad-brimmed sunhat, from the rear of which her copper hair hung in a long ponytail. She'd been mowing the expansive front lawn and was now pruning her roses, which looked distinctly like prize winners. The Bilkses already had everything they could want here. But thanks to the Doom, the new vicar's stock had risen considerably in the eyes of the diocese. After the church re-opening a couple of weeks ago, the bishop, having been treated to an exquisite brandy purchased by Pamela especially for the occasion, had muttered something about Bilks having 'a very enviable future'.

But it was a strange thing to benefit from, the Doom.

Art historians had already come from as far away as Oxford and Cambridge, and had been awed and horrified in equal measure. A local news team had produced a feature on it, which itself had made the headlines because network broadcasters had refused to screen it before the nine o'clock watershed. This had brought it to the attention of the wider public, and a succession of curiosity-seekers had called in over the last few days, which had helped local businesses no end and left the church collection-boxes clinking.

Not, if he was honest, that Bilks liked to think about it this way. The Doom itself illustrated the dangers of such an attitude.

In essence, it was a lesson – and a very lurid one.

At first glance it was difficult to see what was happening: it was a mass of struggling forms with no apparent sense of order; a battle maybe. But when you got closer, it was plain that what you were actually looking at was a multitude of damned souls in the clutches of thousands of grinning devils. Painted a variety of sickly colours – white, yellow, green – the damned were uniformly corpse-like: bald, limp, cadaverously thin. Yet they were clearly alive, as the cringes of agony on their skeletal faces attested. The devils, who displayed a hideous array of gargoyle and dragon-like features, were either red, orange or black and armed with swords, pincers and scourges as they drove their victims like cattle from one horror to the next. Some were being hanged on gibbets or nailed to crosses. Others were roasting on spits or splayed on wheels. There were red-hot kilns with arms and legs poking out through tiny apertures, racks on which bodies had been stretched to inordinate length, rows of upright figures impaled on spears. Every type of suffering imaginable was on view, with nothing left to the imagination.

It was extraordinarily ghoulish for a piece of ecclesiastical art, but in the historical context understandable. The medieval mind was tortured by fear of the afterlife. In an age when violence was rife, when the very forces of law, the kings and barons themselves, were as likely to rob and kill you as provide justice, the Church had had no option but to try and terrify mankind into restraining his baser instincts. Needless to say, Pamela didn't approve. She'd described it variously as 'horrid', 'disgusting', 'revolting'. But Pamela had never been one to look a gift-horse in the mouth either. When Bilks first began toying with the idea of charging visitors to photograph the Doom, it was her suggestion that he charge merely for viewing it. It was unique after all. And if people were prepared to travel to see it, they'd surely be willing to pay.

He went upstairs to finish dressing. Appearances had now become important, so he selected a smart, short-sleeved shirt of pink silk and a freshly-laundered collar. As he did, he happened to look through the bedroom window and spotted that a car, a new model Alpha-Romeo in metallic smoke-grey, had parked on the forecourt. It wasn't yet ten o'clock and visitors were arriving already. By the looks of it, moneyed visitors.

Bilks hurried downstairs and out into the garden. His plan to start charging for viewings hadn't become official yet. For one thing, he hadn't run it by the bishop, but he didn't see there'd be much objection. Presenting an annual accounts book that was in the black could only win him more kudos. But there were no money-handling procedures in place as yet, so he'd have to play it by ear.

The church sat next door with only a low rockery between itself and the vicarage. Bilks skipped over this and hurried up the path to the church's porch door, which stood wide open. Mrs Coulson was in there by six each morning because she had to finish at nine to care for her senile mother. At one time she'd have locked the building up again when leaving, but Bilks had now instructed her to leave it open.

Inside, it was cool and shadowed. Bilks halted in the doorway. At first he had to squint, but then his eyes adjusted. Only one visitor was present: a man in beige slacks (*Armani*, Bilks noted) and a white, short-sleeved shirt (*Yves St Lauren*), with a brown leather jacket draped over one shoulder. He was appraising the Doom from very close up.

'Hello,' Bilks said, approaching in his usual polite, semi-cautious sort of way.

The man glanced around. He was youngish, mid to late thirties. His hair was black and thick, cut with a fringe and sideburns. His dark skin and dark eyes gave him a vaguely Italian look. His torso was wedge-shaped, his arms hairy and firmly muscled. An expensive gold watch occupied one of his wrists.

'Impressive, isn't it?' Bilks said.

'Astonishing.' The man looked back at the mural. 'But I'm more interested in the story behind it.'

'We were in the middle of refurbishment work, when …'

'No, I mean the *real* story. The subtext, if you like.'

Bilks was puzzled. 'I'd have thought the subtext was obvious.'

'Not necessarily. These images here …' The man indicated a row of separate pictures ranged along the top of the Doom. Each one appeared to represent a scene from everyday medieval life. The first showed a woman with flowing hair leaning from the bedroom of a house; a row of monks were passing below, heads bowed, though one at the rear had stepped back and was looking up towards the woman. It was fairly clear what this image, and therefore the others, portrayed.

'The Seven Deadly Sins,' Bilks said.

'Yes. Yet they all appear to be given equal status. I'd have thought that some were worse than others.'

'They're all venial sins, I suppose. But the point is that any one of them could lead to mortal sins.'

'Surely it's the mortal sin that's deemed most deserving of punishment?' the man said.

'I'd imagine so,' Bilks replied. 'In fact yes, yes it is.'

This was an unexpected conversation. It wasn't often that he was required to discuss concepts like these, a couple of which – if he was honest – he found a bit discomforting. One of the seven images depicted a cardinal in the upper room of a palatial residence, counting heaps of coins, while beyond his window naked peasants toiled in a barren field. It clearly represented Avarice. Several times while looking at it, Bilks had needed to forcibly remind himself that it wasn't avaricious to want to rise in your chosen profession; it was not as if he personally could ever be rich. Another picture portrayed a shepherd asleep under a tree, while in the background a bizarre animal, something like a wolf, ran riot among his sheep. It was a disquieting depiction of Sloth, and this too worried Bilks. He'd commenced his career full of idealism, and much of that was now blunted. But wasn't that inevitable? Yes, it was easier to take tea and cakes with well-heeled ladies than to visit the damaged and diseased in the subways and mission halls. But this cosy village was his post; he hadn't asked for it and he could only offer succour to those who lived here. Not that Jesus would have taken that attitude, of course.

'And these are savage punishments,' the visitor said, interrupting Bilks's thoughts.

'Er yes, well … they reflect the attitudes of the time.'

'Ah! So they're Man's punishments rather than God's?'

'They're Man's idea of God's punishments.'

'Based purely on imagination?'

'How could they be anything else?'

'Doesn't the *Book of Revelation* describe scenes like this?'

'Does it? I mean yes, it does.'

'And wasn't that supposed to be based on a vision?'

'Well …' Bilks wasn't especially well up on *Revelation*, and was now finding the questions tiresome.

'Every ancient text we have tells us that sinners will be punished,' the man added.

'That's true.'

'So if this is just imagination, do the punishments come on Earth, maybe?'

'Does God punish us on Earth?' Bilks said, confused by the change of direction but realising that this, at least, he could deal with. 'Officially, what happens on Earth is Man's doing, not God's. We have free will, after all. But in some circumstances it might be God's judgement that a soul has suffered so terribly during its life on Earth that no further punishment is required.'

'I see.' The man gazed at the picture again.

'It might interest you to know how we plan to preserve this amazing piece of art,' Bilks said. 'If you're not a regular churchgoer, you probably won't …'

'But I am. I'm a staunch Anglican.'

'Oh.'

'I'm also a pathological sex-offender.'

It was several moments before Bilks could stutter: 'I … I'm sorry?'

'I've been in prison several times for raping and assaulting women.'

PAUL FINCH

Another moment passed, during which Bilks felt his scalp start to tingle.

'You needn't be concerned,' the man said. 'I'm not wanted for any crime at present. But it's a near-certainty that I'll rape again.'

'In Heaven's name, why?' Bilks hadn't meant to say that; he hadn't meant to say anything. It had come out before he could stop it.

The man shrugged. 'Because I enjoy it. Because it's a temptation I can't resist. Perhaps now you realise why I'm here, asking these questions. If anyone's damned, it's surely me.'

'Not ... er, not necessarily.' Bilks couldn't quite believe the way the conversation had turned. The man was in no way threatening, but suddenly Bilks felt trapped. What was he supposed to do, tell the fellow to leave, order him out of the church when he'd clearly come here for some form of absolution? 'The Lord forgives all who truly ...'

'Repent their sins,' the man agreed. 'But I don't. How can I? They're a source of joy to me. I always say I'm sorry afterwards, but I'm not really sorry. Not in my heart of hearts. Certainly God wouldn't be fooled.'

Bilks's mouth was too dry for him to respond.

'Which brings us back to this.' The man indicated the Doom again. 'I'm currently seeking to find out as much as I can about Hell. Trying to decide whether or not I think an eternity there would be something I could, well, endure.'

'Don't take this the wrong way,' Bilks said, his basic clerical instinct screaming at him to reach out with a placating hand, but a far stronger one advising that he edge away. 'During the time you've been ... offending, have you had any psychiatric help?'

'They've tried to cure me several times, but have always failed. There's nothing wrong with me, you see. It's something I just love doing. Tell me, how terrible do you think my punishment will actually be?'

Humour him, Bilks decided. That was the only way to deal with a madman; you had to humour him. 'The modern view of

164

Hell is not that it's a pit filled with fire. Rather that it's ... well, an absence of God.'

'And when you say "modern view", do you mean trendy Church of England modernism, where no-one actually does anything wrong because personal responsibility is unimportant? Or do you mean a modern theological view based on careful but respectful rationalisation of scripture?'

'Er, modern, theologic ... the latter.'

'An absence of God?' The man pondered this. 'Well there's no God in my life now, so maybe it wouldn't be too bad.'

'For all eternity?' Again, Bilks couldn't help but pose a question.

'An eternity of this life. Would that be so bad?'

'But it won't be *this* life.'

'Why not?' the man asked. 'Everyone else in the country will surely be there. Look at these other sins.'

The image representing Pride showed a woman standing before a mirror, adorning herself with jewels, unconcerned that an infant child crawled out through an open door behind her. For Gluttony, a merchant sat on a donkey, drinking from a goblet and feasting on a full roasted chicken; he was so corpulent that the poor beast's back was bent to breaking point. For Envy, a man clad in the tatters of regal robes begged by the roadside; instead of feeding him, the passers-by mocked him. For Wrath, two men armed with clubs fought violently outside the entrance to a tavern.

'Is there a better précis of modern Britain than this?' the man said.

'It isn't that simple ...'

'What do you think this fellow did here?' The man pointed to a corner of the main mural where one of the damned had been fastened to rings in the ground; clamps held his mouth wide open while a devil shovelled dirt into it. 'I'd imagine he was obsessed with earthly things, and is now being reminded what earth actually is. I wonder what *my* punishment will be?'

'An absence of women.'

The man glanced around, surprised.

'An absence of the thing you desire,' Bilks explained, astonished that he'd been drawn so deeply into the discussion. 'For all eternity.'

'Is that part of doctrine?'

'No, but it would make sense.'

'Yes. Yes it would. Seems I'm caught between a rock and a hard place. Do you have any advice?'

'Advice?'

'That is your function, isn't it? To offer guidance?'

'Well yes,' Bilks said, though it was a while since he'd ever had to perform such a duty. In fact, he wasn't sure he ever had, not for someone so desperately in need. 'Sometimes ... well, sometimes there's solace to be found in prayer.'

'I pray a lot, but I don't get many answers.'

'Have you prayed for the strength to resist your compulsion?'

'I've told you, it's not a compulsion. I'm not like a paedophile who hates himself because of what he can't control. I enjoy doing it. It's my main form of recreation.'

'Then ask for any assistance you can. There must be a way for God to help.'

The man seemed unconvinced, but now slid into a pew and knelt down. 'It'll be a new experience, praying in the shadow of judgement.'

He glanced nervously at the Doom before closing his eyes and joining his hands.

Bilks took the opportunity to backtrack down the aisle. He stepped outside into the sunlight, breathing hard, his forehead damp. He'd taken the easy option of course, passing the buck back to God, but despite his soothing words he had no real interest in saving this chap's soul. Though guilty about breaking the confidence expressed to him, he had no hesitation in whipping the phone from his pocket and tapping out 999.

He was diverted to the nearest police control centre.

'Hello. My name's Lewis Bilks. I'm vicar of St Bronwyn's in Chiddingworth. Listen, there's a chap here who's deranged. He's claiming to be a mass-rapist.'

The voice at the other end was female, but clipped, terse. 'This man's with you now?'

'He's in the church.'

'Is he violent?'

'No, quite the opposite. But to be honest, that's scaring me even more. Please send someone, hurry.'

'What exactly do you mean "he says he's a rapist"?'

'What do you think I mean?' Bilks was sweating hard. 'He says he's been in prison for raping several women, and that he's going to do it again.'

'Do you believe him?'

'Absolutely. Look, he's clearly out of his mind. Please send someone.'

'Is there any way you can isolate him without risk to yourself?'

'I don't understand.'

'If he's alone in the church, can you lock him in?'

'I suppose. Wait, no I can't. The windows – he'll break one and get out easily.' Bilks didn't mention that the Tudor windows were another of the church's pride and joys; any one of them would cost a small fortune to replace.

'The point is, Mr Bilks, Chiddingworth's well out of our way. We can dispatch a patrol, but it's going to take ten minutes at the very least to reach you. And as he's not engaged in crime at this moment, our priority ...'

'You're not listening to me!' Bilks almost shouted. 'I genuinely believe he's dangerous. For God's sake, he says rape is his recreation.'

There was a pause, during which he heard the officer mumbling to somebody else. Then she came back on the line: 'I know this is a lot to ask, but can you possibly keep him talking? We'll be as quick as we can.'

'Dear God. I'll try, yes.'

'Don't worry, sir. He's probably just an attention-seeker. It's very rare that serious criminals walk off the street and confess their crimes, even to men of the cloth.'

Bilks cut the call and went nervously back inside. In a horror story, the church would now be empty. Bilks would search, and the assailant would leap from behind a pillar screaming, having reverted fully to his bestial self.

But that didn't happen.

The man was standing in the aisle, pulling on his leather jacket. Was he leaving? Bilks was absurdly hopeful. The man halted to scrutinise the Doom again.

'I'm sorry you haven't found what you were looking for,' Bilks said, approaching.

'It hasn't been a complete waste of time.'

Bilks didn't ask why.

The man walked in the direction of the door, and Bilks was only too pleased to escort him. The hell with keeping the fellow here till the police arrived. What was he supposed to do, restrain him? Having already admitted to himself that he was no crusader, Lewis Bilks had no trouble admitting that he was no martyr either.

'If it's genuinely true that you don't feel any sorrow for the hurts you cause,' he said, attempting a subtle consolation, 'then I'm not sure it's entirely your fault.'

'I do feel sorrow of a sort. But that doesn't compare with the exhilaration of the hunt, the joy of scheming, the delight I get from the catch …'

'Then you won't go to Hell,' Bilks interrupted. They stepped out onto the church forecourt together. 'You're clearly disturbed. Mentally ill.'

'I told you, I've been thoroughly examined.'

'It's not a scientific thing.' Bilks felt his confidence grow as they approached the parked Alpha-Romeo. The man was listening attentively. 'In my opinion, you were born without a conscience.'

'Is that possible?'

'As possible as being born without an arm or leg. Only a lot more disabling.'

They'd now reached the car. The man looked thoughtful. 'I'm not at fault at all?'

'I don't think we can say that. But if you lack the basic

mechanism that helps other men avoid wickedness, you can't be fully blamed.'

The man slipped a key from his pocket, inserted it into the car door and opened it. A smell of warm leather exhaled. 'Thank you.'

'I've not done anything really,' Bilks said modestly.

'On the contrary. You've helped me a lot.' The man climbed into the vehicle, but he didn't immediately drive away. Even when he closed the door, he powered its window down. 'I have to say, I'm not sure I agree with all your views.'

'Well ...' Bilks made a friendly gesture. The last thing he wanted now was to prolong the conversation.

'It's heartening to hear your opinion that I won't be punished too much.' The man said this with apparent sincerity, as if a genuine burden had been lifted from his shoulders. 'I'm heartened more than you can imagine. But there's one problem.' He turned the ignition of his car; its engine purred to life. He now peered directly ahead, as if concentrating on a long, invisible road. 'I'm afraid I've lied to you. I've never raped a woman in my life.'

At first Bilks thought he'd misheard.

'I've yearned to do it,' the man added. 'Desperately desired it. And now, thanks to your wise words, I realise it's a desire I can surrender to.'

'But, I ...'

'It isn't my fault.'

'Now wait ...'

'Isn't that what you said?' The man put his car into gear. In the better light, his swarthy face was pockmarked, his eyes a curious smoke-grey, almost the exact same colour as his vehicle.

'I was only telling you what you wanted to hear,' Bilks said quickly. After previously keeping a discrete distance, he now pushed himself forward. 'You mustn't listen to me. I'm no-one to make these judgments. Far from it.'

'You're God's representative on Earth, aren't you?'

'Hardly. I'm not a good priest. I'm not even a good man. I only engaged you in conversation in the first place because I wanted to cadge money out of you.'

The man smiled. 'Which ties it all together neatly. It must be fate.'

'Please reconsider this …'

The car edged forward, and the man had to raise his voice to be heard further. 'You also told me that Man might suffer his punishment on Earth.'

'Yes, but …'

'Then that's the way you must view it.'

'What do you mean?'

The man powered his window up as he pulled out onto the lane.

'Wait … what the devil do you mean?' Bilks grabbed for his mobile again, but this time, predictably, its battery was failing. 'Pamela!' He spun round to the garden. 'Go inside, call the police quickly!'

But the garden was empty.

Except for a pair of secateurs.

And a single high-heeled sandal.

Bilks swung back to the road. The car was still visible, but so far ahead that its registration was already unreadable. Frenzied, he raced after it. He ran like a man possessed, screaming his wife's name. His shirt was soon a silk skin wringing with sweat. His clerical collar became restrictive, so he tore it off. But the car pulled further and further ahead. It wasn't speeding, but it vanished all the same.

Only a swirling, sweltering haze remained.

LORD STANHOPE'S HOMONCULI

Like many locations where Home Counties mysteriousness has been reported, Eythrope is not the kind of place one would automatically associate with evil, or even the unusual. A quaint village in the parish of Waddesdon, in the leafy heart of Buckinghamshire, little has changed here for decades and the overriding impression one gets is that little ever will.

However, in 1934, local historian, Horace Harman, was compiling a collection of Buckinghamshire tales, when he came across one that startled him. In a local tavern called The Harrow, which still stands today on the road to Bishopstone, a garrulous old customer told him that the area was notorious for witches. This, in itself, did not surprise Harman. There'd been several well-publicised witch trials in Buckinghamshire between 1580 and 1670. But then the old-timer said that he wasn't talking about this, but about a type of witchery that was much more recent. He claimed that it had happened within his own lifetime, and was witnessed by a local shepherd of his acquaintance. Moreover, this case was especially odd as all the practitioners were apparently male and their sole purpose seemed to be to enchant the local sheep.

Several times, the old chap said, the shepherd had come into the fields, and found his flock standing rigid, as if frozen, their heads all turned in the same direction. On each occasion, he had looked the same way, and had seen either one or two bizarre figures perched on or gambolling along the tops of the sheepfold fences. They were diminutive, he said, no more than two feet high, small-bodied but long-shanked, with ugly faces that resembled squashed vegetables.

On seeing the shepherd, these beings always took off at incredible speed, faster than any man or animal could run. On one occasion, the shepherd thought one of the figures had been riding on a hurdle, which in old country speak means a section of wickerwork fencing.

Those aware of these things will know that, far from exclusively seeking broomsticks as their main mode of transport, it was believed that witches could animate any object of their choosing when they were in need of a ride, be that a person, who would accommodate them on his/her back, an old cupboard, a broken-off door or, in fact, a hurdle.

This possibly explains how the idea was planted in the old pub customer's head that these beings were witches. Because nothing else about them seems to fit that bill. If anything, to Harman's ears at least, what the old man appeared to be describing were goblins or faeries, and this suspicion was reinforced not long afterwards, when, some distance down the road, he interviewed an old villager who had worked in the area as a night watchman. Harman mentioned the curious apparitions that had supposedly enthralled the sheep, expecting to be greeted with laughter, but was surprised when the villager took the tale seriously.

He denied that these beings were witches but added that he didn't know what they actually were. However, he confirmed the story that the area was occupied by a tribe of such eerie, shrunken creatures, and said that he had sometimes seen them dancing frenziedly in the moonlight, and that whenever they realised they were being observed, they would take off at mind-boggling speed, so fast that they vanished almost instantly.

When Harman made the point that this story was not dissimilar to other tales connected to faerie lore, the villager was noncommittal, appearing to believe that this manifestation was somewhat more ominous. He spoke of a particularly frightening occasion when, while working as a night watchman, he was patrolling the grounds of Eythrope House with his dog. He was deep in a laurel coppice when the hound became frantic, yowling and snarling as if it felt threatened. The watchman expected poachers, but the next thing, both man and beast were surrounded by these 'devils', which leapt and danced wildly, and on this occasion made no attempt to flee. Indeed, it was left to the watchman and his dog to make their escape.

It did not go unnoticed by Harman that on this occasion, the witness referred to the beings as 'devils', but when asked what he thought they actually were, he became evasive, saying only that he imagined their origin lay in Lord Stanhope's cellars. After this, no further information was forthcoming.

The cellars under discussion seem to have belonged to Eythrope House, but not the house that stands today or indeed the one the villager was protecting in the 1930s. This was constructed in 1875 and is currently a private home in the ownership of the Rothschild family. Of the older Eythrope House, the one with 'the cellars', there is no longer any trace. It stood in a different location but was completely demolished in 1811 and more importantly, for our purposes, it was indeed once owned by a certain Lord Stanhope.

William Stanhope (1702-1772) served as a Whig politician for 35 years, and led an unremarkable life, though he was said to be 'disagreeable', was often absent from Parliament and once raised gossip when he inexplicably demolished the chapel at Eythrope House and then filled its gardens with curious follies. To those with imagination, some of these deeds may seem suspicious, but there is no proof that he was especially feared or disliked in the district.

Various theories have been put forward since Horace Harman first wrote about the Eythrope mystery. Namely, that the diminutive figures were themselves a product of witchcraft or alchemy, homunculi perhaps, lifeless effigies roused to animation by the unknown arts, or maybe elemental beings summoned from another plane of existence. The notion of a cellar-turned-subterranean laboratory seems vaguely reflective of these ideas. It's also been suggested, perhaps inevitably in modern times, that they were aliens, somehow marooned here on Earth, and forced to live under the protection of one of the local landlords.

Unfortunately, as none of the creatures sticks around long enough to ask, we are unlikely ever to know.

SUMMER HOLIDAY
John Llewellyn Probert

The greenhouse was in darkness.

It should have been silent, too, on this warm summer night, but at that moment a drunk fat man was scratching at the door and tapping at the glass. Eventually he worked out how to depress the handle and staggered in, making as much noise as an inebriated obese individual in his late fifties was capable of, bumping into a tomato plant and knocking over a flowerpot before treading in the spilled earth.

'Hello! Are you here?' The words were a lot more slurred than that but for the purpose of this account they have been rendered intelligible.

No reply.

'Hello!'

He staggered forward, fumbling in the pocket of a fraying tweed waistcoat that had seen better times and far less pressure exerted on its buttons. The lighter he produced was cheap and perfunctory, just like him, and the flame it produced was almost as dim and pathetic as his attempts to negotiate the aisles of exotic plants, lovingly cared for but now at risk of destruction from his advances.

'Is that you?'

His attention had finally been caught by a movement at the other end of the building. A quite severe movement, necessary because previous attempts had done little to distract him from his own bumbling. Now that he was looking in the right direction, a dull red glow appeared to help guide him to his destination.

'Ah! There you are, you little minx! Now you hang on ...'

The 'little minx' in question had to hang on for quite a

while, so inadequate were the older man's attempts to crash his way to where the light was.

But eventually, he got there.

'Now … where are you?'

He swung the lighter left and right, the outlines of the plants that surrounded him creating macabre shadows against the glass. The dull glow from the lamp that had guided him this far suggested a towering something close by. He had yet to notice it. He looked as if he was starting to get out of breath, what with the door opening and then holding up the lighter and the small amount of walking he had needed to do. He forgot all about that when the floodlights came on, though.

'Good God! What's that?'

This in response to his discovery that right beside him was an object of either utter monstrosity or utter beauty, depending on one's artistic outlook. From his expression, he was an individual who tended to the former.

It stood in the corner of the greenhouse, fifteen feet high and as wide as three of the normal-sized coffins the gentleman standing before it would likely be a very snug fit for. Despite his obvious fear, he took a step forward and touched one of the leaves, jerking his fingers back when they encountered the unexpected texture. Then his expression changed from fear to one of amusement. He raised a bunched fist and delivered a sharp rap upon one of the broadest leaves, close to the base.

His efforts were rewarded with a dull clang.

'Well fancy that!' He touched it again, more confidently now. 'Who would put a thing like this here?'

His curiosity aroused, his attention was drawn to the plaque that had been placed close to the ground before it. It, too, had been fashioned in the same copper alloy as the artwork itself.

'*Dionaea muscipula gigantis*,' he read. It's doubtful he appreciated the significance of this but essentially it translated as 'Very Big Venus Fly Trap'.

It was while he was bending over to examine the artwork's label that I took the opportunity to come running up behind him. It took surprisingly little effort to cause him to topple forward and into the waiting jaws of the artwork's largest spiked leaf trap, the one that had been positioned dead centre and at the bottom of the work, its jaws open in mimicry of some bizarre reptilian plant hybrid.

The jaws were hinged.

I had been hoping they would snap shut with a satisfying *clang* but the bulky form of my victim meant that they closed as tightly as possible with more of a *thunk*. The force of the sprung steel hinges was still sufficient to make the specially sharpened outer 'hairs' (they are officially referred to as 'cilia') pierce his body in numerous places, leading to a sufficient quantity of blood being lost and a satisfying death groan from the man trapped between the blades.

Thus died my Uncle Barry, by a method I had been planning for some considerable time.

You can't come up with a fifteen foot bronze Venus fly trap death machine in a weekend, you know. In fact I hadn't come up with it at all. I had borrowed it from the art department of the university I was currently attending, having planted the idea in the mind of one of the department's students who had then spent the better part of six months creating it. I have to say she had done a very fine job indeed, and the finished piece had only needed a few adjustments by myself before it was fit for purpose, something the victim now clenched between its steel sprung jaws had never been. The most difficult part, actually, had been convincing the country hotel at which I, my Uncle Barry, and the rest of my family were currently spending the weekend, that it needed to purchase such a work of art. But it was achieved, eventually.

I allowed myself one more moment to appreciate my handiwork before extinguishing the lights and leaving Uncle Barry among the vegetables to be discovered the following morning. I had no doubt he would feel at home there. I would say I wished I could have spent more time with him, but that would be a lie. Besides, the night was young and there were a considerable number of other members of my family I needed to take care of.

The idea for a weekend family get together had been mine, although I had been careful to ensure it was actually suggested, and organised, and chased up with an inordinate amount of cajoling, by someone else, namely my Aunt Agatha who, being an unhappy spinster with too much time on her hands, revelled in the opportunity to coordinate the lives of others as her own possessed so little with which to occupy her. I had been the one to suggest (and indeed insist on) the location, however, because it was vital to my plan. Unknown to the rest of my family, Oakley Court, nestling by the River Thames in the county of Berkshire, and recently opened as a hotel, had throughout the 1960s and 1970s been used as a location for some of the most memorable horror films to be made in Britain. After much deliberation concerning the practicalities of such a venture I had decided that it would be the ideal venue in which to murder the remaining living members of my family, thus ensuring that the not inconsiderable fortune that had been amassed over the years went to what I felt was a most deserving cause. My only weakness, as Ernest Thesiger's Dr Pretorius would have termed it in James Whale's classic *The Bride of Frankenstein*, is that I harbour something of an obsession for British horror films. I had therefore decided that if the members of my family were to meet their ends, those ends should be in the style of such films, and specifically those which had a connection to the hotel in which I had arranged we all stay for the weekend.

There had then followed an inordinate, exhausting but ultimately exhilarating amount of planning. Aunt Agatha's arranging for everyone to turn up to the location, plus the mode of despatch of my Uncle Barry have already been dealt with. Of course I haven't mentioned Uncle Barry's film, which is *The Mutations*, a 1973 production starring Donald Pleasence as a mad scientist creating human plant hybrids. He also has a huge Venus flytrap-type thing in his laboratory that he feeds live rabbits to. The one that gobbled up Uncle Barry looked far better.

But back to the murders. Uncle Barry had been lured outside by a scribbled note, allegedly written by one of the young waitresses he had been groping all evening but of course actually penned by yours truly. I suspect if the inappropriately fondled parties in question knew of his fate I would have been greeted by a round of applause upon my return to the hotel. Sadly sometimes the cost of success is the sacrifice of the adoration of one's public. No matter. The evening was still young (just a little after ten) and I still had a lot of work to do.

If you ever plan to murder a group of people might I suggest the above method of having them gathered together in one place by someone who is none the wiser as to your intentions?

As long as you carry out your plan during the hours of darkness, most of your intended victims will have had sufficient to drink that your task will be considerably easier. Admittedly in the case of Uncle Barry one could have probably stuck his head in a bucket of manure over brunch and he would have smothered to death none the wiser. But such a method lacked finesse and besides, there is no such death in a film made at Oakley Court. My only concern had been the other paying guests, those who were not part of my scheme. However, a local health scare (something to do with a polluted water supply – I can't be more specific because that was all I had told a local newspaper reporter over the telephone a few days previously) had ensured there were far fewer residents than there would have been otherwise.

So let us return to the scene of the (proposed) crimes, and older brother Nigel, twenty-five and in terrible debt. It had started while he was a Classics student at Oxford, spending all his money on champagne and silk ties. He had a fetish for draping them around the necks of his many girlfriends while they were naked, ensuring their breasts were covered with the tapering ends of the high class designer material before taking

Polaroid photographs of them. Whether it was the ties, the girls, or an abhorrence of nipples that drove him to this we shall now never know, but Nigel was of such a psychological disposition that I was not the only member of my family to harbour concern that his little hobby might one day lead to him tying one of those ties very tightly, with the intention of cutting off the air supply of his model. Who knows? Perhaps I saved the world from the attentions of the 'Surrey Strangler' after I had crept up to his bedroom that night. If he had pursued such a career I would have expected him to live somewhere that would allow him an alliterative title. Anything else would have shown a worrying lack of creativity and dedication to the profession of serial killer.

I had a pass key, naturally. He was asleep, of course. His little white hands were clutching a silk tie in one hand (Fifth Battalion Royal Artillery, I think – all the ties he owned had to have some sort of significance, which is partly why he was in so much debt) and a girl's nightdress in the other. Did that mean he had a companion? A quick check of the bathroom revealed not. A quick further check of the nightdress held tightly in my comatose brother's paw revealed it was of a size to suit a rather large lady or, far more likely, a Nigel-sized man.

Curiouser and curiouser. I took the spray cans of silver paint from where I had left them in the bottom of his wardrobe that afternoon. I ensured he was fully sedated (easy), removed his clothing (also easy but far more distasteful), and then ensured that every inch of my brother's exposed skin was coated in a good thickness of the paint. Do I need to mention I had on a surgical mask and apron to avoid contaminating myself? I thought not. To pass the time as I worked, I reminded myself of the plot of Daniel Haller's 1965 Lovecraft adaptation *Die, Monster, Die*, based on the author's novella, *The Colour Out of Space*. Boris Karloff lives in a gloomy gothic mansion (guess where). A meteorite lands and the radiation mutates everything, including Karloff who ends up turning silver and going on the rampage. There's a marvellous scene in a greenhouse with all the mutated creatures but we'd already done greenhouses so I thought this method of despatch equally appropriate to my design.

I left Nigel to slowly succumb to the toxic effects of what he had been coated with, removed the mask and balled up the apron (both small enough to fit in my pocket) and made my way down the corridor to Aunt Agatha, dear Aunt Agatha, whose only crime was to be a potential inheritor of at least part of my proposed fortune. Oh, and knowing it was I who originally came up with the idea of this little weekend getaway.

Oh yes, unfortunately Aunt Agatha had to go.

Some years before, the Spanish director José Larraz had filmed his extremely low budget *Vampyres* at Oakley Court. While there was no specific death scene that one could identify with that film, Aunt Agatha certainly liked her wine (there is a prolonged segment featuring wine tasting in the movie) and she was thin enough that her veins would be easily accessible for a neat and hopefully fuss-free exsanguination. There was only one problem when I let myself into her bedroom.

She wasn't there.

The room was in darkness but with the light of my pen torch I could see that the bed was empty. My thoughts raced. Could she still be downstairs? If so it was best if I hid here and waited. There was enough room beneath the four poster for me to conceal myself. I popped the apron and mask back on, and took my tourniquet, needles, tubing and the first glass jar I intended to fill with her blood from above the bed.

I was just about to crawl beneath it when the bathroom door opened.

What on earth had she been doing there in the dark? Was she one of those individuals so embarrassed by their own bodily functions that they can only comfortably empty their bowels with the lights turned off? I never had the chance to ask her because right at that moment she turned the bedroom light on and stood there in all her face-creamed and hair-curlered bizarreness.

She immediately saw me standing next to the bed wearing a surgical mask, surgical apron stained silver, and holding some enormous needles.

I think we both got a bit of a shock.

It took her longer to react, however. By the time she had opened her mouth and was taking a deep breath I was over there with the chloroform I had placed in another pocket for just such an emergency. Her cry came out as little more than a muffled groan as she fell into my arms. I carried her to the bed and reached up for the rest of my containers before inserting four of the large bore intravenous cannulae, one into each arm, one into each leg. It took a bit of encouragement to produce a siphon effect but soon blood was splashing into the four bottles with enthusiastic aplomb.

I switched the lights off before I left.

I paused to take a breath on the stairs. By now the entire endeavour was beginning to take it out of me, and the last encounter had proved somewhat distressing. Whether it was her face-pack that had caused her to resemble one of the living dead from John Gilling's *Plague of the Zombies* (also filmed at Oakley Court, so in her own special way Aunt Agatha had actually been joining in) or the fact that I had quite liked her and hadn't expected to find her awake I couldn't be sure. Nor did I have the time to deliberate it as I checked my watch. If I was to complete my task and be out of here in good time I had to stick to my pre-arranged timetable.

My father was next.

I have no intention of embarking on a lengthy diatribe regarding how little time I had for him. Suffice to say he was a man wholly without ambition, content to live off the money he had inherited from his own father and with no aim in life other than to avoid anything that might impair such a carefree, if interminably dull, existence. Sadly such an inconvenience had raised its head in the form of my mother's terminal disease, prompting a quick divorce before palliative care measures were instigated, followed by a funeral which he did not attend.

He was waiting for me, paralysed, in the master bedroom, which on other, happier (one hopes) occasions was known as the bridal suite, although after tonight the room would likely carry such a stigma that there might be considerable difficulty getting anyone to spend the night in it ever again.

I had instilled a paralysing agent into the passion fruit *creme brûlée* he had enjoyed for dessert. It provided loss of voluntary movement without increasing muscle tone or diminishing sensation. Consequently he was wide awake and alert as I strapped his wrists and ankles to the bedposts. I explained everything I was going to do to him as I went.

In the Richard Gordon-produced 1966 film *The Projected Man*, Bryant Haliday plays a scientist experimenting with matter transmission. When he tests his new device on himself something goes terribly wrong and, while he does end up beamed to a location outside his laboratory, half of his body is turned inside out in the process.

The whole procedure took me seventy-seven minutes, precisely the running time of the commonly available cut of the film. Of course the room was in quite a mess by the time I had finished, and the drugs I had used were starting to wear off. I wish I could have allowed him to live, if only as a quite remarkable (and dare I say artistic) example of what surgical techniques can achieve, but if I was to enjoy my newfound fortune such a dream was impossible. By the time I left the room my father was no more.

I made my way down to the main entrance to see the night porter – the only member of staff here at this time – still asleep from the nice big cup of coffee laced with a heavy dose of a phenothiazine compound that I had given him. I was preparing to unlock the main doors when the handle was depressed from the other side.

Then the doors rattled.

Then came a loud knock.

I froze. It was well after midnight. Who on earth could that be?

There was a rumble of thunder as I rapidly considered my options. The bodies were meant to be discovered in the morning, when I would be far away from this place. My alibi for the evening was already established but was dependent upon me getting away now.

Another loud knock.

Damn.

The storm was breaking as I opened the door to behold a young woman not much older than myself, outfitted in the kind of knee high boots, orange short skirt and garish blouse that should have long gone out of style but which was apparently the latest Paris fashion. I only knew this because I also happened to know who she was.

My father's girlfriend, Vanessa.

'You're wet,' was all I could think of to say.

'Yes,' she replied. 'It's raining.'

Was it fate that she was quoting from yet another film made using this very location? I like to think not. Sadly my tiring brain was unable to rapidly come up with a suitable mode of despatch that would suit it. In fact my tiring brain had just about had enough for the night, so much so that before I had time to react she had pushed past me.

I closed the door and locked it. Vanessa failed to notice. She was too busy setting down her hideous matching orange leather suitcases as she stared at the night porter. She only once again registered my presence when my polite cough reminded her I was there.

'Why is he asleep?'

'It's very late.' I pointed at the clock.

'That's no bloody excuse.' She went to shake him but I gently prevented her. 'Get off me! What the fuck do you think you're doing?'

'I didn't know you were coming, Vanessa.' She wouldn't be leaving, either, not now that she had seen me. But the exact method of her not leaving was yet to be determined.

'I wasn't supposed to be, but your bloody father begged me at the last minute. "Oh my coochie-lumpkins you should see this great big bed and it would look so much better with you in it wearing those new outfits I bought you. Pwease, pwease, pwease come".' She was actually quite good at impersonating my father at his whiniest. I now realised I should have cut the telephone lines much earlier in the evening but I refused to be too hard on myself about it, especially as I had this new problem to deal with. 'Oh never mind. I'll just go straight up. When sleeping beauty's awake can you tell him to bring the bags?'

She was already halfway up the stairs when I realised my father must have told her which room he was in, the one whose door I had deliberately left unlocked so he could be discovered in the morning. I followed her at a speed I hoped was just slow enough that she wouldn't think I was chasing her, deliberating as I went. My father's bedroom was at the front of the building. It looked out directly over the car park. I could hear him now, complaining about the works vehicles there blocking his view.

The works vehicles …

Perhaps the night could be saved after all.

My thoughts were disturbed by what sounded like a very small hen attempting to lay an especially gargantuan egg.

She'd found him, then.

I was in the room by the time Vanessa was drawing her next breath. It just isn't in my nature to strike a woman, so instead I grabbed part of my father (it was difficult to tell exactly what) and placed it over her mouth while I manhandled her in the right direction. It is remarkably difficult to open a Victorian sash window with one hand while holding the wrists of a fit and healthy (and extremely objectionable) young woman behind her with the other, but somehow I managed it. I could not have wished for a noisier storm as I pushed my father's exceedingly irritating girlfriend out of the window. I am convinced I heard a pleasing crash as she landed on one of the diggers below.

Back down the stairs I went. I unlocked the front door and walked out into the rain.

The weather was really quite dreadful.

Vanessa, however, looked worse.

She must have landed head first on the seat of a bulldozer, the force of her fall driving her face down onto the floor and snapping her cervical spine. All one could see from a distance were two legs sticking up in the air. I swiftly relieved her of this inelegant position, dragging her body over to the hole that had recently been dug. Wet gravel and dirt are not the most manageable of substances and it took me some time and effort to fill the hole in, hoping that whatever repairs that had been intended on the now no longer-exposed gas main had been carried out, and that some workman tomorrow morning would scratch his head but remain essentially grateful that he had one less job to do.

And the film?

Witchcraft, a Robert Lippert production from 1964, in which Yvette Rees memorably plays a witch brought back from the dead when building works disturb the ground in which she was buried. Admittedly I was taking considerable liberties (and running the film backwards by burying a threatening witch rather than unearthing one), but under the circumstances I think I can be forgiven.

I still managed to get away in plenty of time.

I will never forget the solicitor informing me that my family's fortune was now mine and mine alone. I will never forget him reading out that document, his precisely clipped words stating that all funds, investments and properties pertaining to the name of Valentine now fell to the family's only surviving son, Edward. Perhaps most of all I will never forget how much hard work it had been to achieve my goal, and in that solicitor's office I vowed to myself that I would never go to such lengths again.

Unless, of course, I had a very good reason.

In the meantime, I still had four weeks of holiday to enjoy before I returned to medical school, and after the memory of that rain-drenched night I hope the reader of this account will forgive me for the film tune I found myself whistling once I was out of earshot of any and all interested legal parties. It was not a horror film and it was not made at Oakley Court, but then I felt I had rather exhausted that avenue. It was, nevertheless, from a famous British film of the 1960s and under the circumstances most apt

Oh yes indeed – I was going where the sun shines brightly …

THE COLDEST CHRISTMAS OF ALL

An old phrase popular with landlords of supposedly haunted pubs goes as follows: 'It's not the dead you need to fear in this game, it's the living.'

It isn't difficult to understand, especially as most ghosts are works of fiction, and even those that may actually be real tend to appear so rarely – almost never when there are cameras or other recording devices around – that they constitute a negligible problem, especially in comparison to thugs, drunkards, drug dealers and the sort of general-purpose hooligans who wreck pubs and break up bars for the sheer fun of it.

Surely the best illustration of this can be found in the Hertfordshire village of Thundridge, where a supposedly spectacular haunting in former ages has allegedly led to all manner of trouble in the present day from visiting bands of ghost-hunters, sensation seekers and Halloween Night rowdies.

The origins of the difficulty lie with the deconsecrated ruins of a medieval-era church, All Hallows and Little St Mary, which stands just outside the village on the eerily named Cold Christmas Lane. As the original church was built in 1086, it ought to be a place of keen archaeological interest in modern times, but, in truth, nothing of the original structure remains. The graffiti covered tower and graveyard are 15th century in origin at the earliest, and in a poor condition, and even when older, more venerable sections of it were still standing, local folk supposedly avoided the place, which rejection led to its demolition in 1853.

All kinds of stories apparently lie at the root of this.

To start with, the village of Thundridge dates back to the pre-Norman era, when it was known as Thor's Ridge, and one theory holds that this may indicate a prevalence of pre-Christian influence in the district at the time of the church's construction. This might explain why the original building was aligned north to south rather than east to west, which in the eyes of some made it an evil place rather than a holy one, and a very good reason not to attend Masses there. Even if that didn't worry people on its own, the church was either built or protected (or both) by a Norman baron, Hugh de Grentmesnil, and this wasn't long after his countrymen had committed a whole range of atrocities across the conquered land, which included ravaging the southern shires during the autumn of 1066, massacring a huge crowd in London that Christmas Day, Harrying the North in 1070 (still regarded as the worst assault on the English people by their own rulers in the nation's history!), imposing the ultra-harsh Forest Laws, which condemned the rural population to starve, and generally torturing and killing anyone who dared even to voice dissent. It's perhaps no surprise that local people regarded Hugh de Grentmesnil's church as a totem of disgusting Norman hypocrisy.

Even the cheerier legend that in the 12th century, a local knight, Piers Shonks (also a Norman), fought and slew a dragon that was terrorising the district, and for his reward, was buried in an alcove inside the church, which supposedly guaranteed his ascent to Heaven, did little to lighten the district's solemn reputation.

The final confirmation that this was an unlucky place came later in the Middle Ages on an unspecified date, when a particularly savage winter led to the deaths over the Christmas period of most of the village children. They were said to have been buried together in an unmarked mass-grave, the road leading to which was rechristened Cold Christmas Lane, a route that can still be followed today.

By all accounts, the haunting this created was intense, the weeping and wailing of innumerable childlike voices said to be heard nightly in the graveyard and inside the church itself, and even today, in and around the isolated ruins. The problem was apparently exacerbated in the 1960s, when so-called witch cults and Satanists began to hold ceremonies there, the lurid activities of which allegedly summoned an aggressive, bestial spirit that still growls in the darkness of the church tower.

So go the various legends, though now we come to the part about the visiting bands of hooligans (of whom the hippy Satanists might well have been the forebears). Local folk are, to be blunt, pig-sick of *the sensationalism surrounding Cold Christmas Lane, arguing that the story of the dead children is most likely myth and that even if it isn't, it's hardly worth the litter and (aforementioned) vandalism at the site, or the endless gangs of drunken, shouting thrill-seekers who trample all over it on the eve of every occult festival in the calendar.*

The place should be quiet and peaceful, they argue, the ideal venue for a genteel picnic on a balmy summer afternoon. And it probably would be, if only it wasn't for that distant but cursed crying of unseen children.

CHESHAM
Helen Grant

I shouldn't be exploring the High Street because I have things to do, but it's difficult to resist the temptation, and it's somewhere between the curry house and the post office that I suddenly remember her. I think we must have seen her around about this spot, all those years ago: a woman of perhaps seventy-five or eighty, dressed in black, pushing a big Silver Cross pram. I suppose I was only about six at the time, and I was a little bit afraid of her. She had a lot of makeup on, but it was carelessly applied, the lipstick not quite following the lines of her lips, the rouge forming two scarlet spots on papery cheeks that were otherwise rather white. Her clothes were dowdy and distinctly formal. That was the way old people dressed back then. I think she may even have had gloves on. The pram was carefully decked out with frilly covers and lace edging and it was absolutely empty.

I looked into the pram and I was puzzled. We had not gone very much further down the street before I looked up at my mother and said, 'Mum, why was that lady pushing a pram with no baby in it?'

My mother glanced back, swiftly and furtively, to make sure that the old lady was out of earshot. She had her own hands on the pushchair with my brother in it, the handles laden with shopping bags.

She said, 'Shhh. I think she's a bit ... you know, in the head.'

'But why?'

I suppose my mother saw there was going to be no end to the questions if she didn't answer them. She said, 'I expect she had a baby of her own, and lost it.'

189

'Lost it?'

'It died.'

'Oh.'

I turned to look after the old woman, who was now some distance away from us. It was a new idea, to think that babies could die. Normally it was only old people who did that. I wanted to ask more questions, but at that point we reached some shop or other, a fishmonger's or a grocer's, and my mother went inside. I was left outside to guard my brother. Yes, I was only six or so, but those were different times.

The High Street has changed. It wasn't pedestrianised back then. There were other shops, notably an old-fashioned toy shop I always wanted to go into but wasn't often allowed to. My parents didn't have a lot of spare cash, but more importantly my mother didn't have a car; it was a long walk into the town from where we lived, especially with kids in tow, so she wasn't disposed to linger. The toy shop is not there anymore.

I ought to get on; the sooner I get everything done, the sooner I can leave. So I go into a shop and buy myself lunch: a wrap, a chocolate bar and a soft drink. I eat them on a bench near the war memorial, and then I set off back to the house.

It's a big Edwardian semi at the very top of the hill, with a small front garden and a very long back one. It was a wonderful house to live in when we were growing up. It wasn't so good for two, and then one old person living alone. Both gardens are jungles now, and the house feels shabby and ill-maintained. Worse, it is full of *stuff*. I open cupboards and they are crammed with old jigsaws, telephone directories, dried-up art supplies. It would take a million years to sort it all out properly. Instead, I am going to sort through as much of it as I can, and salvage anything of real or sentimental value. Then the house clearers will have to take the rest.

My brother and sister won't want very much of it. They're both affluent; they have good jobs. They don't need chipped china or wooden furniture with scuffed legs. If they want anything, it's probably for the house to be cleared and transformed into cash. It's in everyone's interests to get this job done. I just wish it wasn't me, on my own, listening to the flies buzzing at the windows on this hot sticky afternoon, my ears ringing with the silence in the house.

I suppose I deserve it. I didn't come back often, or for long. It was as though whenever I got out of Chesham, I somehow *forgot* it. I was the wayward child, too; I never got on well with my parents. There is a great deal that is unsaid in the fact that I am here on my own, tackling this grisly job, which is depressing and boring in turns. My siblings did their bit when my mother was still alive. Now I have to do mine. I sigh, brushing dust from my hands.

In one of the bedrooms, where a single bed sags in the middle, I open a cupboard and a torrent of photographs slide out, spilling all over the grimy carpet. I look at them, faded and discoloured and *old*, and for a moment I am tempted to bin the whole lot, or else walk out of the room and pretend I didn't see them. But I suppose this is precisely the sort of thing I should be looking at. I should send some of them to my brother and sister as keepsakes. So I get down on my hands and knees and start looking through them in a desultory way. There's one of my brother as a baby, in which the future corporate lawyer is gnawing on a teething ring shaped like a duck, and one of my sister looking deceptively adorable in a princess outfit. Here are my parents, too – my mother looking weirdly young in a hideously patterned '80s outfit and big hair, and my father up a ladder, determinedly slapping paint on. Odd moments of family life.

I pick out one with my mother and a baby. There are various other people in the picture too – my father (his torso and bits of his legs, anyway), me, my sister, my brother. I backtrack. Me, my sister, my brother. So who is the baby? My mother is cradling it very carefully, stroking its little head with a forefinger. She looks loving. I chew my lip, thinking. I don't have any cousins; both my parents were only children. Perhaps it was a friend's baby. I slide the photograph back into the heap. I suppose it's one of those mysteries that will never be solved, like the sepia snaps of older relatives with no names attached.

Much later, I go for a walk to clear my head and find something for dinner. I remember that there used to be a little grocery store right on the very edge of town – a small, scruffy place, given more to longlife ready meals than fresh produce. So I walk out that way, enjoying the chance to stretch my legs. The route is very familiar, but somehow everything seems smaller than before, the distances shorter. I remember coming along here in the '80s, when the leaves on the bushes were thick with the residue of leaded petrol, and the not infrequent dogs' messes were chalky white from some constituent of dog food that has since been banned.

The shop has closed down. I'll have to go back down the hill, into the town centre. On the way back from the shop-that-is-no-more, I pass a large house set slightly back from the road in a tangle of garden. I remember that house from when I was a child. It was always shut up, and we never saw anyone go in or out of it. We made up our minds that it was haunted, or inhabited by some eldritch creature. Now, it simply looks derelict. I pause to gaze at it.

It's strange how all these things seemed so important at the time, but have simply vanished from my memory in the years away. We were so frightened of that house that we would never have done any of those things kids normally do, like running up and slapping the front door. We left well alone. I stare for a bit, and then I keep walking. It's a funny thing, but a lot of the stuff I can recall from my childhood seems to be things like that. There was a little copse, probably built over by now, called the Grove, where nobody liked to play because something or other was supposed to happen to you if you went in there alone. And the old air raid shelters in the park, long gone now I should think, there was some story about those too. Maybe it's my dismal state of mind, but I find myself dwelling on those stories. The children who wandered in. The infants who vanished. As though the town is honeycombed with something we don't want to think about too closely, with doorways leading somewhere we don't want to go …

I shake my head. I should have bought something for dinner earlier. It's very tiresome walking down the hill again, knowing I'll have to walk back up later. In the end, I decide to get fish and chips, which you can buy without going the whole way into the centre. It's a warm evening, so I sit on a wall to eat them. They're good – the fish tastes fresh and the chips are very hot. For a while I give myself over to the pleasure of eating them. Something is bothering me, though. I can't think what it is. Just something at the back of my mind, a little out of reach. I pat my pockets: phone, wallet, keys. Everything is there. I scrunch up the fish and chip paper and put it carefully in the bin. Then I set off – not for *home*, it hasn't been that for ages, but for the house.

Tonight I was going to sleep in one of the bedrooms, but none of them looks remotely appealing. There's hot water, although it takes an eternity to run, so I start a bath and while it's running I go hunting through all the cabinets and the sideboard in the dining room. My mother wasn't a great drinker, but my Dad liked a good malt, and sure enough, there's half a bottle, hidden behind a bottle of sherry and something else that looks like Blue Curaçao but could equally be dishwasher rinse aid. There are tumblers too, though they are very dusty, so I carry one through to the kitchen and rinse it. I pour myself a generous measure, and take it up to enjoy in the bath. I have to climb over a few things in the hallway. Then I go up the stairs, carefully holding my whisky, and the treads creak under my feet, a sad cacophony of age and disrepair. I've found a towel, but it feels kind of crispy, as though it was line dried rather than tumbled. The soap is like a stone. The hot water is nice, though, even if it's rather peculiar sitting in an avocado-coloured bath installed in around 1980.

After the bath, I settle myself on the sofa. I still have that strange feeling that there's something I've forgotten, but perhaps it's just the déjà vu that comes from returning somewhere you used to know very well. I keep meaning to get up and clean my teeth, but the whisky has burned a pleasurable trail down my throat and after a while I just nod off.

Perhaps it was seeing that derelict house again, or perhaps it was simply the whisky before I went to sleep, but I doze fitfully. My mind is populated with scraps of memory intertwined with what can only be nightmares. From those taboo spaces, the abandoned mansion, the lonely copse, the mouldering shelters, things not distinctly seen come creeping. Something shifts stealthily within the empty house. A child wanders into the copse and does not come out again. A Silver Cross pram stands in the shade under a tree in the park – the mother returns with an ice cream, gazes inside, and screams and screams. In all these scenes, people drift by, not reacting, not noticing. Not *seeing*.

I wake up feeling grim and unrefreshed, and find that it's morning. Time to get started again if I ever want to get away from here, which I do, very badly. So once I've had breakfast, which is mainly black coffee, I start making piles of things: books, ornaments, photographs. Those are the things I want to save. The things I don't want to save, or can't, outweigh them a thousand times. They still have to be gone through, though: I don't want to miss some critical item.

Halfway through the morning, I slide open the bottom drawer of a bureau and find a lot of school books, and it's down the rabbit-hole again. Some of them have names inexpertly inked on the front: Jon, Sally, Kay. Others don't, and I amuse myself trying to think who they belonged to. They contain ill-spelled stories, and pictures of completely unidentifiable animals. I turn the pages onto their sides and squint at the drawings. Ducks, horses, cats?

Fragments of memory come back from my school days: netball in the playground, painting with bright poster paints, singing hymns in the school hall, which smelled of plimsolls and chalk. Once, a man from the zoo came to give us a talk, bringing a dwarf crocodile with him. I can't believe you'd be allowed to do that now. I remember my sister performing a turn in the Christmas show on that same stage. She was remarkably self-possessed for a girl of nine; she did all the right movements and didn't flinch when the audience laughed. And I remember – I remember the headmistress giving us a very serious talk about a boy in the school whose sister wouldn't be coming back. I suppose she'd had an accident or an illness, leukaemia or something. At any rate, she impressed it on us very forcefully that we should not mention this to him when he reappeared. I don't think we did, either, although children can be little brutes. There it is again, a feeling like a twang on some hidden nerve. The child who didn't come back to school … I close the exercise book I am holding.

These books, I think. *I should throw them all out. Nobody is going to want to look at them again.*

I decide to go and tackle the rest of the photographs. Those are the things we might want to keep – some of them, at any rate. So I make myself another cup of black coffee, and upstairs I go.

The photographs are still spread out all over the floor. I sit down on the worn carpet, and recommence going through them. I am brisk now, setting the ones we want to one side, and pushing the rest into another heap. Nobody wants blurry shots of unrecognisable people on a beach, or faded snaps of drab-looking places. I find one of Jon in his graduation gown, clutching a diploma. He has an absolutely execrable haircut, and a cluster of spots at the corner of his mouth, and if it were me I'd probably burn that photograph, but I suppose he might like it, so I put it aside. There's one of Sally and me, Sally wearing a fairy outfit and me wearing a suit of armour. The armour is plastic, and not terrifically convincing. The sword I am flourishing, gravely, has a dent in the middle.

The next photo I examine is a family group. Mum is in the middle, flanked by my father and Sally on one side, myself and Jon on the other. She is massively pregnant.

I wonder which of us that was, I think. Then I look at the picture again. Mum, Dad, me, Jon, Sally. That's all of us.

I stare at the photo, wondering if I've got it wrong, if she isn't pregnant at all. But she very clearly is. The eighth or even the ninth month, I would say. There's no mistaking that enormously taut round belly, clearly defined in pink floral cotton. She has her hands folded over it, a classic protective gesture.

I think about the photo I found yesterday, of Mum holding a tiny baby. For a moment, I think I am going crazy. There are three of us children. Me (Kay), Jon and Sally. There is no fourth child. There *was* no fourth child. I don't think it's possible that my mother had a fourth one, and we somehow didn't *notice.* Anyway, where is it? Did it *die*? I think I'd remember something like that. I was old enough by then. And my mother wasn't the sort of person to cover up something like that. She'd have talked about it, cemented it into our family history.

I decide to put that photograph in the *keep* pile. I can't ask my parents about it anymore, but when I've finished here I'm going to ask Jon and Sally if they can remember anything. My eyes keep being drawn back to it. It's weird, and somehow unsettling. I know that something has escaped me here, but I can't think what. I pick the photo up again, and study it. The extra pregnancy. The missing baby. I think about the other children, too. The girl who never came back to school. The old woman with the empty pram. The lonely places, waiting, gaping open like mouths.

I rub my face, screwing up my eyes. It isn't possible, surely, that children could vanish … *Or be taken,* says a voice at the back of my mind. That an entire town would just kind of *gloss over* what was happening – not see it. That we would all live alongside it, accommodating it somehow, giving up a few here and there so that the rest of us could live in peace. I do not want to think about the derelict house, or the Grove, because those are too close by. But I think about the old air raid shelters in the park. I think about something down there in the dark, under the damp soil. Something as pale as a grub, and horribly thin. And hungry.

No, I say to myself. *You have been alone for too long; your imagination is running riot. Imagination, not memory. People would never. Your mother would never. You would never…*

It takes me until late morning to finish with the photographs, and until mid-afternoon to finish picking out anything else I think we ought to hang onto. I make a pile in the middle of the sitting-room carpet, carrying things around the stuff in the hall so that I can deposit them in there. There's too much for a single person to carry, which I expected, so I'll have to come back with a hire car. As well as the photographs, there are some books, and pieces of jewellery, and a single Famille Rose punch bowl; I can't think how *that* survived two decades of children running about the house.

So, that's the job finished. Outside, it's a glorious afternoon; in the sunshine, even the overgrown garden looks pretty, with its long grass and rambling roses. I collect up my few things, and head into the hallway. I have the keys in my hand. Sunshine is streaming through the dusty stained glass windows set into the door. My hand on the door, I look at what is standing in the hallway.

I *really* look at it, in a way I somehow haven't managed to before now. It's a pushchair. Not an old one, a relic of the 1980s; a brand spanking new one. It's all done out in pink and grey, the hood up to shield its tiny occupant from the sun. There is a little board book on a clip attached to the side. Underneath it, there is a basket, which is full of baby things: spare nappies, nappy sacks, wipes, a bottle, a tin of formula.

I have had to climb over this pushchair every time I've wanted to go upstairs; I've had to walk round it to go in and out of the sitting room. But somehow – somehow I haven't really seen it. I do now, though. I let go of the door and take a few steps towards it, so I can peer in. It's empty, of course.

My head is throbbing. It's not a headache; it's memories, and not-memories, fighting for dominance. I look at the pushchair, and for a moment I seem to look *past* it; I think I should be turning my back and going. Then I look again, and it's still there.

I remember being on the train from London. I was talking, and singing. The sun was coming in through the window, and I was busying myself with something. I was smiling. The train passed Rickmansworth and Chorleywood. At Chalfont and Latimer you have to change; you have to get off the train that's going through to Amersham, and go through the underpass to get the Chesham train. There are stairs on both sides. That's quite difficult if …

I frown. I recall the Chesham train, waiting at the platform. I feel as though I wasn't quite alone when I got on that train. And when it got to the terminus – I remember being interested, because I hadn't come back this way for years, and everything looked smaller than it had before, and I was kind of preoccupied … And there was a barrier, I remember that, and the man standing there, in a London Transport uniform. When he saw me coming, he pressed a button so that the biggest gate would open, the one for people with big luggage and things like that. He gave me a big smile. He had very white teeth, I remember. He looked down into the pushchair and said, 'She's a gorgeous girl. What's her name?'

And I scream, 'Lily!'

THE RAVEN

In 1885 in West Drayton, Buckinghamshire, another picturesque village fated in due course to be consumed by the westward march of Greater London, the local vicar, the Rev Frederick Lee, commenced a scholarly work in which he both investigated the history of the local church and at the same time underlined a series of past supernatural events, which allegedly were manifesting again during his own period of tenure.

Lee explained how, in 1749, the local villagers became concerned that their church was haunted. The events he describes initially sound like archetypal poltergeist activity: bangs and crashes sounding from the church vaults, though they only occurred on Fridays. In antiquity, Friday was held to be the unluckiest day of the week as it was the day of Christ's death. But if all this sounds rather fanciful, the witnesses to these sensational events included the church sexton and several well-regarded heads of the local community. According to Lee, explorations of the vaults were regularly held, and they were always discovered to be empty – until a group of four men peered down through a grating one Friday evening and were startled to see a large raven fluttering around in the spaces under the chancel. When attempts were made to shoo it out, the bird simply disappeared. But from now on, sightings of the creature continued. Several respected persons, including the wife of the parish clerk, reported seeing the raven, a huge, belligerent creature, fluttering about in other parts of the building: the chancel itself, the sacristy, the nave. Even the bell-ringers were driven from the church tower one wintry Friday night when the aggressive beast attacked them, squawking and clawing at their faces.

On all occasions, the witnesses returned to the church with reinforcements, but then there was never any trace of the bird. One of the last events recorded in 1749 involved an entire gang of local men, who threw sticks and stones at the beast in the main body of the church, appearing to break its wing. It fell to the ground but scuttled away on its talons and hid beneath the pews. The men continued to hunt for it, but several hours later gave up. Yet again, the raven had vanished.

In his treatise on the matter, Frederick Lee expands on several theories at the time, the most prominent being that the raven was the damned soul of an unknown murderer or suicide, who, possibly through the connivance of the local authorities, maybe because his family were well-bred, was buried on sanctified ground rather than in some unmarked grave beyond the church precincts with a stake hammered through his heart.

It seems that Lee's own troubles were not dissimilar to these events, and most likely were the reason behind his investigations. It was in 1869 when two flower-arrangers entered the church and were badly alarmed by the sight of a huge, menacing raven with the most fearsome eyes they'd ever seen perched at the end of one of the pews. From this moment on, it was seen and heard sporadically. Lee himself encountered it in 1883.

The case has never been satisfactorily explained. The fact that the bird was injured in one confrontation suggests there was nothing supernatural about it, and indeed some suggestion was made at the time that maybe it had escaped from local private ownership and was lurking around the church because it knew nowhere else to go, though that would not explain why it only appeared on Fridays and how it always seemed to evade capture, much less how it reappeared in the same place over a century later.

One thing is certain: Frederick Lee was regarded as a serious, sober-minded individual, and a scholar to boot, which one can only assume is the reason his written testimonies were taken so seriously.

LOVE LEAVES LAST
Mick Sims

Unseen. Under cover of darkness. She was the first out of the huge house. Her long flowing nightdress billowed around her, and she feared it had caught in the heavy oak doors as they closed behind. Then she was free, and running barefoot across the damp grass. Running towards the summerhouse, with its open windows, enticing scents, and those precious few moments when she would be hidden away from the spying eyes.

She dared a glance behind her as she ran. The doors of the house opened. Her hand touched her mouth. She had been seen. If not, surely, her absence had been sensed. She stood still, the night sounds familiar around her. The rustling in the woods, the owl taking flight, small animals foraging in the undergrowth.

If it came for her, from the house, she would let it take her. She could hide no more. Not after all this time. She was so tired of shielding the truth.

She hadn't realised she had been holding her breath until it escaped from her chest in a frantic outpouring of relief. It was him, the man she had arranged to meet in the summerhouse. The man she was risking such torments to spend a few precious moments with. The man she could be alone with for a brief time. Her husband.

Her feet danced across the neatly trimmed lawn. The summerhouse was in darkness, but she knew it well enough. She pulled open the thin wooden door and slipped inside. It was a warm evening. Dressed in flimsy lace and satin, she was hot from the race from the house. The moon flooded the interior with a white light that made her momentarily think about death, and perhaps Heaven.

She sat on the couch, and ran a hand over the plump cushions. Then the doorway was filled with a large shadow, and for a second she worried she had been mistaken. Worried it wasn't the man she loved at all. Worried that it was far worse. That what lived in the house had seen them leave. But it was him of course, her husband; they had been careful.

'We won't have long,' he said.

She stood and embraced him, feeling the strength and affection as his arms wrapped around her. They had been married for more than thirty years, and yet they were reduced to sneaking into the vast grounds to display their love. To do what should have been a natural part of their marriage.

She looked over his shoulder at the Manor. It seemed to be breathing in the moonlight.

He sensed her preoccupation. 'You don't think we were seen?'

'Relax, Ian, I'm sure we got out safely.'

He turned and faced the Manor. 'It really is quite beautiful.'

She shuddered. 'I loathe it.'

'Family heritage,' he said. 'A curse maybe, but a legacy all the same.'

She was certain she saw the upper floors moving, as if they swayed.

'Can we just do what we came here for, and get back?'

He watched her as she backed towards the couch. Her face was a mask he couldn't pierce, a code he could never decipher.

'Well, May,' he said. 'Who said romance was dead?'

'The house may be your duty, and this is mine. I'm here aren't I? I want to get back before we're discovered.'

'You make it sound as if the place has eyes.'

'Doesn't it? Perhaps not the house, though I'm not so sure. But what lives in it has eyes, ears ...'

He pulled roughly at her nightdress, and drew it down her shoulders until it pooled at her feet. 'Enough talking.'

'Then make me forget it. Forget it all.'

In the darkness outside, the Manor stood sentinel.

'How the hell do you know a Lord?'

Rob glanced quickly at his wife, before turning his eyes back to the road. Casey had asked the same question, in different versions, at least three times since they had received the invitation for the weekend in the country.

'We were at school together. I told you.'

Casey snorted. It wasn't an attractive sound. 'You went to Eton?'

'It was Harrow, and yes I did, as you well know.'

'Boarding school.' She made it sound like a satanic institution.

'Made me the man I am today … and no jokes, thanks. I've heard them all before.'

She patted his leg. 'I'm happy with the man you are … even if nightly buggery was the price you had to pay.'

He laughed. 'It was only monthly, and I quite enjoyed it.'

'Christ, too much information.' This came from the back seat of the Mercedes.

Rob looked in the rear view mirror at his son. Scott was approaching his mid-twenties, and was working with his father, learning the way the family business operated.

'Aren't you glad we schooled you locally?'

Scott said, 'All I had to endure was the kids from the estate, and the bullying.'

'"Made me the man I am today".' Scott's girlfriend did a good impression of Rob.

Casey laughed. 'Nice one, Selina.'

Rob said, 'I have enough trouble with these two without you joining in. Scott, why did you have to bring her with you?' Then he laughed. In truth he enjoyed it when they used him as the butt of their jokes. It let him know their affection for him. That was what he told himself.

'Sorry, Mr Williams,' Selina said. 'How can you ever forgive my impertinence?'

'I'd give up now, Rob, if I were you,' Casey said. 'She's got your measure.'

Rob turned on the radio, only to flip it off again. 'Bloody Adele.'

He looked out as the countryside passed by. It was a warm summer. The county of Hertfordshire was green at this time of year. The fields were filled with ripening wheat. Wild flowers dotted the edges, splashes of red, white and yellow. Pastures held black and white cows, white fluffs of sheep. Trees were tall, proud and ancient.

His mind began to run over the business he hoped to conduct this weekend, but Scott interrupted his thoughts.

'Do you think Lord Hertmoor will invest?'

Rob took a moment to gather his thread before he spoke. 'He has to. The East Europeans are impressed with the title, but it will be the cash that seals the deal. The land is secured, deposit paid. It's the loan terms and the long leases that need to be finalised. Ian has the documents. I only hope he's read them through.'

'And approves of them.'

'He gets a big enough percentage. Should keep that crumbling pile of his afloat for a few more years.'

'That's no way to talk about Lady Hertmoor,' Casey said.

Rob laughed. Coierit Manor had been in the Hertmoor family for centuries. Generations had lived and prospered there. It was now a successful working estate of hundreds of acres of prime Hertfordshire land. Fishing, shooting, wedding parties, woodland pursuits, each contributed an uncertain income to the finances, but Rob knew the business deal he was brokering was a lifeline for his old friend. It was why they were all staying at the Manor for a long weekend. Seal the deal over a meal.

'Of course he was Ian Churchill at school.'

'Churchill?' Casey said. 'Related to …'

'Winston? No, just a coincidence, but one he took full advantage of as often as he could.'

'Are you sure it's secured?'

May looked at her husband, and saw the strain on his face. Old before its time. 'I checked it all myself. The doors, the bolts, the alarms. It can't escape.'

Ian shook his head, and felt the first footholds of a migraine pinching at his temples. 'We thought that last time.'

'That was all sorted out.'

His temper flared. 'Only because both of them were killed.'

'Because they ignored what we told them.'

'We couldn't have been more specific. No sex in this house.'

'You can't say they brought it on themselves?'

'We should never have guests. It's as simple as that. It's bad enough we have to live here, without bringing others into it.'

May walked the final few steps down the grand staircase, and joined her husband in the vast entrance hall, with its black and white marbled floor and its oak panelled walls.

'You invited them, darling.'

Ian took her arm and squeezed it slightly too hard. 'Let's have a drink in the drawing room before they arrive. These guests that I have invited. Against both our better judgements.'

The drawing room was filled with sunlight flooding in from the floor to ceiling windows. Three sofas were pulled into a cosy circle around an unlit, open fire. Paintings hung on the walls, ancestors peering down on the home they had endured, before passing it to the next generation. The ceiling was adorned with ornate frescos of vibrant colours.

May took a seat on a sofa, and watched as Ian poured two generous measures of brandy. He sat opposite and handed her a glass.

'To a trouble-free weekend.'

'You know them better than I do. Is that likely?'

Ian sighed long and hard. 'We need the money this deal will bring in. I was at school with Rob. He's a good man. The construction company he runs with his wife is a big player. I've read through the plans he sent, and by investing now we can secure the future of the Manor for about ten more years I'd say.'

'What's she like? The wife?'

'Never met her. I'm sure she'll be good company for you. It's only a few days.'

'They should be fine with house rules. What about the son? You said he's coming. And with a girlfriend.'

The room went dark as clouds passed in front of the sun. They both looked up, but as soon as they did the darkness diminished and the room was summer bright again.

'Scott. I don't know the girl's name. I'm sure we'll have no trouble. We can't afford any. We managed to keep it quiet the last time, but Rob and his family are a bit too high profile to sweep it under the carpet.'

'Or ditch into the lake.'

'Don't remind me.'

'Do we have time for another?' May held up her glass in anticipation of a refill.

'Bit early to be knocking it back quite so spectacularly isn't it?'

'Never too early to dull the pain, darling.'

She accepted the second glass, and noticed he had also quite generously topped up his own.

'A toast?' she said.

'To us?'

'To surviving.'

Coierit Manor was a large manor house of the late fourteenth century. Many additions and alterations had been attempted over the years, mostly with success. It was set out over two storeys with attic rooms. There were myriad chimneys, and the original structure had been expanded beyond all recognition. Two huge wings had been added through the centuries, and the overall impression was of wounded grandeur. It had been decorated to bring it into line with the 'Grecian' taste of the late eighteenth, although that excess had been modified in later years. The pristine portico remained, with tri-cornered pediment and ornamental entablature, but the original stucco had been covered with a modern paint substance on the main building. The long wings were built from brick and stone, and lent the perception that the Manor was a thing of nature. The impressive double front doors were polished oak, with a gleaming lion's head knocker in brass. Mullioned windows sparkled as the sun rose higher in the sky, a strong heat warming the grounds.

An observant onlooker might notice that the attic windows of the west wing were boarded against the light. Bars, apparently of wrought iron, covered each pane of glass, and there was what looked like wire meshing over the metal. It begged the question: were the defences intended to keep intruders out, or to keep what was in the attic locked inside?

As the rest of the house was open and inviting, doors and windows welcoming the summer warmth as well as visitors, it seemed to indicate that the top of the house contained something that the rest of the building was ashamed of.

Rob Williams and his family weren't overly observant. They were far too stunned at the size of the house and the grounds to take in much of the detail.

'God, it's like a stately home,' Casey said.

'They really are a Lord and Lady aren't they?' Selina said.

'Nothing but the best for my family,' Rob said. 'I told you I move in the finest circles of society.'

'I am not worthy,' Selina said.

'I've been telling you that for weeks.' Scott winced as his girlfriend dug him in the ribs.

'Watch it, Mister. Or no cuddles for you this weekend.'

'Now who's providing too much information,' Casey said.

'We'll all be far too tired from the activities Ian will have planned for us to think of anything other than falling exhausted into bed at night.' Rob drove the car carefully down the winding lane that connected the outside world to this paradise of privilege. Either side, trees he didn't know the name of crowded over the drive, branches reaching out like fingers to caress the paintwork.

As they neared the Manor the change in the grounds was noticeable. Near the road, around the perimeter wall, were unkempt woods, bushes that had been allowed to grow tall and wide. Closer to the house the grass was neatly trimmed, the bushes shaped and controlled, the flowerbeds overflowing with colour and variety.

'They must have a staff of thousands,' Scott said.

'That, and the upkeep of the house itself, is why Ian always needs an injection of cash.'

'This would be a great place to get married,' Selina said, and when the others looked at her she added, 'Sorry, did I say that out loud?'

'I didn't know you two were thinking …' Casey began.

'We're not …' Scott and Selina spoke almost simultaneously, and both a bit too quickly to convince.

'Well,' Casey said. 'I always find the countryside romantic.' She placed a hand onto her husband's thigh, and rubbed it gently.

Rob pulled the car to a halt on the gravel in front of the house. There were no other vehicles.

'I guess we're the only ones staying this weekend?' Casey said.

'Business before pleasure, that'll be Ian.'

The front doors opened, and two figures appeared at the top of the stone steps.

Before Rob could reach for the door handle, Ian and May had descended. Car doors were dragged open, and the occupants encouraged out onto the warm, shifting stones.

'Rob,' Ian said, as he hugged him. 'Good to see you. Good man.'

Rob shook the proffered hand once he had extricated himself. 'I'd better introduce the group.'

'We're already undergoing that social nicety over here,' May said.

Rob watched as first Casey, and then Selina, were seduced by the embrace of their hostess. Scott walked over to join the men and introduced himself to Ian.

'Quite a place you've got here, Lord Hertmoor.'

'Ian, please. Ian and May. None of this titled nonsense between friends. It helps open a few doors when it needs to, but apart from that it stays locked in a cupboard with all the other family skeletons.'

May looked at him sharply, and Rob wondered what that look might imply. All families held secrets, and one that had lived in the same house for seven centuries was bound to have more than most. It might be fun trying to uncover some of them while they were here.

Rob opened the rear of the car, and between them they took out the luggage. As they carried the bags to the house Rob said, 'You got the papers I emailed?'

'Absolutely. Lots to talk about, but plenty of time for all that. Let's get you settled in, and then we can have some croquet on the side lawn. Nothing shouts upper class twerps like a good old game of croquet.'

'We're "new money",' Casey said. 'We look up to you posh lot. Don't spoil it by talking yourself down.'

May linked her arm through Casey's. 'There's room enough for all of us. Ian's family has lived in Hertfordshire for donkey's years, but we've always welcomed the changes we've seen. Friends in London sometimes look down on us in the Home Counties as being too suburban, but we've got it made as far as I'm concerned. We've seen the commuter belt around London share in the buoyant economic life of the capital. We've got the wealth of London without the inflated prices, and we've got so many lovely little market towns and pretty villages.'

'Don't forget the countryside,' Ian said. 'Maybe not as dramatic as some parts of the country, but it does tend to be lush, green, and prosperously farmed. And there is almost no heavy industry to spoil the scenery.'

Rob laughed. 'Certainly not within view of the Manor.'

'I like the summerhouse,' Selina said.

'We'll talk to you about that when we run through the house rules,' May said.

Rob frowned as he looked at Ian. 'We're not aristocrats, but we are house trained.'

'Nothing to worry about. It's a large house and the grounds are extensive. We don't want any accidents. Insurance is expensive you know.'

'Your safety is our prime concern,' Scott said in a robotic voice.

Selina punched his arm. 'We'll have a great time. Thanks so much for inviting us. Please ignore my ignorant boyfriend.'

The front doors stood open, like a hungry mouth waiting to devour them.

Ian stepped aside, and let the four of them enter. As May went inside he took her shoulder, and gave her what he hoped was a meaningful stare.

It was cool inside the house. Rob and the others marvelled at the lavish interior. Understated, but quietly opulent. Corridors disappeared into the shadows, and doors remained shut. They were grouped in the entrance hall, and ahead of them the grandeur of the winding staircase beckoned.

'Come on up,' May said. 'I'll show you to your rooms.'

'That will be pretty much the only house rule actually,' Ian said.

At the top of the stairs, a wide landing opened onto a long hallway that meandered into the distance, towards large windows.

May stopped as they came to the first door. She opened it, and indicated that Casey should enter ahead of her. When Rob tried to follow May placed a manicured hand on his chest. Gentle but insistent.

'This is Casey's bedroom.'

'We're married, so obviously it's *our* room.'

Behind him Ian coughed. 'We all sleep separately here. Family tradition and all that.'

Rob turned to see if there was a grin on his friend's face, but there wasn't. If anything Ian looked deadly serious. Worried possibly. Scared maybe.

'Casey and I haven't spent a night apart … well I can't remember the last time.'

'I'm sorry, Rob,' May said. She stood between Rob and Casey, blocking Rob from gaining access, and also stopping Casey from leaving.

'Ian,' Rob said. 'This is crazy isn't it? Don't you and … sorry, I don't mean to be personal, but don't you …'

'May and I have separate rooms, but if you're asking me for more intimate details then forget it. That is our house rule. The main one. The only one. I'm afraid you'll all have to abide by it.'

Casey said, 'Don't worry, Rob. It's only for the weekend. It'll be a nice change not to have to put up with your snoring.'

'I don't want to be rude, Ian. I respect tradition, and it's your house, so your decision, but I mean. This is the twenty-first century.'

'Sorry, Rob. Come on. May can help Casey to settle in while I show you all to your rooms.'

'I half expected you to put us in separate rooms,' Selina said. 'After all you don't know us, or our status.'

'Thanks for being so understanding,' Ian said.

'For the life of me,' Rob said. 'I *don't* understand.'

The other three rooms were further down the winding hallway. Each was within shouting distance of the other, but far enough away for privacy. Once Selina had been given hers, and Scott his room, Ian and Rob walked to the end of the hall, close to the window.

'And here's yours.'

Ian opened the door and walked in. Rob followed.

The room was furnished much as it would have been a hundred years before. Four-poster bed, curtains and cushion covers of patterned brocade. A carpet of many colours. Dark wood chest, wardrobe and side table.

'There's a bathroom through there,' Ian said. 'We are up with the times in some respects.'

'What's it all about? This bedroom business? Come on, man

to man. It's more than family heritage isn't it?'

Ian sat on the window seat, and stared out at the expanse of lawn leading to the edge of the woods. 'I was born here, I've lived here all my life, and I'll probably die here. The grounds have got a small chapel and a cemetery. I'll end up there, buried next to Lords from hundreds of years ago. Children have been born here, like I was. But none have ever been conceived here. None that lived at any rate.'

'That's a bit mysterious. What do you mean by that?'

Ian rubbed his hands over his face. 'The house doesn't like it.'

'Doesn't like what? How can a house like or dislike anything? You've lived here too long, old son, you need to get out into the real world for a change. A holiday would do you good.'

'A holiday! Ha! The only time I leave this house is to walk the grounds of the estate, or to visit the summerhouse. Is that man to man enough for you? When May and I want to act like man and wife, we sneak off to the summerhouse.'

'Why on earth can't you just behave normally in your own house?'

'My house? If only it was. Look, I need to get things ready downstairs. I expect you to honour what you've been asked, Rob. I intend to support your project, but if you can't … well, there will be dire consequences.'

'Dire … come on, man.'

When Ian had left, Rob unpacked his bag, and then stood by the window looking out. He could see the roof of the summerhouse to the left. Maybe it *would* be romantic to slip away later with Casey.

There was a knock, followed by the door being opened, and Casey walked in.

'Nice room, much the same as mine, though I've got a vase of flowers.'

'May's little feminine touch no doubt.'

'Can you believe the separate rooms? Like Selina said, I thought they'd keep the youngsters apart, but Ian knows we're married. Where's the harm in us sharing a bed?'

'There's always the summerhouse.'

'May mentioned that, but it seems a bit sordid to slope off in the dead of night. I was looking forward to snuggling up in a room full of history, and making some memories of our own.'

Rob drew her into his arms and kissed the top of her head. 'We will just have to see about that. You know what I'm like with rules.'

It was warm out on the lawn as they went through the motions of playing croquet. The jugs of chilled Pimms helped, and soon everyone was laughing and relaxing.

One by one they let the afternoon sun decide when they took a breather. Without the game having reached anything like a conclusion, they all ended slumped in garden chairs around a large wooden table that was laden with drinks and glasses and enough canapés to feed an army.

Several times Rob tried to guide the conversation onto business, but Ian wasn't to be tempted.

'Time enough for that when we send the ladies off as we enjoy our port and cigars, old boy.'

May slapped his thigh. 'There will be none of that, thank you very much.'

'Quite right,' Casey said. 'We have to keep these men in their place.'

'Even if that place isn't the bedroom,' Rob said.

May ignored the comment, and poured out more drinks. Ian had a face that threatened to cast a shadow over the sunlit scene.

'Rob. It's a couple of days, three nights at most. Surely you can keep your libido in check that long. For your business, if not out of respect for my wishes.'

Rob raised his glass in a gesture of surrender. 'It all seems a bit dramatic that's all. Family secrets, and talk of the house not liking stuff.'

He saw the look that passed between May and Ian, and

perceived it as a warning from wife to husband. *Don't say too much.*

'I don't know what Ian has said to you, Rob, but his family have been tied to this house for far too long for us to ever consider breaking the bonds.'

'However much we may want to,' Ian said quietly.

'I get that …'

'No, Rob, no you couldn't possibly,' May said. 'Traditions, legacies, they all build over generations. They develop over the centuries until they have a life of their own. They become as much a part of the fabric of the house as the stucco and the roof tiles.'

Casey drained her glass. 'You make it sound as if the house is a living, breathing entity.'

Rob watched as May's face turned pale. Ian's fingers stiffened around the stem of his glass.

'Ian,' May said. 'I think we had better go in, and make sure dinner is being prepared. You all stay out here as long as you like. Enjoy the early evening sun. It will stay warm for ages yet. Dinner is at seven.'

When they were gone, Selina said, 'Has Ian changed since you knew him, Rob? Or has he always been weird?'

'It's not just him though is it?' Scott said. 'She's clearly calling the shots.'

'Okay,' Rob said. 'That's enough. I agree the room arrangements are a bit strange, but I need to do business with these people.' He looked at Casey. 'I have to say, though, that he isn't quite the man I used to know. It's as if he's under some kind of threat.'

'Running scared I would have said.'

Selina stood. 'I'm going up for a shower. In my room. Alone. By myself.'

Scott started to push back his chair, but Rob took hold of his arm. 'Whether we like it or not, we will have to abide by their rules.'

'Sure, no problem. No, seriously. I'm a guest in someone else's house. You want their money for your business. I'm not going to rock the boat.'

When they were gone, Casey took Rob's hand. 'Does that apply to us as well?'

'Rules are made for breaking.'

The sun was lower in the sky, but it was still bright sunshine that coated the lawn. If the edge of the woods were plagued by shadows that shouldn't have been there, Rob didn't notice.

When he and Casey entered the house, he wasn't aware of the movement, or the sounds that seemed to emanate from the attic.

He escorted Casey up the grand staircase, and along the hallway. Outside her room, he took her in his arms and kissed her.

Dinner was served in the dining room, in the oldest part of the house, the west wing.

It was a room that might have been constructed recently rather than seven hundred years ago. The oak panelled walls were adorned with tapestries depicting boar and stag hunts. The huge fireplace was cold and open, and large enough for two men to be devoured at a time. The floor was uneven flagstones, which had been polished to a high sheen by the feet of thousands of diners. Scattered about were threadbare rugs.

The table was big enough to seat at least thirty people, although it was set for the more modest party who were beginning to seat themselves.

'Sit anywhere,' May said. 'We don't stand on ceremony. I know it all sounds a bit grand, but we have excellent staff here. Many of them have been with us for years.'

'And their families before them,' Ian said.

'So you didn't do the cooking, May?' Casey said.

'I do sometimes, of course, but we have a wonderful chef, and she's done everything tonight.'

'It's all ready to be served,' Ian said. 'We've given her the night off, and once the three courses have been brought in – they'll leave it all on the warming plates over there – all of the staff are leaving.'

'So there's no live-in help?' Selina said.

'No, there are cottages on the estate where many of them live, so close enough if we need them. But, tonight it's just the six of us.'

'And the secrets and traditions,' Rob said.

The door opened, and four young men and women entered. Some were carrying trays of food, while two of them pushed carts that held metal serving domes on two levels of shelves. The carts were wheeled to the edge of the room, beneath the windows, and the domes were covered with white cloths.

The trays were brought to the table, and plates of food were placed in front of each of them.

'Looks great,' Scott said, as the four servers walked to the door.

'Thanks everyone,' May said. 'We'll see you tomorrow.'

After they had gone and the door was shut, Ian said, 'It's a salad with most of the ingredients sourced from the estate.'

'Apart from the halloumi,' May said.

'Did you get some rest after the rigours of the croquet?' Ian said.

Rob couldn't stop himself glancing at Casey.

'What does that look mean?' May asked.

'Nothing at all,' Rob said. 'My room is very peaceful.'

Conversation flowed in tandem with the wine. The first course was accompanied by chilled Chablis. As May, with Casey helping, served everyone with the main course of beef, potatoes and vegetables, Ian poured out generous measures of Malbec.

The meal was halfway through when the intrusion of liquid was first noticed.

Initially Ian thought it was normal perspiration, and brushed a finger over his forehead. It was warm in the room, even with the windows open. When the next few drops dampened his hair, he looked up.

Rob felt something wet on his head as well. He flicked his hand over his scalp, and when he looked at his palm it was covered in a viscous, opaque liquid.

'What's that?'

Ian pushed away from the table, throwing his cutlery to the floor.

'Who was it?'

May was whimpering from fear.

'What's happening?' Selina said.

'Was it you?' Ian said to her. 'Scott, did you and Selina …'

Scott stared at him, and then realised what he meant. 'Did we have sex? No, of course not. It's none of your business as it happens, but we respected your wishes.'

A sound like liquid flesh squeezing and pulling made them all look upwards. From the ceiling, indistinct shadows were erupting and dropping like rain. Globules of darkness forced their way out through the plaster, until they were in the open, and then as they floated down they coalesced into shapes that were nearly human.

'It was us,' Casey shouted. 'Rob and me. We thought it would be a bit … naughty.'

May was screaming now.

Selina huddled close to Scott.

'Naughty?' Ian's fury was unbridled. 'You have no idea what you've done.'

'What are they?' Rob said, as the shuffling shadows around them milled and swayed as if caught in a breeze.

The ceiling was dripping with moisture. It was as though a dozen baths had been left to overflow, and the water was cascading down onto them.

'Come on,' Ian said. 'We should be able to get out of the window before it gets here.' He grabbed May by the hand, and hauled her out of her chair. 'Come on,' he said to the others. 'We need to get out.'

'Before what gets here?' Rob said. 'You said "before it gets here". What?'

There was a loud crash from above, and the sound of wood splintering, as something strong and large smashed through doors.

Ian helped May to step onto a chair, and manoeuvred her up to the open window. 'Scott, help me.'

With Selina hanging onto his arm, Scott rushed across to give Ian the extra lift he needed to push May out.

'You next,' he said to Selina. Between them, Ian and Scott lifted Selina, and all but propelled her out of the room.

The ceiling cracked open and a liquescent waterfall rained over the table.

More of the shadow shapes dripped down, and lay flopping on the floor. Some were nearly fully formed into a human semblance. Others were barely recognisable as people.

'What the hell are those things?' Rob said.

There was the thundering noise of some immense thing crashing down the staircase. Banisters were ripped away, as the bulk of it tore off everything in its path.

'Quick,' Selina shouted through the window. 'Get out now.'

'Casey,' Ian said. 'Get her out first.'

A heavy body smashed against the doors to the dining room.

They had managed to get Casey's head and shoulders through the window when the doors broke from their hinges, and what had escaped reached a claw inside and grabbed Scott.

Rob took hold of his son's arm, but he would never be strong enough to resist.

Casey squirmed in the window opening, half in and half out. 'Scott!'

Ian had picked up a chair and was holding it like a lion tamer from a circus. He was making quiet, reassuring noises, much as a parent might to a fractious child. Soothing, calming, trying to prevent the inevitable.

Rob ran across to Casey, and was hanging onto her hand when the doorframe splintered, and the mass spilled into the room.

'Ian, help me.'

It was huge, misshapen, and yet there was about it a human essence. Holding Scott by his leg, the creature was pawing at his body, much like an animal would play with its food.

'Scott!' Casey screamed but Rob and Ian pushed her unceremoniously through the open window. 'Rob, you next.'

'I can't leave my son.'

Ian grasped his friend's arm. 'It's too late. The moment you broke the rules it was too late.'

'Rules … why?'

Ian was whispering to the creature, soft crooning noises that a parent might make to their infant baby. He still held the chair in one hand, and with the other was trying to propel Rob to the window.

'If you try to help Scott it will take you as well. It's the way it always is.'

'What is it for …you knew about this didn't you?'

Ian let out a cry of despair that echoed around the room. The sound of his agony soaked into the centuries old tapestries, slid down the oak panels of the walls.

'Knew? Of course I knew. I was so specific. Your arrogance in being … *naughty* … this is the result. Why do you think May and I have no children? Once we are both dead the house can rot for all I care.'

Before Rob could say another word, Ian manhandled him out of the window and leapt out after him.

'I can't leave Scott.'

Ian grabbed his arm and dragged him away. 'We've got to get clear of the house. It's our only chance.'

Stumbling and resisting as best he could, Rob said, 'Why the hell did you want the investment? You went on about your heritage and legacy.'

Ian ran slowly and clumsily, hampered by his friend's efforts to get loose. 'Each father in my family passes on the secret to their son and heir. I won't have to do that. I can let the tradition fade and die.'

Rob dropped to his knees, forcing Ian to pause. 'What on earth is it?'

'Locked away in the attic, no one to feed and protect it, eventually even that thing should disappear.'

Rob clambered to his feet and stared back at the house.

'How long has it been here?'

Ian started to walk away but realised Rob wasn't moving. He was breathing heavily.

'I can't say for certain. The history has become porous over the years. My father hinted at a pact to produce a son, a pact that went badly wrong. I don't think he truly knew the provenance. All I know is sex in the house ignites it. Conception would be fatal.'

'And it kills?'

Ian took hold of Rob's arm and pulled him further away from the house.

'I think ... May disagrees, but I think it is the spawn of one of my ancestors that was either unwanted, or so imperfect when born that it was hidden away. Who knows what people believed then, even the aristocracy.'

Rob was barely listening.

He was abandoning his son to a monster. He couldn't do it.

He struck out and Ian fell to the ground.

'Rob, no!'

It was too late. Rob was running fast. Back to the house.

Ian started to follow.

'I have to save my son.'

At the broken window Ian tried to pull him back but Rob yanked his arm from Ian's grasp, vaulted inside and ran towards the creature.

Ian hauled himself to the window and stared through.

Rob was hugging what was left of Scott.

The creature held both of them in a parental embrace.

THE THING BY THE ROADSIDE

Ghostly incidents that seemingly occur without apparent rhyme or reason are often the most terrifying, usually because their sheer illogicality, at a subconscious level at least, makes them seem all too real.

One of the biggest problems facing folklorists seeking the truth behind popular myths is that it's always been easy to fabricate eerie stories, mainly because audiences tend to want to believe. It's a trick that's been employed for centuries, sometimes for practical reasons: to dissuade trespassers from entering private property, to keep children from danger, to immortalise terrible events, to imply that some kind of final judgement has been passed on deceased felons; and occasionally for the sheer devilment of it, the pure, intoxicating fun of making up horror stories.

However, there are usually indicators when stories have been invented.

For example, are they too pat? Do they have a beginning, a middle and an end? Are they a complete tale, perhaps with a subtext, maybe with the clear purpose of delivering a lesson? All these things are deemed by investigators to be the hallmarks of fertile imaginations, the work of sophisticated tall-tale tellers who know their audience will not be satisfied (or reassured) unless the whole thing is neatly sewn up at the end.

Reality, if there is such a thing in this realm of mystery, is usually quite different. A good case in point is the haunting of the road running between Wilden and Ravensden in north Bedfordshire.

Ask any local in this district and it's highly likely they'll be able to tell you that the road is haunted. What is less likely is that they'll know what it's haunted by, while it's a certainty that none will know how long it has supposedly been haunted for. It's not even the case that this quiet rural lane is regularly haunted. In fact, only on one

221

occasion has an incident been recorded here.

In the year 1872, Wilden was a remote hamlet, but two genteel ladies of the parish, a Mrs Goodhall and her daughter, were out for a ride in their pony and trap. It was late evening and they'd strayed perhaps further from home than they'd intended. Dusk was falling and they were on their way back to Wilden when they were surprised to see a figure standing on the verge with its back turned. From its shape, the figure was quite clearly female, and it wore a tattered, black gown and had long, unkempt black hair. The ladies drove past, unconcerned; they were much more interested in getting home. However, a couple of minutes later, perhaps half a mile further along, they spied another figure standing on the verge with its back turned. It was identical to the previous one: female, with long, untidy black hair, wearing tattered black robes. Despite this, the ladies drove on past. But about a mile from home, when they saw the figure a third time, in exactly the same garb and same posture, they drew their trap to the side of the road and climbed down, cautiously approaching, at which point, the figure, without warning, spun to look at them.

Later on, when they returned to Wilden in hysterics, the ladies told anyone who would listen that it was the most terrible face they had ever seen. To begin with it was male, a man's face on a woman's body, but brutish and scarred, snarling hideously and fixing them with a stare so malevolent that it surely threatened murder.

When a search was made of the district, no such person was found. Members of a psychical research society, who interviewed the ladies many years later, were firmly convinced that this was an account of a true event and concluded that the two women had beheld some kind of apparition. They did not believe, as some suggested, that three demented persons had been at large in the neighbourhood, perhaps three escapees from an asylum. The two witnesses agreed, certain they had encountered a demonic being.

Whatever the thing by the roadside was, it has never been seen since, and though historians have searched for explanations behind it – had someone been murdered in that place, someone evil buried, a witch or warlock hanged or gibbeted? – the answer in all cases was a resounding 'no'.

THE TOPSY-TURVY ONES
Tom Johnstone

'As fondly as he anticipated the Restoration, it seems likely that Sir Francis did not live long enough to see Charles II's triumphant coronation. I say "seems likely" advisedly, for there is no actual record of his passing, though there are various unsubstantiated rumours about his fading from history in a manner most uncharacteristically quiet for this colourful figure. Certainly he was cruel, something of a local despot, and there must have been plenty that wanted him dead and with the wherewithal to carry out such a wish, with probable impunity in those chaotic and lawless times. There is a report, probably apocryphal, of him meeting the radical preacher John Pordage, something that again seems rather uncharacteristic for such a staunch Royalist. The only primary sources we have are certain papers he left to his heirs pertaining to some family curse, a tale drawn from shreds and patches of myth and legend, of Hydra's teeth and Mandrake roots, as luridly colourful as the man himself, and suggestive of some bizarre epiphany of interest only to medical practitioners in the field of mental illness.'

From *Forgotten Figures of the Cromwellian Era*
by Sir Henry Hobday (Oxford University Press, 1954)

1999

The fading ghosts of her dream danced in tatters before her eyes. Scraps of words and images that had formed part of an unbroken whole now splintered into disparate fragments; mercifully she thought, for these remnants were bad enough: the tip of terror's iceberg, the thin end of its wedge. A man's voice howling of silver rust burning flesh. A hand inserting a finger through the hole in a tongue. Blood pouring from the toothless chasm a woman's mouth had become. Moonlit shoots sprouting pallid, muddied heels and toes from grey soil, then ankles and shins and knees and …

But she mustn't think of what followed the strange, fleshy efflorescence, or she'd start screaming again. She hadn't even known she was doing it, thinking a shrill alarm had woken her, until she felt Richard's arms around her, heard him calling to her over the noise that she now realised was her own voice, telling her it was all right, it was just a dream.

Once she'd calmed down, forcing herself to breathe deeply, she made herself remember what had frightened her into shrieking wakefulness. Something about the face that had followed the spidery legs and body out of the loamy earth …

'What was it, Marisa?' he asked. 'A bad memory from … back home?'

'Richard,' she said, with a sigh on the edge of irritability, 'it's not my home. I left when I was three.'

She hated it when he acted all concerned and right-on about her past, like he thought he was that bus driver in that Ken Loach movie he'd taken her to see. Well, he wasn't a bus driver, he was a wannabe film maker with a trust fund, and she was from Chile, not Nicaragua. Her mother had got them out before anything really terrible could happen to them – bad enough to cause nightmares at least, though some of the things she'd subsequently heard or read about had induced them. Maybe this dream *was* linked to the horrors of her past. She had just heard the old generalissimo was holed up in some privately-rented mansion in Surrey, awaiting a decision on extradition. She didn't want to mention that to Richard. He'd only get all worried and over-solicitous, and that would be annoying.

This was something different. The garbled words and images seemed disconnected both from reality and each other. Yet, she reminded herself, while the dream had been playing inside her sleeping brain, they must have had some strange, internal logic. Somehow that passing thought was far from reassuring.

1649

A passing strange occurrence did take place at the crossroads near Iver on the first day of April, in the Year of Our Lord, Sixteen Hundred and Forty Nine. A crowd was gathering around a preacher, who did utter forth great sermons and prophecies. Not so unusual perhaps, for there be all manner of strange doings hereabouts since the Body Politic lost its divinely-anointed Head, but for one thing. This mighty testifier, whose words did impudently storm the very Heavens, was a woman! I wondered if 'twere some All Fools' Day jest, yet 'twas not so – she was in earnest. Some laughed at her, and jeered at the impertinence of such as she thinking she could speak the Word of the Lord. Others, like this one – a man, mark you! – set forth an apology for her, saying unto me: 'Why should she not preach? Did not the Maid of Orleans take divine revelation and with it lead men forth into battle?'

'Aye,' said I. 'And mark what happened to her!'

He turned his long, pock-marked face away from me. I think him one of these pamphleteers that have of late been prating hereabouts of 'Light Shining in Buckinghamshire'. No wonder the world hath gone topsy-turvy, for these 'True Levellers' would have it so. Were it not for their ideas spreading abroad, she'd have been hanged for a witch, I have no doubt. The times are so out of joint, I have betimes had to go abroad in rags or face the vengeance of the mob, and thus seem to level myself afore they level me into the ground!

1999

'There's a patch of flat ground over there,' he murmured. 'That might do.'

Glancing towards Marisa, he edged the car closer to the fence, tugged the handbrake into position and eased into neutral. As he turned the ignition off and started climbing out of the battered green and white 2CV, she called out to him: 'Hey! Richard! Won't we need to get permission to film in this field …' Then she added, more to herself than him, as he'd already vaulted over the fence: 'Especially if we're going to have them digging it up?'

Eventually, she sighed and got out of the passenger seat, leaning over the fence and glaring at him. He seemed oblivious. He was standing in the middle of the field, grinning his stupid grin under his stupid, golden-blond halo.

'Richard!' she called, dark eyes still irritated but with a half-smile tweaking a corner of her mouth. 'You must be trespassing.' He turned round, smiling back at her, probably at the way she put the stress on the syllable 'pass': Though she'd lived in England since she was three, she still had a few odd inflections, maybe from her mother.

He walked, almost strutted, over to her.

'Kind of apt,' he said, when he reached the fence, kissing her on the mouth. 'Yes,' he went on, his eyes blazing with a kind of fierce humour, 'the heartland of Tory England, once the home of primitive communism!'

'What do you know about communism, posh boy?' she snorted. 'Anyway, didn't the Diggers set up their commune on some hill in Surrey, not a flat field in Berkshire?'

'Buckinghamshire,' he corrected her. 'St George's Hill's the one everyone's heard of; the Diggers just called it George Hill of course – they didn't recognise the established canon of Saints. But…'

'Yeah, yeah, I know, there were Digger settlements everywhere from here to Northampton. They were spreading. That's why the Parliamentarians crushed them, etc, etc. You don't need to explain it all to me. I have read up on this shit too! I was just taking the piss.'

He nodded, a little crestfallen at her outburst. Had she gone too far? She didn't want to go to Surrey anyway – couldn't stand to be in the same county as that sick old bastard. But she wasn't going to tell Richard that. She also knew he had his own reasons not to want to go to the site of the more famous encampment. Right now it was crawling with would-be latter-day 'diggers' from the Land Is Ours group, who'd commemorated Winstanley's stand by setting up an 'eco-village' on St George's Hill. That would hinder filming.

'You're still trespassing though,' she added with a smile. 'And you'll definitely be trespassing if you try to film here without permission.'

'Will you forgive my trespasses?' he smiled, leaning over the fence for another kiss.

'I don't know why,' she murmured, 'but yes …'

1649

Such is the anarchy loose abroad since the King lost his head and thus deprived Albion of hers, that the trespasses of these wretches do go unpunished. I know not why, for Cromwell's treachery did not extend to depriving great ones of their birth-rights. Yet some of his rag-tag army have taken his declaration of a Commonwealth a little too much in earnest. The very day that Mistress Preacher did wander abroad proclaiming signs and wonders, Winstanley did establish his beggar's commonwealth, stirring up every yeoman and ploughboy hereabouts to defy the authority of his master, so that the cart doth draw the horse.

This morning I rode to Iver Heath, and beheld men, some women too, some of them strangers to this parish, grubbing in the grey earth with picks and spades. I thought them mere thieves, seeking provender in the soil, thinking to glean turnips overlooked in the last harvest or some such, and drew closer to them, thinking to remonstrate with them. Yet watching them through gaps in the trees, I saw that what I thought had been a mere half dozen of the round-headed rogues had now swollen to thirty or more. Presently, they were joined by another twenty leading a horse that drew a plough, to a raucous cheer that stayed my hand upon the bridle. Something in their bearing gave me pause, and warned me that they might not scatter meekly from my chastising tongue, nor yet doff their caps to me, even had I worn my most splendid garb, not the mean garments I was wearing. Besides, some bore arms, a few even wearing the uniforms and cage-visored helmets of the Parliamentarian army, though I'll wager their officers hadn't given them licence to dally here. So it seemed politic to remain in the cover of the poplar trees, watching the rabble set about its work, for these rascals did not mean merely to rob the unharvested fruits of the earth in a desperate and incontinent fashion but to cultivate it according to Winstanley's pernicious, levelling creed that deems it a 'common treasury'.

I turned in disgust from the sight of these mean creatures ill-using the land God had given to their masters without a benign guiding hand to instruct them in its best employment. Did they think themselves great ones, to take possession of what was mine? The Lord of Misrule should renounce his garland of coltsfoot and cowslip when his day is done. Not these! They have made every day an All Fools' Day. As I rode through the woods, I came upon the wench I spied preaching on the first of this month, standing feet apart before my mount, dark eyes issuing a challenge.

'Let me pass, Mistress Preacher,' I said.

'Do not mock me, sir,' she replied. 'My name be Meg Henfrey. But why goest thou in beggars' weeds, my lord?'

'Why, I am but a humble one like yourself, Mistress,' I said. 'Why sayest thou that I am a great one?'

'By the way thou sits so haughty astride thy horse, my lord,' she said, hands on hips, a slight smile upon her red lips.

'If thou thinkst me a Lord,' said I, 'should I not have thee whipped for calling me "thou"?'

'We do call all folk "thou",' said she, with no trace of womanly meekness in her voice. 'Didst see the diggers at worship in the fields?' she asked.

'At worship?' said I with a laugh. 'Surely the church is the place for that, Mistress.'

'They do the Lord's work there.'

'They do trespass on their lord's land there.'

'So thou art their lord then,' she laughed, 'for only their lord would forbid them.'

'And yet still thou givest me a clownish thou,' I said. 'I am but one that believes that what belonged to his ancestors should go to his issue. I am no more a lord than thee a priest. Who ordained thee a minister to preach at the crossroads as I saw thee doing?'

'Christ is in all of us,' she said. 'He is in Abiezer Coppe, in Jacob Bauthumley, him they lashed to a tree and bored through the tongue, who suffered me to pass my finger through the hole like Saint Thomas did to our Lord's hands. Christ is in the seed they cast on the soil *yonder, to rise again so that we may feast upon his flesh!'*

'Jesus in John Barleycorn?' I laughed, though inwardly I was far from amused. 'How is this so? Explain carefully, Mistress Henfrey, lest thou find thyself put to the question by the magistrate, or even Master Hopkins.'

'Only a lord would make such speeches,' she said, with an impudent snort. 'If thou art a commoner as thou pretends, get thee down off that horse and speak to me face to face, not from that lofty perch. Then maybe I'll tell thee more of my gospel.'

'Very well,' I said, God help me, for I now saw her design in wanting to level me down thus. As I jumped down to stand before her, tying my horse to a tree, her eyes fixed upon mine, enabling the Devil that dwelt in those dark pools to take aim, finding it easier so at point-blank range.

I have heard tell of the lasciviousness of them as do claim to need no chapel. The body is where they do worship, so they say, and they do go naked when the spirit moves them.

'Now that I have descended from my horse, I needs must mount something else,' were the words he sent forth from my mouth, and my hands were about her waist and delving below her rough garment to do the Devil's work.

'Away, sir!' she hissed, grabbing my jerkin, but using her grip to cast me away not pull me closer. Then did she strike my face as if she were a fine lady and I an impudent vassal. 'Thou wanted to hear what gospel I preach. Thou shalt not whilst thou uses me thus!'

'I have heard that thy gospel is community in all things,' I said, my hand upon my smarting cheek.

'Sir, I am no common treasury,' she replied, 'unless I wish it, and I do not.'

Thus she did put on a show of injured virtue after her saucy words and looks.

1999

'What was that?' he gasped. As he'd sat up, something had shot out of a gorse bush near where they had been lying.

'You're very jumpy all of a sudden!' she laughed,

stretching languidly.

'And you're very relaxed for someone who was worried about trespassing a quarter of an hour ago.'

'Maybe I was just tense,' she teased, trying to keep the mood light, though she had to admit to an underlying sense of unease. It suddenly felt cold in the woods. When they'd rushed in here to quench their mutual heat, the shade of the beeches had seemed a relief from the intense heat of the sun, but now black clouds had bubbled up, adding to the chill. 'But you've helped me with that …' She gave a low, guttural laugh.

'Look, I'd rather get done for trespassing than public indecency,' he snapped.

'All right, all right.'

She straightened her skirt and buttoned up her blouse, thinking it was a bit late for him to be worried about his virtue. 'Why are you so tense? Did my stress just go into you? Didn't you …?'

'What? Shoot my bolt?'

'Well, that's a nice way of putting it,' she said, forcing a smile.

'You know I did. That reminds me …'

He picked up the used condom, hiding it inside his hand as if it was evidence. She felt a dismaying sense of deflation at his brusqueness, as if he was trying to rub her nose in the sordid aspects of their impromptu outdoor coupling. Perhaps her face had fallen, though usually she was quite good at hiding when his tone of voice or his gestures made her feel small.

'What?' he asked, his tone still sharp and irritable. 'I don't want to leave rubbish lying around, do I?'

From the way he was talking, and striding off ahead of her, forcing her almost to break into a jog in order to catch up, she felt as if 'rubbish' included her. No, she was being paranoid, wasn't she? But he was already out of the woods and into the field they'd crossed to get here. She could hear more rustlings, more animals rushing from one cover to a safer one. Something in the noise gave her the impression they were taller and thinner than most of the wildlife she thought of as living in a place like this. But her imagination must be running away with her at the speed the unseen creatures were, for something in the rhythm of their footfalls suggested they went on two legs, not four.

1649

What is it plagues me? I heard them in the woods at dusk, with the double tread of men but unshod like to basest animals, within a month after I brought Mistress Preacher to heel. When Cornets Holborn and Bagley presented her to me, I asked her who I was, knowing there could be no mistake as I now wore the fine apparel that befits my station.

'Why, thou art Francis Hearn, sir,' she said, with the same damnable impudence as she addressed me when I met her in the woods at Iver Heath and, I marked well, omitting my title and still addressing me as 'thou', though this time we were within my portals – in the cellar, that is, where rank dew dripped down the damp walls.

'Very well, Mistress Henfrey,' I said to her. Then I looked hard at the two men and spake to them: 'Remove her shift.'

They glanced the one to the other and at the implements ranged upon the table before me, hesitating to act upon my command, but they could see the very Devil that skulked behind my eyes, the one they had already seen at work when that round-headed knave refused to take off his hat before me. I ensured he would get his wish to keep his cap on always. Thanks to a hammer and several stout nails, he need never remove it again! It has had the unhappy effect of making him a worse ranter than before, as he wanders the woods howling and prating of how the silver I wear about me shall rust and sear my flesh when the Day of Judgement does come. Perhaps 'tis he that makes those weird noises at dusk then.

No doubt the cornets also remembered what I had put to them, about the punishment Parliament metes out to deserters, for they did as I bid them. It must have been that same Devil that spake next through my dry, cracked lips, as I looked hard at the two tremulous men and pointed at the great, black-iron pincers on the table. She had but herself to blame, for she put that Devil in me. And besides, if

Satan bids me do God's work of afflicting heretics, why then, he is no Devil at all!

What I said was: 'Hold her fast. Let us see if thou can still say "thou", without thy teeth.'

1999

'Richard!' she called. 'Hold on! No need to go that fast!'

He was almost half way across the field they had crossed to get to the woods. It was open but for the gorse bushes growing throughout, in full flower, whose buttery-yellow colour and coconut fragrance disguised the cruel sharpness of their thorns. He had stopped now, so now was the best chance she had to catch up with him. But something in his stance, the way he stood so breathlessly still, made her hesitate.

'Richard?' she said.

Slowly, he turned.

She let out a little gasp of relief when she saw his cheerier expression.

'Come on then!' he called.

She almost bounded over the stile dividing the wood from the field, which looked so inviting with the gorse flowers glowing in the renewed sunlight and Richard's stupid grin beaming at her. He was like that, Richard. 'Sunshine and showers', she called him, though some of her girlfriends were inclined to say 'moody'. They asked her why a tough cookie like her put up with his bouts of sullenness, to which would just give a secretive smile that made them laugh in half-envious embarrassment. One or two of them weren't her friends any more.

'I'm coming,' she called.

'What? Again?' he grinned.

'Oh, ha ha.'

'Car's still there,' he said, pointing to the 2CV.

'Sorry for being moody,' he said when she reached him. 'Worried something might have bashed into it because of where it was parked.'

'So you weren't really worried about getting caught *in flagrante* then?'

'No. If the worst came to the worst, I could always get Uncle Percy to put in a good word for me with the local beak.'

'Really? So your uncle's a local VIP then?'

'Well, sort of. Stockbroker anyway.'

They both laughed.

'He's pally with one of the magistrates round here,' he added. 'He's got an amazing place, the old Tory bastard. Practically next door to Pinewood Studios. When my folks used to take us there for visits, sometimes we'd see movie stars hanging around nearby ...'

'Wow,' she said. 'So you looked at them and thought 'I want to be in pictures when I grow up'?'

More laughter, though there was an odd, scared look in Richard's eyes that made her feel as if she'd overstepped the mark.

'It was more the other lot over in Bray,' he corrected her. 'When we used to go on family outings to Black Park, I used to love playing at being Count Dracula ...'

He hissed, and made a playful lunge at her neck. Squealing, she backed away and felt gorse teeth biting into her flesh through the thin fabric of her blouse.

'Hands off!' she laughed. 'It's virgins you vampires like, isn't it?'

'I don't know that Christopher Lee was that fussy. Anyway, you know I see myself more in the mould of Mike Reeves than Terry Fisher.'

With an inward rolling of her eyes at his slightly pompous tone, she asked: 'The guy who made that *Witchfinder General* film?'

He nodded. She gave a little exhalation of disgust. She hadn't been able to sit through the video, and he'd spent the rest of the evening sulking. It had taken some doing to get him to understand why: that the chaos and savagery portrayed was too close to home – to the place and time she had been forced to flee as a child. It was all very well for him, born into a comfortable background, in a country where the last time something like that had happened was the seventeenth century. She hadn't said that then of course. She'd chosen her words more carefully, the mood he'd been in.

Later they'd both read the Christopher Hill book, *World Turned Upside Down*, and discovered that there was another side to the English Civil War: more than two sides in fact, not just Roundheads and Cavaliers; new ideas were fermenting, and ordinary people were trying to use the breakdown of traditional authority, not just to give vent to their worst instincts as suggested in the Reeves film, but to test alternative ways of living and create a better world. That was why they were here. They'd both started work on a tentative film script, working title *Jerusalem*, and had come out here to scout potential locations. Well, that was one way of putting it, she thought drily …

'Look, I know you're not keen,' he said. 'But the way that guy used the English landscape …'

'Richard, I get that we can save money using real locations, but we still need *some* money for this project. Are you going to ask your Tory uncle for that too? Somehow I don't think it'll be up his –'

'Sshh!' Richard hissed. 'Did you hear that?'

1649

'Speak up, Mistress,' I said again, 'for I cannot hear thee!'

I would have her address me in the correct fashion, but still she persisted in calling me 'Thou'. Without teeth to harden the sound, it did lend due deference to her speech, so that she did gurgle out 'Yow'. But her haughty air of defiance did take the lustre off my triumph. Suddenly I did feel a terrible disgust at what I had wrought. Even she did blush for shame. Crouching on the crimson-stained floor, she began to collect up the bloodied pegs my cruel instrument had ripped from her gums.

'Why, Mistress?' I asked. 'Thinkst thou to fit them back into thy mouth?'

And I did laugh heartily at this, but 'twas a counterfeit of laughter, and I did glare at my two unwilling disciples to bid them echo my example, yet they did look away in shame at their part in my atrocity. When she had gathered every single tooth into a scrap of her rent shift and tied it up as 'twere a bag, she gave me a look, a most dreadful look of wrath that made me turn away.

1999

They turned back towards the woods. It had all gone quiet again, but she had definitely heard the sound, a rustling of soil shifting under her feet. She looked around in shock at the sudden absence of the bright-yellow gorse bushes that had punctuated the landscape, turning it into a ploughed open field, from which small white shoots were poking out, wriggling like worms. When she saw from the nails that they were big toes, she shut her eyes tight to drive the image from her waking mind back into the dream-world it came from. That was where it belonged, not out here in the daylight. She screwed them tighter. She didn't want to see the rest of the maggot-fleshed feet emerge …

Opening them again, she saw the gorse had returned, but when she reached out to Richard to tell him about what she thought had to be some kind of hallucination, she saw that he had walked back towards the trees. Her unease compounded by the vision, Marisa was more hesitant in following him. Anyway, she was tired of trailing around after him when he walked off like that. She could hear Karen's voice warning her about going along with 'controlling behaviour like that'. Marisa had been meaning to get back in touch with her friend and eat humble pie about the hurtful things she'd said back to her, but she kept stalling over how to phrase the apology. In any case, Karen's accusation smarted. How dare she call Marisa a doormat! But would following him now prove she was one?

Maybe she should head back to the car and wait for him there, though that prospect made her feel almost as irritated as the idea of running off after Richard again. What was he doing? She could hear scuffling noises from the undergrowth around the trees.

'Richard?' she called.

The sounds weren't just that of movement. There were voices too, muttering some kind of gibberish that sounded like sentences said backwards, something like: 'Ours is land until … Again and again rise shall …' More hallucinations, auditory this time? But the absent gorse bushes and the weird shoots had been as vivid as life, and Richard had heard the noises. That was what he'd gone off to investigate, wasn't it? She wondered if he'd seen anything unusual too. She had to find him first, and he was nowhere to be seen. She moved closer to the dark shade of the trees, still hesitant. A pale shape danced before her in the shadows with a face she couldn't make out clearly, but there was something wrong about it, profoundly wrong.

It couldn't be Richard.

She gasped. The figure was naked, hairless, sexless, limbs spindly, like something not long born, half-finished. When her eyes focused on the face, she grasped the thorns of a gorse bush near her, the pain screaming at her brain that she wasn't dreaming, that the black pools of eyes really stared out of the place where the mouth should be, at the base of the head, the nostrils pointing upwards towards a mouth gaping toothlessly in a frown that was a smile turned upside down.

But before she could confirm this, the figure cartwheeled into the darkness, turning its topsy-turvy face upright for the instant the splayed hands touched the ground, then leaving her standing there, gaping at the silent trees.

1649

In the forest, there is for the most part utter silence. That doth make for a yet more uneasy night as I lie there awaiting the next sudden, furtive noise from the darkness. I should hire cottagers to hew down the trees that do close into my chamber window, but methinks none will work for me now. This watching at night began when I did release the wench I had so intemperately ill-used, thinking I did the Lord's work when in truth I obeyed the Fiend's commands. A tinker did discover her corpse at the crossroads where first I spied her preaching, all bloody at the mouth. She must have fallen into an endless sleep there while trudging the road. According to the report my steward brought to me, they found no parcel of teeth on her person. I did not fear that I might be arraigned for her death. She fell far enough away from my house that none might connect me to her, save those two deserters whom I think have fled. I do not think they dare accuse me for fear of bringing retribution on their own heads for assisting me in my misdeeds and also for absenting themselves from their own martial duties without leave. Nevertheless they may yet do so out of spite or remorse. So, for safety, if they do remain in this parish, I needs must accuse them lest they do likewise unto me.

I have but one servant remaining, the others having quit my service to join with the Diggers on the Heath. I sent him forth to ride out and determine if my two former associates were lurking hereabouts. He saw them not, he said, but this he did tell me.

'My lord,' he said, 'I did see that fellow whose cap you did nail onto his pate when in his impertinence he did forbear to remove it before you. Scraps of it still remained about the rusty nail heads, with patches of wild hair sprouting forth between them. He did caper and gambol about the fields hither and thither, gibbering like Tom a' Bedlam, casting what I took for seeds about him.'

'Were they seeds, sirrah?' said I, for he did seem doubtful when he spake the word 'seeds'. 'Speak, man!'

'Aye, my lord,' said he. 'Seeds of corn, methinks. This chant he did make as he scattered them: "Jane Barleycorn is dead" as he hurled one seed; "Jane Barleycorn is risen" as he flung the next; and so on until of corn he had no more. It did not take long. He had not many seeds. Not more than I have teeth in my mouth!'

He grinned his foolish gap-toothed smile, but stopped doing so when I asked him sharply why he prattled of teeth.

'I do think the rusty nails in the fellow's head have curdled his wits, my lord,' my servant said. 'It should be John Barleycorn, not

Jane, should it not?'
    'Indeed,' I said. 'Indeed.'
    But 'twas a week after his report that I began to hear the nocturnal comings and goings hither and thither outside my chamber window, those sounds that are like beasts, but beasts that walk abroad on their hind legs.

1999

Not a sound came from the woods.

She walked forward cautiously, expecting to hear renewed rustling in the undergrowth as she surprised some animal, or worse, the thing she'd seen, or thought she'd seen. The silence was like someone holding their breath. The birds seemed to be holding theirs too. Come to think of it, she couldn't remember hearing them at all since she'd been here.

She stepped into the shade of the trees, trembling at her memory of that thing. She still couldn't believe it, that upside down face. It seemed so unreal now, mere moments later, though it had seemed real enough at the time.

Most of the trees were still bare, but for tiny spikes of young, pale-green foliage peeking out of their branches and the occasional snowy bloom of hawthorn blossom. The exception was the gnarled, overgrown horse chestnut, whose floppy leaves dangled like flat, green hands.

Despite the undeveloped forest canopy, it still felt damp and shady amid the vegetation, as if some invisible force repelled the heat of the day.

She shivered. The involuntary reflex gave itself voice, becoming a gasp as she felt a hand on her shoulder.

1649

I clapped him on the shoulder. He turned with a little gasp. He wore plain clothes, though I had heard tell he was once a man of the cloth until he fell in with the Ranters.

'Dr John Pordage?' I asked.

'The same,' said he. His eyes were narrowed, and who could blame him in these treacherous times, which have turned son against father, servant against master? 'And who art thou, sir?'

'Sir Francis Hearn,' I said, assuming a haughty mien, my chin held aloft. 'I have heard, sir, that thou art no stranger to the esoteric arts.'

He turned from me as if to take flight, saying: 'I know not of what you speak, my lord.'

'Fie, sir, come back!' I entreated him. 'Be not afraid! Master Hopkins' harsh witch-finding wind doth blow in the east, not here. I wish to hire thy services, not chastise thee for them. I would pay thee well …'

'Think you I am of the Devil's party?' he asked, turning upon his heel, his pale blue eyes still narrowed against me.

'Thou art Doctor John Pordage, art thou not?' I did press him.

'Aye, my lord,' said he. 'I have never denied this.'

'Wert thou not a curate in Reading and latterly rector of Bradfield?' I asked.

'Well, indeed,' he said, his downcast eyes closing further. 'What makes you of this, my lord?'

'Thy father was a merchant,' I said, lowering my countenance to try to catch his errant gaze. 'Bradfield is one of the richest livings in the realm. And yet thou art garbed like to a rude mechanic preacher. It must go hard with thee to exist so meanly after such high living.'

'I have no regrets,' he said. 'I have followed my conscience wheresoever it has led me, while you, my lord, have followed my career equally conscientiously.'

He smiled thinly.

'Be not saucy with me, sir!' I said. Then I softened my tone, pointing out that I could help alleviate his straitened circumstances.

'I have no need of thy gold, sir,' said he, adding an impudent, clownish 'thy' to his insult. 'The Lord provides…'

His pale lips formed another faint smile as his long arm did trace a half circle about him, pointing to the trees whose leaves did begin to shrivel around us in readiness for Autumn's shredding winds.

'Herne the Hunter is said to ride forth in these woods, protecting the King's game from the hungry poor. But the King is dead, so poor Herne wants employment. Dost thou think to usurp him, Sir Francis?'

I would not be provoked into another rage by his sauciness, but simply said: 'I can see a long day's ride to the Eastern counties awaits me. It shall be hard and I shall be saddle-sore at the end of it, but not as sore as thou shalt be when Master Sterne has finished with thee ...'

And I made as if to begin untying my horse.

'What makes you think I practise sorcery, my lord?' he asked.

'Were there not wondrous apparitions at your dwelling in Bradfield this harvest time just gone?' I put to him. 'Noisome poisonous smells? Loathsome, hellish tastes of sulphur?'

'Aye, aye, my lord,' he confirmed, 'but there were sweet, angelic fragrances and ambrosial flavours as well as those devilish ones you mentioned. I saw a giant with a great sword in his hand, a dragon with great teeth and open jaws whence he hurled fire at me. These wonders have made me take to the virgin's life, thus to avoid the kingdom of the Dragon. But these conjurations were none of my own doing.'

'Indeed, sir,' I said. 'Then whose were they?'

'I cannot say, my lord.'

'Very well,' I said. 'Thou sayest thou dost not need my gold, for the Lord provides. Or is it the Devil that does so? Hast thou discovered the secret of alchemy?'

At this, he gave a strange laugh, and said: 'Nay, my lord. Had I done so, all your gold would be as dross for being commonplace, as someday soon all that lucre shall be!'

And with that, he turned upon his heel and trudged onwards through the forest.

1999

She turned to see him close at her heels, silently appearing from the forest like a sprite. There was a strange smile upon his face, where blood bloomed in a hectic flush on his cheeks and also in spots that welled from a scratch along his jawline.

'Richard?'

His anorak was torn and there were patches of sweat staining the T-shirt underneath. His walking boots were daubed pale brown with wet mud, which also spattered the ankles of his jeans.

'Richard, what's happened to you? You look –'

'Like I've been dragged through a hedge backwards? But come and look what I've found …'

Something about the feverish light in his eyes made her hesitate, but she couldn't put her finger on what. Besides, she couldn't very well put her finger on anything, with her wrist now gripped tight in his fist as he pulled her towards his discovery.

She stared at the fluffy, pale-brown lumps, flecked with straw.

'Horse shit,' she said, rubbing her wrist, wondering if there'd be visible bruising on it, hating herself for worrying what Karen might think if there was. 'So what?' She couldn't be bothered to hide the annoyance in her voice. He blinked, but recovered quickly.

'I followed the trail though,' he grinned. 'Wait 'til you see what I found at the end of it!'

'I can't wait,' she said drily.

'You won't have to wait long,' he told her, in a tone of voice she didn't entirely like but tried to ignore. 'It's not far. Come on!'

She pulled her arm back from his attempt to grasp her wrist again, saying, 'It's all right, officer, I'll come quietly.'

He must have sensed the reproof behind her humour, for he said, 'Sorry, did I hurt you?'

'No! Not at all!'

'Don't know my own strength!' He let out a forced, nervous laugh.

'I'm not dressed for this,' she said, as he led her through a tangle of briars that caught on her skirt. 'Is it really as close as you said?'

'Yes, not far now,' he said, an edge of irritation in his

voice.

They carried on for a few minutes in a silence broken only by the snapping of twigs underfoot and the rustling of leaves as they pushed through the thick, damp vegetation. To Marisa, this didn't look like somewhere anyone would want to walk, let alone ride a horse. And yet the dung kept occurring at regular intervals. It was steaming.

'It's fresh,' Richard muttered. 'How about that …?'

When she failed to reply, he added: 'Makes you think, doesn't it?'

'What?' she said with a sigh.

'All sorts of things could go on round here without anyone knowing, hidden away behind all this growth …'

'Yeah,' she agreed, thinking of the old, moustached man hiding in a rented mansion not far from here, as if he'd followed her from her homeland. He no longer strutted around in his braided generalissimo's uniform, and was pleading age and ill health to avoid extradition.

All of a sudden, the space opened up. She saw the clearing and in its dim, bluish light what was hanging there.

1649

Deep in the heart of the woods, the trees do open up to form a glade where the sun's rays do penetrate but dimly. That is where he would have me meet him. Wherefore I can only guess. Perhaps this Everard, the true author of the apparitions visited upon Pordage, wishes to keep either his occult dabblings or his dealings with me a close secret, or both. I should have asked the man with the holes in his skull what spells he cast over those teeth that their issue plagues me as I think they do. But he was mad, now dead. My cruel nails must have penetrated further than I did think. So I can but hope that Everard hath the remedy, that he might disconnect the strands of the web that begins to enfold me.

1999

'Everard was the link between the Diggers and the Ranters. Christopher Hill said so!' Richard hissed, a strange, feverish lustre in his eyes in the dank shade of the clearing. 'You've read it, Marisa … Do you remember those passages?'

But Marisa wasn't really listening. Indeed she was wondering how he could ramble on about history books in a clearing hung with upside down corpses, though their faces weren't. She felt as if she didn't know him anymore, if she ever had.

'But don't you see?' he went on, as if he couldn't understand why her attention was focussed on the freakish charnel display instead of his monologue. 'Winstanley's God was Reason! Not so Coppe and his ilk … Their science was alchemy, prophecy! You did read Hill's book, didn't you? Didn't you?' His rant continued, as she failed to turn her gaze back towards him from the spindly, dangling arms turning slowly. 'You do remember the bit about Everard's magic show at Pordage's place, don't you?' He grabbed her shoulders, shaking them with the same febrile energy that burned in his eyes.

Then they softened, and he released them, leaving her wondering vaguely if they'd bruise like her wrist probably would. But not as much as she was wondering why the faces, each with a stark hole between the black eyes staring at her from the white, sexless bodies, were the right way up unlike the rest of the creatures.

'I'm sorry,' he said, and his voice sounded a little more like his old self, the one she thought she knew at least. 'I know I've been getting a bit obsessed with this film, a bit too far into the research side of it. It's just … Well, there's a special connection for me, a family connection, I believe!'

'Richard,' she said, her eyes widening at something out of his line of vision. 'Look!'

She didn't mean the shrunken parodies of humanity festooning the clearing, though that had been enough of a shock for her, sickening her to the core of her being both with their bizarre facial abnormalities and the casual inhumanity with which someone had strung them up like prize partridges. That someone, she suspected, was the figure now towering before her astride a black stallion, the branching latticework of a pair of antlers sprouting from his grimacing death's head, dark spots staining the huntsman's red coat, a rifle slung over the shoulder. The clearing suddenly felt dreadfully isolated.

1649

As I wait in this dread and lonely place, I feel a terrible burden upon my shoulders, for methinks I have indirectly become the progenitor of a terrible infestation upon the land. The nocturnal sounds in the woods near my house have increased of late, suggesting the creatures have multiplied, and this after I set about them with horse and hound. It may be that the measures I took to exterminate these pests have given them increase!

Where is this Everard?

The longer he delays his arrival, the more I do suspect he hath lured me here to ambush me with confederates and do me foul play. Nor would it be undeserved, for methinks I have done deeds of darkness for which I must answer before Heaven ere long. 'Twas with this belief in mind that lately I set myself to setting my house in order, with edicts to my issue on dealing with the monsters, though I fear my instructions may not be precise enough, so that they that come after me shall perpetuate the curse they mean to exorcise.

I hear noises now. Is that steel glinting in the shadows? I fear that whoever comes upon me thus shall leave garbed in scarlet.

1999

'Why's he wearing a red coat?' was all she could think of to say. She hoped that those weren't going to be her last words. What stupid last words those would be.

'Pink coat,' he corrected her.

'OK. Why's he wearing a pink coat?' she asked. 'And shouldn't he have dogs then?' she added, by way of another irrelevant question, since ignoring the dangling elephants in the room seemed to be the order of the day, though anything less like elephants she had difficulty imagining. What *were* they like? That was the trouble. The slaughtered creatures with their topsy-turvy heads were like nothing she'd ever seen before, neither man nor beast. Neither man nor woman either, their blank groins suggested, nor born of man or woman, their navel-less bellies told her.

'Not dogs. Hounds.'

It was the muffled, echoing voice behind what she now understood to be an antlered skull mask. There was an odd look of recognition in her boyfriend's haunted eyes at the sound of the voice.

'It's traditional to ride to hounds of course,' it said, 'but they proved rather counter-productive. You see, they're rather like bindweed – and after all, the vermin did grow out of the ground. When the pack ripped the creatures up, you just got more of the damn things!'

The dam holding back Marisa's rising gorge finally burst. It seemed like an age since she and Richard had shared the picnic lunch she now watched spatter the already-sodden leaf mould at her feet.

The newcomer went on: 'Tradition, ritual. These are important things for our sort, eh, Richard?'

The young man he was addressing looked up with dawning understanding; somehow Marisa now thought of him as 'the young man', a stranger, not her boyfriend. Something told her she must get away from this awful place, run, but in which direction? There might be more of those things out there, and though she pitied these dead ones, she couldn't face meeting a live one face to upside-down face.

'Our school had its initiation rites, though of course I imagine they'd watered them down by your time, my boy! That's political correctness for you … This particular ritual's been going on since the seventeenth century, though we've had to … not water it down exactly … Adapt it, for more practical reasons; so no hounds, just a bullet between the eyes. Bit quick, but far more efficient …'

'Uncle Percy!' Richard gasped.

The antlers shook as the huntsman nodded his head. 'But I've always thought of you more as a son to me, not having children of my own. Listen, lad, not to put too fine a point on it – your old man's going to pop his clogs soon, so how's this for an idea. Why not come and join me in the family business?'

'What? Stockbroking?' said Richard with an incredulous laugh.

'No, no, no!' said his uncle, suddenly whipping his rifle from his shoulder, taking aim and firing at the source of a rustling from the edge of the clearing, the report followed by a mewling whimper like that of a beaten dog, a sound more terrible than anything Marisa had ever heard before, even in Chile. Then, the silence was broken only by Uncle Percy's muffled breathing inside the mask. 'Pest control. You'd need a bit of training of course. Reactions and a sure aim like mine don't come overnight. Sure you'd pick it up though. Right sort of stock.' He slung the rifle back on his back, then added: 'Well, boy? What do you say?'

Richard lowered his eyes, and Marisa saw him glancing nervously in her direction, as if for support or advice. Maybe he wasn't such a stranger after all.

'Richard!' she whispered to him, instantly regretting it as the antlered death's head turned in her direction, as if the huntsman had noticed her for the first time. 'You're not like him!'

'Oh, but he is. Same stock, you see. I'm sorry. We haven't been introduced. Richard? Who's your lady friend? Not from round here, is she?'

She gave a contemptuous little laugh, and was glad her fear was giving way to anger and contempt. She guessed he was directing his jibe at her hint of an accent and her dark colouring.

'She's right,' said Richard, his eyes narrowed. 'I'm not like you.'

'Look, I understand the need to rebel. Everyone's a bit of a lefty when they're young. Even I grew my hair long and dabbled in a bit of pot during my misspent youth. But there comes a time when you have to put aside childish things, decide which side you're on. There's a war going on out here, you see. Our illustrious ancestor, Sir Francis Hearn, understood that, so he took steps to try to remedy the situation. These wretched creatures were the unfortunate by-product. They're not all bad of course. As long as you keep the population down and give the remainder what they want, some of them can even be quite useful.'

'What are you talking about?' Richard asked.

'Come on,' said Marisa, trying to take his arm, though it felt unyielding. 'Let's go. Your uncle's obviously insane.'

'I wouldn't expect you to understand,' he said to her, then addressed Richard again: 'The Civil War never ended. It just went cold. As you probably know, Sir Francis went missing at some point around that time, so it was left to his descendants to try to control their spread. *Noblesse oblige*, if you will! As I said, it's possible to domesticate some of them, but they still need feeding. Now if you wouldn't mind helping me restrain your lady-friend ...'

'You leave her out of this!' Richard said, his eyes narrowing, but his uncle just laughed at his heroics, a horrible hollow sound reverberating behind his skeletal mask.

'Come now, Richard,' he said. 'I know she's a bit of a looker in a swarthy sort of way, but surely you understand that ties of blood outweigh such considerations!'

The look of uncertainty in Richard's eyes was enough.

She gave up any thought of trying to persuade him to escape with her, and bolted for it. She had to put herself first, and couldn't be sure that he would choose her over his family with its terrible legacy. This thought drove her through the brambles and branches, tearing her clothes, until the foliage grew sparser. All she had to do was keep going, though her breath came in gasps and her skin stung where thorns had torn at her as though the long, straggling, pale-green blackberry shoots were themselves agents of Richard's unhinged uncle, devoid of human consciousness, yet possessed of a weird intelligence. Didn't he say that the creatures had grown from the ground like 'bindweed', whose roots their pale, spindly limbs resembled, implying they were actually plants of some kind?

Now that she was out of the passageway that led to the clearing, she dismissed such thoughts from her mind. Whatever she'd seen, or thought she'd seen, must simply be the result of the huntsman's demented power of suggestion. She'd worked in mental hospitals in the past, and knew how persuasive some of the patients with psychosis could be, drawing you into their delusions by sheer force of will.

But she had seen those creatures, hadn't she?

Nevertheless, now she was out of the clearing and his sphere of influence, it all seemed so unreal. She couldn't even hear a hue and cry of pursuit. All she had to do was somehow get back to civilisation. Not that it was far away. London wasn't much more than a stone's throw away after all. It would seem a lot further on foot of course, but she'd manage it. If her mother could escape from Pinochet's Chile, she could surely get out of some woods in the Home Counties of England. Maybe she could break into Richard's car and get that going, but right now she just had to put as much distance as possible between her and that madman on the horse.

She climbed the stile and was back in the open field with the gorse bushes.

A man stepped out from behind one of them.

He was wearing a flat cap, a tweed waistcoat and a collarless shirt, for all the world like an old-fashioned gamekeeper. She assumed the strange, paddle-shaped stick he was carrying was for beating pheasants out of the bushes or something. But the most notable thing about him was that his hat was perched on a chin that pointed skyward.

Then she remembered what Uncle Percy had said about 'domesticating' and 'feeding' some of the creatures. No wonder he hadn't bothered to chase her.

She was about to make a break for it to get past the man, whose grim frown was actually a terrible smile, when another one stepped out from behind a gorse bush, blocking off that potential escape route.

Then another one appeared from another direction. And another one. She spun round to see others closing in on her from behind, all carrying the paddles, which she now saw were studded at the end, like meat tenderisers.

They'd need them, the last rational thought in her head told her, with those toothless, black mouths, which had begun sucking in expectation, leaving her wondering what form their 'feeding' might take.

KNOCKING KNOLL

An eerie tale comes to us from Shillington, a farming community on the Bedfordshire / Hertfordshire border, which concerns a large circular barrow that has long been a central feature of the district.

There have always been curious legends concerning 'Knocking Knoll', as it is known, but they appeared to reach their height in the mid-19th century, when enthusiastic treasure hunters took it on themselves to cut the knoll open. Most stories connected to the site hold that, throughout the ages, villagers and farmworkers, few of whom were comfortable in the vicinity of this enigmatic landmark, had reported the sound of someone knocking deep inside it. The knoll is about 14 feet high and approximately 45 feet in diameter, while its composition must mainly be earth and stone, so how such sounds could be heard in the outside world has never been completely established, though in the realm of supernatural tales logical explanations for the weird are seldom required.

If there was any story behind the creepy rumour it was that an ancient but unnamed king or chieftain had been laid to rest there and for some reason best known to himself was now seeking to return to the world. The extensive presence on the knoll of the purple pasque flower, Anemone pulsatilla, which in rural English tradition was said to grow thickly at sites where Danish blood had been shed, connected it in the minds of many with the Vikings. However, there was also a belief in Victorian times that most mounds and knolls of antique origin were creations of the Celts, even though many of them are much older than that, so it was also felt possible that this mysterious king had been an Ancient Briton. An alternative myth held that, whoever he was, he had buried his treasure in the knoll, and occasionally his invisible spirit would return, enter the structure and to check that his concealed caskets were still full, strike them repeatedly with the flat of his hand.

In due course, the latter story excited more than antiquarian interest, and in 1856 a bunch of amateur excavators took it on themselves to dig around the site, uncovering a few seemingly worthless Bronze Age trinkets, which at least put paid to the Viking theory. The fortune hunters went away disappointed, but according to a magazine feature 40 years later, local villagers claimed that the very night after the amateur excavation was abandoned, a spectral figure in heavy armour was seen approaching what remained of the mound and beating the top of it with the pommel of his sword, knocking to ensure that the echo from within indicated that his treasures were still in place, and then drifting away as a skein of summer mist.

Knocking Knoll, or 'Money Knoll' or even 'Bump Hillock' depending on which of the locals you talk to, is not quite the dominant feature on the landscape that it once was. Modern intensive farming methods have damaged it considerably, but thanks to its long-lasting paranormal associations, it remains a visitor attraction for folklorists and the like.

TAKING TUSK MOUNTAIN
Allen Ashley

I was hopeful that I had started to turn my life around. My new girlfriend Mel – and, perhaps just as much so, her cute and chatty six year old son Leo – were a part of this new-found optimism. My employment situation was still best described as 'intermittent' but I would soon be out of the contract on my flat in a scrubby part of Luton and ensconced with Mel so money wouldn't be quite as tight.

On the other hand, there were my mate Brandon's schemes. Go along with them and I'd be quids in. They were illegal, of course. But victimless … apparently. Sure-fire? Naturally.

'Nah, I've been burned before, Brandon. Count me out.'

Brandon looked at the dregs of his Jaeger bomb and then directly at me as if debating which was the more pathetic. 'Trouble with you, Jason, is you too often look a gift horse in the mouth. You're too much of a pussy … cat.'

'Listen, I don't regret those pranks we got up to back in the day but … my record is wiped clean now. I want to stay out of trouble for Mel's sake. And for Leo.'

'He's not even your kid. Wow, you really have got it bad. Like a moon-eyed moon cow, all lovey dovey.'

'You're just jealous, Brand.'

'No way. Love 'em and leave 'em's what I say. Don't even love 'em if you can help it. Anyway, think about the scheme, eh? You know you'll come round to it. And after that, I'm working on a secret plan called Tusk Mountain.'

I laughed into my beer. 'And you say I'm the dreamer.'

The king of the jungle surveyed his entourage and said, 'Yes, I may have to kill to feed my family but I don't kill unnecessarily. With great power comes great responsibility. It is my duty to look after my subjects.'

Leo screwed up his face a while before smiling and saying, 'I think he was the good guy.'

'Very much so,' I answered. 'Time for shut-eye now, though.'

I wondered what dreams he might have when he finally settled. Often they seemed to be some sort of amalgam of *The Lion King*, *Bambi* and *Dumbo* – all favourite downloads that we'd watched together in the few months that I'd been seeing his mother.

I tiptoed into the kitchen where Melissa was busy clearing away dishes. 'Are you hungry?' she asked. 'I can make you some vegetarian pasta bake.'

I leaned across and kissed the top of her head. Her hair smelled of mango shampoo. I could close my eyes and become an animal padding through the edge of the warm jungle.

Pulling back, I had the impression that her light brown, very loose Afro caught the kitchen light with a halo effect, making her look like Aslan. Yes Aslan was male and Melissa was very definitely female. It was a bit of a worrying comparison. I should get some fresh air.

'I need to pop out and see Brandon,' I answered. 'He wants to tell me about his latest scheme to make some quick cash.'

'I don't trust him, Jason; he'll get you into trouble.'

'He's my oldest friend.'

'And? Romulus and Remus were brothers. So were King Richard and King Henry.'

'It was Richard the Lionheart and King John.'

'Whoever. I've just got your back, is all.'

'I won't be late,' I muttered, pulling on my old leather jacket.

Would this be what a long-term relationship would be like? Maybe it wouldn't be too bad at all – someone always caring.

We were meeting in a pub called The Fox and Grapes. I

doubted that the brewery knew the Aesop reference. Previously it had been The Hen and Farmer and once, rather briefly, The Strangled Cockerel. It was within cheering distance of Kenilworth Road, home of my boyhood football team Luton Town. As much as I was glad to see the Hatters moving back up the divisions, I had somewhat fallen out of love with them lately as a contingent of their fans had started chanting their support for Tommy Robinson, leader of the English Defence League. Melissa was of mixed heritage and so, of course, was Leo. She'd faced enough grief for her skin colour without the local football wannabe hooligans creating even more.

The situation summed up my ambivalence about my neighbourhood. I'd grown up and always lived in this tough part of Bedfordshire and felt a loyalty to the area but you couldn't be surprised at anyone bypassing us and staying on the M1 all the way to London.

Brandon had just a trickle of beer left in his pint glass when I arrived so it was down to me to get the next round in. He was intent on something on his smartphone.

'Look at this, Jase. I mean, talk about sex and death. I can barely stop the table from levitating!'

I focused on the image. A white woman in combat gear, dyed blonde hair, automatic rifle at her feet and the draped carcass of a juvenile giraffe around her shoulders. It was horrible and certainly didn't give me the horn.

'She'll get crucified on Facebook,' I stated.

'Ah, Feckbook. Just think about being faced with the power and might of one of these beasts, a rampaging elephant or a stampeding rhino and you only have your rifle between you and certain death. What a buzz. Which reminds me, Jase, I have more details about my little scheme that's going to make us rich.'

'I'm not shooting any elephants. Or giraffes or nothing. I like African wildlife.'

Brandon snorted into the froth at the top of his lager. 'You won't be popping your pistol at Dumbo, dummy, don't you worry about it. Thing is, Chinese Charlie's got a contact who's after some ivory. And I know where to get it.'

Chinese Charlie was about as Cantonese as a plate of Peking wildebeest. I don't know how he acquired the nickname. Doubtless some casually racist term of endearment from our spotty teenage years.

'Right, Jase, lean in and listen. I told you I'd tell you about Tusk Mountain. So, ZSL – the Zoological Society of London, don't you know? – have recently been collecting stacks of elephant tusks, rhino horn and similar from the glory days of the safari. It's in a temporary storeroom at Whipsnade and I hear they haven't started cataloguing it yet. I mean, they're just asking for somebody to take it off their hands.'

'But, hang on, that will all be old stuff, ivory well past its sell-by date. You can't crush that up for medicine, it will probably kill people.'

'Not our problem, pal. And don't get all squeamish on me, this is a victimless crime. All those rhinoceroses, elephants, walruses, mastodons, whatever are long gone to dust so why shouldn't we make a little profit out of their leftovers?'

'We're not going to harm any living creatures? Leo would never forgive me.'

'These guys are decades dead, you soft vegan pillock. I mean, I'm not above poisoning or clubbing a vicious guard dog if it's life and death but … the money on offer is mind-boggling.'

'How much? … Really? What's your plan, Brandon?'

And the white lion said, 'I am not a cruel creature but, day or night, I will patrol and protect my kingdom. Woe betide any who cross my path. These will be your final steps …'

'Wot's "woe beside", Uncle Jason?'

'It's "woe betide", Leo. It means watch out because you're in big trouble. In the story. I think … some of the language is a bit too grown-up. Maybe we should put this book aside for a while.'

'No, please, I love it. I want to grow up to be a white lion. Or a brown or yellow one and lead an army of animals.'

'I thought you wanted to be a footballer. Anyhow, come on, it's lights-out time.'

Melissa gave me a huge hug as I joined her in the kitchen. 'He keeps you longer every night,' she said. 'You know I really like you, Jason, but … it's even more important that you and Leo hit it off.' She disengaged, slipped back into her apron and began serving dinner. 'It's Quorn and lentils. And lots of veg.'

'Food is the way to a man's heart,' I answered. I wasn't missing cheap meat but I still craved the occasional treat of chili con carne or rump steak.

'I thought you'd be working tonight.'

'They didn't need me. Warehouse isn't very busy at the moment.'

'That means you don't get paid, though. I picked up this leaflet at the supermarket. It's a government thing – "Fresh Beginnings". "Get paid and learn a new trade" is what it says.'

'It would be nice to get paid properly for all the skills I've already got. Also, I may be doing some work with Brandon over the next few days.'

'Be careful with that, Jase. I know he's your mate an' all but … let's just say not all his schemes are strictly legit.'

I didn't want her worrying about me. It was enough that I was worrying about myself. I'd had a couple of awkward moments as a teen but those charges were 'spent' now. And they'd been 'civil' not criminal matters. Brandon had told me the job couldn't go wrong, he just needed a wingman. I didn't want to scupper my future with a criminal record. But if you didn't get caught and no-one else knew … then there was no record.

I finished a slow chew, like an ox with a tough tuft of grass, before I answered, 'It's just some fetching and carrying, hon. I'm clearly the man for the job. You've felt my muscles.'

She giggled, poured herself some Evian and I managed to avoid her gaze.

Brandon was my longest-lasting friend – we went back all the way to the upper stages of primary school. Shared history is always a bond; yet sometimes I wondered whether we really had that much in common anymore.

'I hear they're going to reopen The Panther Lounge,' he stated. 'No bands or DJs this time. Gonna be a strip club. Should save up your pennies for a good night out.'

'Not into it, mate. Melissa wouldn't approve.'

'Whoa, she's got you right pinned by the apron strings, or whatever the expression is. When am I gonna meet her?'

'Probably not any time soon.'

'You got a photo, Jase?'

I pulled up a couple of images on my phone. I watched him pull a weasel face and chew his lip like he had some distressing news to impart.

'Well?'

'She's got a nice smile. But not my type. I mean, I like a big brown arse as much as the next guy but she's a bit well-padded around the mid-rift.'

'It's midriff. No "t". I don't know whether to be relieved or offended. I thought you shagged any female with a pulse.'

'That's just the journey, Jase. I have this recurring dream where I meet her, you know, the one. She's got these big brown doe eyes that melt you. And when she swings those supple hips … wow.'

'Decent fantasy.'

'But I've seen her once or twice. In real life. Not enough to catch her attention but I know now she's truly out there. Somewhere in the wilds of Luton, Dunstable, Bedfordshire …'

We returned to our pints. I decided to feel sorry for my old pal. I had found Melissa and – fuck it, I worshipped her. But

Brandon was still pissing away his life searching for Doe the Deer Woman.

We were ready to go on a recce to Whipsnade when my phone buzzed. Brandon.

'We'll have to postpone by a day,' he stated. 'Some people are getting married and having a late-running wedding reception at the conference centre. How inconsiderate. Honestly, who would get married in a zoo?'

'Maybe Melman the giraffe and Gloria the hippo or Marty the zebra from *Madagascar*.'

'You watch too many kids' films, I don't know why I hang out with you. Be ready tomorrow.'

At a loose end, I popped back to my grotty flat, put a few more possessions into cardboard boxes ahead of shipping them over to Melissa's or into temporary storage. Then I phoned work and was offered a four-hour shift. Putting things into cardboard boxes before shipping them out.

I stayed over at Mel's. Leo was already asleep when I arrived. I loved the warm comfort of Mel's body next to mine but I must have been overtired because I had a run of strange dreams about being a prehistoric man hunting wild boar and sabretooths; except very soon they were hunting me. I was calling out warnings in a prehistoric language of grunts and clicks not that dissimilar to animal calls. Melissa shook me awake. I was sweating.

'You're not used to my spicy home cooking,' she said.

Even though all I'd eaten was a sandwich from Tesco Metro on the way home.

Reconnoitre Day.

I was always amazed to see Brandon's beaten-up old Volvo still functioning. Whether it was actually roadworthy was another matter. As we sat in traffic, I shared some of my research on the history of ZSL Whipsnade: the date it opened, its acreage, the number of species represented. I told him all about the giant chalk lion carved into the Downs: the aerial symbol of the zoo and also in some ways its protective mascot. I even added the details of how my parents remembered its patron Peter Scott and his programme *Survival* as a TV staple from their childhood. Blimey, I could have taken Whipsnade as my specialist subject on *Mastermind.* The criminal mastermind in the driving seat had other concerns, though.

'You print out those maps?' he barked.

'Sure.'

'And bring those sketchbooks and pencils in case we need a cover story?'

I grunted. I didn't want to tell him that I had the artistic abilities of a two-month old chimpanzee.

'Listen, Jase, this job can't go wrong. It's my scheme, so I may take the lion's share but you'll get a more than decent cut. I saw you all right with those iPhones, didn't I?' Yeah, until the screens came loose, I sub-vocalised. 'I'm not gonna drive into Whipsnade,' he continued. 'It's not the expense but … you know those TV shows they have on at eleven in the morning? They always catch people through number plate recognition. So, we'll park in the overspill and then leg it round the zoo.'

'There's a complimentary bus service,' I piped up.

'We need to be on foot to find what we need to find, Jase. Pay attention. I'm top dog on this.'

It was an odd afternoon when we finally got to Whipsnade. Part of me was simply set on enjoying seeing the animals up close, whereas part of me was in tune with Brandon's demands to take note of any clues or information that would determine where the loot lay in this vast, breeze-blown expanse. To keep up appearances, we made a couple of sketches in the giraffe house and at Cheetah Rock. Splotchy, patchy skin suited for camouflage. I couldn't see my effort troubling the judges for next year's Royal Academy showing.

I think Brandon might have been happier planning a bank heist. He moaned constantly – about the mud, the cold wind, the rich and foetid animal smells in several of the enclosures. And his aching feet. We jumped on the striped bus, stayed on for a couple of circuits, sitting on the top deck on a level with the vultures, eyes peeled for private portacabins and tucked away research labs. Eventually, our grumbling stomachs forced us off again in search of overpriced refreshments. Even then, Brandon's cup of tea was too watery and his chips too crispy. He was being about as much fun as a polluted fish tank and I told him so.

'I should've brought little Leo with me. He would appreciate seeing all the wildlife.'

'He'd probably be more use than you. But you'd have to bunk him off school. Come on, let's make another tour.'

As we exited the refectory, a gust wetly warmed my face and I heard a low growl – sustained, resonant, rumbling through my body as well as bothering the eardrums. Probably from the *Lions of the Serengeti* enclosure.

'Your stepson would like this,' Brandon muttered.

I wanted to say that he wasn't my stepson as yet but instead watched as the green-shirted keepers marched a line of elephants along the tarmac. Trunks and tails intertwined, it really was like a scene from *The Jungle Book*.

'Let's follow,' Brandon said, sore toes currently forgotten.

Soon we were at the further edge of the park, near the white rhino, just beyond a café closed for the winter and close to where the Downs rolled away beneath our vantage point.

'The chalk lion I told you about is just down that way,' I stated.

'Shh, stop. What's that guy doing?'

A young man in a liveried fleece was carrying a plastic crate. The wind – stronger here – whipped his cap off and he put down his burden in order to chase and retrieve it. I sauntered past the box and – yep, there it was: a jumbled pile of tusks and horns. Jackpot. Brandon busied himself in the shrubbery, bending down as if he'd mislaid something. We watched zoo guy pick up the crate again and head off towards – oh, double Euromillions winner! – a hut partway down the hill. He fiddled with a small padlock then disappeared inside.

The look on Brandon's face could have lit up the whole of Oxford Street. He was still beaming when the zookeeper arrived back in our vicinity and said, 'Can I help you guys?'

'Oh, I dropped my phone,' I answered. 'I was taking a picture of one of those reindeer you have running around.'

'Muntjac,' he responded. 'Too small for Santa's sleigh.'

'Hey, Ja – er, John,' Brandon called. 'I found your Samsung.'

'Oh, uh, great stuff, Br – Bill.' Then to fleece boy: 'I got some shots of them kangaroos as well.'

'Wallabies,' he muttered.

Life had grown even tougher in Luton and its surroundings over the past several years. Austerity, council cutbacks and the shifting global economy had turned once-thriving high streets of independent shops and acceptable retail chains into hollow funnels of boarded-up windows, punctuated by occasional clusters of takeaways, tattoo parlours and Cash Converters. Sure, I'd flogged them a couple of old laptops and my once-prized shiny school days trumpet. I was off the habit now but ten years of weed, tobacco and vaping had taken its toll.

The downturn and divisions had been exacerbated by the Brexit vote in 2016. I loved my parents dearly but their view of Britain seemed to have been forged some time at the cusp of victory in 'The War' and just before the loss of Empire. Neither of them had even been born then, of course.

I know they had placed their hopes on me and I wish I'd been able to do more with the qualifications and skills I had. I wish I'd had enough money or the debt-accruing effrontery to complete my history degree. But …

If you were local – and, really, this area was hardly a Mecca for tourists – you knew the places to avoid. That needle-strewn alley, this shortcut to Hades; cross to the other side of the road as the leery teen lads congregated in and around a favourite fried-chicken shop, like squabbling hyenas over a kill.

I was on call for a warehouse job. Sometimes this meant working through the night; other times I was twiddling my thumbs or overdosing on *Assassin's Creed* through jobless days.

At least Melissa was understanding. We'd met when I got some cash in hand work doing a bit of plastering and decorating and the like at her dad's place. He was an ex-boxer, a gentle giant with a calm demeanour. And here was his daughter – divorced, early thirties, no boob jobs or Kardashian fixation – bringing me cups of unsugared tea and chatting about songs, politics and museums she'd one day like to visit. I cancelled my Tinder subscription before I'd even asked her out properly.

We've had homeless people and street beggars since I can remember. But even they seem to have changed their tune of late. Where once they might have huddled in a piss-ridden shop doorway along with a duvet and a dog on a string, now one of them was on his not so sprightly feet, half-following and calling out to me, 'Hey, son, steer clear. Don't get involved.'

Was he retraining as a life coach? Would you take advice from this grizzled old sucker with a shock of leonine white hair around his head?

As I reached the corner of Mel's street, I saw a car pull up a few doors down, its windows tinted against the darkness, its low thrum of bass music attracting a couple of youngsters in hoodies keen to score a wrap or a rock. I resolved again that I would do whatever it took to get us out of this dodgy neighbourhood, even if it meant co-piloting Brandon's fantastical get rich quick schemes.

She gave me a peck on the lips, wrinkled her cute brown nose and said, 'You smell of the great outdoors. And …

animals?'

'Oh, we had a package to deliver. To a farm.'

'Jason, you're … not being some sort of drugs mule, are you?'

I laughed. 'I'm not any kind of mule, babe, you know that. Hee-haw! And there's no cocaine shoved up my arse to fool airport security.'

'Hmm. Seems to me you know a little too much about those processes.'

I had bought Leo a toy plastic lion from the souvenir shop. He felt its solid weight in his small hand but was gazing at it rather doubtfully.

'Don't you like it, little guy?'

'It should be white like the one in the story.'

'Most lions are yellowy-brown, you know.'

'I'll get some of Mummy's make-up and paint it. Thank you. What shall we call him?'

'The same as the one in the stories: Rex. It's Latin – Ancient Roman – for king.'

He gave me a big hug.

Heist Night.

'This is their weak spot, security-wise,' Brandon stated. 'You've got to be a nutter to climb up this hill past the chalk lion and break in this way.'

'We're certainly that.'

'Here – take one of these masks.'

I chose a fox. He went with a tiger. It was hard enough and dark enough finding our way without the encumbrance of a cardboard face-covering with tiny slits for eyeholes.

'We can remove them when we get up the hill and beyond the perimeter CCTV cameras. Come on, Let's climb. Oh and keep silent. Understood?'

I pictured myself as Tom Cruise in a new chapter of

Mission Impossible. But then he'd have been helicoptered in or swung in on wires like some macho human spider. Just focus on maintaining your footing, Jason.

At least the wind had dropped a little. At one stage, the Moon broke free from her cloud prison and shone her silvery love down upon the recently restored chalk lion. I could see one of its limbs and it seemed to shiver and move. As if there wasn't enough actual danger already abroad, now I was conjuring supernatural felines.

Keep moving. Think of the treasure I was going to stash in the expandable holdall strapped to my back.

An increase in the strength of the wind carried further cries and scents into our senses. I was sure I could see animals moving about on the periphery of my vision. During the day they had a couple of free-ranging species – wallabies and muntjac – so maybe they didn't tether them up at night, either. Nothing to worry about.

'We should've come properly tooled up, not just a big wrench,' said Brandon. 'Here, grab one of those branches from that pile. Whack anything that comes your way.'

I kept my gloves on, wary of leaving fingerprints on the dark wood. Not that I was 'known' to the rozzers. Unless … there had been that time way back in primary school when a community policeman had given a talk in assembly and then invited everybody in my class to ink their thumbs on his spare charge sheet. Would they have preserved that somehow? No, I was surely being paranoid. And there was a more pressing concern:

'Brandon, are you certain we're headed in the right direction? This is a big and confusing place.'

'I've got a phone app. It's retracing our footsteps.'

'You numpty! They'll have a tracker on your phone or GPS or something. We're done for.'

'Shut up, Jason, and trust me for once. Anyhow, once I sell that ivory, I'm gonna upgrade to the latest Apple iPhone. And change my number.'

He hadn't reassured me. Even when his geographical tool brought us in sight of what looked like the right store room, I still had my doubts.

A deep, throaty growl punched holes in the air.

'Shit,' I said.

'Try not to,' Brandon replied.

The king lion gathered all his subjects together with one mighty proclamation. Many shivered in fear at such close proximity. Life was short and precious and maybe today, perhaps tomorrow, certainly not too far down the line, the king would be taking a few of them to fill his meat larder. For now, though, he had other concerns:

'There is conflict in the land of people,' he announced. 'This is of a greater significance than their usual petty squabbles, which impact on us quite enough. We are all in grave danger and it is necessary for us all to go under cover and into hiding. This may remain the situation for many revolutions of the sun. Those of you who can hibernate should do so. For the rest of you: the most important matter is not to be visible from the air.'

'They have wings now?' one of the hyenas interrupted.

'They have had flying contraptions for more than a generation of their kind. They use them to drop deathly fire on each other's settlements. Do not ask me why; the humans' ways are inscrutable even to one as wise as I. But it means we must vacate the hill. Be neither seen nor heard nor smelt. This man-conflict – something they term a "World War" – will one day end. I hope we all survive long enough to greet that happy day.'

Even Brandon was starting to get spooked by now.

'What was that?' he asked. 'It sounded like a retriever being strangled by a goose with the stomach of a polar bear.'

Madly, his description felt accurate. I didn't want to indulge in 'I told you so' but I found myself muttering, 'We should have chosen a fully moonlit night or come in the summer when the skies are lighter.'

'Stuff will be gone by then. Man up, you pussy, and keep an eye out for guards or cameras.'

I kept the beam of my torch facing down so as not to reveal our features. This part of the zoo was covered in scrubby grass with the occasional bush or bramble. At least the weather had been dry of late so not much mud.

We would have to pretty much exactly retrace our steps with our booty. Brandon claimed the app on his phone would enable us to do so tread for tread. I wasn't entirely sure that I believed him.

Once again, I felt a warm breath on my neck and face. Could have just been the breeze but it felt like it had a tang of animal about it. I tried not to make my turning around and squinting all about too obvious. I couldn't see or hear anyone or anything other than ourselves in the immediate vicinity. Yet I sort of perceived accompanying movements. Like we were being tracked. Or stalked.

'Come on, Jase, keep up. Christ, I shoulda done this on my own …'

There was the warm, meaty breath. There was the throat-catching smell of sweaty pits and pelts. The sound of softly padding feet – no, *paws* – keeping track with us, ready to intercept soon.

In the best tradition of some sci-fi or horror film tag line, we were not alone. And I didn't mean muntjacs or marsupials.

I realised that I was lagging a little behind Brandon and his brazen bubble of bravado. Would there be safety in numbers or was I subtly letting the leader be the sacrifice?

And I could see flashes of white amongst the trees and the other surroundings – fences, footpaths, enclosures. It was not an effect of the fickle moonlight. The only description that fitted properly was: ghostly. An old, lined, chalky face surrounded by a dandelion halo of hair. I knew him. From books, from dreams … from real life. He opened his mouth and where I expected a roar, instead I heard some throaty words:

'Jason, turn around. This is not a place you should be.'

But where should I be? I felt half in one world – Brandon's get rich quick zoo heist – and half in another – a sort of Disney on drugs where an ancient white lion spoke into my brain without actually making a sound.

Somehow, my legs had carried me forward and we were at the hut. Brandon had the big wrench in his hands and was about to make mincemeat of the padlock.

Oblivious to my visions, he said, 'Right, keep an eye out. Let me know if you see or hear anything.'

The lion was gathering his subjects around him. Yet Brandon was unaware of this hypnotic activity. If I told him, he would just think me mad and probably save one swing of the wrench to knock some sense into my head.

A couple of ear-splitting clangs then the combined sound of the padlock falling and the thin wooden door giving way.

We were in, like Howard Carter stumbling into King Tut's tomb.

Like hungry rodents walking into a trap.

Surrounded. Optionless.

Brandon even had the gall to flick on the light switch.

'Here we go,' he crowed. 'Look at those tusks. Right gives me the horn, ha-ha!'

The place was a bit of a mess with boxes and containers of specimens, scientific equipment, journals, DVDs, USB sticks and the like all arranged higgledy-piggledy. Brandon's eagle eyes had spotted what we'd come for and he was busy sorting out swag before I'd even remembered to breathe. Should it have been this easy? Howard Carter found Tutankhamun's treasures stacked floor to ceiling and retrieved the crowning glory of the death mask pretty early on. But then the curse struck.

I could hear animals – creatures – gathering outside the hut. We were sitting ducks; but not for the mundane enemy we might have expected.

'Come and help, for fuck's sake, Jason.'

The pieces were lighter, sometimes yellower, often smoother and shinier than I had anticipated. A few were already fortuitously protected by bubble wrap and as that weighed almost nothing I used it in my re-packing so as to prevent any unfortunate breakages. There were what I took to be rhino horns, elephant and walrus tusks, even some beautifully curved and edged African antelope horns. Everything went into the holdall.

It was when I picked up a brown-stained, slightly chipped canine tooth that I had the weirdest experience. Like in a sci-fi film or some clever video, everything around me froze. Brandon's hands paused mid-air, his haul precarious. My vision misted and after several moments – moments *out of time* – I perceived the off-white craggy face of an ancient lion, hair matted and eyes a little milky but still inherently regal. I understood then that the brand new hill carving was just for show, a snazzy piece of much-needed publicity for the wildlife park. But the old chalk lion was still around and just about active and it was he who was protecting all those left in his charge. I had encountered his history in the books I was reading to Leo; I had even met his avatar through the homeless guy near Luton railway station. He hadn't said, 'Hey, son!' No, it was definitely, 'Ja-son.'

A calm came over me like sinking into a warm, tropical pool. However things turned out, I would be all right. To an extent, at least.

Everyday survival should always be counted as a victory.

I didn't notice the moment when all the gears started clicking again but suddenly Brandon was busy once more and my own fingers grabbed the last of the loot.

'Let's scuttle,' Brandon suggested.

We pulled back the door and emerged not into searchlights but not into complete darkness either. Like some sort of ghostly projection against the scrubby trees at the top of the hill, I could perceive brief dioramas of hunting and safaris. The majority of times, the humans came out on top and the noble beasts fell and were hefted away as trophies. I didn't really need to be shown this, I knew it as self-evident history. When the pictures cleared, I could see lines of magnificent wild animals parading away into the distance like a spectral army. I would mourn each one if I had the energy but what good would that do?

At last I was transfixed by the watery gaze of the old chalk lion himself. Should I bow or abase myself? Running seemed futile.

Brandon broke the spell with an exclaimed, 'Hey, there she is!'

There who was? In the periphery, I caught a glimpse of doe eyes, a brown rump and my erstwhile companion hurrying off through the long grass in search of his own personal nirvana. Wow, I mean, hang on, heck, that was straight out of left field!

'It's the dream,' Brandon cooed; and then he was off on the chase.

Brandon … WTF? We were supposed to stick together but now he'd run off after Deer-Woman and …

What next for me?

I was licked. Breathed upon. Pushed gently but firmly by tough paws with the sharp nails temporarily tucked away.

I walked. I stumbled. I progressed. I retraced my steps through the half-darkness. I slipped and slid when I reached the hill. Lost my incriminating holdall at some hapless point.

I don't remember all the details of how I made it home to a concerned but solicitous Melissa. I was walking in dark, muddy clothes along an unlit country road. One unlucky moment or one encounter with the local boy racers and I would be as dead as the dodo.

Someone stopped and gave me a lift, claiming to have recognised me from the sleazy club The Panther Room way back in the decade. I think I spun him some line about having DJed there a couple of times. His eyes were as wide as saucers and, though I was glad about whatever happy drug he was on that made him want to help me, I might have been safer taking my chances as a solitary, nocturnal pedestrian.

Home sweet home. Well, Melissa's flat. I blabbered something about how much I loved her and that I wanted to adopt Leo.

'You already have,' she grinned. Then: 'Listen, I know you're tired but you need to freshen up in the bathroom before I let you under the duvet. You smell like the giraffe house.'

And with the intrusion of the mundane world, the reckless adventure and the grand heist were effectively over and done; with nothing to show for my efforts.

Except one browny yellow lion tooth snagged in my trouser pocket.

I tossed and turned in bed for a couple of days, my mind infected with vivid yet confusing dreams the like of which I hadn't experienced since an episode with some dodgy gear when I was briefly a teenage tearaway on a rundown estate. The white lion dominated my visions. Sometimes I felt that I got the message; at other times I was swept along for the ride.

I missed some shifts at the warehouse and was worried that they might terminate my contract. To my surprise, my manager told Mel that they had assumed that I was seeking employment elsewhere and would like to discuss a supervisory role when I recovered.

Which seemed a long way off during those forty-eight hours or so.

Melissa made a nest for herself on the couch. She brought me cups of tea and slices of wholemeal toast smothered in Marmite whenever I re-emerged into consciousness. This must be love from a different angle.

Leo lent me his toy lion. He had used a little dab of magnolia on the character's face. The paint was poorly applied and still a bit sticky. The likeness was thus made more acute.

At the end of the week, I got a call from Brandon. I'd been scouring the news and Google and stuff over the past couple of days: not a mention of anything.

'What happened to you?' he asked.

'I've had a fever. I only just got out alive. Zoos are dangerous places for humans.'

'Tell me about it,' he responded; although I knew he wasn't really that interested. 'I … had … a weird experience, Jase. It felt vivid and real at the time. Now I'm not so sure.'

'I know what you mean. But what about … the luggage?'

'Oh don't remind me of it. I took it to Charlie and he said it was useless. Wouldn't even take it off my hands. Ceramics.'

'Ceramics?'

'Yeah, plaster casts and teaching models of the real thing. Made to wow the schoolchildren or for vets and stuff to practise on.'

'I almost wish I'd kept some now,' I muttered.

'What's that?'

'I said shall we just forget this little escapade?'

'Going to have to. Well, see you around.'

Not if I see you first, fam.

I pulled out and examined my lucky lion tooth. Should I give it to Mel or to Leo? Maybe buy a nice jewellery box to keep it in. wish upon it when necessary.

With a few quick moves before I lost the leonine nerve, I deleted Brandon's number from my friends' list.

The lion gathered his subjects around him and said, 'We must unite together and be wary of the coming of the trickster-thief.'

'But how will we know him?' a young elephant asked.

'It is true that he may disguise his form. Yet you shall know him by his wheedling words and his wicked actions.'

'I am scared,' said a mouse; and many of the other creatures great

and small confirmed their agreement.

'I am your wise ruler,' answered the lion. 'Listen carefully for I have a plan.'

When the trickster-thief arrived, he was tall on his two legs and charming with his sweet voice and smiling with his devil eyes.

The lion sent out the oldest of the zebras. So ancient was he that his black stripes had turned to grey and his white stripes also had turned to grey and his galloping and trotting days were over.

'You make an easy catch,' muttered the trickster-thief, 'but your meat will be wrinkled and chewy. I shall wait for better.'

After a time, the lion sent out a young rabbit. Smooth, sleek and promising good eating.

'But too small,' decided the trickster-thief. 'I would eat and then be hungry again well before sunset. I shall wait for something more substantial.'

'It's like the Billy Goats Gruff,' Leo blurted.

'It's what they call the rule of three,' I answered.

At last the lion sent out a female deer. This doe was fleet of foot, firm of skin, dappled and delightful. Her big wide eyes were enchanting and the trickster-thief knew he had to follow her.

Follow he did. Underneath the shade of the fruit trees; passing the briar thorns and the wizened bushes. Along the dried-up river bed and then up into the wooded glade. And all the time he followed, the trickster-thief's excitement and appetite grew.

Now the doe knew where she was headed and every footstep she made was certain. Soon she had taken the trickster-thief to the top of the crumbly mountain and here she rested as if exhausted from the chase and ready to submit to her fate.

But just as the trickster-thief reached for his prize, his leather-shod feet slipped on some small stones and he tumbled head over heels down that crumbly mountain.

And that was the last time the kingdom of animals was ever bothered by one such as him.

THE DROWNED

In or around the year 1190, in the parish of Shere in the heavily forested shire of Surrey, a recently widowed woodcutter lived with his son and daughter in a woodland hovel on the shore of a tranquil and secluded lake. They possessed nothing of value, but in the tradition of the medieval English peasantry, believed in sharing what little they had with strangers.

One day, a horseman in fine clothing turned up at the cottage, claiming that he had lost his way. The woodcutter directed him back to the nearest highway, and then offered him some small refreshment. Rather to the woodcutter's surprise, because there was nothing fine on offer, the stranger accepted his hospitality. The woodcutter didn't know it yet, but the newcomer had set his lustful eye on the householder's handsome daughter.

Later, after the stranger had apparently left, the daughter took herself to a quiet corner of the lake and there stripped naked in order to bathe. A few moments later, she sensed that someone was watching from the trees. Nervous, she moved to the shore, only for the well-dressed horseman to appear alongside her clothes. Embarrassed, the girl took to deeper waters, but the horseman rode in after her, laughing. Whether he knew that she couldn't swim is unknown, but when she found herself out of her depth and began to scream, he made no effort to rescue her. In fact, when her younger brother heard the commotion, ran into the lake himself to help and also began to sink, the stranger still watched. Eventually, when both youngsters had drowned, the horseman took himself away and headed for the London road.

Later that day, the woodcutter returned home and was worried to find his children missing. Only when he searched did he spy their bodies floating beneath the lake's surface. He also discovered a feather, which he recognised as coming from the hat of the well-dressed horseman. Determined to have revenge, the woodcutter searched the forest for days and days until he finally received information that the man who had visited his home was none less than Count John, the wicked brother of King Richard the Lionheart, who only one year earlier had led his great army to the Holy Land as part of the Third Crusade.

Still demented with grief, the woodcutter sought an audience with Count John at Guildford Castle. Only a short time had passed since the original incident, but the mighty nobleman did not recognise the woodcutter, and in fact expressed fury when he learned that a pair of innocent youngsters had been drowned by an arrogant cur on a horse. He told the woodcutter to name the villain so that he could punish him, at which point the woodcutter produced the feather and named the Count … earning himself the noose and kick-starting the baronial rebellion that ultimately would lead to John being forced to sign the Magna Carta.

This is the story attached to Shere Pool, and it most likely owes more to romance than history. To begin with, John would not be king for another nine years and the baronial revolt would not gather steam for another ten years after that. In addition, Count John – better known to the modern world due to countless Robin Hood television dramas as 'Prince John' – was blamed, often unfairly, for every evil deed that was done during the time he was alive and for quite a considerable time afterwards. Though he was vain and treacherous, John was mainly reviled for his failure to retain the duchy of Normandy (which infuriated the baronage as it meant they lost much of their income), and, thanks to his having inherited an empty treasury from his warlike older brother, Richard, his ceaseless and ever more callous attempts to extort money (which alienated him from his ordinary subjects). Even so, the stories that John endlessly plotted against Richard, and while Richard was away murdered, raped and stole with astonishing abandon, not to mention the legend that, after his death, God punished his wickedness by transforming him into a werewolf that would terrorise the Home Counties for decades, seem a little over the top.

The explanation perhaps lies in what was a deliberate attempt to demonise John after his death in order to justify the fact that England's barons had dared lay their mailed hands on one of the crowned heads of Europe and forced him to sign what was in effect an early bill of rights.

So, did his attempt to ravish a simple village girl lead to the drowning of both she and her young brother? And did he stand by and laugh while they choked and screamed and sank beneath the water?

Probably not, and yet Shere Pool, the eerily quiet stretch of water in the leafy heart of the Surrey countryside, is infamous for its haunting atmosphere and occasional reports that a milk-pale form has been spotted drifting there – so much so that people have even kicked their shoes off and gone running in to help, only to find themselves alone in the water.

MOSES
David J Howe

The moonlight barely made it through the tree branches overhead, but Toby was glad of the darkness. He listened intently, but there was no sound, just the gentle rustling of the trees in the wind. Maybe soon he'd be able to move away from here …

For the hundredth time he wondered why he had gone out that night at all. It was all Simon's fault. If his school friend hadn't double-dared him to spend the night in their hideaway by the river he wouldn't be there … and now look at where this stupid adventure had got them.

Toby drew in as much breath as his eleven-year-old lungs could manage. He had to stay calm or the *thing* might come for him. Toby settled his back against the tree trunk and let the breath out in a silent huff. He focussed on holding the panic in, all the time wondering how he would escape this awful nightmare.

It was about five o'clock in the afternoon the previous day, when Simon and Toby had made their way down to the Hogsmill River. They lived in a small block of flats alongside the A3 road – one of the main routes into London from the Home Counties. About a mile away they could see the stark outline of Tolworth Tower. Office blocks for the most part, though with a large Marks and Spencer's shop underneath.

The Hogsmill was a small stream, which flowed under the A3, heading for Kingston, where it joined the Thames. Where it came from no one seemed to know – explorations upstream tended to end where the river diverged from the footpath –

certainly there was a large hill here, but where the river emerged was something of a mystery.

But down by the flats where Simon and Toby lived, it was easily accessible, and there was also a strip of green land all the way alongside it. Various exploratory trips had revealed the presence of old hiding places and camp sites, sometimes with the remains of fires still in them.

The boys had never seen anyone else use them, but this didn't mean there was no-one about. The sites were often well hidden right on the bank on the edge of the river within enclaves of fallen trees and branches, and could be entered by crawling through hidden tunnels which were often themselves blocked with wood or foliage. It was a paradise for Toby and Simon. They loved the idea of their own secret hiding places, and often headed down there with sandwiches and bottles of drink.

On this particular evening, Toby had managed to smuggle a blanket out of the flat, and some crisps, and a bag containing a couple of Mars bars and an apple. Simon was to bring his own supplies, which included a battery powered radio. It was summertime, so the weather was warm, and there seemed to be no issue with what they planned. Just some harmless excitement for the summer holidays. They'd each told their parents that they were going to the other's home for the night, so their families would not be worried.

They met at the gates into the greenbelt beside the river, and made their way to the hiding place.

Simon even had a box of matches and a tightly rolled wad of newspaper in case they decided to light a fire, but both boys were wary of that. Both were in the Cubs, and had gone camping with their troop. They had seen first-hand how hard it could be to get a fire going, and also how hard it could be to control once it was lit.

Neither wanted the whole of the area to go up in flames and for it to be their fault.

So this was brought as an emergency measure only.

They settled down in the den, and busied themselves

throwing pebbles into the river. One side of their lair opened to the side of the river, so it was perfect for watching the water and idling away the day. The river had fish too, which could be seen flitting in between the algae and plants, but despite various attempts with rods made from old sticks, and line from bits of string with bent paperclips on the end, and the occasional bait of worms or other pieces of food, they had never managed to catch anything.

The evening drifted by and the boys were calm and relaxed.

All was fine until darkness fell.

Toby looked out of the den again. It was pitch dark outside, and there was no movement at all. Maybe he should try and make a break for it.

Simon had run. He had taken his chance and raced for the exit to the greenbelt area. Toby had heard him go and the last he had seen had been his heels flashing in the faint light. He hoped he had got out.

Toby stirred and moved slowly, trying hard not to make any noise. When he got to the entrance to the den, he paused.

The night was silent and still.

He pushed aside the brush that partially covered the entrance and stepped out.

His foot cracked a twig.

Just a gentle *snap*.

Toby froze. Foot poised.

From somewhere in the darkness he heard something moving, something careful and predatory getting closer once more.

He pulled his leg back and retreated to the den again, pulling the brushwood over the entrance behind him with a rustle.

He wasn't sure if whatever it was in the dark would hear that. But it was close now and making a gentle crunching sound as it moved around.

The smell was awful. A rotting, noxious mixture of everything that was bad. Toby had once found a rabbit killed by the side of the road, and the smell from the decayed corpse as he and Simon investigated it with sticks had been similar. But even that wasn't as bad as the miasma which accompanied the thing.

The creature was snuffling around outside now, stirring the dry leaves and grit as it went. There was a scraping sound. Toby saw what seemed to be a giant spider leg, thin and segmented, with lots of large hairs or thorns growing from it.

This went on for a few minutes. Something big and heavy moving about outside, shifting things noisily. Toby clamped his hands over his mouth and nose to still his whimpering and his breathing and to keep the stench from his nostrils. The worst thing he could do now was make a sound.

Toby could hear his own heart beating. Thumping in his ears. He was sure that whatever was outside could hear it too.

He forced himself to calm down. He shut his eyes tight and took in a deep breath and let it out as slowly as he could. This helped and after a few more breaths, he opened his eyes. The darkness was still there, but there was silence outside now.

He looked around. Nothing to see. The box of matches and paper was still on the floor. Toby picked up the matches and shook the box. There was a soft rattle as the matches moved. His eyes shifted to the river, still flowing gently past. The sound was relaxing somehow. Maybe he could wade along the river and get out where there was more light and open ground, perhaps by the main road?

He leaned out of the hide and looked upstream. It was no more than a couple of hundred yards to where the water passed under the road. He could do it.

He crouched still, listening.

There was nothing to hear. No night-birdsong, or insect noise. There was usually some sound but tonight there was nothing. He suspected that all the usual night creatures had the right idea and had stayed at home … nothing wanted to be outside at the same time as whatever the thing was that he had heard.

Toby made up his mind and returned to the riverbank. He took off his shoes and socks and rolled up his trousers. There was no sense in getting everything saturated. He dipped his toe into the water and the sharp cold bit him. He scrunched up his face and put his whole foot in the water. It was chilly, but not unbearably so.

He was pleased that the water was at least clean. The river was fairly well maintained by various associations. They would come every year and pull out all the rubbish that accumulated there, old bicycles, bottles, traffic cones, supermarket trolleys and the like, and generally keep it neat, tidy and healthy for the fish and the ducks.

He slid his other foot in and smiled. It wasn't so bad.

Something moved against his foot and he jerked. It was just a fish or something. Having a little nibble on his toes. Nothing to be worried about, he told himself.

He picked up the matches and paper and his shoes and socks, and gently pushed himself away from the bank. The river bed was uneven and slimy, and every time he moved his feet they slipped a little. With the current pushing against his legs, it was tricky to stay upright. Every time he looked down at his feet, the patterns on the black water running past gave him a sort of dizzy feeling and he had to either close his eyes or look back up to stop himself falling over.

He fixed his eyes on the lights of the road, and started wading slowly in that direction. With each step he put his foot down carefully, waggling it a little to ensure he had a firm perch before moving the other one. He didn't think there was any glass on the bed, but there were rocks and stones and other unidentifiable objects, and the last thing he wanted was to trip and fall. The water gurgled and bubbled as it ran past him, and the sound of his legs cutting the surface was hushed and quiet. He hoped that nothing could see him, smell him or hear him.

He looked across at the bank. It was pitch dark there. There was no moon tonight and no stars – clouds had come in – and so apart from the lights ahead on the main road, there was no source of illumination.

He pushed on through the water, one foot after the other, slowly and steadily.

As he moved he could hear the gentle drone of cars on the A3 increase. There weren't too many at this time of night, but the road was so busy that there were always cars passing.

At this moment though, Toby was pleased to see any sign of normal life.

There was a *crack* and a rushing sound on the bank, as though something large had just moved past him. Toby stopped and stood still in the water.

Silence.

He turned his head and in the light from the road he saw something moving among the bushes and reeds that lined the bank. He couldn't make out exactly what it was but it was big and quiet, and the light seemed to fall off it.

He stepped forward again, toes searching for a hold underwater. The water sloshed around him, and he felt rather than saw the thing on the bank pause and listen.

He stopped moving again.

The current run of traffic on the road passed, and there was silence as no cars approached. In that stillness, Toby thought he heard something breathing. Then more cars cruised past and the sound of their engines overpowered the slow, heavy exhalations.

He moved forward again, every step bringing him closer to the traffic bridge.

Toby realised that his feet were growing numb. He could barely feel his toes as they sought out the best footing, and the chill was extending up his legs. He shivered, gripping his belongings against his chest as though they would help to keep the heat in his small body.

He started to count in his head as he stepped. One, two, three … Every step brought him closer and closer to the bridge. And every step was a success.

Eventually Toby was standing by the black mouth of the

tunnel under the road. Up above he could hear the sound of the occasional car passing. In between the sounds of the cars, there was silence.

Toby swallowed and looked around. There was nothing to be seen in the inky gloom. The streetlights far overhead shone a yellow glow over the grass and river, but the shadow of the bridge was dark.

Toby took a further step under the bridge, the water washing up his legs. His foot hit something on the concrete base of the riverbed under the bridge, and it gave. Something moved beside him ... and shifted above him, and Toby instinctively jumped back as a wooden plank of some sort clattered from the bridge roof and splashed into the river. He had obviously dislodged something and the plank had fallen from above

There was a movement over on the field, and in the yellow glow Toby saw the thing that had been hunting him. It was hard to make out any shape, except a large, dark, multi-legged shadow that moved swiftly across the grass, heading for the bridge.

Toby let out a squeal of terror and scrambled into the tunnel.

His feet stumbled on bricks and other rubbish there, and the concrete was slippery too. He managed to get further under when he heard the splashing of something coming up behind him. He could dimly see the slightly lighter arch at the other side of the bridge, and he headed for it as fast as he could. His feet slipped with every step on the mossy and treacherous concrete; his few possessions were clamped to his chest.

Suddenly, something loomed out ahead of him, something man-sized.

There was a splashing sound, and as Toby continued his way to the other end of the tunnel, he heard someone clearly say, 'No-one's gonna take children from Kingston town. No. Not happening.'

Then there was a swoosh of air and a muffled *crunch*. There was more splashing, and a growling, keening sound echoed around the tunnel.

Toby paused and looked back. Silhouetted in the tunnel entrance, a black shadow on a grey background, was the figure of a man.

He was large and stocky, and had a plank of wood in his hands. Toby could see in the gloom that it seemed to have nails protruding from the end. The figure braced itself and swung the wood as a shape that Toby could not make sense of leaped out of the darkness. The wood connected with the monster with a solid thump and a sound like breaking twigs. There was a hiss and the creature rapidly backed away towards the far entrance to the tunnel. It had more legs than Toby wanted to count, and one of them was dragging behind it.

The creature lunged back and the man swung the plank again, missing the monster narrowly, his weapon swishing through the air.

Toby pressed himself to the side of the tunnel. There was a slight indent here, and a flat area on which to stand. No water went over this, so Toby's footing was firmer.

He realised that he was still holding the newspaper in his hand. He hooked his shoes over his arm and pulled the matches from his pocket. The first match scraped on the side of the box but wouldn't light. But the second caught with a fizzing flare, and Toby lit the top of the wadded roll of newspaper.

There was more splashing and hissing from where the man and the creature were still holding each other off. With a rush, something came through the blackness at Toby and he held the burning paper up in front of him.

He caught sight of a hideous mouth with fangs, multiple eyes and legs, and an alien intelligence, before the stranger took advantage of the distraction and caught the creature full on with the nails and plank of wood.

In the flickering light from his makeshift torch, Toby saw the thing convulse and shake. The man took another smack at it with the wood, and it fell back, hissing and mewling like some baby. Toby took a shuddering breath as it backed away down the tunnel, the water splashing around its legs.

With a final hiss, the thing vanished beyond the entrance, and over the man's breathing, Toby could hear splashing and the cracking and breaking of the trees along the riverbank as it departed. The man walked to the end of the tunnel and checked outside. He paused, listening, and then, after a moment, returned to where Toby was crouching at the side.

'You okay?' he asked.

'Yes,' Toby said. 'I think so.'

'Come on then. We can't stay here. Gonna get you out of here.'

Toby allowed the man to help him up. He held out his hand and it was almost engulfed in a large paw.

The two moved to the other end of the tunnel on the far side of the main road above.

There was a low barrier there of wooden railway sleepers with a section of wire mesh above it. This seemed to be there to stop rubbish from flowing down river under the bridge, and there was indeed a traffic cone wedged in the wire along with some large pieces of wood and other flotsam.

The man moved a section of the wire, creating a clear path through and he and Toby emerged on the other side of the bridge.

'It can't get over the top,' said the man, nodding upwards. 'And if it tries to come under … well I'm waiting.'

He helped Toby cross the water, which was fairly still here due to the barrier created by the mesh, and the two of them stumbled up the bank.

Once they were standing safely on dry ground, Toby got his first good look at the man who had saved him. He was stocky, maybe just under six feet tall, but what intrigued Toby most was that his skin was black as coal. The man smiled down at Toby, his teeth gleaming yellow in the light from the road above them.

'You OK?'

Toby nodded, and as his eyes took in what the man was wearing, he realised that he had seen him before. Even in the yellowed light from the lamps, Toby could see that the chap was wearing a crazy mixture of clothes, most of them wildly patterned and coloured pink, red and white. Slightly farther up the bank, Toby saw a supermarket trolley festooned with items ranging from a pink skateboard to a child's brightly coloured pull-along luggage.

The man grinned again. 'You got nice skin,' he commented. 'Gotta keep it that way.'

'I know you,' Toby said. 'I see you in Kingston on the way to school sometimes.'

The man nodded. 'Kingston, yes. I'm Moses.'

Toby nodded. Moses was something of a local legend. He was most often to be found in the centre of Kingston, sitting on one of the benches, or standing on a street corner, dressed in the maddest and craziest outfits. Toby remembered one that was all red and white stripes. Moses was currently wearing a clown wig that was similarly patterned. Another time he had been dressed all in black, with a highwayman hat on … but regardless of what he wore, Moses always had time for everyone. He wasn't a beggar, he never asked for money, but he smiled and talked and told everyone how wonderful everything was … he was a legend. You couldn't see Moses without a smile coming to your face.

Toby looked around as Moses smiled at him. He hoped that the thing wasn't going to come back.

'Should we get away from here?' he asked.

Moses smiled. 'You can get away,' he said. 'You could.'

Then Moses seemed to stop for a moment. Toby saw his face crease as though he was trying to think of something important. His eyes darted around and narrowed, but then he relaxed. His lips parted in a wide grin.

'Yes,' the man said. 'Let's move away.'

They made their way up to where the trolley was standing. Moses reached into it and pulled out a bright red hat. He swept his hand over his curly hair and crammed the hat down.

Toby smiled. He looked so ridiculous that you had to smile.

Moses glanced at Toby. 'You smilin',' he said, and his own grin returned. 'That's good. Keep smilin'.'

Toby looked back at the river tunnel under the A3. 'What was that ... that thing?'

Moses' smile dropped. 'That's the bad thing,' he said, suddenly serious. 'That's why I'm here, keepin' a look out, and a watch. It's why I'm an inventor and not a builder, why I know about the animals and the flowers and rhododendrons and people ...'

His eyes clouded slightly once more, and Toby realised that Moses was affected by the battles with this dark creature. He was struggling to stay focussed.

'Come on, Moses,' said Toby. 'Let's get you back to Kingston.'

Moses grinned and took hold of his trolley. 'It won't be back,' he said. 'Tonight, anyway.'

He looked at Toby, again suddenly serious. 'You shouldn't be out. Not at night. There are ... things ... which you don't want to meet or see.'

Toby thought of his friend Simon. He hoped he had got back home safely.

'Come on,' he said.

The two made their way back up to the main road. There were hardly any cars, and they walked together along the pavement towards one of the footbridges over the road. The bridge happened to be right by the flats where Toby lived.

Once they had crossed the footbridge, Moses took Toby's hands again.

'You stay safe little friend.'

Toby nodded.

Moses moved off, walking back along the road towards Tolworth where he could jump on a bus towards Kingston and home. Most bus drivers knew him and allowed him free rides. Moses, it seemed, was allowed to go wherever he wanted. As he walked, he talked. Even on his own. He was Moses.

Toby nodded to himself. That was only right, he thought. After all, if a town or a city has a protector, whether it's someone from the comics like Batman or Spider Man, then they *ought* to have the freedom of the place for all the good work they did.

But sometimes, the person doing all the good work was unknown. Sometimes he was an apparent itinerant called Moses, who never had a bad word about anyone, but who lightened the day for everyone who met him. Someone who just made you feel good.

And who kept the monsters at bay.

EERIE IN OIL

Tadworth Court, a listed building currently used by a national charity to provide care for disabled children, is an eighteenth century country house located in Tadworth itself, a suburban village in northeast Surrey, quite close to Reigate. It's a pleasant enough structure, which suits its current role admirably, and there is nothing frightening or distressing about it ... unless you consider the supposed antecedents of a large, handsome oil painting that hangs in one of its many galleries.

The painting, which appears to date to the 17th century and is the work of an unknown artist, depicts a beautiful young woman in a shimmering white wedding dress, standing outdoors amid flowers and fruit and looking radiantly happy. To all intents and purposes, it's the lovely memory of a special day captured in oils.

Except for one curious detail: the scowling face of another young woman peeping at the bride through the trees behind her

Visitors to Tadworth Court have often commented that this part of the picture seems so out-of-place that it's always the first thing that strikes them. In the 1920s, the historian, Frances Leaning, was so captivated by this curiosity that she decided to look into the matter and trace the painting's origins.

What she finally learned was hair-raising.

Apparently, two sisters living in Tadworth Court were rivals for the hand of the same eligible bachelor. This rivalry became bitter and the sisters began to feud. But things only really got out of hand when their beau finally chose one of the two to be his wife. The lucky sister was over the moon with happiness, while the unlucky one was grief-stricken to the point of derangement. Shortly before the wedding, when the handsome chap arrived at the house, his bride-to-be came rushing to an upstairs balcony to call down to him, only for her sister to appear behind her, slip arms around her waist and upend her over the balustrade.

The unfortunate girl fell headfirst to her death on the flagstones some 20 feet below. Appalled at what she had done, the surviving sister then climbed to an even higher point of the house, and threw herself to her own death.

A grim tale to be sure, and highly melodramatic. But the melodrama continues, because a local artist had previously been commissioned to create a portrait of the engaged sister in her wedding gown, which would be presented to the happy couple on their big day. The family still had this painting, but when they unwrapped it a short time later, they were stunned to see the murderous sister also depicted.

It was her angry visage that peeked through the bushes at the bride's rear.

When confronted, the artist swore blindly that he had never added that latter detail and that in fact, when the painting had left his studio, there'd been no second woman there at all.

It seems that the evil sister had appeared of her own accord.

Frances Leaning didn't take this tale seriously, assuming it a bit of romantic countryside drivel. But as hard as she looked into the painting's history, she was unable to find any other explanation. Always she was brought back to the two sisters who were love-rivals. Likewise, she was unable to discover anything else about them, what their names were or when exactly they had died.

If anything, the uncanny tale grew with the telling, local people insisting that not only was the story true but that the painting had hung in the family home ever since because any effort to remove it would cause the sounds of the original disaster, a terrible scream followed by the thump of a body striking stone, to replay itself night after night, all night, until the portrait was returned.

THE OLD MAN IN APARTMENT NINETY
Jason Gould

Let me tell you about the old man who lives at the dark end of the hall. Listen, and listen good.

Do you remember I showed you the door to his apartment? It's the type of door you might walk past and not think twice – nondescript, unremarkable. To look at, it's the same as every other door to every other apartment in the tower block, including our own. It is made from wood, uncared for in recent years, flakes of brown paint beginning to lift from the surface.

But the door to the old man's apartment is different. It is dangerous. Unlike the door to our own apartment, which will keep you safe, you would not feel safe if you found yourself on the opposite side of the door to apartment ninety, removed from the security of the communal hallway, removed from the stairwell that leads back down to where we live, removed from the world you know and understand.

Do you remember the gap beneath the old man's door? I showed you it. I showed you it after the first time I found you down that end of the corridor, playing in the shadows. Do you remember that gap? I pointed it out. I knelt down beside you, quietly so he wouldn't hear us, and I showed you the thin gap between the bottom of his door and the stained strip of carpet that runs the length of the hallway, from apartment ninety back to the disused lift, and beside the lift, the staircase.

What did I say about that gap? Do you remember?

It glows – that's what I said. The gap beneath the door to

the old man's apartment flickers and glows.

And do you remember how dangerous I said it was – that glow? Tell me. Do you remember?

You must never look at it, that glow. You must never allow your gaze to be lured. And you must not, under any circumstances, ask yourself what it is, that shimmering light, what it might be.

Do I make myself clear? I'm not joking. I am deadly serious. It's not a game. Listen to me, please …

If you were to look beneath the door to apartment ninety – or, God forbid, if you went inside that apartment – you would feel sad – very, very sad. In fact, you would feel sadder than you ever felt in your life. You would feel more sad than if you woke up one morning and I was no longer here, as if I had gone away, never to return, and you – only six years old – left with no one, nobody, not a single soul in the whole wide world, no one to love you, no one to hold you at night, not even your mother.

That's how sad you'd feel. Pretty sad, huh?

And that is why you must never, ever play near the old man's door. And why you must never look at the glow beneath that door. And why you must never, ever turn the handle – or even think about what might be inside.

Promise? Good. Now, into bed. No need to cry. I know you're sorry. I know you get bored in here all day with nothing to do, no friends to play with. I know you didn't mean to wander down the dark end of the hall. And I know you won't play down there again.

But he had a problem, this boy. He was not made that way. He was not made of the stuff that keeps kids safe from peril. He was made of the stuff that urged him toward rather than back from danger.

In fact, the very thought of sneaking up the stairs to the ninth floor and down the corridor to where the light began to fade, to stand outside the forbidden door to apartment ninety

– the very thought sent droplets of excitement down his spine as if from some exquisite icicle. If his mother told him not to venture into prohibited territory, to stay away from the dark end of the hallway on floor nine, then it was into that prohibited territory he felt compelled to tread, into the very darkness itself.

It was, of course, pointless attempting to resist. He had no choice in the matter. He was a boy of six for God's sake. Surely his mother – understanding, forgiving, maternal – surely she knew that. And surely she knew he loved her. And surely she knew that he planned to climb the stairs not because he intended to defy her but because he had something inside him, some indescribable thing he could not explain, that said he had to see behind that door.

His mother permitted herself to fall asleep only when she thought he, himself, was asleep. But he had the ability to feign sleep, to be still for hours until he knew by her breathing that she would not feel him move out from beside her. So he waited. And he waited. And when he was certain she was in a deep sleep, he slipped out of the bed, out of the room and out of their apartment.

Like an urgent shadow he slid along the corridor toward the stairwell. It was dark in the stairwell. It was always dark. Each window in the stairwell was painted black – thick black paint that couldn't be scraped off. It was night as he crept up the stairs, but even in the daytime it was not permitted for light to come in from the outside. Every window in the tower block was the same. It had been like that as long as he could remember.

And so he climbed the stairs. He climbed by the light of the car and motorbike headlamps that hung from the ceiling. Each floor in the tower block was lit in that manner, each corridor, powered by the crude electricity cables that looped their way across the ceiling and walls and vanished through the holes smashed into the brickwork, down to the generator that hummed in the basement. His mother said it reminded her of the lamps in a coal mine. But he had never seen a coal mine. He had never seen anywhere except their apartment, this tower block.

As he climbed the stairs, beneath the pale lamps, he wondered if it would be nice to live in a coal mine, nicer than, say, a tower block like this – a tower block that had its exterior doors barricaded, its exits sealed up, its windows blacked out. He wondered if a coal mine was nicer than an apartment that plunged into darkness if too many people switched on their electric stove at the same time. If it would be warmer than this tower block, less hollow. If the people who lived there would be less crazy.

He wondered many things. He had plenty of time to wonder. Most of all – every day, every hour – he wondered what it would be like to go outside, to leave the tower block and step beyond its walls, into the world he had never seen.

But tonight he focused his thoughts on apartment ninety. What would it be like inside? Why had his mother warned him his whole life to stay away from that place, the door to the old man's residence?

What was in there? Why did it terrify his mother? And why did it make his heart beat faster?

He climbed from floor three, where he and his mother lived their quiet life, keeping themselves to themselves. He climbed up to floor four, and five. Floor six …

He paused, between floors seven and eight. Some of the headlamps had short-circuited and the dark was thicker up here. He could see the route but if it continued like this he would be in full darkness by the time he reached floor number nine and the old man's apartment.

He had not been up here at night. Every time he'd been caught up here it had been during the day. Not that it made much difference – the tower block relied on the daisy-chained system of lamps twenty-four seven – but somehow it seemed darker at this hour, as if night came out of the walls, up from the floor.

It reminded him of something his mother had said, about the old man. She had said, 'He is most dangerous at night. For it is at night when he feels most sad. And when he is sad, he is dangerous.'

He'd expected it to be dark on floor nine but it was bright – very bright. Sometimes the generator malfunctioned and a surge of electricity flooded part of the building, and the lights – normally dim – would burn incandescent.

He left the stairwell and entered the corridor. Each lamp hummed and fizzed and he thought they might explode, one by one, as he passed by. They were painful to look at. They hurt his eyes and he averted his gaze, trained it on the reason for his trip up here tonight – the door to apartment ninety.

Which was ajar …

As if it had known he was coming.

Inside, the layout was identical to the boy's own apartment. A short, narrow vestibule with doors that led off to the left and right, presumably the bedroom and bathroom. And at the end, a closed door. Because the layout was the same he knew that on the other side of that closed door he would find the living room. And, he assumed, in that living room, he would find the old man, of whom his mother was so terribly afraid.

This was the last point at which he could turn back. He could still heed his mother's warning. He could flee the apartment, sprint along the corridor, down the stairs from level nine to level three, slip back behind his own front door and slowly, gently pull back the covers on the bed and slide into the warmth beside his mother – and if she stirred, he would mumble he had been to the toilet, or for a glass of water.

But he had to see beyond that door. He had to see inside the living room. He had to meet the old man.

Like every other window in the block the window in the living room was painted black to block out the view. Thick, gritty paint, like sand. Once it was applied it might never be removed, regardless of how much you chipped and scratched. Artificial light – from a floor-standing lamp beside the armchair – attempted to compensate for the lack of natural light in the room, but it was weak, overburdened by the barrier daubed on the glass. The room had many unlit corners.

The old man failed to respond when the boy crept through the door and into the living room. The boy stood behind and to one side of the old man's tattered wing-back armchair. He could see only part of the old man's profile – unshaven, emaciated. It was unclear if the old man even realised someone else had stepped inside. He was still, motionless. And he looked very, very sad.

'Sadness,' he remembered his mother had said. 'When he is sad he is at his most dangerous.'

But the old man was pre-occupied. He was staring at the television set – a large, old, heavy television set – his gaze focused intently on the screen as if nothing else in the world existed.

And the boy realised this was the source of the glow his mother had warned him about. It was the glow that reached beneath the door, and flickered and pulsed in the corridor outside.

It was the glow his mother had said carried such danger – the glow of the pictures that moved on the television screen.

You say he was sitting in his old, worn armchair. The lamp dimmed. The room in disarray. Unwashed plates, mugs. Thick dust on every surface. I've been inside. I know what it's like in there. It's as if the whole place has been stopped by an unseen hand that swept through the air and paused time.

He is incapable of anything, the old man in apartment ninety. He can only watch the television. And watch. And watch.

Did you look at the screen? Tell me, my son. Be honest. Did you look at the pictures on his television screen?

It had lured his gaze, the television screen, just as his mother had said it would. He had unfixed his line of sight from the old man, who simply sat in his armchair with tears on his cheeks, and looked toward the source of the light.

And the boy had stared, and stared, and stared. But no matter how much he stared it was impossible to make sense of what he saw on the screen.

He had never seen anything like it in his life.

You did not understand what you saw. You saw pictures moving on the television screen, pictures of things you did not understand.

And that is why you ran. Not because of the old man, but because of the pictures on the screen.

That is why you ran out of his apartment and back downstairs to me, your mother.

You're shaking. It's natural to be afraid. Come here. Let me hold you. And I will explain what you saw.

In the days before we locked and barricaded the doors and blacked out the windows, he was young, the man you saw tonight. He lived a full and happy life. As did most of us. As did I.

It was before you were born. You were born right here, in this apartment. And this – the time I refer to – was long before we lived in this apartment. Long before we had to live in this way.

In those days, the old man, who at the time was not old but young, he had what was called a video camera. It was a piece of equipment that would record … well, it would record the world, whatever you pointed it at. Do you understand? If you had a video camera now, and you pointed it at me, it would record me. And then you could play that recording back on a television screen. Like the television screen we have in our apartment. Yes, the television screen that only shows the emergency broadcast. And plays the classical music.

So back then, the old man liked to record footage. He would walk around the town where he lived, where I lived, and record whatever he saw. You see, he loved the town. He was what they called an urban planner. What's an urban planner? It means he decided where they would build new buildings, where they would make roads, and where people could go to the shops, or the cinema.

I'm sorry, yes … shops and cinema. I know you don't understand. God, how I wish this day had never come. Why did you play up there? Why did you defy me!

I'm sorry. I don't mean to shout. Come here. Hold me, your mother. I need to feel you in my arms.

Let's see if I can explain. Come on, dry your eyes.

We lived among the things you saw on the screen in the old man's apartment. We did not watch them on a television, on videotape, watched enough times for the picture to fade and flicker, grow grainy and fall apart. We did not watch them as you did tonight. We saw them for real. We lived among them – for real.

We lived in a place that looked like that. It was our home. Just as you and I live in this tower block, so I lived in that place. We walked among the cold wet streets, through the

dreary canyons of concrete, the windswept municipal
buildings.

And the old man, he captured footage of the city. People
shopping. Old folk sitting on park benches. A car's tail-lights
vanishing into the dusk. The midday sun caught in a pool of
rainwater.

It was beautiful. So beautiful.

What you saw, my son. What you saw on the television screen
in the old man's apartment – it was called Stevenage.

When it was first constructed – when Stevenage was first
constructed – it was intended to be perfect. They said it would
be Utopia – that means ideal, faultless. And the critics – the
people who wanted to disagree – they said it was boring,
empty, soulless.

And to us – young kids at the time, twenty, twenty-five –
we thought it soulless too. My friends and I yearned to escape.
We longed to run away to somewhere with more energy, more
history, more … soul. A place like London. Or Manchester. Or
even America.

But we were incarcerated in our modern-day concrete
jungle. Every day we stared out at the dour streets, the
identical walkways, the rubbish-strewn squares and
playgrounds, the grim overhead gantries. It looked as if it had
been designed by a computer programme, constructed from a
mathematical algorithm, put together by robots.

It was Hell on Earth.

Until …

Until the accident, or what they said was an accident,
nuclear rods exposed to the sky, and death blowing on the
breeze.

And then we fled, hid wherever we could: abandoned
schools, office blocks, warehouses. And, eventually, this place
– our new home.

THE OLD MAN IN APARTMENT NINETY

And as we blacked out the windows, boarded up the doors, tried to forget the world that had become too deformed to gaze upon, too sad to contemplate, it was then we realised we hadn't been living in Hell on Earth – in a brick-built metropolis that had no heart or soul. Quite the opposite.

We had been living in paradise.

You see, my son. A happy past is a terrible thing to live with. It's enough to turn any of us insane.

I hoped you would never have to see the things I've seen. I hoped you would never have to see the beauty of Stevenage city centre dappled in the midday sun. I hoped you would go your whole life without seeing that.

You must never see those things again. The things on that television screen should not be seen by anyone, and certainly not by someone your age. Once they're inside your head you will never be free of them. They will haunt you your whole life. They will make you long for a world you never had, and never will have.

I cannot let that be. You have had a glimpse of the promised land that we lost, and it is too much. You are more precious to me than life itself. And since I cannot stop your inquisitive nature, since I cannot stop you sneaking up to the old man's apartment again, I have no choice.

I cannot help you forget what you have already seen. But what you have seen will fade in your mind, as you grow older.

It is my duty, though, to stop you seeing more.

Come, sit on my knee. Tilt back your head. Let me fix your eyes …

SOURCES

All the stories in *Terror Tales of the Home Counties* are original to this publication, with the exception of 'The Doom' by Paul Finch, which was first published *The Sixth Black Book of Horror* (2010).

OTHER TELOS TITLES YOU MAY LIKE

PAUL FINCH
Cape Wrath & The Hellion
Terror Tales of Cornwall
Terror Tales of Northwest England

RAVEN DANE
THE MISADVENTURES OF CYRUS DARIAN
Steampunk Adventure Series
1: Cyrus Darian and the Technomicron
2: Cyrus Darian and the Ghastly Horde
3: Cyrus Darian and the Wicked Wraith

Death's Dark Wings
Standalone alternative history novel

Absinthe and Arsenic
13 Horror and Fantasy Short Story Collection

HELEN MCCABE
THE PIPER TRILOGY
1: Piper
2: The Piercing
3: The Codex

GRAHAM MASTERTON
The Djinn
The Wells of Hell
Rules Of Duel (with WILLIAM S BURROUGHS)
The Hell Candidate

TANITH LEE
Blood 20
20 Vampire stories through the ages

Death of the Day
Standalone crime novel

Tanith Lee A-Z
An A-Z collection of short fiction
by renowned writer Tanith Lee

SIMON CLARK
Humpty's Bones
The Fall

FREDA WARRINGTON
Nights of Blood Wine
Vampire horror short story collection

PAUL LEWIS
Small Ghosts
Horror novella

STEPHEN LAWS
Spectre

RHYS HUGHES
Captains Stupendous

DAVID J HOWE
Talespinning
Horror collection of stories, novels and more

SOLOMON STRANGE
The Haunting of Gospall

DAWN G HARRIS
Diviner

SAM STONE
KAT LIGHTFOOT MYSTERIES
Steampunk Adventure Series
1: Zombies at Tiffany's
2: Kat on a Hot Tin Airship
3: What's Dead PussyKat
4: Kat of Green Tentacles
5: Kat and the Pendulum
6: Ten Little Demons

THE COMPLETE LIGHTFOOT
Hardback limited-edition compendium of all Kat Lightfoot books with bonus extras.

THE JINX CHRONICLES
Dark Science Fiction and Fantasy, dystopian future
1: Jinx Town
2: Jinx Magic
3: Jinx Bound

THE VAMPIRE GENE SERIES
Vampire, Historical and Time Travel Series
1: Killing Kiss
2: Futile Flame
3: Demon Dance
4: Hateful Heart
5: Silent Sand
6: Jaded Jewel

Zombies In New York And Other Bloody Jottings
Horror Story Collection

TELOS PUBLISHING
www.telos.co.uk